Tom Holland is the author of *The Vampyre, Supping with Panthers* and *Attis*.

He lives in London.

Tom Holland

DELIVER US FROM EVIL

WARNER BOOKS

A *Warner* Book

First published in Great Britain by
Little, Brown and Company 1997
First published by Warner 1998

Copyright © Tom Holland 1997

A CIP catalogue record for this book
is available from the British Library.

Endpapers © British Library

ISBN 0 7515 1861 1

Typeset by Solidus (Bristol) Limited
Printed and bound in Great Britain by
Clays Ltd, St Ives plc

Warner
A Division of
Little, Brown and Company (UK)
Brettenham House
Lancaster Place
London WC2E 7EN

... SATAN, HE WHO ENVIES NOW THY STATE,
WHO NOW IS PLOTTING HOW HE MAY SEDUCE
THEE ALSO FROM OBEDIENCE, THAT WITH HIM
BEREAVED OF HAPPINESS THOU MAYST PARTAKE
HIS PUNISHMENT, ETERNAL MISERY;
WHICH WOULD BE ALL HIS SOLACE AND REVENGE,
AS A DESPITE DONE AGAINST THE MOST HIGH,
THE ONCE TO GAIN COMPANION OF HIS WOE.
BUT LISTEN NOT TO HIS TEMPTATIONS ...

John Milton, *Paradise Lost*

For Bro – a true swash-buckler

I

It was always said that animals would never cross spilled blood. Mr Aubrey considered this, then tried to spur his horse forward one last time. Again the horse whinnied and backed away from the rampart of Clearbury Ring, its nostrils flaring with unmistakable fear. Mr Aubrey scratched his head, then swung down on to the frozen ground. It had to be a coincidence, of course. The sacrifices had been offered up a long, long time ago. There could be no blood now for his horse to smell. Nevertheless, as he had often found in the course of his studies, there were many ancient sites in Wiltshire which bore an evil reputation, and he doubted that all such reports could be merely credulous invention. For it was a constant maxim of Mr Aubrey's that, in the study of the dim and uncertain past, even superstitions might hint at some truth.

Why else, after all, was he standing where he was? Because he had heard a tale from the women in the village below, that on Yuletide ghosts might be seen on Clearbury Ring. And now it was Yuletide – the twenty-second of the month of December the year of our Lord,

1659 – and a bitter, freezing cold day it was too. Mr Aubrey shivered, then drew his notebook out from his coat. He studied it briefly. If his researches were correct, then the Druids would have gathered to make their sacrifices on this very date, drenching the soil with their victims' blood, attempting to appease the wrath of their mysterious god. He studied his scribblings for the last time, then slipped his book away. He did not expect to see ghosts, of course. Village people were always timorous and gullible – they did not see, as he could, that their legend was doubtless nothing but an echo of the Druids' ancient practice. And yet perhaps ghosts might be seen. Mr Aubrey peered into the darkness of the wood ahead. Perhaps they might. He braced himself. Whatever lay ahead, it was his duty, as an antiquarian chronicling his county's past, to investigate it.

He clambered up the outer rampart, then down into the ditch. As he did so, he became aware how still the trees were ahead of him. He passed into their shadow and, although he walked quietly, the snapping of twigs and the rustling of leaves seemed all of a sudden frighteningly loud. Mr Aubrey froze; he turned and glanced round. He could just make out Salisbury Cathedral through the trees, and saw to his surprise how it was perfectly aligned with the ancient hill town of Old Sarum, which rose hunched behind the spire on the opposite hill. He would have to make a note of such an interesting detail, Mr Aubrey thought. He reached in his pocket for his handkerchief, and tied a knot in it to remind himself. Then, his courage and his enthusiasm for research restored, he continued on his way, pushing through the brambles towards the centre of the Ring.

He saw no ghosts. Instead, to his initial relief, the still-

ness which had enveloped him on his first entry into the
trees was soon broken by the cawing of birds, and he
began to observe them perched on branches, or wheeling
overhead. He continued forward, and soon discovered a
great flock of ravens gathered on what appeared to be the
branch of a tree. Then Mr Aubrey realised that the birds
were pecking at something; and as he stared at them, he
saw one of the ravens swallow down a gobbet of flesh.
The bird pecked again, and seemed to hold in its beak, for
a second, a human eye. Mr Aubrey shrieked; he rushed
forward, and the birds flapped reluctantly up into the air.
The corpse could be seen quite clearly now. It had been
left beneath a tree, an old man, stripped of all his clothes.
Numb with horror and scarcely conscious of what he was
doing, Mr Aubrey bent down beside the body. It was
possible, of course, that the birds had inflicted most of
the wounds: pecked out the eyes, certainly; punctured the
skin with the points of their beaks; but the worst
mutilations could only have been inflicted by a human
hand. There were terrible slashes across the stomach,
face and limbs; and yet there was a mystery, Mr Aubrey
realised, for the wounds themselves seemed utterly dry.
The flesh was blanched; it was as though every drop of
blood had been drained away ... and yet when he
inspected the soil below the corpse, there was not a trace
of blood – not a single splash.

Mr Aubrey rose to his feet again. He removed his coat
and draped it over the corpse. Unsure now whether he
was shuddering with the cold or with his fear, he began
to run, breaking through the branches and out on to the
open fields beyond the Ring, screaming all the time for
help as loudly as he could. Behind him, in the silent
trees, the ravens began to settle again upon their

interrupted meal. The coat did not impede their hungry beaks for long.

∽✺∾

'AND NOT ONLY AMONG THE ROMANS AND JEWS, BUT ALSO AMONG CHRISTIANS, A LIKE CUSTOM OF OBSERVING DAYS AS EVIL IS USED, ESPECIALLY CHILDERMAS OR INNOCENTS' DAY . . . WE DREAD TO DO BUSINESS ON CHILDERMAS DAY.'

John Aubrey, *Miscellanies Upon Various Subjects*

Robert Foxe had been with his father when the old man had been found. They had been riding across the fields that stretched below the hill. He had not been allowed to climb up to Clearbury Ring and see the corpse, but he knew that whatever his father had witnessed there, the sight had affected him badly. Captain Foxe, his son realised, must have been half-dreading, half-expecting further news. And now, eight days later, it seemed to have been brought.

The trooper from the militia hurried across to his captain, and began to whisper into his ear. Only the faintest frown of surprise darkened Captain Foxe's face. He muttered a short prayer beneath his breath, then reached at once for his sword and gathered up his cloak. As he strode to the door, he paused and glanced back. His son, naturally, was still sitting with Emily Vaughan. Captain Foxe smiled. He thought, as he often did, how like a brother and sister they seemed. Both were rosy-cheeked, fine-featured, with golden hair, Robert's cropped short and Emily's an untamed flow of ringlets and curls. They were holding each other's hands, inseparable as they always had been, it seemed, since they had been born just days apart thirteen years before.

'You are to wait here,' Captain Foxe ordered them sternly. He brought out a coin from his purse. 'You may send for a pastry,' he added, a note of vague apology in his voice. Robert took the coin reluctantly, and fingered it with distrust. It was growing late now – almost time for dinner. They were meant to be leaving for Woodton very soon. Despite his father's gift, he had no wish to spoil his appetite: they had already bought provisions in Salisbury that day, and tonight Hannah, their servant, would cook them a goose. It was to be the most delicious meal they had ever had. His mother had promised him as much. It was to be his reward – his reward for attaining a scholar's rank. Hannah had whispered the same promise in his ear. When they had left for Salisbury, she had added a kiss. She was very fond of Robert – he smiled at the thought – and he was fond of her.

He wished, though, as he remembered how she had held him, that she were not quite so large. He did not like large women. Indeed, as he considered Hannah's size, he realised that he had almost forgotten what she looked like when not on the point of giving birth. He offered up a quick prayer that she would not have had her baby while he was away in town. She had promised him before they left that she would not – for after all, didn't she have his goose to prepare? – but when he had asked his mother, she had said that babies were sometimes hard to put off. This news had only confirmed his darkest suspicions, and all day he had been worrying that time was not on their side, that the baby was waiting, any moment, to be born. Robert watched darkly as his father left the room. He didn't want a baby – he wanted his goose. He wondered if they would have to remain in Salisbury for long now. He sighed, suspecting that they would. For he had guessed at once on what business his father had been called.

He waited until Captain Foxe's footsteps had faded away, then jumped to his feet and turned to Emily. 'We must go,' he said.

Emily frowned. 'But we were told to wait.'

Robert shrugged, then made a face.

Emily stared at him a moment more, before she tossed her head and clambered off her stool. Robert realised that he was still holding her hand. He squeezed it. Together, they crept on tiptoes down the stairs.

Outside the Council Hall, snow had muffled everything. The market-place was almost empty. Only a few dark figures could be made out slipping like ghosts across the square, or into the gloom of the adjacent streets. Robert searched for his father. He just caught him, a cloaked shadow, as he turned and disappeared towards the Poultry Cross. Captain Foxe's footprints were clearly before them, leading through the otherwise undisturbed snow. Robert and Emily followed them.

The trail, they soon realised, was heading towards the Cathedral. Robert stared up from his father's prints. High above the snow-hushed town, the spire seemed almost a phantom of the mist, as insubstantial as the darkening clouds. Robert remembered something his father had told him – of a ghostly battle he had seen in the sky, he and countless others, on the eve before Naseby, when they had fought the King and destroyed his cause forever. And now, Robert thought, the Cathedral and the dark streets seemed as spectral as that vision in the clouds must have been. A ghost-haunted place. Unreal. He shivered; then returned his gaze to the footprints in the snow. He could barely make them out now, the street was so narrow and dark. Then, as they passed St Thomas's, he saw from within the church the barest flickering of light. He turned aside and stared in through the doors. The candles could not have been lit to illuminate the building: they were far too tiny and delicate for that. There were people beside them, kneeling in prayer.

'It is Childermas,' whispered Emily.

'Childermas?'

'When Herod killed the babies in Bethlehem. The candles – they are for the babies, to remember them.'

'Why?'

Emily shrugged. 'It is just what we do.'

Robert looked at her, surprised. Emily's parents were not like his own. Her father had fought against the Parliament – he was said to be almost a Catholic. 'We,' Robert repeated slowly. He glanced into the church again, at the figures bent before the candle flames. 'So those people' – he pointed at them – 'they are worshipping according to the practice of your parents?'

Emily shrugged again. 'They must be, I suppose. If they have lit the candles, I mean.'

'But . . . in a church . . .' Robert frowned and shook his head. 'It is forbidden, you know it is.'

Emily smiled shyly. 'Have you not heard, Robert? The King is coming back. That is what my father says.'

'No.' He broke away from her angrily. 'The time of kings has passed away. There will never be kings in England again.'

'Do not worry.' She hurried after him, and took his hand again. 'My father will look after you. Just as your father has looked after us.'

Robert did not answer her. Instead, he stared back down the street towards the Cathedral Close. His father, passing here, must have seen the candles as well. He was a kind, a tolerant, a compassionate man. He would not have stopped to interfere. It was true, he had fought in the war, but only for the right to worship as he wished; it was no business of his, he had always told Robert, to prescribe how others should worship in turn. Yet for all that, Robert thought, he served as Commissioner in the local militia and it must have disturbed him, at the very least, to see the laws being flouted so openly. He had seemed much distracted, the past few days. Robert had assumed it was memories of the body he had found. But then he remembered something his father had said, as the corpse was being borne away. 'The times are cracking,' he had whispered, barely above his breath. What had he seen in the horror of the old man's wounds? A foreboding of the rumours that even Emily had heard, of the King's return, of the overthrow of everything he had fought for and believed? Suddenly, tracking the footprints, Robert felt afraid for him – and of what might lie waiting beyond the Cathedral doors.

For he could see now how his father's trail led without deviation across the expanse of the Close. Together, he and Emily advanced carefully, since there were no shadows of buildings to conceal them now and, as they crossed the snow, the clouds thinned and were stained with a sudden, weak red. The snow, reflecting the dying sun, seemed almost to shimmer beneath the unexpected light, but there was no one to see them, not a soul abroad, and they reached the Cathedral doors unobserved. Emily shuddered, and clasped her companion's arm. 'Robert,' she whispered, 'I don't like it here. Please, let's not go inside.'

Robert understood her fear. He could feel it himself; it was almost palpable in the gloom of the nave. But then, from beyond the choir-screen, he heard the sound of voices, and he wanted to know what his father had found. As they crept down the aisles, he had to force his way against the terror almost as though it were a gale, and the further they went, the greater the terror grew. Not until they had continued along the entire length of the aisle did they see Captain Foxe, for he was standing in the Lady Chapel, the Cathedral's easternmost and oldest point. Two ministers were hunched together by his side.

Robert tried to peer into the Chapel's darkness; and as he did so, the terror rose and grew within him so that he felt almost ready to suffocate. He swallowed, then choked. Captain Foxe glanced round; Robert froze; he clasped a pillar, breathing in deeply, and at length his father turned back again. Emily was clutching on to Robert in turn, her eyes wide, her face unbearably pale, and he could feel her body shaking against his. She had been right, he thought; he wished they had not come. But even in the grip of his terror, he wondered what it was which could reduce him to such fear; and so he began to stare again, to try and penetrate the dark.

His father and the two ministers were still standing with their backs to him, staring at something which lay at their feet. Captain Foxe bent down to inspect it more closely. Still Robert could not see what he was looking at, but when he turned round to look up at the ministers, there was an expression of revulsion and pity on his face.

'Who would – who could – do such a thing?' he murmured.

One of the ministers shook his head. 'And in the Cathedral itself.'

'Most cruel anywhere,' replied Captain Foxe. But Robert knew that he too would be feeling the shock of sacrilege, for he loved the Cathedral with a deep and secret passion, despite what he had often affirmed – that all places must be equally holy before God. After a long while staring at what lay before him, he rose to his feet. 'And you found her?' he asked, addressing the minister who had spoken before.

'Not more than half an hour ago. Naturally, I sent for you at once.'

'And before that, do we know when anyone was last about here?'

'I was, an hour ago,' said the second minister. 'I was lighting the candles . . .'

'Good,' said Captain Foxe, interrupting him. 'So we can be certain that the body was deposited during the half hour after that.'

'Deposited?'

'Yes,' said Captain Foxe shortly. 'These wounds' – he crouched down again – 'they are not fresh. She was not killed here. Feel her. She has been dead these several hours now.'

'Then you think . . . but . . . oh no. Oh no.' The minister wiped his brow with his sleeve. 'What is happening, Commissioner?' he whispered. 'If the poor soul was not killed in the Lady Chapel – then *why* was she brought here? What does it mean?'

'That,' said Captain Foxe slowly, 'is what we need to find out.'

'Do you think . . .?' Again, the minister's voice trailed away. He swallowed. 'Could this be . . .?'

'Sorcery.' His companion completed his question, then just as decisively answered it. 'There can be no doubt about it. To mutilate a body – any body – but especially one such as this – it is sorcerer's work. See! What can these wounds be, but the glutting of the thirst of malignant spirits? Oh, dread – oh, mighty dread! The Evil One is abroad in the Cathedral tonight . . .'

'No!' Captain Foxe only rarely raised his voice, and the two ministers must have known of his reputation for calmness, for they both stared at him in the utmost surprise. 'No,' Captain Foxe repeated, less vehemently now. 'Please' – he addressed his appeal to both men – 'we cannot allow talk of this kind to go beyond these walls.'

The minister he had interrupted began to frown, and Captain Foxe lowered his voice still more. 'You know,' he whispered urgently, 'how dangerous a fear of the black arts can be. It unsettles the multitudes, who in their superstition and cruelty will always seek to find witches on which to blame their own sense of sin. For it is rarely, if ever, the true sorcerers who are burned, but only poor old women who are guilty of nothing, perhaps, beyond seeming a little crazed in their wits.' He bowed to the first minister. 'I know, sir, that you agree with me on this matter, for we have discussed it before.'

The minister glanced at his colleague, then inclined his head. 'It is true,' he acknowledged, 'that I dread the effect of the news of this crime.'

'But you would not deny,' exclaimed the second minister indignantly, 'that this must indeed be the work of a sorcerer, for who but the Evil One could inspire such a work of horror – such an *abomination* – as this?'

'I would not deny it, sir,' agreed Captain Foxe. 'Indeed, it appears exceedingly probable. And yet that is my very point, for so hellish, so brazen is the crime that I would not see lonely old women being harried for the fault,

when our adversary is clearly a man of deadly cunning
and skill.'

'You said a man,' asked the first minister. 'You have
certain proof of this?'

'I do, sir.'

'Then this is not the first such murder you have come
across? There has been a previous one?'

Captain Foxe's rugged, handsome face, which could
seem almost simple to those who did not know him well,
appeared suddenly drained and impenetrable. 'I would
like to ask you first,' he said eventually, 'before I say anything more, the obvious question – have either of you
seen a stranger in the Cathedral today? He would needs
be well built. A strong-looking man.'

The first minister swallowed. 'Needs be?' he asked.

'On the evidence I have witnessed,' Captain Foxe
replied. 'In the previous case.'

The first minister swallowed again. He shrugged. 'I
have seen no one,' he said.

His colleague, though, as he thought, began to frown.
'I remember,' he said at length, 'that there was a man I
saw this morning about this very place.'

'This very place? You mean here, the Lady Chapel?'

'Yes. But he had nothing with him, no bundle.'

'Describe him,' ordered Captain Foxe.

'It is difficult.'

'Why?'

'It was dark. His eyes, though, I remember his
eyes. They were piercing, exceedingly bright. And his
clothes . . .'

'What of them?'

'Gaudy, again, like his eyes, very bright. It struck me
that they seemed curiously old-fashioned, for he had the

appearance of one of the old Cavaliers, those who fought for the King in the war. I assumed that he was someone returned from abroad, perhaps on the seditious rumours current in the air, that the Commonwealth is shortly to be overthrown.'

'Possibly,' was all that Captain Foxe replied. But he appeared very troubled by what the minister had said, and did not attempt to conceal his unease.

'You have heard reports of such a man, then?' the minister asked him at length.

'Possibly,' said Captain Foxe once again. He continued to stare at the body by his feet. 'A man dressed and bearded very like a Cavalier was seen last week,' he murmured softly, 'by Clearbury Ring.'

'Clearbury Ring?' Both ministers seemed scarcely to recognise the name.

'There was an old man found there last week as well. Mr William Yorke – a scholar and antiquarian from my own village. He had taught Latin and Greek to my son. I knew him well. He was dead though, when I saw him last. He had been murdered – very horribly.'

'May the Lord have mercy on us all!' exclaimed the first minister. 'Why had I not heard of this before?'

'The details have been kept secret on my own instructions.'

'May I ask why, Commissioner?'

Captain Foxe grimaced, and glanced down at his feet again. 'For the same reason,' he said at last, 'that we must conceal the news of this death as well.'

'No!' The minister began to wring his hands and his voice, when he spoke again, was almost a wail. 'Not signs of sorcery again?'

'So it appeared.'

'And what were they, these signs?'

'The wounds, the ... mutilations ... they were very similar to those inflicted on this poor soul.' Captain Foxe crouched down. 'Identical, indeed. Violent cruelties – and the body, like this one, drained of all its blood.'

Emily had started to shudder. Robert turned and held her as tightly as she was clinging to him; he could feel her silent tears scalding his cheeks. 'We must take her to a physician,' he heard his father say, 'so that we may have her injuries exactly determined. Poor child. Poor child! May the good Lord receive her innocent soul.'

Robert stared hurriedly back around, as his father spoke the word 'child'. Captain Foxe had risen to his feet again, and was nestling a little bundle in his arms. 'A cloak,' he whispered, 'please, sir, your cloak.' One of the ministers unfastened his mantle; he handed it across; as Captain Foxe raised his tiny burden so that it could be wrapped in the cloak, Robert and Emily caught their first glimpse of the murdered child. They both gasped. It was a baby; no, too small even to be a baby – as small, Robert thought, as one of Emily's old rag dolls. Its face was blue and its arm, as it hung from over Captain Foxe's hand, seemed almost purple. The fingers were so tiny that Robert could barely see them; and then, when he looked closer, he realised that each one had been snapped, so that they were bent backwards across the hand. He heard Emily cry out, 'No, no, no!'; and then he heard a second noise in his ears, a second sob of mourning and fear. It was himself.

He had expected his father to be angry. They had broken his direct instructions, after all. But Captain Foxe said nothing to them; instead, he handed his tiny burden across to one of the ministers, then walked from the

Chapel to the pillar where the children were hiding. He gathered them in his arms; and as they shook, so beneath the protecting folds of his cloak, he sheltered them.

∾⧫∾

'I FLED, AND CRIED OUT, *DEATH*;
HELL TREMBLED AT THE HIDEOUS NAME, AND SIGHED
FROM ALL HER CAVES, AND BACK RESOUNDED, *DEATH*.'
JOHN MILTON, *Paradise Lost*

The journey back to Woodton was bitterly cold. But if they shivered, Emily and Robert, as they rode behind Captain Foxe's charger, it was not the wind which reached deepest into their bones. Emily stared resolutely at the track ahead of her, Robert all about him at the bleak, dark snows of Salisbury Plain, but both were thinking of the killer, how he might be ahead of them, behind them, anywhere that night. As the winds shrieked, Robert imagined he was hearing a baby's dying wail; as the burial mounds of ancient kings loomed ahead of them off the track, he flinched, lest their shadows be those of lurking fiends. Even Captain Foxe, who had been promoted from the ranks for his courage in the war, and was a byword amongst his men for bravery, seemed unsettled by their journey on that night.

They began to draw nearer to Woodton – but between them and home there was first Stonehenge, and as they approached it, Captain Foxe reined in his horse, peering ahead as though expecting some danger to be awaiting them there. Emily and Robert both halted as well; their eyes by now were adjusted to the dark, and they could easily make out the giant stones, black against the

screaming eddies of snow. Captain Foxe rested his palm
upon the handle of his pistol; then, as though suddenly
embarrassed, he smiled back at the children and, shaking
out his reins, spurred his charger on. As he cantered
forward, Emily followed him.

Ever more looming now, the ancient stones rose out
from the dark. Robert stayed where he was, and wiped at
his brow where, despite the cold, a sweat had formed. He
gazed up at the stones with surprise, for he felt, as he had
never sensed before, how malignant was the circle's
mystery, how implacable and blank, as though some
monstrous secret lay veiled behind it, which might not,
perhaps, be yet altogether dead. He remembered the
terror which had filled him in the Cathedral: like the echo
of some violent theme, he felt it again now. Suddenly,
there was silence: the sound of hooves on the snow, the
wailing of the wind, all dropped away, and he imagined
he was alone, for everything else seemed absorbed by the
stones and their stillness, all the world. He forced himself
to turn. He called out his father's name. Captain Foxe
looked round. He too had been gazing at the circle; his
stare was very wide, and his skin so pale and tight across
his bones that his face seemed like a skull. 'I felt it!'
Robert screamed at him above the wind. 'I felt it too!' But
his father only shook his head, and urged his horse on.
Then he cried out suddenly, and pointed. Robert and
Emily stared into the snow as it was blown into their
faces. Dimly, through the gusts, they could make out a
lamp. It was approaching them.

Captain Foxe spurred his horse on once more. Robert
heard him shout something, but his words were lost on
the gale.

'It is Father!' cried Emily suddenly, her voice light with

relief. She shouted his name, waving her arms, and as the horseman drew level with her, she reached out for him. Robert could distinguish Sir Henry Vaughan clearly now: his thin, handsome face, his old-fashioned Cavalier's beard and moustache. He swept up his daughter from her pony's back, and hugged her tightly, so tightly indeed that he seemed almost to be convincing himself that she was truly in his arms. Robert wondered what news there was, to have persuaded Sir Henry to ride out on such a terrible night; for that some dread was haunting him could easily be read in his face. He kissed Emily once more, and settled her back on her horse; then he turned to Captain Foxe, and beckoned him aside. He began to whisper in a low, urgent manner; Robert couldn't hear what was said above the screaming of the gale, but as he watched his father, he saw him start, and shake his head, and grow very pale. Sir Henry did not speak for long; Captain Foxe asked him some further questions and then sat, head bowed in silence, frozen in his saddle. He seemed to whisper a prayer; then he turned to Emily and Robert, and beckoned them on. Robert thought that he had never seen his father's face set so angry and grim – unless, perhaps, in the Cathedral that same afternoon.

Captain Foxe glanced round at him. 'Robert.' He reached out to stroke his son's hair. 'We must always trust in God to fulfil His ways,' he murmured, as though to himself. Then he turned in his saddle again, staring directly at the road ahead. Woodton lay beyond the next ridge. 'You must guard your mother closely tonight,' he said. 'I may have much to do, and she will need you by her side.'

Robert waited. 'Will you not be with us when Hannah cooks the goose?' he finally dared to ask.

'There will be no goose.'

Captain Foxe said nothing more and, as they approached the brow of the ridge, he began to ride faster again. The full horror of what he had said only gradually registered with Robert. No goose? *No goose.* And to be told so abruptly. It was not his father's usual habit to dispense his decisions in such a brutal manner. What could have happened? He wondered again what news Sir Henry had brought to his father. Robert looked for them both; they had passed into the small wood which lay ahead of them on the track. Calling out to Emily to do the same, Robert dug in his spurs. Beneath the bare, dank boughs, they cantered through the mud.

Following the path which brought them out of the wood, Robert reined in his horse. Ahead of him he could make out the hearth-fires of Woodton, but Captain Foxe and Sir Henry had both turned aside from the path, and were heading towards a gateway in an old, decaying wall. Beyond it, Robert knew, lay Wolverton Hall, where a Cavalier lord had once lived; but he had been killed in the war, and his seat had lain deserted ever since. Robert called out to Emily, and together they followed their fathers down the track; they had thought they would be ordered back, but Captain Foxe seemed scarcely aware of anyone now, and Sir Henry did not even look round, and so the four of them together approached the wall.

Behind it, entombed beneath snow, lay the old gardens. Emily and Robert had sometimes played in them; but both their fathers had discouraged them and, indeed, the children had observed how little any of the villagers spoke of the place, still less visited it. Robert's father, as Commissioner for the district, might by rights have settled in the Hall, but he had preferred to return to his old home after the war; and everyone, it seemed, was content to see the estate fall into decay. Even Robert and Emily, while exploring the grounds, had never dared to penetrate the house; why, Robert couldn't say; save that they were only young and had been influenced, perhaps, by the whisperings of their elders, although they were neither of them naturally cowards in their play, and delighted, indeed, in exploring deserted ruins, enjoying the pleasure that they found in their fear. But there would be no pleasure felt that night, Robert knew, no pleasure at all – for his fear was damper and colder than the snow, and reached deep into the very marrow of his bones. And Robert remembered what the minister in the Cathedral had said, that the Devil was abroad; and he thought of the Dark Spirit not as he had been taught to do, enthroned amongst Hell flames, but as a god of ice, beneath whose touch all the world must grow chill. He stared before him and prayed, but it did not comfort his spirits, for the chill seemed on his soul and his words could not rise up to God; and so Robert thought then – which as a child he had never felt before – how he was lost amidst the vale of Mortality.

Emily made a face at him. 'You look even gloomier than you did before,' she said. 'It frightens me, Robert, when you look so solemn.' She rode up closer so that she could shelter beside him. 'Can you tell what has happened?'

But Robert shook his head. And indeed, despite the sudden despair he had felt, there was nothing he could see which he immediately understood. The snow-storm was abating now. Ahead of them, a stretch of level ground which must once have been a lawn extended as far as the house; the snow was much churned up with tracks. Directly before the empty doorway of the house, a group of some six or seven men was gathered. Robert recognised one of them as Mr Gerrard Webbe, who preached universal salvation to the villages about Salisbury, calling for the levelling of privilege and wealth so that the oppressed might establish a heaven on earth. Once, though, in the days before the war, he had been a surgeon; and sometimes, as he went from place to place, Mr Webbe would still be called on to minister to the sick. Robert suddenly wondered in what capacity, whether as a surgeon or a man of God, he was serving now; for as Mr Webbe knelt with his back to him in the snow, Robert was unmistakably reminded of how his father had knelt in the Cathedral, head bowed, gazing down at the body of the murdered child. As then, so now, the view was obscured; but Robert felt, with a sudden shudder of certainty, that he scarcely needed to see what Mr Webbe was examining. Another person was dead: the killer – the sorcerer . . . whatever he might be . . . the *demon* – had killed again. And at the same moment as he understood this, he realised how clearly he could see all that lay before him; he gazed up at the front of the house, and saw how every window was illumined by candle flames, so that a patchwork of shadow and gold lit up the snows.

'Hannah,' he cried aloud.

He had not meant to speak. His father turned in his saddle, and frowned. He opened his mouth, as though to ask Robert a question; but then his frown deepened still further, and when he did speak it was to order his son away. Robert went without complaint; indeed, with relief. He had no wish to break his father's commands a second time. He glanced back at the candles again – and then thought of Hannah: imagined her dead; her belly ripped open for the life inside. He did not want to believe it, but he did – for he was certain now whose baby they had seen, scooped up in his father's arms; and he remembered the anguished cry of the Cathedral minister, his despairing question, 'Why?'

As Robert looked about him, they passed out from the gardens, and left the candle flames behind. All was black again. Suddenly, a fresh eddy of snow scudded across his face. The wind screamed through the trees, but he could only hear, not see, the boughs as they creaked; and beyond them, no matter how terrible the gale, the stones would be standing silent on the plain. Robert shivered; and when Emily met his gaze, not asking any questions now, he could think only of how he did not want her to be dead as Hannah was: her bright eyes to dim – her plump, soft body to turn cold and blue like the snow. He reached out to squeeze her arm, but at their backs the wind continued to moan; and when Emily whispered that she was scared, Robert could think of nothing comforting to say.

Emily's father was riding ahead of them, and it was he who broke the silence at last. He did not speak of the scene they had just left, but when he mentioned that Mrs Foxe was staying with Lady Vaughan, Robert knew for certain that it was Hannah who was dead. Only a terrible tragedy could have persuaded his mother to leave her home on such a night; certainly, nothing else could have persuaded her to stay with Lady Vaughan, who always reduced her to a state of nervous over-awe. Robert's mother had worked as a servant in Salisbury before her marriage, whereas Lady Vaughan was the wife of a gentleman. Mrs Foxe could never forget this; not even though her husband and Sir Henry were the best of

friends, not even though, since the war, all the world was
turned upside down, the small made great and the great
made small. It was Captain Foxe, after all, who had saved
the Vaughans from being utterly beggared after the war,
for Sir Henry had been a tireless partisan of the King,
and might have had his property confiscated had not
Captain Foxe pleaded his cause. Although it was never
spoken of by his parents, Robert knew this, because
Emily had told him everything; and in truth, his mother
had no cause to be timid, for Lady Vaughan had always
shown her the utmost affection and respect. Robert knew
it was she who had refused to discourage Emily from
playing with him; and for that alone, he would always
honour her.

And indeed, when he arrived at the Vaughans' house
to discover his mother folded in Lady Vaughan's
embrace, his sense of gratitude was reinforced, for
although his mother's face was white and pinched with
grief, he knew that without her neighbour's comforting
she would have been paler still. Lady Vaughan surrendered her; Mrs Foxe's relief at seeing her son was very
evident, but he saw her flinch when he was offered
supper and, although she encouraged him to eat, Robert
knew she was thinking of the goose they would never
now have cooked. She said nothing, however, about
Hannah, and continued silent as they returned to their
home; only once Robert's horse had been stabled and he
held her in his arms, did she at last start to talk. She
confirmed, what he had almost forgotten needed confirmation, that it was indeed Hannah who was dead. All
day, Sir Henry and a group of villagers had been
searching, ever since the alarm had first been raised that
morning – at which point Hannah had already been

missing for several hours. Not until after sunset had the body finally been found. Robert asked if it was the candles which had first drawn the search party to Wolverton Manor; but his mother looked blank. She had heard no mention of candles. Robert let the matter drop.

Mrs Foxe rose at length and drew out her Bible. She hugged it to herself; then began to turn the much-thumbed pages, like someone lost who is scanning a map. Together, she and her son studied them for several hours. Mrs Foxe could not read, but she knew the words of scripture almost by heart, and those parts she could not remember she would narrate as she saw fit. In this way, she found a gradual balm for her grief; and for Hannah, the servant who had also been her dearest friend, a tribute of tender and heartfelt love.

It began to grow late. At length, as they sat there together at their reading, Robert and his mother were joined by Mr Webbe. Mrs Foxe rose to greet him, but he gestured her to sit down. Gently, he kissed her on her brow. ' "He that is without sin among you," ' he murmured, ' "let him first cast a stone at her." ' Mrs Foxe stared up at him, then reached for the Bible from Robert's lap, to find the place where the verse could be found. But she did not need her son to read the story to her; she knew it well enough; for she had quoted it often in defence of Hannah who, like the woman brought before Jesus, had been taken in adultery. Mrs Foxe spoke the verses again now, and when she repeated Christ's words of forgiveness and hope, Mr Webbe joined with her: ' "I am the light of the world," ' they proclaimed together; ' "he that followeth me shall not walk in darkness, but shall have the light of life." ' Mrs Foxe began to smile. 'She has reached her journey's end, Mr Webbe,' she said. 'My Hannah and her child, they are at rest now, with Him whose company is Peace-after-life.' Then she turned to Robert, and hugged him tightly. She was still smiling. But down her cheeks, tears were flowing in silent tracks.

∽∾∾

'. . . A PROWLING WOLF,
WHOM HUNGER DRIVES TO SEEK NEW HAUNT FOR PREY,
WATCHING WHERE SHEPHERDS PEN THEIR FLOCKS AT EVE
IN HURDLED COTES AMID THE FIELD SECURE,
LEAPS O'ER THE FENCE WITH EASE INTO THE FIELD!'

John Milton, *Paradise Lost*

Captain Foxe joined them later that same night. His face was perfectly blank. He kissed his wife, and then his son; but he said nothing of what he had been doing, nor of what success his investigation might have had. He caught Mr Webbe's eye, though, and almost imperceptibly shook his head; Robert, observing this, doubted his father had discovered much. Mr Webbe, who rarely spoke a word when the spirit of the Lord was not upon him, only shrugged; he rose and, crossing to a dark corner of the room, rolled out a bedding mat. He had no need to ask if he could stay. He was an old acquaintance of Captain Foxe's; how old, Robert had never presumed to ask, but he knew the two men had served together in the army, and doubtless had shared much. For the purposes of his own curiosity, he wished that Mr Webbe would sometimes be less close; but it was the preacher's habit of silence, Robert knew, which did most to recommend him to Captain Foxe's good opinion. Mrs Foxe too, when she woke the next day, would be glad of Mr Webbe's company. For he was a good man; and gifted, she believed, with prophecy. He would help as he had already done, to guide her through the courses of her bereavement and grief.

Robert, as he lay in bed later, wished that he too could be so comforted. For unlike his mother, he had found little solace in the scriptures they had read; he had seen the Devil's mark stamped too clearly on the world, and its print had seemed more terrible than any mark of God. That night, although he lay with his eyes closed for many hours, sleep would not come to him, and the shadow of darkness lay thick on his soul. He tried to picture Hannah in his mind as Mr Webbe had described her, one amongst the company of saints; but instead, he could see her only as a mess of stinking corruption, and her dead baby too, slung upon the dunghill to be the blowflies' meat; and he dreaded to think how feeble was life, that could be reduced so easily to rottenness. At length, he rose from his bed, for he had found it impossible to banish such imaginings from his mind; he lit a candle and turned to his Greek, but as he read, he came to a passage describing the fall of Troy, and how Hector's baby child had been flung from the walls to be fed upon by dogs, and he could not bear to read the poet any further, and so he tossed the book aside. He rose to his feet again, for he knew that he needed to escape the closeness of the room and walk his nervous humour away. As he crossed to the doorway, he wondered if his parents at least had obtained their rest, and he turned back to look. His mother was asleep, and he was glad to see it, but the place beside her was empty, and he saw that his father's riding-boots were gone. Robert was not alarmed, for it was often his father's habit, when oppressed by a matter of business, to sleep barely at all – and the business before him now, it seemed likely, was as great as any he might ever have confronted.

As he returned to the doorway, Robert noticed that Mr Webbe's place was empty as well, and when he looked through the window at the stable doors, he saw that two of them were hanging open, and the horses were gone. Folding his cloak about him, he hurried outside. The snow was no longer falling, and the clouds had been blown away so that the sky was lit a crisp, cold blue by the blaze of the stars. Robert gazed up and down the village road, but he could neither see nor hear his father, although the snows gleamed as blue as the sky and the crunch of his own footsteps was loud in the air. He walked down the road until he was past the village, and approaching the wood; an owl called out once from the bare boughs of the trees, but otherwise the world seemed wholly embalmed beneath the snow. Robert reached the first line of trees, and called out his father's name; then Mr Webbe's. Again, no reply but the screeching of the owl. Robert sighed and turned – he was growing cold. He began to walk back.

Then, as he left the trees, he heard the distant sound of hoofbeats ringing through the air, and stared back down the road. From the shadows of the village, he saw a horseman emerge. The rider was cloaked in black, with a hood pulled close so that his face was obscured, and his horse, like his cloak, was a deep, coal-black. At the first sound of the hoofbeats, Robert had begun to run along the road; but when he saw the horseman, he immediately shrank back into the trees, and the nearer the horseman approached the faster he retreated, stumbling through the undergrowth, his heart beating louder and louder in his ears. At the point where the road first plunged into the trees, the rider reined in his horse. The path forked there, Robert knew – there was a track to the left, which led to Wolverton Hall. He dropped to the ground and froze, sheltering behind the branches of an old toppled elm. Then, slowly, he raised his head above the trunk again.

The rider was still sitting perfectly motionless, a cowled silhouette against the burning stars. Robert imagined all the wood must be pulsing with his heart, so loudly was it beating now, and he placed a hand on his chest to try to calm himself. As he did so, the rider looked round. He sniffed the air; the hood he wore fell fractionally back, and the light of the stars caught his face. He wore a thin beard and moustache, much like Sir Henry's; but in all other respects his face was like no one's Robert had ever seen before, and the merest sight of it filled him with disgust. It was deathly pale, with not a hint of colour in either the cheeks or lips; the mouth was thin and very cruel; the nose nothing but nostrils, the flesh around the bones having rotted utterly away. But it was the eyes which revolted and astonished Robert the most, for they were at once as piercing and silver as the brightest moon, and yet utterly dead, and he wondered what manner of thing might possess such a stare, and he shook his head, for he did not care to know. Then he shuddered, knowing that such eyes had seen him once before, and he prayed silently with all his soul that they would not see him a second time now, defenceless as he was, alone amidst the trees, on so cruel a night.

Robert held his breath. The rider pricked his horse forward a few paces and sat still again for a few moments underneath the trees. Still Robert did not breathe. He thought he would expire. Then the rider turned suddenly and, with a clattering of iron on frozen mud, the horse cantered away down the opposite lane – the lane which led towards Wolverton Hall. Robert waited where he was, sheltering behind the branches of the tree. Minutes passed until, very cautiously, he rose up to his feet. He looked about him; then he crept out past the trees and back on to the path. It was empty, although the trail of hoofprints was clear in the snow. Robert wondered if he should follow them. Not for long, though. He turned round and, his teeth chattering, began to run towards Wolverton, and the safety of his bed.

∽◦◦∼

'. . . ONE OF THE BANISHED CREW,
I FEAR, HATH VENTURED FROM THE DEEP, TO RAISE
NEW TROUBLES . . .'

John Milton, *Paradise Lost*

The next morning, when his father had still not returned, Robert went to visit Emily, and told her all he had seen. As he finished, she shook her head. 'No, no,' she complained, 'you are missing things out.'

'What things?' he asked.

'You said you had seen the horseman before. But you haven't said anything at all about that.'

'Oh.' Robert closed his eyes, then smiled guiltily. 'But I am not meant to tell you. Father swore me to keep it quiet.'

'Even with me?'

Robert smiled again.

Emily mimicked him. She paused. 'Anyhow,' she said, 'it is too late now. I know you have a secret, and if you will not tell me then I shall bother you until you do.'

Robert considered this point for a few moments.

Emily wrapped her arms round his neck. 'Well?' she asked.

'I should not,' he said at last.

'Of course not,' she replied.

'It was last week,' he said, after another pause. 'The Winter Solstice ... ' – he frowned – 'the feast-day of Yule.'

'Where were you?'

'Can you not guess?'

'Why should I?'

'It was on the fields below Clearbury Ring.'

'Clearbury Ring.' Emily hugged herself. 'Where your tutor was found.'

Robert inclined his head.

'What had you been doing there?'

'Riding. I was with my father. We were practising.'

'And so that was where you saw him?' Despite her solemn expression, Emily's eyes began to gleam. 'That was where you saw the horseman?'

'He was in his saddle ... ' – Robert paused – 'in his saddle,' he continued, 'not moving, just watching us. He was in black again, just like last night, with his hood pulled low across his face. That was how I recognised him yesterday night, when I saw him coming from the village – that was how I knew I had to run.'

'But why?' Emily hugged herself again. 'What had he done the first time, to frighten you so much?'

Robert wondered. 'I am not certain,' he said at last. 'He sat where he was for a long while – then he rode down towards us, and galloped past.'

Emily looked disappointed. 'And that was all?'

'Yes.'

'Where was the terror in that?'

'But you have not seen him, Emily. For if you had . . . ' Robert paused. He remembered the crawling terror he had felt, like lice across his skin, and knew that he could never hope to explain. 'I did not want to continue with the riding after that,' he said finally, 'but my father insisted – even though he seemed unsettled as well. And then, not long after, we heard shouting, and a man came hurrying down the hill waving at us. He was screaming there had been a murder, a body found in the centre of the Ring.'

Emily said nothing for a moment. Then she swallowed. 'Your tutor?'

Robert nodded.

'Who was the man who had come running down the hill?'

'Mr John Aubrey. A scholar, from Broadchalke, on the other side of Salisbury.'

Emily narrowed her eyes. 'And what had he been doing on Clearbury Ring?'

'My father asked him that immediately, of course.'

'And?'

'He said he was interested in ancient monuments.'

Emily frowned. 'Why?'

Robert shrugged. 'Because . . . I suppose that some people are. Mr Aubrey had gone to Clearbury Ring because he was looking for ghosts. They are meant to appear on the feast-day of Yule.'

'Why?' asked Emily again.

'Because the day was sacred to the pagans who lived

upon the Ring. They killed people as a sacrifice to the anger of their god.'

'Just like your tutor was killed.'

Robert paused. 'Perhaps,' he said at last.

Emily stared at him, her eyes very wide. 'And Mr Aubrey . . . ' She hesitated. 'Does your father think he might be guilty of the crime?'

'No, I don't think so. No, no, I am certain he doesn't.'

'So who does he suspect?'

Robert's stare was unblinking. 'Only the one,' he said finally.

Emily leaned forward. 'And last night, Robert,' she whispered, 'the horseman you saw . . . you are certain – quite certain – it *was* the same man?'

Robert turned from her. He crossed to the doorway and gazed out at the road, as it wound through the village up towards the wood. He closed his eyes. 'Quite certain,' he said at last.

Emily joined him. 'When will your father be back?' she asked.

Robert shook his head.

Emily reached to hold his cheeks and met his stare. 'The tracks you saw him leave,' she whispered with a sudden tense excitement, 'they will melt with the snow.'

Robert shrugged. 'Doubtless.'

'So . . .'

'So?'

'We should follow them now.'

Robert looked away again; but he did not disagree.

Emily pointed at the sun. 'Midday,' she said. 'It will not be dark for several hours yet.' She took his arm. 'We shall not go far. We will only follow the tracks.'

'Only?' Robert made a face. But although he felt

uneasy, he did not protest, and indeed the excitement of
their quest, and his sense of its possible value to his
father, made him hurry as he climbed with Emily up to
the wood. He showed her the spot where the horseman
had stopped. She studied it. 'Look,' she said, pointing.
There was a trail of hoofprints, still clear in the snow.
Emily took Robert's hand, then she glanced up at the sun
again. 'Not too late,' she murmured. She began to run.
'Come on.'

They followed the trail as far as they could. They lost it
shortly before the gateway to Wolverton Hall: the snow
was very churned up there from the evening before, and
it was impossible to distinguish all the various tracks.

'Well,' whispered Emily, 'I suppose we should go
back.' She gripped Robert's hand, and squeezed it tightly.
'For remember what we saw yesterday, when we followed
your father's trail.'

Robert nodded. He too wanted to turn. But as though
frozen to the ground, both children remained where they
stood. Then Emily walked forward and Robert followed
her. Dread tasted sickly and sweet in his mouth and, as
he drew nearer to the gateway, he began to feel it in his
blood, lightening his stomach and the bones in his legs.
'Emily,' he called out. But she did not stop; and he knew
she must be feeling as drawn as he was.

Stillness hung deathly over the gardens as the two
children crossed to where Hannah's body had been
found. There was nothing there now; brushing away the
snow, Robert imagined that he could see brown stains
upon the frozen soil, but he did not care to inspect too
closely, and he and Emily both rose and hurried on. 'The
stables,' said Emily, as they rounded the house. 'Surely, if
he came here, that is where his horse is going to be.' At

first they had hopes of discovering something, for a covered cart was standing in the yard, and although it was unhitched it must have been drawn there recently, for its paintwork was still fresh and its ropes unfrayed. Robert and Emily peered in through the back: but there was nothing there, save only a scattering of dirt. This disappointment was succeeded by an even greater one, however, for when they turned from the cart, they saw that the snow around the stables was undisturbed and the stalls themselves were rotten with disuse. The odour of damp wood hung thick in the air; and the mud across the floor was slimy with moss. Emily made a face. 'Eeugh!' she exclaimed. 'No one has been in here for many years.' She held her nose as she stared round at the dripping stalls again, then back at Robert. 'What about the house?'

Robert frowned. 'What about it?' he said at last.

'If he came here at all last night, then that is where he will be.' Again, she glanced round and up at the sun, which hung pale above the ridge of a western hill. 'Do you not think?' she asked.

'I suppose so,' agreed Robert reluctantly.

Emily shivered. But the glint of excitement was unmistakable in her eyes. She should not have said it, Robert thought. They would not then have had to go inside – there would not have been any challenge to their pride. But it was too late now. He looked up at the house. Every window was black. 'It may still be light outside,' he murmured, 'but in there . . .' And then he remembered the candles, how they had been placed by the windows the night before – and he realised that someone must have been inside to have lit them all.

They crossed the stable-yard to the rear of the house. When Emily pushed at a window frame, the wood snapped and crumbled at once. As quietly as they could, they clambered through. The room inside smelt worse than the stables, thick with mould, and dampness, and rot. They could feel weeds beneath their feet as they crept forward, and hear the crunch of frozen animal droppings; ahead of them loomed the skeletons of chairs, their fabric hanging like tatters of skin, and feathery to the touch with spiders' webs. Emily looked around. 'Eeugh!' she said, pulling an even worse face than she had done before. '*No one* could live here.'

'Then why are you whispering?' Robert asked.

'Eeugh!' she repeated, more loudly this time. She bent down, and picked up a broken piece of wood. 'Eeugh!' she cried out again several times, as though challenging the darkness. But although her voice echoed, there was no other reply. Emily flung the piece of wood through the nearest door.

There was a clattering, and the sound of china smashing. Both children scurried through to see what was broken. The light was much dimmer; even so, they could just make out the shattered fragments of a vase. Robert stared about him in amazement. Crockery and ornaments were everywhere. The house, he realised, must have been left utterly untouched – for almost fifteen years it had stood abandoned, and yet not a single thief had dared to pilfer it, not a single beggar had sheltered in its rooms. And then suddenly, he heard Emily whispering to him. 'Robert, come quick, through here, there's a light!'

She was in the next room and Robert hurried through to her. He realised they were standing in the hall. An oaken stairway rose ahead of them; it was still imposing, although spiders had woven the tapestries silver and fungus was oozing like sores from the wood. At the summit of the stairway stretched a gallery, where portraits could be made out dimly on the wall. Only one was lit so that the face could be seen; four candles, in a row, had been placed before it on the floor. 'No,' Robert whispered. 'No.' But though he wanted to shrink back, he had to make sure.

'What is it?' Emily hissed.

He pointed; then began to climb the stairs.

'Robert!'

She wasn't following him. He glanced back at her; her face, in the candlelight, seemed very pale. 'Can you not see it?' she whispered. 'There are no other footprints – none at all.' He looked down at where he had trodden, across the floor and up the steps; the trail was perfectly clear; for all around it, the dust and mould remained thick and undisturbed. Robert ran to the top and looked down either side of the gallery – again, his footprints were the only ones to be seen. And yet someone must have lit the candles – very recently too, for the wax had barely begun to flow. Robert looked up at the portrait, gazing at it in horror – and yet not in utter surprise. For he knew the face at once – he had seen it cowled and deathlike, the night before. It was the same man . . . there could be no mistake.

Robert stared at it a moment more; then shuddered violently, and turned and ran. As he did so, two of the candles were knocked to the floor, and in the sudden gloom, he almost fell down the stairs. He crashed into the side of the wall. As he struggled to regain his balance, he saw a cloaked form approaching him. It had risen from the darkness of the floor below, and was climbing the stairs. 'Emily,' Robert screamed, 'Emily, are you there?'

But the blood was pounding in his ears, and he couldn't hear what she said – if she said anything at all. The figure was on him now. He thrashed out blindly – he struck it once – and then it seized his arms. 'Robert.' He froze. 'Robert,' he heard again, 'in the name of our dear Lord Jesus Christ – please!'

He looked up into his father's face. Captain Foxe smiled. 'You are safe,' he said.

Robert half-laughed, half-sobbed. He hugged his father as tightly as he could.

Captain Foxe lifted his son up in his arms, and clasped him in turn. 'What was it?' he asked. 'What was it made you scream?'

Robert turned and pointed at the portrait on the wall. His father inspected it briefly; then glanced round. Mr Webbe was just behind him; Emily was folded in the preacher's arms. The eyes of the two men met, and a shadow crossed the faces of both.

'Who is he?' Robert asked, still gazing at the portrait. 'I saw him last night.'

Again, Captain Foxe met Mr Webbe's eye; then he nodded. Mr Webbe set down Emily, and climbed the stairs; he heaved the painting down from the wall. As he did so, he shuddered, and held it as though its very touch might poison him. Neither he nor Captain Foxe spoke a further word; and Robert's question hung unanswered in the damp and mouldy air.

They left the house through the open front door. There were a couple of troopers standing on the lawn, Robert saw; they saluted Captain Foxe, and then one of them waved with his arms, beckoning to something in the darkness behind the house. Robert heard the faint clopping of horse hooves, and a rumbling of wheels;

there were more shouts, and then the cart which he and Emily had seen before emerged from round the house. Captain Foxe stood watching its progress across the lawn; he nodded to his troopers, and gestured with his arm towards the gateway in the wall. He watched the cart pass; then he frowned and turned, and stood for a moment frozen in thought. He studied the front of the house, barely visible now in the twilight gloom.

'Robert . . . ' He paused. 'Yesterday – you never saw poor Hannah – and yet you knew at once, it seemed, that it was she who was dead.'

'Yes,' his son agreed.

'How?'

'It was the candles.'

'Candles?'

'Yes. The candles in every window of the house. It made me think of the dead child we had seen. I did not know for certain, but I suddenly feared that the baby had been torn from Hannah's womb.'

'Why?'

'It was Childermas,' said Emily suddenly. 'When we remember the slaughter of the Innocents. I told you that, didn't I, Robert, when we saw the candles lit yesterday?'

Captain Foxe glanced at her briefly, then turned back to his son. 'But why should you associate that with Hannah's murder?' he asked.

Robert swallowed, not wanting to answer. The darkness suddenly seemed very cold again.

'Robert,' his father coaxed him.

'It was the same, wasn't it?' he blurted out at last. 'Like with Mr Yorke. The way he was killed. Like a sacrifice.'

Mr Webbe furrowed his brow. 'Sacrifice?' he asked in his low, soft voice.

'Yes.' Robert turned and appealed to his father. 'You remember? You must do. Just like Mr Aubrey said. A sacrifice must be offered on the feast-day of Yule. Well, it was. And now a child has been killed on Innocents' Day.' His voice trailed away. 'Anyway,' he continued weakly, 'that was how I knew. I just remembered what Mr Aubrey had said.'

'Yes,' said Captain Foxe slowly. 'You remembered what Mr Aubrey had said.' He pondered in silence for a moment; then glanced across to Mr Webbe. 'Perhaps we should see what else he might have to say.'

Mr Webbe made no reply.

Captain Foxe shrugged. He reached for Emily's and then for Robert's hand. Together they trudged through the snow, meeting no one on the track, towards the blessed flickering of the village lights.

∽⌒∾

'THESE LOOKS OF THINE CAN HARBOUR NAUGHT BUT DEATH;
I SEE MY TRAGEDY WRITTEN IN THY BROWS.'
Christopher Marlowe, *Edward II*

For the next three days, Captain Foxe was absent again. When he finally returned, it was late at night, and his household had to rise from their beds to greet him. Mrs Foxe and Robert found him sitting by the doorway, pulling off his boots. He looked exhausted and tense; he was streaked with mud, and his clothes were sodden through. At the sight of his wife, however, his face lit up and he reached up to fold her in his arms. 'How I have missed you, my dearest love,' he whispered softly. 'I have kept you much in my thoughts, as a comfort to my soul,

for there is great evil abroad, and devilry.' He closed his
eyes and kissed her; then he turned to his son. 'Would
you care to go fishing tomorrow?' he asked.

Robert stared at him in surprise.

Captain Foxe smiled. 'Would you care to go fishing?'
he asked a second time.

Robert nodded slowly. The promise had originally
been made to him as a reward for his achievements in
Greek; he had assumed – in the wake of Hannah's death
– that the fishing trip had gone the way of the goose. He
nodded again, very fast. He did not want his father
changing his mind.

But Captain Foxe, having given it, kept to his word. He
had a meeting, he told his son as they set off early the
next morning, with a man whose stretch of river was
famous for its chub; the man had personally insisted that
Robert should come and try out his luck. Captain Foxe
did not say who the man was, nor what his interest in
him might be; and Robert knew better than to pry. But he
observed his father's set expression, and the brace of
pistols in his belt; and he doubted it was fish his father
hoped to catch that day.

They travelled by way of Salisbury. Captain Foxe had
business there; he apologised to his son, and insisted it
would not delay them very long. Outside the Council
Hall, he dismounted, and was pleased to see two of his
men come hurrying towards him immediately. 'We've
found him, sir,' said one of them. 'We've got him round
the back with Sergeant Everard.'

Captain Foxe nodded. 'Excellent.' He ordered his men
to follow him, and led the way round the side of the
Council Hall. They entered a yard where the soldiers'

horses were quartered and, in its very rear, a covered cart. It had been brought there three days before, when Captain Foxe ordered its removal from Wolverton Hall. Two men were inspecting it. One, to judge by his clothes, was a driver or stablehand; the other wore the uniform of a militiaman.

Captain Foxe smiled. 'Samuel!' he called out.

The militiaman glanced round. He answered Captain Foxe's smile, then stood to attention. 'This is our man, sir,' he said with a wave of his hand. 'He's the one who sold the cart.'

The journeyman scowled and shrank back. 'I haven't done anything wrong,' he muttered.

'No one is saying you have,' replied Sergeant Everard pleasantly. 'The Captain here just wants to have a word with you, that is all.'

Captain Foxe, meanwhile, had wandered to the front of the cart. He reached out beneath the awning, and ran a finger along one of the boards, then held it to the light. 'Mud.' He frowned and, turning back, inspected below the covering again. 'A great deal of mud.' He stared at the journeyman. 'How did it get there?'

The man shrugged uneasily. 'That was what he wanted taken.'

'*Mud?*'

'Well – soil. Earth. In boxes. Some of it must have spilled.'

'Why did he want earth carried?' asked Sergeant Everard.

'I don't know,' said the journeyman, clearly surprised that it should be considered any of his business.

'And this "he" – what was his name?'

Again, the man shrugged.

'He must have given you a name,' said Sergeant Everard disbelievingly. 'Where he was staying, at least, where you could contact him.'

The journeyman shook his head. 'He just paid in coin, and I took it. I barely had a look at him.'

'But could you remember his face?', asked Captain Foxe urgently. 'If you saw him now?'

The journeyman shrugged yet again. Captain Foxe, suddenly losing his patience, took him by the arm and dragged him across the yard. The journeyman began to shout angrily; but Captain Foxe merely tightened his grip. 'I want to show you something,' he said quietly; and the journeyman, sensing something in his captor's tone, allowed himself to be led into the Council Hall without further complaint. 'Here,' said Captain Foxe, unlocking the door to a small, paper-littered room and crossing to the far corner. 'Was this the man who bought your cart?'

He lifted a purple cloth to reveal the painting which Mr Webbe had removed from Wolverton Hall. The journeyman studied it. He shuddered suddenly, then shook his head.

'You are certain?'

The journeyman shook his head again. 'The man I saw, his beard was very curling and thick.'

'Might it not have grown since this portrait was painted?'

'No, sir – the face is quite different. And the man I met with – he was dressed very strange – like a foreigner, sir. Didn't speak like an Englishman at all.'

This news startled Captain Foxe. He continued to frown, and stare at the portrait.

The journeyman glanced at the picture again nervously. 'Can I leave now?' he asked.

Captain Foxe waved his hand. The journeyman muttered an exclamation of relief and, turning on his heels at once, clattered down the stairs. But Captain Foxe barely heard him go; he continued to study the painting, his frown deepening, his knuckles whitening as he clenched his fists. At length, he bent down, and turned the portrait to the wall. He swathed it in its cloth; then he shut the door on it, and secured the padlock on the bolt.

Robert sat hunched by the river bank. He felt oddly unsettled, which annoyed him, for by rights he should have been feeling pleased with himself. He had only been fishing for half an hour, and already he had caught more than enough for his family's supper – two plump chub, laid out neatly on the grass. He sighed and shifted, and glanced about him. All was calm. The river flowed by with a glassy quiet, the bare-boughed trees were still beneath a silver sheen of frost. To Robert's right lay the grey-stoned tower of Broadchalke church, and beyond the trees thin plumes of smoke wisped from the village hearth fires, rising almost straight into the clear blue sky. It was a scene of wondrous, hushed beauty; and yet still Robert felt uneasy, and he did not know why.

He inspected his hands. They looked clean enough; but even though he had washed them again and again, he still seemed to feel the dirt behind his nails and on his skin. He wished he had never clambered on to the cart. It was as though the filth it had been carrying had clung to him. He bent down to wash his hands again, then dried them on the grass of the bank. He closed his eyes; and at once, he imagined that the dirt was still on his skin, thickening, feeding, like some living thing. He looked down in horror – but saw that his hands were as clean as before. He shook his head and sighed, then rose to his feet. As he did so, he heard the clattering of hooves on distant stone.

Robert clambered up the frozen mud of the river bank. A lawn stretched away from him, and at its far end stood the Old Rectory, the Broadchalke home of Mr Aubrey, who two weeks before had found the corpse on Clearbury Ring. Robert crept forward, using bushes and trees as cover, until he had reached the stables by the side of the house. He peered out at the yard, and saw his father standing with Mr Webbe. They had their backs to him, and were greeting the horseman who had clearly just arrived. Robert recognised him at once. He frowned. What was Colonel Sexton doing here? He was an important man: in command of the militia for the entire county and beyond. Clearly, Robert thought, his father's business was more urgent than he had ever dared to think.

He watched as the three men crossed the yard, and passed through a low door into the house. Robert scurried after them, then crept along the side of the garden-facing wall. He had gone half-way when he passed a large window and, peering in, saw the glow of a fire. He watched as his father walked into the room; then Colonel Sexton and Mr Webbe. A fourth man rose from a chair, where he was surrounded by books and stacks of papers; as he was introduced to Colonel Sexton, Robert recognised Mr Aubrey.

The four men took their places at a long oaken table. Kneeling outside, Robert made himself as comfortable as the cold would allow. Then he pressed his ear to the window-pane.

'MY GREAT GRANDFATHER, WILL: AUBREY, AND HE WERE
COUSINS, AND INTIMATE ACQUAINTANCE. DR. A.'S COUNTRY-
HOUSE WAS AT KEW, AND J. DEE LIVED AT MORTLAKE, NOT A
MILE DISTANT . . . AMONG HIS MANUSCRIPTS, WERE SEVERAL
LETTERS BETWEEN HIM AND JOHN DEE, OF CHEMISTRY AND
MAGICAL SECRETS.'

John Aubrey, *Brief Lives*

'I trust,' said Colonel Sexton, leaning forward in his
chair, 'that you have brought me to this place for a
purpose. I will not conceal from you that I was reluctant
to come. There are great disturbances abroad in the
Commonwealth, of which none of you yet can have any
idea.'

'There are lives at stake,' replied Captain Foxe shortly,
'perhaps many lives. It is my hope today that we may
attempt to save them.'

'Then that is purpose enough,' said the Colonel. He
nodded, and gestured with his hand. 'Proceed.'

'I believe,' said Captain Foxe, after a lengthy pause,
'that there is a great residue of evil which waits in the
darkness of the long-forgotten past, in the stones, and
tombs, and ancient places hereabouts, which may seem
to be silent and yet, for our sins, is sometimes not.'

Colonel Sexton stirred uneasily. 'Perhaps you are
right,' he muttered, 'but such considerations are scarcely
the business of a militiaman.'

Captain Foxe ignored the reproof. 'You have read my
report, of course,' he asked, 'on the murders committed
these past two weeks?'

'Of course.'

'And you recall the dates, and their significance?'

Colonel Sexton waved his hand disdainfully. 'Fancy, as I have warned you before, the merest fancy . . .'

'No.' Captain Foxe spoke quietly, but with such cold intensity that he froze his superior's words upon his tongue. Both men stared at each other; and for a moment they seemed like blocks of ice, lit only by the flickerings of colour from the fire. 'She was a child, sir,' whispered Captain Foxe at last, 'unborn, ripped from her mother's womb – an innocent, murdered on Innocents' Day. And then my son's tutor – an old man killed when the year itself is nearest death, on the Winter Solstice, the feast-day of Yule. Fancy, sir? No. *Such coincidences are more than mere coincidence.*'

Colonel Sexton met his captain's stare. 'What, then,' he asked at length, 'if not coincidence?'

'You know, sir, full well.'

'You have proof, Captain, beyond the mere fact of these murders and their dates?'

'Of witchcraft, sir? Of the worship of demons and blood-steeped, ancient gods?' Captain Foxe glanced across the table at Mr Aubrey. 'I do.'

'Then produce it. For you know full well, Captain, and have often argued so yourself, what terror the charges of witchcraft can inspire, and what persecutions of the innocent, whom we are charged to protect. Be very careful before you press your accusations. I beg you, John.' Colonel Sexton leaned forward. 'Be wary what you say.'

'You are right, of course, sir' – Captain Foxe bowed his head – 'to counsel caution. But I am certain of my case. For you see – I would never have spoken of witchcraft to you, had I not known already who the murderer was.'

'You know?' The Colonel stared at him in disbelief. 'How?'

'The cloaked rider we saw by Clearbury Ring – my son has since seen his face and has identified it with an authenticated portrait of the man.'

'And who was it?'

Captain Foxe swallowed. He glanced at Mr Webbe. 'Sir Charles Wolverton,' he said.

There was a sudden silence, save only for the crackling of the fire.

'Impossible,' said Colonel Sexton at last. 'Quite impossible.' Despite himself, he ran his hands through his hair. 'Sir Charles has been dead these past fifteen years.' He jabbed a sudden finger at Captain Foxe. 'You, John, your company, you reported him dead.'

Silence settled on the room again. Then Mr Aubrey cleared his throat. 'I count myself a not unenterprising historian of these parts,' he said hesitantly, 'and yet, alas, I must confess it – I have never heard of any Sir Charles Wolverton.'

'You were young,' answered Captain Foxe shortly, 'before the war broke out – otherwise you would certainly have heard of him. But since the war, his name has been buried. Men do not speak of it. No, sir, please . . .' He raised his hand, seeing that Mr Aubrey had reached for his pen. 'Do not make notes, for the oblivion which has descended upon Wolverton's memory was all too well-deserved. And yet, in truth, why should I stop you? For now his name, like his body, walks abroad once again.'

'And how can this be, Captain,' asked Colonel Sexton ominously, 'that Sir Charles has risen from his grave?'

'Because, sir' – Captain Foxe glanced at Mr Webbe, then bowed his head – 'he was never laid in it.'

'What?' exclaimed Colonel Sexton.

'The fault was mine.'

The Colonel glanced round in surprise, for it was Mr Webbe who had spoken. He did not meet Colonel Sexton's stare. Instead, he sat hunched over the table, gazing distantly into the depths of the fire. 'I would not be a judge over a fellow man,' he murmured at last. 'I would not condemn, and kill in cold blood. For what was it I had been fighting against, if not the power of the King's men to commit such crimes? How could I have been so wicked and arrogant as to judge what was sin, and what was not?'

'How indeed, sir?' Colonel Sexton spoke with icy restraint. 'Even though Sir Charles Wolverton was rumoured to have satisfied his lusts through torture and vile cruelties – yes, even against children, as was later discovered. Would you not call that sin? And yet what are you telling me?' He stared at Mr Webbe in disbelief. 'That you had the man, and then set him free?'

Mr Webbe continued to stare into the fire. 'I did not know then what was later proven true,' he whispered in a distant voice. He buried his face in his hands. '*I did not know.*'

Captain Foxe reached out to touch Mr Webbe on the arm. 'The fault was with us both.'

'Then explain yourself, Captain.'

Captain Foxe met Mr Webbe's stare; he breathed in deeply. 'You will remember, sir,' he began, 'how at the end of the war, I and my men were ordered to Salisbury.'

'Naturally, for it was I who sent you there.'

Captain Foxe nodded; then he turned to Mr Aubrey, to explain to him. 'The armies of the King had been scattered – and yet their power to inflict mischief had not been utterly destroyed. It was therefore the responsibility of myself and my men to disarm those Cavaliers who were still at large, both in Salisbury and in the countryside surrounding the town. We duly arrived; and yet the rumours were so conflicting and confused that we could not be certain where to start our search. Then Sir Henry Vaughan, whom I had known from before the war, was brought unexpectedly before me, streaked with dust and gashed with wounds. He had always been a loyal partisan of the King, and had fought throughout the war in a unit of horse, Sir Charles Wolverton's regiment, in which he had served as the second-in-command. He had long sought to restrain the viciousness of his superior; but now, with the war ended, he had abandoned the attempt, for Wolverton's cruelty and rage had grown worse with defeat, and he and Sir Henry had at last come to blows. Sir Henry had escaped; and he urged me to pursue Wolverton at once, for he was afraid that his commander might be plotting some revenge.

'Sir Henry had fled Wolverton and his men by the London road, not far from Stonehenge and Wolverton Hall. Accordingly, I headed to the same place as fast as I could; Mr Webbe was with me, and twenty other troopers, all brave, good men. There was a trail, easily distinguished, leading across the Plain, and so we followed it at once; it took us, not surprisingly, to Wolverton Hall. We found the house deserted, however – and then suddenly, from the distance, we heard the muffled beating of a drum, and saw a plume of heavy smoke. It was rising from Woodton: my own village, and Sir Henry's. I felt a numb horror seize me, and my heart began to quicken with the rhythm of the drum, for the beat was sounding faster the closer I approached. I was riding forward as quietly as I could by now, for I had ordered my men to surround the village without being seen. But no one observed us – for the simple reason that no one was abroad who could have done. The approaches to Woodton were wholly empty; as were the outer limits of the village itself. We were thus soon in our positions in a circle round the square.

'That was where I found the villagers. They had been herded together in a panic-stricken huddle. A great bonfire was raging, and along either side of it gallows had been raised. Wolverton and his men were gathered on horseback by the fire; one of the horsemen was beating the drum and, when it had reached its climax, Wolverton raised his hand and began to address the weeping crowd. He told them that they were accursed, that they and their village were to be utterly destroyed. In revenge for Sir Henry's betrayal, and for my own treachery towards the King, the men were to be hanged and the women condemned to the bonfire's flames. There were screams and cries of despair at these words, but Wolverton only closed his eyes and smiled, as though indulging himself in some profound pleasure which the terror of his victims was arousing in him. 'Those two whores first,' he cried, opening his eyes again and pointing towards the flames. Two women were dragged forward. They had refused to scream or plead for their lives, and so it was only when I saw their faces that I realised who they were. 'No!' I cried, galloping forward. 'No!' My men at once followed my lead; they burst from their hiding places and surrounded the startled Cavaliers, but I had no concern save to rescue my wife, to rescue her and Lady Vaughan from the threat of the flames. Mr Webbe rode to join me; and it was he who fought with Wolverton, who had crossed to prevent me from saving the women. The Cavalier guarding her and Lady Vaughan, I killed in my rage; Mr Webbe merely wounded his adversary. Wolverton was left in the mud, clutching at his side; and as we began the process of disarming his men, I was content to leave him there. It was my hope that, untreated, he might bleed to death.'

'But he did not,' said Colonel Sexton.

'No,' said Mr Webbe. He shook his head, still staring at the fire. 'He did not.'

'What did you do with him?'

'What we did with the others – stripped him of his arms and money.' Captain Foxe shrugged. 'Then Mr Webbe and I escorted him to the coast. There was a ship at Portsmouth, bound for the port of Lübeck in Germany; we put him aboard it, and paid his passage. There was no chance he could have slipped ashore again – his wound was very bad. And when he arrived in Germany, he would have been possessionless, moneyless, one of God's poor – those poor whom he had formerly despised so much.'

'And may yet,' said Mr Webbe, 'for our sins.'

There was a brief silence. Then Colonel Sexton suddenly scraped back his chair. 'No,' he said brusquely, as he rose to his feet. 'I do not think so.'

Captain Foxe stared up at him angrily. 'You have no reason, sir, to doubt what we have said.'

'Not the facts you have given me; but the interpretation you have put upon them, yes, John, I do. For instance' – he began to pace across the floor – 'you have said that your son glimpsed Sir Charles' face, and then recognised it again when he saw a portrait of the man. But when would that portrait have been painted? Before the war, at the very least. Twenty years ago? Twenty-five, perhaps? Sir Charles, if he were indeed still alive, would be an old man by now.'

'That is true,' said Mr Webbe slowly, as his face brightened. But Captain Foxe frowned, and shook his head. 'Then whom did my son see?' he asked. 'What other theory can you possibly have?'

'One which your own confession now makes certain.' Colonel Sexton reached inside his coat, and drew out a sheaf of papers. He dropped it on to the table. 'This is a deed of inheritance. It establishes the right of Edward Wolverton, son of the late Sir Charles, to those properties and lands held by his father, and left unconfiscate by Parliament.'

'But Edward Wolverton is dead.'

'It would seem not.'

Captain Foxe glanced at Mr Aubrey. 'But ...' He swallowed, and turned to look up at the Colonel. 'I found him,' he whispered violently. 'All of Wolverton's children – I found them. You remember, sir. They were dead, all dead.'

'Their remains were' – Colonel Sexton swallowed, and then he too lowered his voice – 'very much decayed.'

Mr Aubrey stirred uneasily. 'If you wish,' he said, half rising, 'I can leave ...'

'No, no,' said Colonel Sexton as brusquely as he could, 'we need not discuss this matter any further, for your own words, Captain, have established that Edward must surely be alive. These papers' – he held them aloft – 'were drafted in and sent to us from the city of Prague. That is why they were brought to my attention – it was felt that such an origin must brand them a definite fraud. But now, since we know that Sir Charles was in Germany after the war, and was clearly joined there by his son at least, we can be confident that the papers are genuine indeed.'

Silence, doubtful and uneasy, fell on the room.

'Who was it, then,' Captain Foxe asked at length, 'whom Robert saw, cloaked in black, with a face which seemed to be that of Sir Charles?'

'Why, John, it is obvious – Edward, his son.' Colonel Sexton brandished the papers. 'For we know he was planning to return to England.'

'But has anyone else seen him, apart from Robert?'

'No. He must be lying low. He has an agent, though, who has been very active for him.'

Captain Foxe frowned. 'A foreigner? Very pale, with a large, black beard?'

'You have seen him?'

'The man who bought the cart to transport the soil . . .' Captain Foxe had been speaking almost to himself; as his voice trailed away, so his frown deepened and he closed his eyes. He seemed to be rehearsing an argument beneath his breath. Then suddenly, he clapped his hands together, and leaned back in his chair. 'It makes no difference, Sir Charles or Edward Wolverton – the man must be seized. He was seen heading towards Wolverton Hall. Where else can he be but skulking in its cellars? I need your permission, sir, to flush the rat out from its lair.'

Colonel Sexton shook his head. 'Edward Wolverton has done no wrong.'

'He has killed two people.'

'You have no evidence for that.'

'We have evidence of witchcraft.'

'But I repeat, Captain – none to connect it with Edward Wolverton.'

'Is he not his father's son?' Captain Foxe brought his fist crashing down; then he leaned across the table. 'Do I need to remind you, sir, of what we found in the cellars of Wolverton Hall? The books, the drawings, the . . .' – he swallowed – 'the . . . other . . . evidence . . . of . . . unspeakable rites?' He paused to control himself; then leaned back in his chair. 'Such a man,' he whispered, 'would pass down to his son not only the poison of evil in his blood, but also his teachings, his books, his hellish beliefs.'

Colonel Sexton sighed, and shook his head; but as he did so, Mr Aubrey lifted up his hand. 'If I may just add . . .' he said nervously.

'Yes?'

'These Wolvertons – they would have lived, you think, in the city of Prague?'

'Yes,' said Colonel Sexton impatiently, glancing down at the papers. 'What of it?'

'Prague is a most notorious place. A man raised there, especially by a father such as you paint Sir Charles to have been, would have had many opportunities to study the black arts. I know this, sir, because I have a book . . .' – he rose excitedly, and searched through his shelves – 'yes, here it is – here – just have a look at this . . .' He removed the book from its place, and smoothed out its pages. They were covered with a strange, hand-written script, which Mr Aubrey pointed to with pride. 'Incomprehensible!' he boasted. 'Utterly incomprehensible. A script which has defied my every effort to translate.'

Colonel Sexton shook his head in bemusement. 'But what has this to do with Prague?'

'Because' – Mr Aubrey took a deep breath – 'I had this from my great-grandfather, Mr William Aubrey, who was the cousin and confidant of Dr John Dee – you have heard of him, no doubt? – the great astrologer to Queen Elizabeth? – who travelled to Prague – and brought many books back. You see, sir?' He pushed the book forward. 'It illustrates a woman in a bath of flowing blood . . .'

'Enough!'

'But it is proving my point, how in Prague . . .'

'I have told you, sir – enough!'

Mr Aubrey fell into a reluctant silence. He stared reproachfully at Colonel Sexton, then reached for his books and placed them back on the shelf. No one spoke as he returned to the table. He opened his mouth once; then closed it again and sat hunched in his place.

Colonel Sexton sighed. He rubbed his eyes; then began to pace slowly up and down in front of the fire. 'I should not be telling you this,' he said at length, addressing Captain Foxe in a low, sombre voice. 'I fear, though, it will be common knowledge all too soon enough. The Commonwealth is collapsing, John. Parliament, it is said, will shortly be dissolved. The army is preparing to march upon London.' He paused. 'The King waits in Holland to be restored to his throne.'

Captain Foxe shrugged. 'As he has been waiting these eleven years now.'

'Do not be naïve.' Colonel Sexton rounded the table to meet his deputy's stare. 'You know full well what I mean. If the King is restored, John – then so are all his men.'

'That is not certain,' said Captain Foxe obstinately.

'No. But it is probable.'

'All the more reason, then, why we must act at once.'

'I cannot allow you into Wolverton Hall.'

'Why not, sir?'

'I have told you.'

Captain Foxe narrowed his eyes. 'Because the King's

men may be returning, and you are afraid for your post? As I remember, sir, you used not to be so scared of Cavaliers.'

The blood had at once left Colonel Sexton's face. He clenched his fists; then, very slowly, unclenched them again. 'I would not have taken that,' he whispered, 'from any other man.'

'Of course not, sir.' Captain Foxe bowed his head. 'So I have your permission then, do I, to enter the house?'

A smile, very faint, flickered on Colonel Sexton's lips. 'You always did ride your luck, Captain.'

'Yes, sir.'

'But it is not luck altogether, I think. The Spirit of the Lord watches over you.'

'He watches over us all, sir.'

Colonel Sexton smiled faintly again. 'And if you find nothing?' he asked at length. 'If Wolverton Hall is empty – what then?'

Captain Foxe glanced at Mr Aubrey. 'We shall still not be wholly lost,' he said, 'God willing.' He turned back to face his superior. 'It may be, sir,' he explained, 'there will be a further trail we can follow. That is why I asked that we should have our meeting here, and have free discussion before Mr Aubrey so that he may learn what we know about the author of the crimes, and be equal with us in our pursuit of the fiend, whose evil otherwise may overwhelm us all.'

'Otherwise, Captain?' asked Colonel Sexton, '*otherwise*? So Mr Aubrey's presence is truly that important? I agreed to your request that he be in attendance with us, but without understanding why, for I was content to trust to your good sense, and thought the reason for it would soon become clear. It has not, though.' Turning to study Mr

Aubrey, who sat sulking in his chair, the Colonel
frowned. 'I still do not see how he can help us,' he
murmured. He turned back to Captain Foxe. 'And yet you
tell me he will lead us to Wolverton?'

'He may, should we require him to.'

'How?'

'He is a chronicler of Wiltshire's monuments.'

'Why should that be of any concern to us?'

'I told you before, Colonel. We are hunting evil – and
there is evil waiting in the monuments hereabouts. Is
that not so, Mr Aubrey?'

Mr Aubrey shrugged, and twisted, and scratched at his
head. 'It is possible,' he stammered, 'in a sense, I suppose. There is much uncertainty on the matter. I really
couldn't say.' But he began to nod to himself; and at once
it was as though the motion of his head was shaking up
his ideas, so that when he spoke again, he seemed barely
able to keep pace with his thoughts. 'The antiquities are
so very ancient,' he explained, 'and so few records of
them survive, that it really is very difficult to say. . . and
yet I think – yes, I really do – that if one surveys them on
the spot, and interprets what legends and old stories say –
and allows one's speculations free wing – then . . . yes . . .
one could argue – *please* don't smile – that they were used
by the priests of terrible gods – by the Druids, perhaps –
as places of sacrifice – in dark groves, or beneath the
shadow of stones – to spill out their victims' living blood.'

Colonel Sexton frowned. 'As the blood of victims is
being spilled out now?'

Captain Foxe shrugged. 'We know that Wolverton was
a sorcerer, and worshipper of evil spirits.'

'But the girl – the tiny baby – she was left in the
Cathedral itself.'

'In the Lady Chapel, I believe?' Mr Aubrey turned to Captain Foxe for confirmation; received it; then continued. 'The Lady Chapel was the first part of the Cathedral to be built,' he explained. 'Why was it started there? We know – from the old records – how churches were often built on ancient pagan sites. It is a theory I offer – with humble submission to better judgements – that the Cathedral itself was built on just such a site.'

The Colonel considered this point. 'So what are you suggesting?' he asked. 'That there is significance not only in the dates of the murders, but in the locations as well?'

Captain Foxe nodded. 'Does that not seem possible? In the architecture of our world, is there not a pattern of evil, as there is a pattern of good? Might not this pattern – by a follower of the Accursed One – be discerned and traced, and then marked out, as it was in ancient times, with innocent blood?'

'You are certain, then, there will be another killing?'

'I am certain of that, whether there is a pattern or not.'

'And if the pattern does exist – what shape does it take?'

Captain Foxe gestured towards Mr Aubrey. 'You understand now, sir, the need for an antiquarian's presence at our conference. For Mr Aubrey, it seems to me, is best placed of all the men in England to divine when – and where – the next killing will take place.'

'Then, sir – you have a heavy charge.' Colonel Sexton stared at Mr Aubrey; he rose and laid a hand upon his shoulder. 'May God's light guide you in your studies. May He bring you to a truth that may serve us all.'

'And may He render your studies unnecessary,' added Captain Foxe. 'May He permit us to capture and confound the man we seek.'

'Amen.' Colonel Sexton bowed his head. 'Amen, indeed.'

∽◌∾

'LET NONE ADMIRE
THAT RICHES GROW IN HELL; THAT SOIL MAY BEST
DESERVE THE PRECIOUS BANE.'

John Milton, *Paradise Lost*

Emily Vaughan sat crouched behind the wall, peering through a gap in the masonry. She could make out two covered wagons, stationed in front of Wolverton Hall. A horseman was next to them. His skin seemed to gleam; the pallor of his face set off the curling thick blackness of his beard. Emily shivered. Something in his presence chilled her. She was not sure what; but she had felt it at once when she had first seen him, riding down the village road. As she shrank closer against the wall, she began to wish that she had never followed the man.

A couple of figures came shambling out from the main doorway of the Hall. They were as pale as the man with the beard, but otherwise quite unlike him. Indeed, so malformed they appeared, so dead-eyed and numb-faced, that they scarcely seemed to be human at all. The bearded man glanced at them. He did not speak or even nod; but at once, it was as though he had issued orders to the men. They shuffled across to one of the wagons. As they lifted the awning, Emily caught a glimpse of wooden boxes stacked in neat rows. The two strange figures eased one of them out. The box was about six feet long, made from rough, unpainted planks. It seemed heavy, but the two creatures bore it as though it were no weight at all.

They carried it up the steps and into the Hall.

The horseman watched them, absolutely motionless; then he felt in his pockets and pulled out what appeared to be a couple of heavy purses. He tossed one of them up and down in his palm; even from where she was hiding, Emily could hear the clinking of coins. The drivers of the two carts must have heard the sound as well. Emily watched them as they clambered down from their seats, and came hurrying across to where the horseman sat. He laughed. He tossed one of the purses into the mud, then a second; then, reaching again into his pockets, a third and fourth. The drivers scrabbled after them; the horseman waited, then threw out a fifth purse, and lolled in his saddle as the drivers began to fight. At length, growing bored, he rode across and separated the brawlers with his riding crop. He gestured them away. The two drivers picked themselves up, and turned to withdraw. As they did so, Emily saw their faces for the first time. She recognised them at once. They were labourers from Woodton, Jonas Brockman and Elijah, his son. She had often seen them in her father's fields.

Emily pressed her face closer to the crack in the wall. As she did so, the horseman turned and sniffed the air. The two servants, reappearing from the Hall, also paused and seemed to breathe in. Their eyes, which before had seemed nothing but sockets, now began to gleam like cats' from the dark. They knew she was there . . . they knew where she was. She saw the horseman smile. He was staring at her, where she lay hidden behind the wall. Emily was certain he would cross to her – she would be discovered, exposed. But the horseman did nothing. Instead, still smiling, he turned his back on her again. The servants resumed their work. The

Brockmans, oblivious to her presence, were counting out their gold.

Emily jumped to her feet. She began to run as fast as she could. No one followed her and she reached the village without being stopped. But even there the terror remained, a scent from the Hall she could not wash away.

That night, they told each other everything. When they had finished, Robert hugged Emily as tightly as he could. Her warmth, and her softness against his skin comforted him. He kissed her as his mother always used to kiss him, when he had been frightened by dreams. It made him feel better. 'It will be all right,' he whispered. And he believed it. For some reason he did not understand, the touch of Emily's lips against his own had dissolved all his fears. 'It *will* be all right,' he repeated. Stroking the blonde curls of Emily's hair, he hugged her tighter. Then he kissed her again.

⤳⤳

'HELL HATH NO LIMITS, NOR IS CIRCUMSCRIB'D
IN ONE PLACE; FOR WHERE WE ARE IS HELL.'

Christopher Marlowe, *Doctor Faustus*

The next morning, Captain Foxe climbed the front steps to Wolverton Hall. Behind him was Sergeant Everard and four militiamen. All six were armed; all carried lanterns. All six, more than fifteen years before, had been part of an investigation which had searched every room of the place.

Captain Foxe paused as he walked inside; then he left

the rectangle of light cast by the open door, and entered the dark beyond it. He paused again, and called out loudly. His voice barely echoed, swallowed by the dampness he could feel against his skin. He swung his lantern around. Doorways waited to the left and to the right; behind him rose the stairway which his son had recently climbed. The rooms beyond were as thick with blackness as the air was with the damp.

Captain Foxe allocated his men to search various rooms – two upstairs, two beyond the doorway to the left of the hall. He watched them salute and set off; then he turned to Sergeant Everard. 'And we shall take the right.'

'Yes, sir.' Sergeant Everard paused, and tried to stare beyond the door. 'Is that not where the entrance to the cellars may be found?'

'As I recall it,' answered Captain Foxe, walking into the room beyond the hall. He did not meet his Sergeant's eye – but he did not need to. It was Everard who had been beside him fifteen years before. They both knew exactly where the cellars' entrance lay.

They began to make their way through the darkness of the house. Captain Foxe felt dread stirring like a worm in his guts, and he prayed, knowing that he was mortal and ripe to be food for worms of all kinds. Yet there was nothing to be found; no sign of anyone; and Captain Foxe could not explain his fear, for – picking his way across the rubble, brushing aside the clumps of slimy weeds – it seemed certain he had been wrong, and there was no one there at all. What living thing could endure in such a place? He shuddered, then stumbled forward into a further room where he swung the lantern about him. Still nothing – only the silence, and the darkness, and the cold. The worms in his stomach were breeding faster now. He paused for a moment, almost tempted to turn and head back. And then, from the room ahead, he caught the flickering of a light.

He called out . . .

No answer.

He summoned Everard. They both drew their swords, then crossed into the room. It had once been a library, and books were still lined in shelves along the wall; but mould in silver patches had spread across their spines, and the stench of rotting paper hung dank in the air. A chair, with a table beside it, was stationed at the far end of the room. It was impossible to see who might be sitting in it, for the back was turned so that it faced the wall. On the table, a lamp was flickering. Books and parchments were strewn across the floor.

Captain Foxe took a step forward. As he did so, he heard the sound of a page being turned.

At once, he froze. 'Who is there?' he called out. 'Who are you?'

There was silence, then a voice spoke. Its accent was foreign; and yet it was not that which explained the strangeness of its effect, but rather its tone, which was at once enchanting and immeasurably cold, so that it seemed to Captain Foxe like a shard of silver cutting pure through the air, pure and icy, deep into his mind. ' "Divinity, adieu!" ' whispered the voice. ' "These metaphysics of magicians, And necromantic books are heavenly; Lines, circles, scenes, letters, and characters . . ." '

The voice rose and, as it did so, so also did the man, who stood and turned to face Captain Foxe. It was not Sir Charles, nor anyone like him, for though his face was gleaming pale, his beard was thick and very black.

' "Ay," ' he nodded, glancing down at the book, ' "these are those that Faustus most desires!" ' He smiled; then snapped the book shut. 'I have been expecting you, Captain Foxe.'

'You have the advantage of me, then, sir.'

'My name ... no – you would find it hard to pronounce. So call me' – the foreigner glanced down at his book – 'Faustus.'

The Captain stared at him coldly. 'You are a magician, then,' he asked, 'like that Faustus whose ambitions you have just been reciting to us?'

'I have been many things.'

'And now – Faustus?'

'You know full well, Captain. I am here to prepare this house for Edward Wolverton, the son of my late friend. No other purpose.'

Captain Foxe continued to study him, meeting the stranger's stare, which was very bright, and cruel like a snake's. 'You are lying, Faustus,' he said at last. 'Sir Charles Wolverton is not dead.'

'I was in Prague with him, Captain. I saw him die.'

'No.' Captain Foxe raised his lantern, and walked across to a doorway in the far wall. 'Wolverton is here. I can feel him in the air.'

'I had not expected to find you so womanish, Captain,' the stranger sneered, 'startled by shadows.'

'What is a shadow,' answered Captain Foxe, 'if not a warning that the man who casts it is nearby?' He held his lantern up high again, and beckoned Everard across; then he turned back to the stranger. 'Two wagons were seen here yesterday,' he said, 'loaded with boxes. What was inside them?'

'The goods of Edward Wolverton, inherited from his

father, and brought here from Prague.'

'And where are the boxes now?'

'Why, Captain, in the cellar.' The stranger smiled slowly; he pointed towards the doorway in the wall. 'You know how to get there, I believe?'

Captain Foxe glanced at his companion; then led the way along a damp narrow corridor, through a second door and down the waiting steps. The stone underfoot was greasy, and he almost fell; he paused, straining to see an end to the passageway ahead of him, but the blackness seemed to rise from the depths like a fog, and Captain Foxe could never see further than two or three steps. And yet in his mind's eye, scenes were starting to crowd each other. He remembered Faustus' words: lines, circles, characters. He could picture them all, just as they had been those fifteen years before, chalked upon the floor or smeared in blood across the walls. He could almost believe, when he reached the cellars, that the marks of witchcraft would still be there, waiting for him; the marks – and worse. The stones had been slippery then – just as the steps were now. He bent down, touched the step, raised his fingertip to the light. Only mud. Captain Foxe bowed his head. Desperately, he prayed. 'Yea,' he whispered, 'though I walk through the valley of the shadow of death, I will fear no evil – for thou art with me. *For thou art with me.*' For a moment, the memories were gone; yet still, as he continued on his way, the fear remained, and his light could not penetrate the vomit of the dark.

'You will find the boxes ahead of you.'

Captain Foxe glanced round. Behind Everard he could just make out Faustus' silhouette following them down the steps. Captain Foxe quickened his pace; and when he had reached the first cellar, he found the boxes stacked where he had been told they would be, in rows against the wall. Everard joined him. 'Help me,' said Captain Foxe. Together they lugged down one of the boxes, and inspected the lid; it had been secured with nails. Everard began to kick at the boards with his boot.

'There is no need to look. The boxes have all been emptied.'

Captain Foxe glanced back at Faustus again, then joined with his sergeant in smashing the lid. The boards soon gave: an odour like that of damp earth mingled with rottenness rose up from the box. But when Captain Foxe inspected inside, he found that whatever had been transported had indeed since been removed. He turned to the remaining boxes, pulling them down at random and kicking in their lids. All were empty – all shared the same stench of rottenness and mud.

'Storms in the Channel,' said Faustus, seeing Captain Foxe blanch. 'The boxes were drenched by high waves and the fabrics, being so enclosed, have since proved sadly decayed.'

'Your servants,' said Captain Foxe suddenly. 'The creatures who unloaded these boxes for you – where are they?'

'Asleep.'

'All of them?'

'They have been working hard. All night. They are tired.'

'Where are they?'

Faustus gestured towards an archway.

'They sleep in the cellars?'

'Why not? You have seen the condition of the rest of

the house. It is no different down here.'

'There is no light.'

Faustus shrugged.

'And there is also – down here . . .' – Captain Foxe glanced at Everard – 'a legacy of . . . of evil – of horror . . . which still lingers in the air. Can you not feel it? This is a cursed place – but perhaps Sir Charles did not tell you what he did in these cellars, what blood he spilled, what innocents he slew – perhaps he chose not to tell you that, Faustus . . .' He paused. 'Or perhaps he did?'

'He told me,' replied Faustus impassively.

Captain Foxe turned away. His revulsion was suddenly so strong that he could feel it crawling in a sweat across his skin, and he thought he must be sick, for the horror was rising like vomit within him, and again he had to pray, to recover himself and not surrender to the fear. He turned to Everard. The Sergeant's face was covered in a sheen of yellow sweat, and his eyes were bulging as though his throat were being squeezed. Behind them, Faustus laughed. Captain Foxe did not look round. 'Come, Samuel,' he said, clasping his Sergeant on the shoulder. 'We cannot fail in our duty. It is all the more God's work we do here, because we do it in the very entrails of Hell.'

Everard nodded faintly. Together they passed through the archway and into the succeeding room. At once, Captain Foxe recognised the odour from the boxes, but worse, far worse, a stench which seemed to ooze out from the very pores of the wall. He took a further step forward into the darkness, and the stench hit him like a blast of hot air against his face. He held up his lantern; and saw a glimpse of things unbearably white. Something stirred; a waxy, naked body; soft, pale limbs.

They gleamed from the dark, ten of the creatures, twenty . . . Captain Foxe found it impossible to tell. As he held his lantern above them, they writhed beneath its beams, like shell-less things dug up from the soil, to be kept by fishermen as bait for their hooks. And yet they had the form of men; and the Captain wondered how such a horror could be.

'What are they?' exclaimed Everard, his voice almost cracking.

'Creatures of flesh and blood, like you.'

Everard turned to face Faustus. 'Not like me,' he whispered. 'They have the look of the dead.'

Faustus smiled. 'Then it is certain,' he hissed, 'if not now, then one day, you will be like them.' His face froze; his smile too, like the rictus of a skull. 'I can promise you that, sir,' he whispered at length.

Captain Foxe turned slowly to face him. 'Do you dare to threaten us?' he asked.

'Why, no, Captain. It is merely an observation drawn from philosophy. *Stipendium vitae mors est.*'

Captain Foxe shrugged. 'If you wish to talk in Latin, then you must do so to my son, for he is the scholar, not I.'

'Of course. Your son Robert. It was his tutor, was it not, who was recently killed?' Faustus' smile broadened. 'I heard of it. A terrible end – and yet one which proves the observation I only just now made, that *the reward of life must always be death.*'

'Our Saviour teaches us otherwise.'

'Then you must trust he will save you. But for myself' – Faustus paused, then sneered in open challenge – 'I would not put much faith in a dead Jewish trickster. Look about you, Captain. Remember what you found the last time you were here. Where, do you think, was your bastard-god then?'

Captain Foxe seized him suddenly, ramming him against the wall. As he stared into the gleam of Faustus' eyes, he heard a stirring from behind him and, glancing round, saw the creatures shuffling dumbly to their feet. But Captain Foxe ignored them, and turned back to Faustus. 'Where is he?' he whispered. 'Where is he hidden?'

'If he is here,' answered Faustus, his face suddenly a mask, 'then find him.'

'Sergeant,' said Captain Foxe, not looking round, 'search amongst those ... creatures ... for one whose face is like Wolverton's.'

He heard Everard cross towards them. There was silence, then a deep intake of breath. 'What is it?' Captain Foxe asked.

'Their skin ...' replied Everard faintly. 'I wonder ... if they are not lepers – for on many of their faces ... the flesh seems almost to be shredding away.'

'Wolverton?'

'No.'

Captain Foxe sighed, and released Faustus from his grip.

'Captain ... ' Everard swallowed as he gestured towards a further archway. 'We have not yet searched all the cellars.'

Captain Foxe stared at the archway. 'No,' he murmured. 'No, we have not.' He paused; then bent down and picked up a stone. Crossing to the archway, he drew a cross in white chalk on either side of it. Faustus, behind him, began to laugh; but Captain Foxe did not turn, only thickened the lines, drawing up and down as though scrubbing the walls, as though the chalk could purge the bricks of all they had seen. He was sweating when he finally tossed the stone aside; he paused for a moment, staring at each cross; then, bowing his head, he passed in through the arch.

He felt the closeness immediately, and remembered it from before. There had been the low buzzing of flies then, and a sticky sweetness in the air. There were no flies now, but the sweetness still seemed to linger, and when he brought his hand up to his nose he felt a strange taste prickling the back of his throat. He dreaded to raise his lantern. The darkness waited, as it had waited before, when it had concealed a glimpse of Hell. There had been a bundle of bone and skin, Captain Foxe remembered, topped with blond hair. Blond, he thought, as Robert was now. He began to shake so that his fingers could barely keep hold of the lantern. Slowly, he raised it above his head. Then he walked, one step, two steps, three, into the dark.

He began to feel himself sinking into earth, and looked about him. Soil was piled everywhere, rising away from him until it reached the cellar's roof. He stepped back instinctively. As he did so, the earth sucked on his legs, and he felt faint, as though it had also been sucking courage from his heart. He bent down. The earth was sticky to the touch, like dust on the verge of becoming mud. It stuck to his fingertips and, seeing it beneath his nails, Captain Foxe began to shudder. He could not explain his terror as he stared at the mounds of earth. They seemed like waves, rising above him, preparing to break, to submerge him and suck him into their depths. He rose to his feet, unable to bear the horror of the place; he had to leave. Then, from behind him, he heard a sudden clattering of metal on stone, and the light in the cellar was immediately dimmed. Captain Foxe turned round. Sergeant Everard's face was cast in shadow, but his eyes were gleaming with terror, bulging from their sockets as they had done before. Everard choked something unintelligible; then he turned, and fled. Captain Foxe heard the footsteps fade; he steeled himself not to flee as Everard had done. 'Faustus!' he called out angrily, so that the rage in his voice might disguise his own fear. 'This earth,' he demanded, 'what is it for?'

'It is from Prague.' Faustus appeared beneath the arch. 'It contains the mortal dust of Sir Charles. He wished it to be transported and buried here, in atonement for his sins. See how we have obeyed his command, Captain. The cellar is filled. It cannot be used again.'

Captain Foxe stared at the mounds of earth. His terror billowed and would not abate.

'You asked where Sir Charles was.' Faustus gestured. 'His remains are mingled with the earth you see there.'

Captain Foxe took a step forward. Again he bent down, and ran the soil through his hands.

'What will you do, Captain? Will you dig up the soil and pan it, so that Sir Charles' dust may be anatomised, and exposed to your godly retribution?' Faustus laughed; he turned and, still laughing, walked across the cellar floor away from Captain Foxe. His footsteps faded until at length, there was silence.

Captain Foxe stood alone. He breathed in deeply. The sweetness still seemed to linger in the air; and when he kicked at a mound of earth, he felt his terror rising inside him even more, for again it seemed to suck and feed on his soul. He paused, irresolute; then shuddered, and turned. As he hurried through the cellars, he did not look back.

ᴏⱷᴏ

'FOR THE TRUE MATHEMATICAL SCIENCE, IS THAT WHICH
MEASURETH THE INVISIBLE LINES, AND IMMORTAL BEAMS,
WHICH CAN PASS THROUGH CLOD, AND TURF; HILL AND DALE.
IT WAS FOR THIS REASON, IT WAS ACCOUNTED BY ALL ANCIENT
PRIESTS THE CHIEFEST SCIENCE; FOR IT GAVE THEM POWER,
BOTH IN THEIR WORDS AND WORKS.'

Dr. John Dee, *Mathematical Preface*

The sense of horror hung dense over Captain Foxe's spirits for several days afterwards. Not until almost a week had passed did he prepare to inform Colonel Sexton of the failure of his investigation; but by then, although the horror still lingered, determination had replaced his initial despair. For Captain Foxe was not a man given to a sense of hopelessness; his faith in the workings of God, which he found expressed every day in the existence beside him of his beloved wife and son, fortified him also in his belief that evil could be conquered. For days he had been appealing to God, speaking in his prayers as he might speak to a friend, asking that the murderer be uncovered and stopped; and he believed that God, like any friend, would surely answer his requests.

He set out, then, on the morning of his visit to Colonel Sexton, with his sense of hope undiminished. For part of the way, he was accompanied by Sir Henry, whose news, given as they rode together, only increased Captain Foxe's resolve. It appeared, from Sir Henry's report, that several of his farmhands had been recruited by the Hall, tempted

by the promise of abundant rewards – for the men who
had driven the carts there had been paid with bags of
coins, and Sir Henry knew this to be true, for he had seen
the money with his very own eyes. Captain Foxe's
questioning of them had not been welcomed; nor his
warning that they should keep away from the Hall. For
what was such advice, Sir Henry asked, when set against
the promise of further gold?

Captain Foxe brooded on this question. He did not
care to think that men he had always known, men from
his own village, might so easily be bought; and yet in his
heart he could not be surprised, for he was a militiaman
and had seen repeatedly in the course of his investigations how life was but a highway through Vanity Fair,
in which the lure of money was hard to resist. Such
greed, he had always believed, would bring its own
punishment; yet Captain Foxe dreaded to think what the
lure of Wolverton gold might bring in its wake, for he
knew for certain that if the Devil tempted, then it was
only to damn; and it was the Devil whose servants he had
seen in the Hall. So convinced of this was Captain Foxe,
that when he met with Colonel Sexton, he would not
admit to even a glimmering of doubt; and when he was
pressed by the Colonel, he would only challenge his
superior to do as he had done, to venture into the cellars
and feel the Devil's breath against his face. Colonel
Sexton sighed at this; but he did not attempt to contradict
his officer any further, nor did he deny him license to
continue watching the Hall. 'You should know, though,'
he warned, 'that I have already started to receive com-
plaints, from my own superior and from the mayor. It
appears this man Faustus has well-connected friends.
They do not approve of your interest in him.'

'I have already discovered, sir, that Faustus is not averse to spending his gold.'

Colonel Sexton shrugged. 'Find what you are searching for quickly, Captain. I may not be in a position to protect you for much longer.'

'I will find him, sir.'

'You have a course of action prepared?'

Captain Foxe paused. His brow creased faintly. 'God will aid us,' he said at last.

'Let us hope so,' murmured Colonel Sexton, rising to clasp his officer's hand. 'Take care, though, John.' He nodded, a gesture of dismissal. 'For God's sake – take care.'

Captain Foxe saluted, then strode through the Council Hall back towards his room. His mood had turned bleak once again. He pondered the silent admission which his colonel had wrung from him, that he was helpless before the killer, that he knew neither where to find him nor how to stop him killing once again. 'Captain Foxe!' a voice called out suddenly; he froze. He looked up the stairs to see a trooper standing there; and at once, he knew what had happened, what the trooper had to say. He was only glad, he thought, as he hurried up the stairs, that Robert and Emily were not with him this time. 'Very well, then,' he said, meeting the trooper's eye, 'tell me the worst. Who is it this time? Where has the body been found?'

The trooper looked puzzled. 'Sir?'

Relief, in a sudden flood of gold, bathed Captain Foxe. 'No murder?' he asked.

The trooper continued to look puzzled. 'No, sir,' he said. 'There is a man in your room.'

'And that is all you wanted to report?'

'Yes, sir.' The trooper looked so baffled by now that Captain Foxe began to laugh. He turned, and hurried towards his room. His despair had vanished as completely as it had arisen; and he was confident once again of God's guidance in his task. As he entered his room, he almost tripped up over a jumble of papers and books; he looked about him in surprise, and recognised the back of Mr Aubrey, who seemed perfectly oblivious to him, crouching over a map. Captain Foxe offered up a silent prayer of thanks, that his faith in God's assistance had been justified so fast; then he cleared his throat. 'You have discovered something which may help us?' he asked.

Mr Aubrey looked round, startled. 'I hope so,' he nodded, as he saw who it was. He jabbed a finger down at his map. 'I believe I know when and where the killer may be trapped.'

'Then that is glad news indeed.' Captain Foxe crossed to join him, picking his way through the scattered piles of books. 'I see you have brought the materials of your research with you,' he observed.

Mr Aubrey coughed modestly. 'There was a great deal to be tracked down,' he agreed as he gazed round at his books. He reached for one of them, smoothed it out, then blew away the dust. 'You see, Captain,' he asked, 'why it is said of we antiquaries that we wipe off the mouldiness we dig, and remove the rubbish?' He reached for another book; he patted it; there was a second cloud of dust. 'These had lain undisturbed a long time on my shelves, with all my father's books, and my grandfather's and my great-grandfather's too, for we have always been a family of collectors. Sadly, however – and you may have observed this for yourself, Captain – ordering these possessions has never been my strength.' He gestured self-reproachfully at all his scattered books and papers. 'It took me time to find these – hence the delay.'

'No, no,' said Captain Foxe, shaking his head, 'you have been remarkably quick.'

Mr Aubrey blushed a pleased shade of pink. 'It was the mention of Prague,' he said, 'which gave me the hint.'

'Of Prague?' frowned Captain Foxe.

Mr Aubrey nodded. He looked around. 'Now curse the thing, where is it?' He began to search through his books, creating a blizzard of papers before he finally found a small vellum-bound manuscript, which he brandished below Captain Foxe's nose. 'You remember?' he asked. 'I showed it to you before. It has the pictures of women bathing in blood.'

'Yes,' said Captain Foxe, nodding slowly. 'It had belonged to a doctor . . . Queen Elizabeth's astrologer?'

'Yes, yes, Dr John Dee, who lived at Mortlake, not a mile distant from my great-grandfather at Kew, with whom he was a very intimate acquaintance, and had great discussions on magical topics; so that when Dr Dee was accused of sorcery, he gave many of his books to my great-grandfather, by which means I have them now.' Mr Aubrey paused for breath and shook his head sternly. 'I told you this before, Captain.'

'I am sorry. Clearly I mistook its significance.' Captain Foxe shrugged. 'Nor do I fully understand it even now.'

'Why, sir,' said Mr Aubrey, flicking through the small vellum book, 'it is said that Dr Dee had penetrated the mysteries of the universe, and sought to discover the philosopher's stone. It was to that end that he travelled to Prague, which as I also told you before, Captain – I remember mentioning it quite specifically – is the

world's university for the magical arts. In the Jewish
Ghetto there was a book which had only just recently
come to light, though in mysterious circumstances – for
how and from where it had appeared no one could say –
and it was rumoured to reveal how the dead might be
raised. Yet no one could read it – and this greatly
frustrated the learned men amongst the Jews, who longed
to master the knowledge the manuscript contained, and
penetrate the secrets of the very grave. Learning that Dr
Dee was in Prague, and knowing of his reputation, the
leader of the Jews invited him to inspect the manuscript,
which the Doctor did, making a copy of the book, with
great expense of effort, so that more than one man might
study it at a time. But the Jew, when he discovered what
Dr Dee had performed, mistook his intentions and complained to the Emperor, who greatly loved the Jew and so
banished Dr Dee. The Doctor's revenge, however, was to
take his copy of the manuscript with him – and here it is,
in my library today.'

Mr Aubrey had been speaking with increasing speed,
and as he reached his triumphant conclusion he waved
the book in the air again. Captain Foxe took it, and
scanned the opening page. He did not recognise the
script; he frowned. 'Is it Latin?' he asked.

Mr Aubrey shrugged. 'I do not have the remotest idea,'
he replied.

'You mean you cannot read it?'

'No.' He laughed cheerfully. 'No one can.'

'But . . . I thought . . .' Captain Foxe shook his head.
'What about this Dr Dee?'

'No, nor him either. For the rest of his life, after his
expulsion from Prague, he tried to decipher the script,
but it was all in vain.'

'Then of what value is it to us? I do not understand, Mr Aubrey, why you have raised my hopes only to dash them in this way.'

'Patience, Captain, patience! Just remember what we do know about this book.' He beamed, and tapped the side of his nose. 'One – it deals with the raising of the dead. Two – it was copied from an original still in Prague. You will understand, perhaps, why my interest was aroused when you described the man you believed your murderer to be: a man who appeared to have risen from the dead – and who was very recently a resident of Prague.'

'Yes, yes,' said Captain Foxe impatiently, 'but the coincidences are merely tantalising, and nothing more, if we cannot read the book.'

'It is true that Dr Dee failed to decipher it – but he appears to have come exceedingly close.'

'How close?'

Mr Aubrey gestured at his scattered papers and books. 'As I said – exceedingly.'

'These are the materials of his research?'

'The materials – and the fruits.'

Very slowly, Captain Foxe sat down in his chair. 'Tell me, then,' he said at length, 'what it is that you have found.'

Mr Aubrey almost skipped across to join him. He scooped up an armful of volumes and maps, and spread them out on the table; then he picked up the books. 'These are histories of the Ancient Britons,' he began. 'I have never come across their like before, and indeed would have considered them the merest knavery, for the arguments they contain are exceedingly strange, had not certain passages been marked by Dr Dee.' He opened one of the books, and passed it across. Captain Foxe studied it. There was an illustration in black ink, of symbols connected by a single straight line. 'And now look at this,' said Mr Aubrey. He opened the vellum-bound manuscript and again, Captain Foxe studied it. An illustration had been drawn in the margin of the page, and when he compared it with the first book, Captain Foxe saw how the two were virtually the same.

'It is in Latin,' said Mr Aubrey, pointing to a block of text by the illustration in the first book. 'It tells how the Druids used to practise their magic on certain sacred days.'

'And these?' asked Captain Foxe, pointing at the symbols. 'What do these mean?'

'They are ancient signs, drawn from the Magical Arts. Dr Dee had a great understanding of such secrets. See, here' – he opened up another book – 'he has written out their meaning. They symbolise the sacrifice days – what we call in this our Christian age, Yuletide, Innocents' Day, Candlemas, and the like.'

'Yuletide,' said Captain Foxe slowly. 'Innocents' Day . . .'

Mr Aubrey nodded. 'But I do not think, Captain, that the symbols refer to the sacred days alone.'

'What do you mean?'

Mr Aubrey closed the book, and slipped it into his pocket; then reached across the table for a bundle of maps, and smoothed them out. 'Some of these Dr Dee brought back from Germany,' he explained, 'and some are in his own hand, for you must understand that the Doctor made many maps and charts for the Queen. Now – observe.' He pointed to one of the maps. 'What do you see?'

Captain Foxe looked; and at once, felt his heart begin to pound. For there, drawn across the map, were the symbols he had already seen in three different books, linked, as before, by a single straight line.

'It is a map of Bohemia,' said Mr Aubrey, 'and all the wonders of that land. But look carefully – observe which places are marked with the symbols. Do you see, Captain? Monuments dating from the most ancient of days, raised in Bohemia as they were also raised here – and my argument would be that these monuments were pagan temples, and built by the Druids.'

Captain Foxe frowned. 'But I do not understand . . .' he said slowly. 'The line which has been drawn through them . . . it is perfectly straight. How is it possible that the monuments should all be so aligned?'

Mr Aubrey shrugged. 'Doubtless it was achieved by the Druids' magic.'

'And the sites around here? What of those?'

Mr Aubrey stared at him, his eyes very wide and his expression solemn. 'Do you have a map of Wiltshire in this place?' he asked.

'Naturally,' replied Captain Foxe.

'Then I wish to see it. The most comprehensive you possess.'

Captain Foxe rose to his feet at once, and led the way to the records room. Mr Aubrey scanned through the various maps available and then, finding one of Salisbury and its neighbourhood, asked Captain Foxe to inspect it closely. 'Murder number one,' he said, pointing with his finger, 'Clearbury Ring. Then murder number two' – he inched his finger upwards – 'the Cathedral – here. We now have a straight line, linking the two sites.'

'And beyond those two sites, if you extend the line?'

Captain Foxe turned to a nearby clerk. 'Quick, man, your pen!'

The clerk handed it to Mr Aubrey, who began carefully to draw a line across the map, from Clearbury Ring to the Cathedral and then beyond.

'Of course,' murmured Captain Foxe, watching as the line was extended. 'Old Sarum.'

'I observed the alignment several weeks ago,' said Mr Aubrey, 'when I climbed to Clearbury Ring, and looked out from its edge, shortly before I discovered the corpse of the old man. But look further – if I continue beyond Old Sarum – there is another monument on this perfectly straight line. You see, Captain? Look!'

With two dramatic scratches, he marked a large cross.

Captain Foxe peered across to see what lay beneath it. 'I should be surprised,' he whispered. 'And yet how can I be? Stonehenge.'

'It was their chiefest temple,' nodded Mr Aubrey.

Captain Foxe stared at him. 'You said that you knew where the killing would be. I assume, from what you have just shown me, that you believe the killer will leave his victim at Old Sarum.'

Mr Aubrey inclined his head.

'And after that?'

'If you do not capture him before?'

'Yes.'

Mr Aubrey swallowed. 'Then doubtless at Stonehenge.'

'And the dates?'

'The dates?'

'Yes,' said Captain Foxe impatiently, 'we must know *when* the killer will strike. You said you knew.' He pointed his finger at Old Sarum on the map. 'When, Mr Aubrey? In the name of Christ – *when*?'

'I have here . . .' Mr Aubrey patted his coat, then drew out the book which he had earlier slipped into his pocket. He handed it over to Captain Foxe. 'You remember them – the symbols drawn by Dr Dee?'

'Symbols?'

'Illustrating the dates. Of the ancient feast days.' Mr Aubrey took back the book, and opened it. 'Here,' he said, pointing at a symbol with his finger, 'Yuletide, the twenty-second of December – we have had that. And here – the twenty-eighth of the same month – Innocents' Day – we have had that as well. So the next . . .' – he traced his finger down the page – 'here.'

'Yes?' pressed Colonel Foxe, as Mr Aubrey read the script. 'Tell me. I am aflame.'

'Candlemas,' said Mr Aubrey. 'So called by we Christians, but doubtless a holy day from very ancient times. February the second, Captain; that is your date.' He studied the map, then rolled it up and handed it across. 'Be at Old Sarum on Candlemas, Captain Foxe, and my presumption is that you will discover the murderer there, with evil purpose in his soul.' He paused, and bowed his head. 'Let us only pray, you do not discover him too late.'

∽✲∾

'That there be good and evil times, days lucky and unlucky, many profane authors mention.'
          John Aubrey, *Miscellanies Upon Various Subjects*

The horses snorted and shook their heads, as though disturbed by the coming of the new day. Captain Foxe bent low in his saddle and whispered soothing words, then, patting his horse's neck, he stared east at the first cold beams of sunlight as they rose behind the distant hump of Clearbury Ring. The mist in the valley beneath was stained purple; and for a moment, all of Salisbury seemed blotted out, save only for the spire, which rose like the mast of a ship above spray. But then the mist began to fade from the valley; and even in the February cold, Captain Foxe could feel the sun against his face. He looked along the ramparts of Old Sarum, where he had stationed his men. He hoped they were ready. Candlemas had dawned.

He turned to Sergeant Everard. 'Take your first patrol now. Around the hill – but not too far.'

Sergeant Everard nodded, and spurred his horse down the rampart side and out across the ditch. Three men accompanied him. Captain Foxe watched them depart, then turned to Sir Henry who had been sitting silent beside him for the past hour. 'I am going to inspect the other men. You should come with me.'

Sir Henry shook his head. 'You are the captain. I do not wish to intrude.'

'But it is you who has been threatened. I am reluctant to leave you alone.'

Sir Henry gestured towards a trooper who had been stationed along the rampart. 'I will stay with him.'

'If that is what you would prefer.'

'I have faced danger before. You need not worry, John. I will be all right.'

'I do not believe you would have been so threatened yesterday, had it not been for a purpose.'

Sir Henry smiled. 'I will be careful.'

Captain Foxe nodded curtly. Then he wheeled his horse and descended the rampart into the ancient town itself, where he was soon lost amidst yews and shapeless grassy mounds.

Robert sat huddled alone in the upstairs room. As he studied his book, he was careful to nestle it in the folds of his cloak, for he did not want to be discovered reading it. Not that his parents would have heard of Ovid, he thought – his father had merely given him the volume, in obedience to Mr York's will, along with the rest of the dead tutor's books. But Robert was worried, now that he was staying with the Vaughans, that Lady Vaughan might find him; for she understood Latin, and would know the kind of poems Ovid had written. She would be amused, no doubt; she might even mention it, as a joke, to his mother.

The very idea made Robert flush; and he was almost moved to hide the book away. But there was no sound of footsteps from outside; and after he had sat in silence for several minutes, he bent forward once again and returned to the book. Two months ago, even had he been able to obtain it, he would not have chosen to read the poem – not before Hannah's death. But since then everything had changed, and all that Robert had been taught – of the goodness of the world, of the vanquishing of sin – had come to seem more and more uncertain, for although he still turned to the scriptures for comfort amidst the terrors of life, he wondered whether this might not be from love of his parents rather than from any love of God. In Ovid, certainly, he found no comfort at all – just the opposite, indeed, for the poetry seemed nothing but a record of depravities and crimes, of a kind that Robert had never heard of before, but which he now suspected, following Hannah's death, to be the very stuff of life.

Doomed passions, strange transformations, the hunger
for infamy, and the terrors of love: all of these were
drawn in Ovid's pages and seemed, to Robert's wondering mind, a glimmering portent of what it might
mean to be alive and no longer a child. For mingled with
his fear there was also guilty pleasure: he knew things
now he had not formerly understood. He knew, for
instance, what Hannah must have done to have grown
her baby; and he knew why he liked to kiss Emily.

He stopped reading. For several minutes he gazed at
nothing, then started suddenly, as though waking from a
trance. He tried to remember what he had been thinking
about and realised, with an embarrassed smile, that it had
been Emily, and the feel of her lips against his own. At
once, he snapped his book shut; then leapt to his feet and
hurried downstairs. He knew she would be in the house.
Since yesterday, when he and his mother had been
brought to the Vaughans', no one had been allowed outside and, just to make certain, there was a militiaman at
every door. Robert wondered again what his father had
discovered, to insist on such precautions; but he did not
doubt that they were justified. Suddenly, he thought of
the danger not as a game, not as an excuse for him to stay
with the Vaughans, but as something terribly imminent
and real. He felt a brutal jolt of self-reproach. It might be
Emily who was threatened; might be Emily who needed
protection the most. And yet what had he been doing?
Reading a book.

He found her in the passageway by the parlour door.
She glanced round, her face screwed up with concentration, and motioned him to be quiet, then pressed her
ear back to the door. 'And now there is silence,' she
complained. 'Nothing to hear.'

'Is that my fault?' Robert asked.

'As everything is.'

He took her in his arms. She allowed him to kiss her, then pushed him away. 'Have you been reading that book again?' she asked.

'It needs no book, Emily.'

'Indeed?'

'It is not poetry which teaches me to love you, but Nature only.'

'We are learning fast from her, then, are we not?'

'So we must.'

'Why?'

'We shall not be children long. We must be married soon.'

'You have not even asked me yet, if I will be your wife.'

'I do so now.'

Emily smiled. She allowed herself to be kissed a second time. 'And yet ...' she murmured suddenly. Robert could feel her stiffen in his arms; she looked up at him, and he saw foreboding reflected in her eyes. 'What if we are never to be married?' she whispered.

'Why do you ask that?'

'Because of what I have heard.' She gestured back at the parlour door, then bent down close again. At length, she frowned and shook her head. 'Still nothing.'

'But what did you hear before?' Robert seized her arms and raised her to her feet. 'Tell me, Emily. What did you hear?'

'It was my mother,' she whispered, 'talking to yours. About the soldiers, about why we all must stay inside.'

'Well? You are being too mysterious. Tell me what you mean.'

Emily took his arm and began to lead him down the

passageway. 'My father,' she whispered, settling on the stairs. 'He is in danger – he has been threatened by the foreigner at Wolverton Hall.'

'Faustus?'

Emily nodded. 'The pale man with the black beard. He was riding yesterday across my father's fields. He had been stopping amidst the labourers, giving out gold, paying them to come and work for him. My father rode up to complain. But Faustus only laughed, and spat in his face.'

'Your father's men should have cudgelled him.'

'Men? What men? You do not understand, Robert – my father has no men, they have all been bought away. And even those who saw what Faustus did, who had only just been hired that day, did nothing to help my father but rather rushed up and held his arms, so that he was powerless to avenge the insult, for he could not move from his saddle. And then Faustus mocked him, and called him traitor for having deserted Sir Charles at the end of the war. Faustus said he would be punished very soon for his faithlessness, for the time of reckoning was close at hand, and there were many accounts that had to be drawn up.' Emily paused, and bit her lip. 'And that is what I heard,' she said at last. 'And that is why I have grown afraid.'

Robert hugged her tightly. 'What do you think might happen, then?' he asked.

She shrugged slightly.

'I swear,' he whispered, 'whatever befalls us, whatever occurs, we shall never be parted.'

She met his eyes. Her own seemed suddenly very solemn and deep. Robert waited for her to blink, but it was as though her expression had been frozen, and would never change. 'I believe you,' she said at last. She squeezed his hand. 'But you must never forget, Robert, what you have just promised me. For I never shall.'

Then she jumped to her feet.

Robert joined her. Together, they looked towards the hall. Robert could hear the dim thud of boots as they approached up the pathway outside; they paused, then there was a rap upon the door. At once, before the maid had appeared, Lady Vaughan emerged from the parlour with Mrs Foxe, to join Robert and her daughter in the passageway. She glanced at them nervously, as the maid came hurrying.

There was a second knock. 'Open it, Sarah,' said Lady Vaughan. 'Let us see who our visitor may be.' The maid curtsied; as she unbolted and opened the door, Lady Vaughan stepped forward.

It was a moment before she could speak. 'Sergeant Everard,' she whispered at last.

He stood in the doorway. He was exceedingly pale, a look of unspoken horror on his face.

'Samuel.' Mrs Foxe walked forward. She took his arm and drew him inside. 'Something has happened.' She swallowed. 'Please, Samuel – tell us what it is.'

Sergeant Everard allowed himself to be guided forward. He stopped before Lady Vaughan; then stood silently.

'It is my husband, is it not?' asked Lady Vaughan after a pause.

'Madam . . .' Sergeant Everard bowed his head. 'I am very sorry.'

'Well, then . . . well . . .' She turned and, for a moment, leaned against the wall. She smoothed back her hair; then reached for Emily, to brush the tears from her daughter's cheeks. Emily began to sob silently; Lady Vaughan rocked her to and fro, not crying herself but staring into space. At length, she looked round at Sergeant Everard again. 'Where did it happen?' she asked.

'Old Sarum, Madam. In the wood that surrounds the outer ring.'

Lady Vaughan glanced at Mrs Foxe. 'As your husband foretold. And in the same way, Sergeant, as the previous two?'

'Aye, Madam.'

'I would like to see him.'

'I have been sent to take you there.'

'What, his body has not been brought back?'

'The Captain wanted him left where he was found. He believes . . . the location – it may be significant.'

Mrs Foxe nodded. 'Yes,' she whispered softly. 'Again, as he has often said it would be.'

Sergeant Everard gestured towards the door. 'Come, we must go at once,' he said numbly. 'All of us. I have two soldiers outside, who will ride by our sides.' He shivered. 'For none of us, I think, should be alone upon this day.'

✦

'. . . LYING IS THY SUSTENANCE, THY FOOD.'

John Milton, *Paradise Regained*

They travelled in virtual silence. Sometimes Emily would choke on her sobs, and Lady Vaughan would whisper words of comfort in her ear; but otherwise not a word was spoken or exchanged. Even the militiamen sat in their saddles as though chiselled from ice, and Robert dreaded to think what horrors must have been inflicted on Sir Henry, for the soldiers' eyes were as glazed as their Sergeant's, and their faces pinched with the same disgust. Soon Old Sarum was visible from the road; and the nearer it loomed, the greater grew Robert's dread. He saw a couple of ravens wheeling above the summit where the castle had stood; and he remembered how the birds had flocked above Clearbury Ring. And yet in truth, he realised, he did not mind what had happened, did not mind that Sir Henry was dead – for it had not been Emily. *It had not been Emily*. This thought kept beating like blood in his ears; and since he could not feel ashamed of such selfishness, he marked it down as a sign of his love.

At length, before the trees which stretched up to Old Sarum's outer ring, Sergeant Everard reined in his horse. He pointed towards the depths of the wood. 'You see, Madam, where the trees start to climb the rampart of the fort . . .'

Lady Vaughan bowed her head. 'I see it,' she nodded. She turned to Emily. 'Come, my darling,' she whispered. 'Let us not put off the evil sight.' She dismounted and, taking her daughter's hand, began to walk slowly through the trees. Sergeant Everard gestured to his men; they dismounted as Lady Vaughan had done, and ran after her into the wood. The Sergeant turned to Mrs Foxe. 'Come,' he said, 'this is an evil place. We should not linger here.'

Mrs Foxe stared at him in surprise. 'But, Samuel, should I not go after Lady Vaughan, so that I may comfort her in her grief?'

'No, Madam. The Captain is in attendance by the body, and will offer the widow consolation, but for yourself and for your son – you should not see what lies in that darkness, for it is not to be borne. Please.' He spurred his horse forward. 'Let us escape the shadow of these trees.'

The Sergeant rode with them until the wood had been left behind, and Salisbury could be seen in the valley below. Then he turned in his saddle, and pointed up at the rampart of Old Sarum where it emerged from the trees. Figures could be seen standing there, in the uniform of militiamen. 'Wait for your husband there, Madam.' He bowed his head. 'Farewell.' He wheeled his horse, and galloped away along the track.

Robert watched him depart; then followed his mother up the hill towards the summit of Old Sarum. He narrowed his eyes as he stared at the militiamen on the rampart; and then suddenly, he started, and seized his mother's arm. 'Is that not Father?' he asked. 'There, coming down?'

For a moment Mrs Foxe sat frozen; then she spurred her horse on, for she could hear her husband's cries – how frantic they were, as he came running towards her, down the rampart and across the open field. 'What are you doing here?' he screamed. 'Both of you, what are you doing in this place?'

Mrs Foxe swung down from her saddle and ran into his arms. 'There was no danger,' she said breathlessly, 'for we were brought here by Sergeant Everard.'

Captain Foxe gazed at her in consternation. 'But Sergeant Everard has been missing since just after dawn, he and his entire patrol, all save one, who has been found just now some miles from here, killed, his skull caved in.'

'But ... but ... Samuel's patrol was with us. They brought us here to see Sir Henry's corpse.'

'Sir Henry is no corpse.' Captain Foxe pointed towards

the rampart. 'See, where he walks and breathes, a living man yet.'

Mrs Foxe shook her head dumbly. She tried to speak, but horror strangled her words.

'Lady Vaughan,' said Robert. 'She and Emily, they are in the wood. We left them there.'

Captain Foxe, like his wife, seemed unable to speak. For a moment, he could only stare at Robert; then he seized his wife's horse and, clambering into its saddle, galloped as fast as he could urge the horse to go. Robert followed him. The meaning of what he had just said still seemed unreal; he could not believe that Emily might truly be in danger – that Emily might be dead. And then, as he felt his stomach rise and become air in his mouth, he did believe it. He looked ahead of him, where his father had already reached the summit of the hill and had dismounted. He was screaming orders to his men, and troopers were spilling out amidst the trees. Robert followed them; he headed into the ruins of the castle, tripping once across a grass-covered stone, then over the root of an old gnarled yew, but never stopping – stumbling forward until he was slipping through the mud down the side of the far rampart, towards the wood where he had last seen Emily alive, and which was waiting for him, menacing, and dark, and still.

He hurried through the trees. Suddenly, the silence was broken. Robert heard a cry of horror, and then a second, both ahead of him, and then from all sides there was the sound of people crashing through the undergrowth, hurrying in the direction of the voices. Robert recognised his father, a dim form through the branches and shadows; he followed him, then shrank back as they approached a clearing where two men were kneeling over something in the mud. The soldiers looked round at the approach of Captain Foxe; they rose to their feet and, as his father walked forward into the glade, Robert felt his own legs give way beneath him. He knelt in the mud, and forced himself to look again. He could barely recognise Lady Vaughan. She was swinging in the breeze, her ankles suspended from the branch of a tree. Her naked body had been mutilated, and disembowelled; she had no eyes; her fingers, just as those of the unborn child had been, were snapped backwards. And yet despite the violence of the attack, and the fact that it could only have happened a few minutes before, there was scarcely any blood – not on the body itself, nor splashed upon the ground. Captain Foxe stared at the corpse in disbelief. 'Dear God,' he murmured, 'receive her sweet soul. She was a noble lady, and a most dear friend.' He unfastened his cloak and placed it tenderly round the naked body. Then he turned to his men. 'Find them,' he ordered. 'Whoever did this – I want them all found.'

As the militiamen dispersed, Robert pushed past them into the clearing. At once, Captain Foxe spun round, as though expecting to be surprised. His face darkened at the sight of his son. 'Have you not followed me enough, Robert,' he asked bitterly, 'to know what you were likely to find on such a trail?'

'No.' Robert pulled on his father's arm. 'Emily.'

'Emily?'

'Yes, you must tell them to search for Emily; she was with her mother, and now she is gone.' Robert gestured frantically at the trampled mud of the clearing. 'Where is she?' he cried.

Captain Foxe closed his eyes a moment; then he seized

his son's hand, and together they plunged into the darkness of the trees. For a while they heard nothing but the splashing of their own feet in mud; then suddenly Captain Foxe held up his hand. 'Quiet,' he whispered and Robert froze. He heard it at once: a slapping sound, like damp washing being smacked up and down upon a stone. Slowly, Captain Foxe drew out his sword; then he crept through the shadows towards the source of the sound.

Two men in militia uniform were squatting on a fallen tree. Even from behind, Robert could recognise them as the escort of Emily and Lady Vaughan, sent by Sergeant Everard as guards into the wood.

'On your feet, troopers,' ordered Captain Foxe.

The two men stirred and glanced round. Their hands and mouths were smeared with blood; their faces, though, wore the same pinched expressions of horror as before; and their eyes were as dead. One sucked on something which he held in his hand; and for a moment, his eyes seemed to light up with greed. The other pulled on it and sucked in his turn; and as he smacked his lips, Robert recognised the slapping sound.

'What has happened to you,' cried Captain Foxe in horror, 'that you are sunk to the level of beasts – no, lower than beasts, to that of demons in Hell?' He crossed to the men and ripped their bloody meal from their hands, tossing the gore away as though it were poison to his touch. On the ground before the men, Robert saw a soup of organs and blood, such as he had often seen in the channels of butchers' yards; and then he realised what the mess was, and he began to retch, retch and retch until he thought that he would faint. But he did not; and always, even as he closed his eyes and prayed for oblivion, he saw Emily before him, and he dreaded that the guts might not be Lady Vaughan's alone.

At length, he spat the taste of vomit from his mouth and stumbled forward, despite his father's cries, for he could not bear to remain in such a place, which had seen such horrors and sheltered such crimes. The wood seemed lighter ahead of him, and as he looked, he caught a glimpse of the road. He recognised it as the stretch where he had last seen Emily, and so he turned and began to run towards it. Then he tripped and tumbled into a tangle of brambles, but he barely noticed the pain of the thorns for, when he turned back, he saw he had fallen across the body of a girl. Feverishly, he scrabbled out from the brambles. The body was wearing Emily's dress. When he pulled her round, he saw that her eyes were closed, and her blonde curls were matted with blood. He touched the wound; it was still damp – and then softly but unmistakably, Emily moaned. Robert stared at her feverishly; he pressed his ear to her heart, for he thought he must have been deceiving himself, but no, the heart was beating, she was still alive. He began to sob: he kissed her once, then lay with her, his cheek pressed against hers, holding in her warmth as though afraid it might escape.

Captain Foxe found them soon afterwards. He turned wordlessly, and brought Sir Henry. The father knelt beside his daughter; he stroked her matted curls, and wept with mingled sorrow and relief. With Robert's help, he gently lifted Emily; then he carried her towards the road, where the body of his wife had already been taken to lie, in the cold and stillness of her death.

~~∽⌒∾~~

'WRONGED SHALL HE LIVE, INSULTED O'ER, OPPRESSED,
WHO DARES BE LESS A VILLAIN THAN THE REST.'
   The Earl of Rochester, 'A Satire Against Mankind'

The injury to Emily's head was not deep, and she
recovered well. But she could offer Captain Foxe little
information. All she could remember was walking with
her mother into the wood, and hearing the militiamen
run up behind them. There had been a sudden blow to
her head . . . and she had seen nothing more.

Nor were the militiamen themselves any help. They
refused to talk; and indeed, it seemed to Captain Foxe as
though they had lost the power of speech altogether, for
they sat wordless in their cells, and almost motionless
save to sniff at their gaolers like wolves smelling blood.
When Captain Foxe himself sat down before them, not a
trace of recognition would cross the men's faces,
although they had served beneath him for many years;
instead their eyes would gleam with hunger and their lips
begin to moisten and smack. Such a transformation alone
would have persuaded Captain Foxe that his men had
been bewitched; and yet with time, their very flesh began
to rot, so that there was nothing left of their noses but the
bone, and their skin had a pallid, maggoty gleam. The
gaolers spoke of leprosy; but Captain Foxe remembered
the creatures he had seen in Wolverton Hall, writhing
like worms in the depth of the cellars, and knew what he
was watching when he saw his soldiers now. They stood
accused of murder, and would doubtless hang; but they
had once been good and gentle men, and Captain Foxe
could not bring himself to believe in their guilt. Instead,

the faster they began to decline, the more he saw them as victims themselves, and of a fate more terrible even than Lady Vaughan's.

Their guilt was pronounced. They were hung in Salisbury market-place, and their corpses tossed into a carrion pit. Colonel Sexton was pleased. On the same day that his troopers were executed, bells were ringing the length of the city and bonfires being lit, for it was rumoured that Parliament would meet and summon back the King. Effigies of Charles Stuart were being displayed, and toasts to his return drunk openly in the streets. In such a time of uncertainty, the apprehension of two vicious murderers was a triumph Colonel Sexton was reluctant to forgo. When Captain Foxe pleaded with him not to believe that the true killer had been found, the Colonel ignored him; and when Captain Foxe begged for permission to continue with his own investigations, it was curtly refused.

But Captain Foxe, who had fought in the war for the right to follow where his conscience led, was not prepared to ignore its urging now. He could not command his troopers to assist him in the search for the killer; but he had time of his own, and the help of Mr Webbe. Together, they began to trace sightings of a horseman cloaked in black, seen galloping along the Old Sarum road on the very day when Lady Vaughan had been killed. To those who had glimpsed the horseman's face, Captain Foxe would show the portrait of Sir Charles; and all were agreed that the likeness was very great. Only in Woodton itself did the trail run cold, for no matter how extensively he inquired, Captain Foxe could find no one there who remembered having seen the man in black. He pressed everyone he could think of who might have been near

Wolverton Hall on the day, but the villagers were surly and taciturn, as though they resented his questions; and in the end he had no choice but to abandon his search.

Captain Foxe would sit with his wife, or watch Robert and Emily playing in the yard, and feel close to despair. He was more certain than ever that the source of the evil he was hunting lay in Wolverton Hall, not half a mile away from everything in the world he most loved; and yet he could neither expose nor counter its threat. As the afternoons lengthened, as winter began to ripen into spring, so Captain Foxe's dread also grew, a malign blossom which darkened with each successive day. Three murders there had been; but on Mr Aubrey's map, the monuments had been four. Captain Foxe would wake in the night, and find himself muttering their names: Clearbury Ring, the Cathedral, Old Sarum – and Stonehenge. One more killing, at the very least – unless he could stop it. One more killing – and one more date. 'May Day,' Mr Aubrey had said, when Captain Foxe had asked him what the feast after Candlemas might be. 'Beltane, it was called by the ancients, when mighty fires would be lit to celebrate the emergence of the new from the old, of long-dead sap rising fresh through frozen veins.'

'Life from death?' Captain Foxe had frowned. 'There can surely be no evil in that.'

But Mr Aubrey had shrugged. 'It depends, might it not, on the nature of the thing that is woken from its grave?'

Captain Foxe had responded to that question with silence; but it continued to haunt him as he thought of what answer might have been supplied. With each day that brought May Day closer, ever darker possibilities bred in his mind; and his dreams were crowded with imaginings. In one, he saw a figure standing by his bed; its face was very pale, and its eyes had the gleam of moonlight on ice. 'Samuel?' he whispered. But Sergeant Everard made no reply. 'Samuel?' repeated Captain Foxe. 'We have been searching for you, Samuel. But we did not find you. Where have you been?'

There was silence. When Sergeant Everard spoke at last, his voice seemed to come from very far away, as though bled of all its life. 'I have been lying in the soil,' he whispered, 'where the worms have their shelter and feed upon buried men.'

'What are you?'

'Dead, sir, and yet not altogether so.'

'Why did you lure Lady Vaughan away?'

'It must come.' His voice now was as faint as a dying wind. 'All are of blood, and all must turn to blood again. No escape, sir.' He bent low across Captain Foxe's chest. 'No escape.' He rested one hand on the Captain's forehead, the other on the neck. With his nail, he began to slice across the throat.

Captain Foxe felt a warm dampness rising from the wound. He shuddered . . . and woke up. Gingerly, he touched where Sergeant Everard had sliced. The dampness was gone. But Mrs Foxe, woken by his nightmare, stared at where he was clutching his throat and asked him to move away his hand. 'There is a line there,' she said, 'a thin welt. What did that to you? What has been here tonight?'

Captain Foxe stared at her, but did not answer, and rose from his bed. The front door was open; he crossed to it, and stared outside. Nothing. He grabbed a cloak, then hurried along the track that led through the village. Ahead of him, on the brow of a ridge, a horseman in militia uniform was riding. He turned, to glance back at Captain Foxe. It seemed to be Everard, it seemed to be his face ... but Captain Foxe could not be certain. A cock crew; and the horseman at once began to fade, as though melting into the light of the coming dawn. At the same time, there was the sound of laughter and raised voices, and Jonas Brockman staggered out from a house into the road, followed by Elijah, his son, and two other men. Elijah bent double and was sick; all appeared to be violently drunk. Nevertheless, Captain Foxe hailed them, for he knew them from the village; but although they heard his greeting, the revellers stared at him with unconcealed dislike and made no reply. Then one of them stumbled and dropped a purse; gold coins spilled out; the men all collapsed into laughter again. They made no attempt to gather up the coins; yet Captain Foxe had never seen such wealth as lay before them now, glinting in the dirt. He shivered, and glanced over his shoulder at the hill beyond which lay Wolverton Hall. The drunks must have seen his gesture, for they began to jeer at him, and Jonas Brockman picked up a coin and flung it at his head. The coin struck him, and drew blood; but he allowed himself to give no sign of pain. Instead, he turned and walked slowly back to his house. The abuse of men he had known for years followed him. He barely heard what they said, though; for above their voices came the crowing of the cock again, and Captain Foxe could think only of how the next morning, when the cock made such a noise, Beltane would have dawned – May Day would have come.

He had no choice, he realised, but to confront Colonel Sexton again – to demand that something, *anything*, be done. Yet he could barely bring himself to leave for

Salisbury; he hugged his wife and son desperately, as
though he would never let them from his arms; and when
he did arrive in the city, it was not to Colonel Sexton he
first went but to Mr Webbe. Captain Foxe found him
preaching to an almost empty square, virtually on his
knees, beseeching his listeners not to permit Charles
Stuart's return; but his audience only laughed, and one
proposed a toast to the health of the King. This was
warmly answered; and Mr Webbe shrugged and stepped
down from his box. 'As a dog returneth to his vomit,' he
sighed, 'so we creep back to the slavery of kingship. See,
John' – he pointed – 'how the Cavaliers return, and walk
openly in the street. God's kingdom of His poor, it
seems, is not to be built in England just yet.'

'Then you must save those who can still be saved.'

'Who do you mean?'

Captain Foxe explained; and Mr Webbe immediately
agreed that he would do all in his mortal power to protect
Mrs Foxe, and Robert, and the Vaughans. He left at once;
and Captain Foxe, crossing the market place to the
Council House, began to believe that God had not
abandoned him yet. Nor were his hopes to be dashed by
Colonel Sexton, although he found the Council House in
chaos and the Colonel himself in a despairing state.
Captain Foxe's request for men was greeted with a
derisory laugh. 'You may take whom you wish, John,'
shrugged the Colonel, 'and take them while you can, for I
shall not be in this seat for very long.'

'You have been saying that for many months now, and
yet you are sitting there still.'

'The end is coming fast, though.' Colonel Sexton grimaced, and leaned forward. 'I have it on good authority that
Parliament will vote tomorrow for the King to be restored.'

'All the more reason, then, why I should be given my soldiers, so that I may achieve what must be achieved while you still have your command.' Captain Foxe saluted. 'I will be back tomorrow, sir, May Day, very early, before the break of dawn.'

He returned to Woodton. The roads in the village were empty, and all was quiet, but it seemed the stillness of foreboding, such as precedes a storm, rather than the calm of a tranquil summer evening, for there were eyes gleaming from within the darkness of doorways, and as Captain Foxe rode along, they would watch and follow him. Passing Sir Henry's manor house, Captain Foxe turned aside to warn his friend of the troubles there might be to come; but Sir Henry seemed to need no warning, for he appeared unsettled and nervous already, and could barely look his companion in the eye. Captain Foxe was not insulted, however, for his friend had seemed much changed since the death of his wife; and he did not doubt that, whatever happened, Emily would be protected to the last drop of Sir Henry's blood. He only prayed that such protection would not be needed in the end – that all would still be well, once May Day had passed.

∽∾∽

'HIS LOYALTY HE KEPT, HIS LOVE, HIS ZEAL;
NOR NUMBER, NOR EXAMPLE WITH HIM WROUGHT
TO SWERVE FROM TRUTH, OR CHANGE HIS CONSTANT MIND
THOUGH SINGLE.'

John Milton, *Paradise Lost*

Captain Foxe ate early that evening with his family and Mr Webbe, then retired to bed. He woke at three. He dressed, then knelt by his wife and kissed her on the brow. She stirred, but did not wake, and he left her to her dreams – her and Robert, whom he likewise knelt by and kissed farewell. The touch, as he rode, seemed to linger on his lips. But he tried not to think too much of his family; he could serve them best by putting them far from his mind. He could not afford to be distracted: it would be May Day very soon.

He rode fast to Salisbury, where his men were to meet him at the Council Hall. He would brief them, and then lead them back to Stonehenge in time for dawn. There could be no delay. Who knew when the killer might not strike? Captain Foxe thought of what his colonel had told him the day before, about how the King was formally to be invited back; and he wondered if he might not be preparing for his final patrol. If so, he prayed, then let it be crowned with success. He spurred his horse on. He could see the Cathedral spire now, dark against the lightening blue of the sky. He was almost there, yet still he rode faster. Today of all days, he could not afford to be late.

But by the approach to the city gate, he pulled suddenly aside. He had seen three soldiers and some instinct, some sudden chilling of his blood, warned him of danger. He rode forward slowly, not along the road but through the shadows afforded by neighbouring buildings, until the city gate was before him and he could see the soldiers clearly. All three wore the uniforms of militiamen; two were hooded, but the third wore nothing on his head and, even before he turned, Captain Foxe knew who he was. Sergeant Everard had changed, but although his flesh was rotting and his eyes seemed dead, there could be no mistaking him this time. Seeing him in uniform, on watch by the gate, Captain Foxe wondered how it was that he had not been captured, for he had been an open accomplice in the murder of Lady Vaughan; any soldier would have known to arrest him. Any soldier. Captain Foxe thought of his patrol, waiting for him at the Council Hall; and he knew he had to reach them without being seen.

He rode down as far as the river, then galloped along its banks and up into the streets of the still sleeping town. The hooves of his horse clattered loud across the cobblestones, ringing his approach to the Council Hall and scattering pigeons as he rode across the square. There seemed to be no one waiting for him; he called out loudly, then climbed down from his horse. Still no sign of his patrol, and so he hurried up the steps. He paused in the doorway; almost without thinking, he drew out his sword.

'Put up your weapon.'

The voice came from the shadows, as chill as it had been before in the library of Wolverton Hall.

'Faustus.' Captain Foxe stepped towards him. 'You dare to come here.'

Faustus smiled, his teeth a gash of bared white above the blackness of his beard. 'I might say the same thing to you, Captain,' he whispered. He held up a scroll of paper. 'Have you not read this?'

'What is it?'

'The warrant for your arrest.'

'Do not play with me, Faustus. You must think me a fool. You expect me to believe that my own commander would sign such a thing?'

'You refer to Colonel Sexton, I presume?' Faustus pulled a mocking expression of regret. 'He is no longer in command here, I am afraid. There is a new Colonel; it is he who has issued the warrant. You are to be apprehended as a traitor – a traitor to the King.'

Captain Foxe took the paper; then he tore it and flung it in Faustus' face. As he turned and ran down the steps, he could hear Faustus following him; and then the sound of steel being drawn. He twisted round, just in time to parry a thrust and answer it back with a thrust of his own. Faustus screamed as blood was drawn; he cried out for help, but Captain Foxe was upon him again, beating down his weapon and then, with a second thrust, stabbing him in the side. As blood began to spill from the wound, Faustus collapsed on to the ground; but although he knew the thrust had not been fatal, Captain Foxe did not stab again. Thou shalt not kill: even now he honoured the commandment, and was content merely to have disabled his foe. He sheathed his sword, untethered his horse; scrabbling up into the saddle, he wheeled the horse round, then bent forward low and rode as fast as he could.

He had seen horsemen approaching him from the far side of the square. But he was well ahead of them; and for a while, he was able to lose them in the tangle of streets which stretched behind the Council Hall. He knew, though, that when he left the city and had to ride into the open, they would be upon him again; and so he paused in an inn yard off St Catherine's Street to consider how best he might make his escape. He had seen how the north gate was being guarded; and he knew that his pursuers would expect him to head that way, towards the Woodton road and his family. But to the south of the city there was no wall, and the roads there would soon be busy with early morning traffic – that, he decided, was the way he would take. Later, when he had shaken off his pursuers, he could wheel back to the north and reach Woodton before the coming of night; for he doubted that much evil could be inflicted in the full light of day.

Salisbury was waking by now. Carefully, Captain Foxe rode out from the inn yard and joined the throngs of people hurrying along the streets. He rode past the Cathedral without being seen; then over the river and into open fields. The track ahead of him was empty; it wound up a hill, and Captain Foxe knew that if only he could make the brow without being seen, then he would most likely be safe. He forced himself to ride slowly, and with his shoulders stooped, so that he might seem to be a merchant or traveller; then, when he had reached the summit of the hill, he turned to look back towards Salisbury. He waited several minutes; but no one seemed to be following him, and he dared to hope that he might have escaped. He rejoined the road; and with a final glance at the city behind him, rode from it as fast as his tired horse could bear.

He covered several miles; and realised suddenly that he was by the turning to Broadchalke. He paused, to consider whether he should not take the path; and as he did so, from behind him he heard the distant beating of hooves. He glanced round: dust was rising from the Salisbury road, and the cloud was drawing ever nearer. Hurriedly, Captain Foxe dismounted, and led his horse up a bank into a dense clump of trees; he hid himself carefully, and stared down at the turning through a veil of branches and leaves. He did not have long to wait. Three riders approached the turning, then reined in their horses and looked about. Two were cloaked; the third, bare-headed, was Sergeant Everard.

He sniffed the air. Captain Foxe crouched lower, and prayed that his horse would not suddenly whinny or stir. For a moment he imagined he had been seen, for the riders all seemed to be staring at him, but then Sergeant Everard shouted something and continued on his way along the Salisbury road. One of the two hooded riders accompanied him; the second took the trackway which led towards Broadchalke. Captain Foxe watched them depart, and waited until all was silent again. Then, slowly, he led his horse out from the trees. Climbing into his saddle once again, he did as the second rider had done and turned aside from the Salisbury road.

The track ahead was much narrower now, and wound through thick woods. Captain Foxe rode carefully, not wanting to be surprised; but for several miles he met no one else, and it was only as he was approaching Broadchalke that he slowed and stopped, to draw out his sword. For he had seen something ahead of him, lying in the road; he spurred his horse forward again and, as he drew closer to the object, he saw that it was covered by a cloak. Leaning over from his saddle to inspect it more closely, he recognised the cloak at once from its hood, for it was a militiaman's, of the kind that the man he was following had worn close about his head. Captain Foxe lifted it gingerly with the point of his sword. It seemed heavy; and he realised that it was sodden through with blood. He flung it aside with a cry of disgust, and then at once brought his hand up to his mouth, for he thought he would retch; he breathed in deeply and yet, even so, it was all he could do to climb, not fall, from his horse.

It was a child who had been killed, no more than thirteen years old – Robert's age, Captain Foxe thought, as he stroked the boy's still warm cheek. And he felt at once, mingled with his pity, a great anger, greater than any he had known before, rising within him like a wall of fire; for he knew why the boy had been killed, merely so that his adversary might surprise him by the corpse and spill his blood as the boy's had been spilt, as that of so many innocent people had been spilt. Captain Foxe felt ready to despair, imagining the world as dark beneath the flood of such a slaughter, and man no better than monsters of the deep, lost forever from the light and love of God. He turned ... and saw, as he had known he would, his enemy behind him. The creature's breath stank of the grave; his eyes bulged dead from naked sockets; the flesh across his skull seemed nothing but a slime of earth and blood. But Captain Foxe knew him for all that; he never forgot his soldiers' faces – and he had last seen this one swinging from a rope, hung for the murder of Lady Vaughan. 'Dear God,' he whispered as he felt soft, clammy fingers press against his throat; but his anger blazed anew, and it gave him strength. Twisting, he picked up a stone from the track and brought it down upon the creature's skull. He heard the bone shatter, and then he was blinded by a fountain of mingled blood and pus, as though the thing's head had been nothing but a bubo ripe with putrefaction. Captain Foxe wiped the matter away from his eyes; the creature was still stirring, reaching up blindly, hungry for blood. The Captain raised his sword; he was sobbing now, he realised. Down he brought the blade, again and again. 'And he looked for judgement,' he panted through his tears, 'but behold oppression. For righteousness – but behold a cry.' And at once there was a shriek, a terrible, inhuman sound, and Captain Foxe realised that his blade had punctured the sac of the creature's heart. Blood in a fountain rose, and fell, and died. The thing twitched one final time; then at last was still. Captain Foxe knelt by his side. 'O Lord,' he whispered. 'O Lord – forgive us all.'

He felt a terrible weariness now, so that when he arrived at Mr Aubrey's door he could barely explain what had occurred. Mr Aubrey led him to a couch and Captain Foxe lay down there, intending only to recapture his breath; but his eyes no longer seemed his own and he fell asleep at once. When he woke again, sharply, he knew that it was late. He crossed to an open door. There was a coolness in the air, and the sun was starting to sink into the west.

He heard footsteps behind him and turned to face Mr Aubrey. 'I must go at once,' he said.

Mr Aubrey shook his head. 'They will find you.'

'They have been here, then? Still hunting for me?'

'Barely two hours before.'

'And no one betrayed me . . .'

Mr Aubrey looked surprised. 'Why should they have done?' He took a step forward, and lowered his voice. 'You were seen, Captain, your struggle, against . . . against the killer of the boy. No one here will betray you. The debt of gratitude is far too great for that.'

'Then is human charity not altogether dead, and I wronged the world when I conceived it to be so.' Captain Foxe nodded to himself; then he crossed suddenly to a writing desk. 'I would have you pen something for me, sir,' he asked, 'if you have the patience.'

Mr Aubrey nodded. 'Of course, Captain. Just tell me what it is you need written down.'

'I would like to leave for my son a true account of all that has occurred, so that he may be armed with the knowledge that I have gained, and be forewarned.'

'Can you not tell him yourself?'

'I have . . .' Captain Foxe paused, and bowed his head. 'I have a strange foreboding within myself,' he continued, 'I shall not see him again. Should it prove true I would have him know in what cause it was I died; and that it was not wholly in vain, for nothing befalls us in this world that God does not somehow bless. For I love him, Mr Aubrey; and I would teach him, as though it were on my parting breath, the best I can – that even in this darkling world, there yet endures within us the lesson of hope.'

Mr Aubrey nodded; he reached for his pen and his pot of ink, and began to write according to Captain Foxe's dictation. When he had finished, he handed the sheaf of papers across; but Captain Foxe refused them and handed them back. 'They will be better protected with you,' he said. 'Promise me, sir, that if I should die, you will hand the papers on to my son.' The promise was given and Captain Foxe received it with a simple word of thanks. Then he turned. 'I must leave now,' he said.

'But if you know yourself to be in danger,' asked Mr Aubrey, 'why risk yourself like this?'

'Tonight of all nights,' Captain Foxe replied, 'and in spite of my foreboding I would not leave my family alone.' He glanced up at the sun. 'And see,' he murmured, 'it is already growing late.'

∽∾

'SEE WITH WHAT HEAT THESE DOGS OF HELL ADVANCE.'
John Milton, *Paradise Lost*

Captain Foxe did not leave Broadchalke by the Salisbury road. Instead he climbed the valley's northern side, until he had reached the chalk trackway along the summit of the downs. He paused there, and admired for a moment the beauty of the landscape stretching far away from him: the woods and hills, the villages and fields, dyed with the colours of the afternoon sun, and all peaceful, so peaceful, with nothing stirring but the sheep cropping at the grass, and the wisps of smoke from far distant hearths. 'As I was born to this land,' thought Captain Foxe to himself, 'so shall I return as dust to it. Where then is the triumph of evil in that, even though I be doomed to die tonight?' But an image of his family swam across his thoughts; and he felt his anger return. He spurred his horse on, and did not stop again; for he had a long way to travel before the setting of the sun.

Even so, he did not ride as fast as he could, for he did not wish to tire his horse; he knew that the final stretch of his journey might be when he would need the fullest speed. He met no one on the ridgeway track; nor, when he ventured back into the valleys, did he permit himself to be seen, for there were many trees along the river banks, and he was able to avoid the villages and towns. Only when the road began to climb again did he start to feel exposed; for the woods were thinning now and ahead of him, desolate and bare, stretched the lonely expanse of Salisbury Plain. Soon he had left the trees behind; and as he began to ride across the downs, so he dug his spurs into his horse's flanks.

He did not look back for a couple of miles, for the wind – even on such a temperate day – came gusting across the Plain, and it was only when the breeze dropped that Captain Foxe heard the first beating of hooves. He stared round and saw three horsemen, black silhouettes on a distant ridge, their cloaks flapping like the wings of crows. He dug his spurs in even further; but he could feel his horse tiring, and he knew it would be close. He glanced round again; he had not been able to shake the horsemen off, but nor had his pursuers made any ground. Captain Foxe smiled grimly; he swung away from the road, and began to ride across the open land.

The grass was rougher than the track, but Captain Foxe was an experienced horseman and well-practised at riding on the Plain. Soon his pursuers were starting to flag, and he felt his hopes revive. The sun was a deep red above the horizon now, and behind him the east was growing dark; but when he stared ahead, he could see the distant silhouette of Stonehenge, and he knew there was only a mile more to go. Nevertheless, he would not take the straightest route, for he had no wish to ride beneath the circle on such a day; and so he swung to the right, and left the stones behind.

He had almost passed Stonehenge when he heard more hoofbeats, ahead of him now, and saw horsemen approaching, blocking off his route. He wheeled again even further to the right, so that he was riding away from Woodton, but once more, above the pounding of his own horse's hooves, he heard other hoofbeats approaching him, and he had no choice but to wheel and turn once more. Now he was riding directly towards the circle. All its stones loomed black against the sky – all save one, touched along its edges by the rays of the sun so that it seemed washed a bloody red. Captain Foxe glanced round involuntarily; and saw how his pursuers were forming an arc, closing in on him, so that he had no choice but to continue straight ahead. The nearest horseman to him was cloaked in black; his face could barely be made out in the twilight, but it gleamed even so, and Captain Foxe could guess who it was. The rider was nearing: for desperately though Captain Foxe urged on his own horse, he could feel how tired it was growing, and he knew that soon, very soon, he was bound to be caught. At least, he thought, let it be once he had passed beyond the stones.

He was approaching them now: under the lintel and into the circle itself. At once, he stopped, for his path was blocked. He recognised the horsemen he had escaped on the road; they sat frozen in their saddles, stationed in the gaps between the giant stones. He would not escape them now. He stared desperately beyond the ring, towards the road that led on to his family. He could see now that there was a giant cloud of smoke rising above the wood which blocked out his view of Woodton. He tensed himself. There was an unmarked gap between two of the stones. He dug his spurs into the flanks of his horse.

Immediately, there was the crack of a pistol shot. Captain Foxe was flung from his saddle as his horse whinnied, rearing upwards, then crashing to the ground. Captain Foxe heard a snapping, and felt a sudden searing pain in his leg as his horse rolled across it in the agony of its death. There was a second pistol shot. The horse rolled once again, then lay suddenly still. Captain Foxe struggled to move, but he couldn't feel his leg and he knew that it was shattered. He closed his eyes. The chase was over. He was snared in the trap.

He felt a shadow pass between his face and the last dying rays of the sun, and he opened his eyes again. Sir Charles Wolverton was standing above him, staring down. He seemed almost unchanged: a little older perhaps – the face more lined, the thin beard more streaked – but otherwise the same. 'If I must die,' said Captain

Foxe, 'then I am ready for death. But my family – spare them. Glut your anger on me.'

Sir Charles gave no sign of having heard him at all; his face remained frozen, a rigid mask of ice. He knelt slowly, until he was squatting on Captain Foxe's chest; but still his expression continued unchanged, and Captain Foxe knew suddenly that it was not Sir Charles at all but a true mask indeed, concealing a different and dreadful breed of thing. Captain Foxe stared into the eyes; and saw only an eternal depth there, blind, and pitiless, and cold as space. 'No,' he whispered, 'no,' before a hand was placed across his open mouth and a blade of steel against the vein in his neck. Life ebbed from the stare of Captain Foxe; but still the expression of his killer did not change.

❧

'. . . THOU PROFOUNDEST HELL,
RECEIVE THY NEW POSSESSOR . . .'

John Milton, *Paradise Lost*

It was early evening when Robert heard the first rolling of the drum. He had been studying in one of his favourite spots with his toes in the stream, his back against a tree, his books in a scattered ring around him on the grass. Mr Webbe had ordered him to stay inside the house all day, but the sky had been so blue, and the sun so warm, that Robert had felt little guilt about slipping away. He knew he would not be punished – Mr Webbe never punished anyone.

The drum roll sounded louder. Robert gathered up his books, and scampered up the bank. Woodton lay before him; and beyond the village, a line of men was descending from a hill. They were dressed as soldiers, but their uniforms were tattered and their breastplates and helmets were stained with mud. One of the men, at the head of the line, was beating the drum; a second held a standard. A light breeze caught it, and for a moment it fluttered in the air. The flag was decorated with a coat of arms; and Robert stared at it wide-eyed. He had seen the arms before: carved above the doorway of Wolverton Hall.

As he ran towards the village, people were starting to gather on the road. Robert pushed and slipped his way past them, but the nearer the column of troops approached, the slower his progress became, and he grew ever more desperate to reach his mother and home. He cursed himself for not having stayed with her, for with each beat of the drum his dread was growing as he thought of what the Wolverton standard might portend. He remembered his father's description of what had happened the last time it had fluttered above Woodton; and how close-run the rescue of the village had been then. Robert stared about him. Where was his father now? It was not possible that he could be away at such a moment of crisis. Suddenly, as he looked, Robert saw a man on horseback, and for a moment mistook him. He waved and shouted; the man turned, and Robert saw that it was Sir Henry. Emily was clinging to his back; she seemed pale and afraid, but when she saw Robert, her face lightened and she slipped from her horse to run across to him. 'Robert!' she cried, as she held him in her arms. She kissed him; but then her head was abruptly pulled away, and she screamed as her father hauled her back by her hair. He seized her in his arms, then roughly placed her where she had been before. Sir Henry leant over from his saddle to hiss in Robert's face. 'Save yourself,' he whispered. 'Find your mother, and both of you, run for your lives.' Then he wheeled his horse around, and cantered away. Robert stared after him; Emily was crying something, her eyes damp with tears, but her father rode on, and they were soon lost amidst the crowds.

Robert did as Sir Henry had advised, and ran for his life. He reached home at last and found his mother with Mr Webbe in the yard; she cried with delight, and held her son tight in her arms. But Mr Webbe pulled them roughly apart. 'We do not have the time,' he said and, picking Robert up, put him in the saddle of a horse. Robert realised that his mother and Mr Webbe had been waiting for him, and he felt a burning flush of shame.

'I have delayed you,' he said.

'It is no matter,' answered Mr Webbe shortly, as he climbed into his saddle.

'Who are the soldiers?' asked Robert.

Mr Webbe stared at him; and his face seemed twisted. 'It is an army of the dead,' he whispered. Then he spurred his horse on, and galloped from the yard.

But it was too late. As Robert followed, he heard the drumbeat stop and a terrible silence fill the evening air. He saw Mr Webbe reining in his horse, and then his mother too; and as Robert emerged on to the village green, he almost fell from his saddle, so great was his shock. For ahead of them, the soldiers he had seen marching on the village were now ordered in a single rank; and the stench of the grave rose heavy from their line. All seemed decay: the flesh rotting on the soldiers' bones, the breastplates smeared with rust, the uniforms streaked with the silver trails of worms. Their eyes met

Robert's stare, and seemed to gleam as though with thirst. Robert turned in his saddle, and looked away.

It was only as he did so that he realised how the villagers too were gathered round the green. They were lined in a ring, so that every course of escape was cut off. Mr Webbe scanned their silent faces. 'In the name of God,' he cried suddenly, 'I beseech you, let us pass.' Some of the villagers looked down at the ground, but most continued to stare as before – coldly, with their lips pressed tight and their faces set. Not a single one of them stepped aside.

But then there was movement from the soldiers' ranks. Robert turned again and saw that a passage was opening through the centre of the lines, and a horseman was approaching through the gap. His face was very pale and appeared to gleam, a pallor offset by the curling blackness of his beard; his eyes were bright, and as hungry as his men's. He passed through the lines, then reined in his horse and sat silently, not looking once at Robert, or his mother, or Mr Webbe, but at the ring of villagers around the edge of the green. He smiled, as though accepting a triumph already won; then lifted up his hand.

'Men and women of Woodton,' he proclaimed. 'The days of rebellion are finished.' His accent was foreign; but he spoke English with perfect command, and although he barely raised his voice, his every word seemed to reach into the depths of Robert's mind. 'My name is Faustus,' the horseman continued. 'In his exile, I was the companion of your master, Sir Charles.'

At the mention of Sir Charles' name, a sobbing moan rose up from the villagers, and they began to shuffle and writhe.

Faustus smiled and raised up his hand again.

'You need fear nothing,' he said softly, 'although all of you, by your traitorous revolt, have well merited a cruel and bloody punishment. But Sir Charles is generous; and he chooses to forgive. Indeed, more than just forgive. You have all of you, I think, during the past few months, benefited from the gold which I – as Sir Charles' steward – have handed out to you. And yet the wealth you have been given so far may be nothing compared with what is still to come. See!' He turned and, at his command, two of his soldiers brought forward a chest. Faustus gestured that it should be opened. As the soldiers obeyed his order, the villagers caught the sudden glint of gold, cast red by the setting sun; and almost as one they began to surge forward, for they could see how the chest was full to its brim with coin, and plate, and treasures of every kind. Faustus smiled mockingly; then lowered his hand. His soldiers raised their muskets, and fired a volley into the air. At once, there was silence. The villagers stood frozen, then shrank guiltily back.

'Patience,' smiled Faustus. He inspected his nails. 'Patience.'

'What would you have us do?' a voice cried out desperately.

'Tell us!' yelled another. 'Tell us what you want!'

'Why,' replied Faustus in a low and silky tone, 'I want nothing but your loyalty. *Your undying obedience.*'

At once, there were shouted protestations from around the green.

'Let us be perfectly clear,' said Faustus, raising his voice so that the cries were stilled at once. 'You must surrender yourselves to the mercy of Sir Charles. You must give yourselves over to him, freely, to serve him as he desires. In return, the wealth I have shown you – and more – will all be yours.'

Again, cries of agreement rose around the green.

Faustus lifted up his hand.

'You agree, then? All of you? Without reserve?'

The answer now was deafening.

'And yet . . .' Faustus frowned; and for the first time he stared at Mrs Foxe and Mr Webbe. 'And yet – there are those, I fear, who do not agree to the terms.'

'I pray the Lord have mercy upon us all,' replied Mr Webbe, his expression as impenetrable as it had ever been. He scanned the faces of the villagers. 'I confess it,' he acknowledged, 'I shall never barter my soul away for gold.'

A low, angry murmur answered him.

'Please!' he cried suddenly. 'I beseech you all – do not destroy yourselves like this! Have you not learned yet, that however sweet the Devil's tongue may sound, his gifts lead only to wretchedness and the flames of that Hell which is known as Despair? You are good people, all of you – or once you were. It is not too late for you to be so again.'

Silence answered his appeal; and then a stone hit him on the shoulder. Mr Webbe raised a hand to protect himself, but a second stone struck him on the back of the head and he toppled from his saddle like a heavy sack of grain. Faustus laughed immoderately at the sight; and, still laughing, rode across to where his enemy lay half-dazed in the dust.

'You have always been a troublemaker,' he sneered. 'You, and this sorry woman's husband together.' He turned to Mrs Foxe and cuffed her across the face, very hard, so that she too was knocked down from her horse. 'No!' cried

Robert, riding forward, but Faustus ducked him easily; seizing him by the neck, he wrestled Robert from his saddle, and thrust him on to his own. Robert struggled to break free; but Faustus' nails dug deep into his arms and he could not escape. Meanwhile, Mrs Foxe was rising slowly to her feet; but she was kicked in the face and collapsed again, to lie by Mr Webbe's side. Faustus wheeled his horse round to address the crowd. 'It is necessary, sometimes,' he cried, 'to lop off rotten branches, that the tree itself be saved. Have not these two – grovelling before us now – always been compounded of rottenness? It was this man, fifteen years ago, who helped expel from Woodton its master, Sir Charles. And it was this woman who was rescued by that crime from the fate she richly merited – to be burnt as a notorious whore, and a witch.'

Cries of agreement answered him, mingled with cheers, and then, as the crowd stared at Mrs Foxe and Mr Webbe, they began to hiss and chant. Some men broke forward, intending to seize the prisoners; but although Faustus smiled at the sight, he shook his head and waved them back.

'Not yet,' he murmured, 'not yet, loyal friends. For there is no crime so terrible that it cannot be forgiven – if only it first be confessed.' He turned to his soldiers, and beckoned with his arm. 'Bring forward the other prisoners.'

Two of the soldiers broke from their line. One led Sir Henry, who had been tethered round his neck; the second was pulling on Emily. 'No!' cried Robert, struggling to escape again, but Faustus' grip was implacable, and still he could not slip it. He stared despairingly at Emily. She had not heard him, and her eyes seemed blind with terror.

'This man too,' proclaimed Faustus, gesturing towards Sir Henry, 'has been a most arrant traitor. Come, sir – confess it.'

'I confess . . .' said Sir Henry. He swallowed. 'I did betray my commanding officer, Sir Charles Wolverton, to the rebel, Captain Foxe.'

'Are you sorry?'

'I am sorry.'

'Are you punished?'

'I am punished.'

Faustus curled his lips into a smile. 'How?' he whispered.

Sir Henry swallowed again; he glanced at his daughter, at her pale, frightened face. 'My wife . . .' he said at last.

'Yes?' prompted Faustus.

'My wife was slain.'

'Yes,' said Faustus. 'Exterminated – lest her womb produce further traitors.' He nodded to the soldier holding Emily. The man twisted her hair violently, so that the girl was forced on to her knees; then he silenced her by placing a knife against her throat.

'You promised!' cried Sir Henry, running forward until throttled by the rope around his neck. 'Please!' he choked. 'Please, not my daughter, no!'

Faustus shrugged. 'I must have proof of your repentance.'

'Yes,' gasped Sir Henry, 'yes, of course!'

'You see these traitors?' Faustus gestured down at Mrs Foxe and Mr Webbe. 'How do you think they should be punished for their crimes?'

Sir Henry stared at them dumbly; he tried to speak, then choked and shook his head.

Faustus turned to the ring of villagers. 'Decide!' he

shrieked suddenly. 'How should they be punished? This heretic – and this witch! The judgment must be yours – and their blood upon your heads!'

There was silence; then a woman stepped forward, her face twisted with hatred. 'Hang them!' she shrieked. 'Hang them both!'

'No!' answered a man from the far side of the green. 'Hanging is too good for them!'

'Stone them!' screamed a third villager.

'Burn them!' answered a fourth.

'There,' said Faustus, turning to Sir Henry. He lolled in his saddle, then bared his teeth in a smile. 'You have heard the sentence of the court.' He waved with his hand. 'See that it is done.'

Sir Henry stood paralysed, and still could not say a word. But there was no need for him to order the execution, for the villagers were already surging across the green, and although Mr Webbe tried to fend them away, he was submerged beneath their fists, and then Mrs Foxe as well. As he saw his mother being seized and dragged along the ground, Robert began to scream. 'Father!' he cried, 'Father, Father, where are you? Mother! No, Mother!' But he was silenced by a laughing Faustus, who ordered him gagged and bound, so that there was now not the faintest chance of his escape. Then Faustus spurred his horse forward, following the crowd to the edge of the green. He glanced down into his prisoner's face, and smiled. Robert's eyes were bulging; he was screaming wordlessly from behind his gag. For on the edge of the green, two stakes had been erected; and around the stakes were great bundles of wood.

Mr Webbe and Mrs Foxe were each secured in turn. The crowd was now baying for their deaths – screaming, spitting, hurling stones. Each prisoner was repeatedly hit; but neither protested, nor even cried out. Then gradually the tumult began to fade, until silence had fallen right across the crowd, for Sir Henry was now standing beneath the stakes; and all were waiting for the fire to be lit.

A torch of burning pitch was passed through the crowd. Sir Henry stared at it with numb horror, until at last it was handed to him, and he began to shake. 'I cannot do it,' he cried; and at once, at Faustus' command, Emily was dragged through the crowd and hauled across the bundles of wood towards the stakes.

'No!' shrieked Sir Henry. He clambered after his daughter and took her in his arms; then he lit the very corner of the pyre. He gazed up at Mrs Foxe. 'I am sorry,' he said.

'Do not be,' she answered. She smiled, despite her tears and the bruising to her face. 'I see behind the multitude a chariot waiting for me, and it will soon take me up through the clouds, with the sound of trumpets, to the Celestial Gate. Do not be sorry, Sir Henry – for I am not.' But even as she said so, she began to weep. 'Farewell, my darling boy!' she cried. 'Robert! In the mansions of the Almighty, we shall be reunited once again – your father – you – and I. Let your life be as a progress to meet with us there . . .' She tried to say more; but she had swallowed smoke and began to cough. The crowd was falling back now, as the heat began to build, and Robert noticed how the soldiers had vanished into the dark. For a moment, his head was filled with wild schemes of wrestling himself free and putting out the flames; but even as he struggled, he felt the knots begin to bite, and he slumped despairingly forward once again. Of his father, he realised, there was still not a trace.

The heat of the flames was soon burning against his cheeks as he stared into the heart of the inferno. His mother and Mr Webbe seemed nothing now, just two streaks of black amidst the oranges and reds, as their blood, and flesh, and bone became smoke. High the clouds billowed, high above the village, so that the brightness of the very stars seemed blotted out, and the dust was scattered on the breeze into the night. Dimly, through his tears, Robert followed its flight.

'It is done,' said Faustus at last. He stared about him at the throng of villagers gathered around the fire. 'All is prepared,' he murmured, 'and all shall be fulfilled.' Then he wheeled his horse round, and left the cheering crowds behind.

๑๐๑

'NOW, BODY, TURN TO AIR,
OR LUCIFER WILL BEAR THEE QUICK TO HELL!
O SOUL, BE CHANG'D INTO LITTLE WATER-DROPS,
AND FALL INTO THE OCEAN, NE'ER BE FOUND!'
Christopher Marlowe, *Doctor Faustus*

As Faustus rode towards the darkness into which the soldiers had vanished, Robert saw Emily crouched beneath a tree, her head in her hands. Sir Henry was kneeling beside her, attempting to make her face him, but she remained hunched in her grief and would not look up. As Faustus' horse rode by, Sir Henry glanced round and he saw Robert. Guilt twisted his face; but although Robert knew that Sir Henry was staring into his eyes for some mark of forgiveness, he had nothing to offer, nothing but his hate. Sir Henry shuddered; and as he did so, Emily looked up. She stared at her father, then followed his gaze and at once leapt to her feet. She would have run after Robert; but she was seized by her father, and held prisoner in his arms. Robert struggled to shout back to her; but the gag was tight in his mouth, and he could make no sound.

'There are finer joys in life than women.' Faustus laughed shortly. 'But you seem very young to require that lesson.'

Robert twisted round in his bonds; tried to believe that his eyes could kill.

Faustus, though, only laughed a second time. 'Of course, you do not thank me now for what I have done, but in time you will.' He glanced back at the pyre. 'It is best to be without love. If you are to voyage where I will lead you, if you are to learn what I shall teach you, then love is nothing, no better than pitch upon an eagle's wings, clogging its flight, dooming its ambition to soar above the clouds. You are your father's son, Robert – and he was strong, and courageous, and full of resolve. But he had the canker of morality in his soul, which debases even the best into mud. He, and your mother, and Lady Vaughan, and Mr Webbe – all would have stopped me, and so all had to go. But you are clever, Robert, cleverer than them – and although you may hate me now, and curse me, in the end you will be mine.'

'So my father, then,' Robert wanted to scream, 'my father too is dead?' He had imagined he was so abandoned upon an ocean of horrors that nothing could have persuaded him to feel any more lost; but he knew now that the ocean was infinite. Tears blinded him; but he could not wipe them away. Instead, they trickled down his cheek, and moistened his gag, and fell on to the ropes which were bound around his chest. He tried to stop crying; but still the hot tears flowed.

'Mewl on,' whispered Faustus suddenly, 'but understand what it is I am offering you.' They had been passing along the track which led through the wood; now they left the trees, and emerged on to the plain. Stonehenge was before them, silhouetted against the blaze of a full moon; and around it, some on horseback, some on foot, was a circle of the dead. 'See this ancient place,' Faustus whispered. 'All its secrets, all its powers will soon be mine. How hard I have laboured – how long I have prepared. Would you not share in my wisdom, Robert? Even if you had as many souls as there are stars in this sky – would you not surrender every last one for just a taste, just a glimpse, of what I offer you for free?' He began to pull at Robert's gag, his fingers shaking with his eagerness. He tugged at the knot violently; and the gag was undone.

Robert stared round. He narrowed his eyes, as though the gleam in Faustus' stare were too bright for him, but he did not look away. For a long time, he said nothing. 'What are you? he whispered at last. 'What nature of thing?'

'Greater than you, or any man.'

'How?'

'I am a compound of impossible things. I am alive and dead; spirit and clay. I own the secrets of the grave – and of ageless immortality.'

Robert struggled to keep his expression perfectly blank. 'You are a demon, then?' he asked. 'A spirit from Hell?'

Faustus shrugged. 'Men might think so, for we prey upon their blood.'

'We? There are many of you?'

Faustus shrugged again. 'More than the common run can know.'

'And Sir Charles? Your *friend*. Is he a demon too?'

'Why do you ask?'

'I saw him once. He was very pale, like you.'

Faustus laughed, and gazed towards the stones. 'You did not see Sir Charles,' he whispered. 'His outward form, perhaps – a shell – but nothing more. Sir Charles was a fool. A man who sold his soul – and discovered he had sold his flesh and blood as well. For he desired to be a vessel for the coming of the Most High – and his wish was duly granted – a vessel he became.'

Robert shook his head. 'No,' he whispered. 'What do you mean?'

Faustus glanced back round. His eyes gleamed brighter than they had ever been; and his skin seemed lit by some inner fire. 'The Great One,' he cried suddenly. 'He will soon be here! Oh, Robert!' He gripped the boy tightly. 'How hard have I worked, and into what depths of learning and necromancy plunged, to discover the rituals that will summon Him here! And with what success have my efforts been crowned! Come!' He wheeled his horse round. 'Come and behold Him – the master of us all!'

'Who?' Robert screamed. 'Who are you talking about?'

Faustus widened his eyes. 'What?' he asked. 'Can you truly not guess?' He laughed at the fear he could see in Robert's face; then spurred his horse forward. At his approach, the dead paraded their arms. Staring into their faces, Robert recognised some as his father's men. One was Sergeant Everard; Robert called out to him, but not a trace of intelligence crossed the soldier's face. Then they were past him, and under the shadow of the giant stones themselves. Faustus reined in his horse. He sat still for a moment; then climbed down from his saddle. He lifted Robert and stood him, still bound, upon the grass. 'Follow me,' he ordered. He led the way into the centre of the ring.

A body was hanging from a lintel of the stones. It was framed by the moon and its naked flesh could be made out quite clearly, for it was cast silver by the light. Robert could see how it had been pierced through its ankles by a hook, and then he saw a drop of something falling from the head, and he heard a soft splash, and he understood why the body appeared so perfectly white, for it was being drained of all its blood. It swayed gently; and then, with a creaking of rope, it swung round in the breeze. For the first time, Robert was able to see the corpse's face. He tried to scream; he could not; no sound would come out. He tried to run; his limbs seemed made of lead. He could do nothing but stare into his father's face. And then at last it came: a shriek of horror, and loss, and disbelieving grief.

Faustus twisted his fingers through Robert's hair and dragged his head back violently, then placed a hand to cut off his scream. All was silent again, save for the creaking of the rope in the breeze. There was another drop of blood from the nose; another splash. Suddenly, Robert jerked himself free. He ran forward, stumbling across the centre of the ring, and shrieked out his father's name. Then he froze. Something was moving ahead of him. Something was stirring, and rising from the ground. It was the figure of a man: naked, drenched in blood; standing beneath his father, staring at the moon. Slowly, the figure turned. Robert stared into the face. He knew it at once; he had seen it before – beneath a black cowl, and in the painting that had hung in Wolverton Hall. But then Robert started. He stared into the man's eyes: he found himself shaking uncontrollably; and he sank to the ground. It was no man before him; nor anything, it seemed, that had ever been a man. Robert could not bear to look at those eyes again; and yet he did, as though drawn. He stared, and at once felt a damp warmth spreading from his groin.

'Feel no shame,' whispered Faustus in his ear, 'for it is right you feel such fear. You can see Him there, then – you can see Him through the outer shell of human clay?'

Robert cowered, bowed his head – anything to escape the void behind the eyes. 'I . . . no . . . ' He swallowed. 'What is it?' he cried.

Faustus spread out his arms. 'He has many names. Some of them you doubtless learned at your mother's knee. But He is older than them all. To those who grovel in a synagogue or church, He is the very Principle of Evil; but to those who dare, He is Eternal Knowledge, the Fountainhead of Truth. When Eve was in Eden, do you think, was she wrong to steal fruit from the forbidden tree? For the serpent did not lie. Eve ate the apple; and as she had been promised, won wisdom from its taste.'

'Yes,' whispered Robert. He stared up at his father. 'As she also won death.'

But Faustus had not heard him – he was stepping forward, then falling to his knees, bowing in worship at the naked man's feet. He began to chant in a strange language, and stood again, reaching feverishly for the arms of Captain Foxe, tugging hard on them, as he continued to chant. With a ripping of tendons, the corpse was pulled down from its hook. 'Three baths there have been,' said Faustus, speaking now in Latin. 'Now receive the fourth. Emerge restored from it. No more a thing of clay!' He shuddered with exaltation and, with his bare hands, ripped apart the stomach of the corpse. He scooped out an armful of guts; and as though they were soap, began to rub them across the naked man's skin. Robert could bear no more. He looked about him for the nearest stone. He struggled to his feet and crossed towards it, determined to have no more of such an existence, to join his parents, to smash out his brains.

He paused by the stone, tensing himself. As he lifted his head back, ready to bring it down, a terrible howling filled his ears. It rose and fell, and Robert froze at once, for it seemed to pierce into his very soul and flay him apart. For a moment, he had thought it was his own scream he heard; for it had seemed to resonate with a pain that could only have been his. But then the howling rose and fell again; and this time, turning round, Robert knew that he was listening to no human sound.

Had Satan, he wondered, made such a cry, when he woke for the first time amidst the fiery wastes of Hell and, looking about him, understood how great had been his fall? Was it really possible, Robert asked himself, was it really true that he was staring at the form of the Evil One? His father had always taught him that Hell existed only within the soul, and the Devil likewise; but his father was dead now; perhaps he had been wrong? For *something* was standing there, lit by the moon, some terrible spirit of great and monstrous power. It howled again; and to Robert, listening, all the world seemed bleached with desolation and pain.

The howling fell away; but the figure still writhed, as though enveloped by the flames of an invisible fire. The gore that had been smeared across his skin appeared to be bubbling and melting into his flesh. The figure ripped at it; and Robert saw how the very limbs had turned viscous, as though there were nothing on the bones but a soup of blood and meat. It was flooding away now, spilling across the grass; still the figure wiped at it, smoothing his fingers across his body and limbs until, below the filth, Robert saw a whiteness as blinding as snow, and he realised it was not bone at all but naked flesh. The figure bent back his head and howled, as though to summon down the stars. Then he ran his fingers across his face, and the features of Sir Charles Wolverton were forever obliterated, wiped away into a mess of gore; and though the eyes remained the same, there was a new face framing their measureless stare, emerging from beneath the shell of Sir Charles.

This new face seemed strangely and terribly deformed. Its nostrils were flared and its lips puckered, but otherwise the face seemed impossibly thin, as though its stare, like some glacier, had worn the cheekbones right away. And yet it was not in any physical deformity that the terror of the face existed, but rather in what it appeared to conceal: that measureless power upon which the eyes alone opened a window. Robert did not dare to meet their stare again; for he feared that, if he did, it would incinerate his soul.

A sound like a gust of wind swept through the stones. It was the creature's sigh. Even Faustus shuddered, and drew his cloak about him, as though the sound had chilled his bones. 'Welcome!' he cried. 'O Lord and Master, O source of all knowledge, of wisdom, of truth – welcome to this home, which I have prepared for You! Welcome.' He laughed, he kissed the figure upon his cheeks, he held him in his arms.

He was answered by silence. The long grass ceased to murmur; the distant bleating of sheep could no longer be heard on the breeze. All was still. And then suddenly Faustus shrieked.

'No,' he cried, 'no!' He tried to stagger back, but he could not escape. The figure seized him by the hair and, forcing back his head, kissed him, not on the cheeks but on the mouth; when he pulled his lips away, they were glistening and red. He licked them; then bent back Faustus' head once again, and bit into his throat. Robert, as he cowered behind a stone, could hear the puncturing of the skin, and then a snapping of bone; he peered round, and saw how Faustus' head was twisted half-way round. For a long time, the figure sucked on the wound; then he dropped his prey. Like a dried insect with broken wings, Faustus crawled across the grass. His flesh had been withered to the bone; as he twitched vainly, his limbs seemed to rustle and his head, as it lolled from the broken spine, to creak. 'But . . . no . . . ' he whispered. 'I am immortal . . . ' He frowned. 'This cannot be . . . '

His eyes grew wide with the shock of his own death. His neck cracked. His skull hit the ground; it crumbled into dust. A wind began to blow, and the ashes of the corpse were blown across Stonehenge. Robert felt them against his face; they were very fine, and scratched his skin. He wiped them away, and saw how all the circle seemed engulfed by a storm, as eddies of dust were blown about the stones, so that the light of the stars and the moon was blotted out. Through the haze, and beyond the stones, Robert could just make out the Plain. It was empty: where the circle of the dead had been, there was nothing but a storm of burning ash. He rubbed his eyes and screwed them shut. He fell to his knees; then buried his face in the coolness of the grass.

When he at last stared up again, the dust was gone. The stars blazed brightly in the heavens; the shadows were cool and lined with silver. From across the open miles, a church bell rang.

He turned round.

The eyes were gazing down on him.

Robert wondered if he could run, but he was drawn into their stare. At once, he was lost: he could feel himself sinking, as the darkness grew cold and eternal all about him. But then the eyes closed, and the face grew twisted. The figure bent forward, as though doubled up with pain. He clutched at his stomach. For the first time, Robert realised that the body was as deformed as the face. The arms and legs were both unnaturally thin, but the hips were like a woman's, and the belly was swollen as though pregnant with a child. Again, the figure clutched at it and bent forward with pain. He knelt; then reached for Robert's arms. The fingers were so cold that they might have been ice. They gripped implacably; and as they did so, Robert felt his arms growing numb. He hoped, when he was fed upon, that his death would be quicker than Faustus' had been.

He stared into the terrible whiteness of the face. For a moment, a shadow appeared to flicker across it; and Robert imagined he saw self-loathing there, and horror, and regret. But he did not really know: for so rapidly did the shadow pass that Robert could not be certain it had been there at all. He searched the face for some sign of pity – but in vain. It was twisted again with agony; and in the eyes, the blankness remained.

The creature's swollen stomach seemed to pulse, as though some force within it were trying to escape. He doubled up again; and Robert found himself suddenly being knocked round. He felt his legs being parted; and then he was being lifted by his thighs. Something hard brushed against them; Robert tried to close his legs, but they were only pushed even further apart, and suddenly he screamed, for he was being impaled, and the stake was growing longer and thicker all the time. Up and down, it thrust; up and down; and Robert felt the world start to swim before his eyes, pulsing and contracting to the rhythm of his pain, quickening and melting, and beginning to dissolve. He blinked and looked again; but still the world was fading. Darkness was seeping in from the margins; darkness was flooding everything. Suddenly, deep within him, Robert felt a spurt of liquid ice; and at the same moment, the world was gone at last, and all was black.

II

'IN WHAT FANTASTIC NEW WORLD HAVE I BEEN,
WHAT HORRORS PASSED, WHAT THREATENING VISIONS SEEN?'
The Earl of Rochester, *Valentinian*

The young lady held on to the side of the carriage window. The curls of her hair were swept back by the breeze, and she had to smooth them with a touch of her slim white hand. As she did so, a shadow passed across her face. 'Why,' she murmured, 'there is almost a menace in the air.'

Her companion stirred, as though woken from a profound lassitude. He frowned. 'Menace?' he asked at length.

'See.' The lady pointed. 'We are drawing near to the standing stones.'

Her companion moved along his seat, and twisted round to stare out of the window. His nostrils dilated faintly. At once, his expression froze.

'You can smell it?' the lady asked.

The man met her eye.

'I was not certain at first,' she continued. 'Yet I am right, am I not, that it is more than merely the aura of the place?' She shivered delicately, and reached across for her companion's hand.

The man studied her for a moment; then he leaned from the window to shout orders to the coachman. 'You may be right,' he admitted, settling back into his place. 'There does seem something almost dangerous in the air.' He closed his eyes and smiled faintly. 'Christ, but I had forgotten what fear might be. Is not its touch golden-fingered? I find that it almost ravishes me.' He shivered, just as the lady had done. 'Rare pleasure,' he whispered, 'to feel my stomach so lightened.' He squeezed his companion's hand; then he turned again, and gazed through the window at the stones as they drew near.

Robert woke. Immediately, he wished he had not. The sun was unbearably bright; it made his pupils feel scalded and raw. He screwed his eyes shut, then turned and cooled his face in the dew.

A hand touched his shoulder.

He screamed; he flailed out blindly, hitting air. 'No!' he cried. 'No, no!' Then he felt the hand again, now gentle and cool against his brow.

He looked up to see a lady standing between him and the light of the sun. He rubbed his eyes; he could see her clearly now. His first thought was, how like a goddess she appeared, for she seemed lovelier than that Venus he had read praised in ancient poems, risen like the surf of murmuring waves, or the dancing sunbeams of early morning, a glimpse of something infinitely beautiful, and dangerous. Her body was slim, her face sweet-turned, oval and very soft; her cheeks the colour of a damask rose; her hair raven black. Her dress was rich: edged with lace, and red like her lips. Young she seemed, and most desirable; save that her skin and her eyes, which were exceedingly golden and bright, had a gleam too cold for a girl of eighteen, which in every other way she appeared to be. Robert had seen such a stare before; he remembered the depths behind Faustus' eyes, and how they had submerged him. He gazed up in dumb horror; then, with an effort of will, he turned his face away.

'He is alive,' he heard the lady call out. Her voice was as he would have expected it to be, thrilling and soft. With a rustle of skirts, she bent down beside him. Gently, she caressed his cheeks, so that he could not help but gaze up once again into the beauty of her face. She studied him closely; a look of puzzlement creased her brow, and she reached out to touch a wound on his head, then tasted the blood. 'Mortal,' she murmured. She shook her head. 'And yet . . .' She began to comb her fingers through his hair. 'What has happened to you?'

Robert wondered. Misery rose on his memory. He had no mother, he had no father. He was alone. He clawed at himself as he began to shudder. He felt so cold. He remembered, from the second before his mind had gone black, the jet of liquid ice. Even now, it seemed to linger in his stomach . . . Robert closed his legs at once, crossing them tightly. He stared wildly about him. He was amongst the stones; he had to escape. The Devil had been there the night before, the Pitiless One, the Lord of Flies. The Devil had been there – and God knew, might be yet.

Robert tried to climb to his feet. At first, he thought he had succeeded. His limbs, though, no longer seemed to be his own. He imagined he was moving, but the world about him was moving as well, rippling like a field of corn in the wind, and as he watched it Robert's head began to spin. He gasped for air. He felt his body arch; and then he was vomiting ice. So freezing was it that his mouth and lips grew numb. Again and again, until he was retching air, he struggled to bring up the coldness from his guts. He was sweating now, he realised, and his blood seemed on fire, but deep inside, so deep that it seemed less in his stomach than in his soul, the ice remained and would not be purged.

'Some terrible thing has happened here.'

The words were coming from a great distance. Robert imagined he was lying in a well, and that the words were falling from the young lady's lips like stones. He was in her arms, he discovered; he had not moved at all. She untucked a handkerchief of lace from her sleeve, then began to mop at his brow.

'The dead have been here.'

Another voice, Robert dimly realised: this time a man's.

'Then where are they now?'

'Burnt into ashes. Can you not smell their dust? It clings to the stones.'

The lady breathed in deeply. She shook her head. 'But who could have done such a thing? One of our kind?'

'It may be.' A pause. The man cleared his throat. 'But there is something else as well. Hanging in the air. I would almost say . . .'

'What?'

No answer; only footsteps across the grass. Robert felt a shadow. Struggling to focus his gaze, he stared up, and saw a second face. The man who had just been talking: auburn-haired, with a short, well-trimmed beard; skin chalky and gleaming; eyes once again uncomfortably bright. Above one of the eyes ran a faint, pink scar.

The man puckered his nostrils; and Robert realised that he was being smelt. Just as the woman had done, the man began to frown. 'You said he was mortal.'

'And so he is. Taste his blood.'

'Then why can I not smell it?'

The lady shrugged very faintly. 'Perhaps,' she suggested, 'it is for the same reason that I cannot sense his thoughts. Try – but to me, it is as though they are walled around by brass.'

The man stared into Robert's eyes; for an eternity, it seemed, he did not look away; then at last he shook his head. 'But how is this possible?' he asked. 'I cannot smell his blood. I cannot read his mind. I have never known such a thing – not since I was changed.' He bent down. He pinched Robert's cheeks between his finger and thumb. For a moment, a cold smile flitted along his lips. 'He is very pretty,' he murmured, 'this mystery boy of ours.'

'Indeed,' the lady replied at once. 'I would not otherwise have claimed him for myself.'

The man met her gaze; then shrugged as she reached across to recapture her prize. As she did so, she gasped suddenly; she raised a hand to her mouth, and looked away, then hugged Robert tightly in her arms. 'See,' she whispered, 'what has been done to him!'

Pillowed upon her breast, Robert knew from its rapid rise and fall that his comforter was struggling to hold back her tears. Dimly, he wondered why. He had thought he read in her eyes what she was: a demon like Faustus – a drinker of blood. Desperately, he tried to think. But fever clouds were rolling across his mind, like banks of warm fog, and he could not understand. Someone was touching his thighs: inspecting his wounds. Robert closed his legs tight. He clung to his protectress; nuzzled his cheek against the lace across her breast.

'Who did this to you?'

The words came so faintly that Robert could barely

hear them at all. He lifted his head, to try to hear; but his skull seemed made of lead, and he could not support its weight. Again, he nuzzled up against the lace. His mother had worn such a piece: a wedding gift from the young Trooper Foxe. Robert smiled. She had always loved it despite herself, for she would never otherwise have worn such a thing, not having the confidence. Dimly, Robert asked himself why; for she had been very lovely. Yes, he thought – a lovely woman – as lovely as she was kind, and strong in her faith . . . his mother. He smiled.

'Who did this to you?'

The voice again. Surely it was his father, come to rescue him? Of course. Who else, at such a time, would be there to comfort him and tend to his wounds? 'Very deep, Father,' Robert muttered. 'Very deep inside.'

'Who, though? Unless you tell me, how can I know?'

'It was the Devil, Father.'

An intake of breath. A silence so long that Robert feared his father was gone. Then a hand upon his shoulder. 'And how was the Devil raised?'

'Faustus did it.'

'*Faustus?*'

'It was Faustus who summoned the Evil One.'

A pause; then sudden laughter, bitter and short. 'And where is this – Faustus – now?'

'Faustus is dead.'

'No. He cannot be.'

'I saw it, Father.'

'But he is a drinker of blood, and a great one at that. You do not understand. A creature such as Faustus can never be slain. *Never!*'

'Yet is he dust. I saw it, Father.' Robert raised his head. He imagined that he too was nothing but ashes in the wind, spinning, spinning, round and round, borne upon the maelstrom that had swept above the stones and now seemed in his head. 'I saw it, I saw it, I saw it . . .' All was growing dark. He laid his cheek again upon the softness of the lace. How gently it lulled him. He turned, to wipe away his tears; then buried his face upon his mother's breast.

For a moment, he remembered it could not be her at all. But then he felt himself being lifted, and the darkness deepened into black. When he woke again, his memories seemed like distant floes of ice, looming through the mists above an Arctic sea; and as though he were some cautious mariner, Robert dreaded them, for he knew that they were cruel. He shivered violently. He tossed and turned, trying not to think, to escape back into sleep; but then there was a jolt, and he opened his eyes. He looked about him and found he was lying in a carriage. Opposite him, cast in shadow, sat a man. His features could not be made out, but his eyes burned like twin sparks of flame. Robert frowned. He had been hoping for his father. 'Who are you?' he asked.

The man leaned forward. Above one of the eyes was a jagged scar which Robert vaguely remembered having seen before. 'You may call me . . .' – the man paused – 'Lightborn.'

Robert sighed. He closed his eyes, and when he opened them again his father was returned. 'I had feared you were lost,' Robert murmured.

His father smiled. His teeth were set in the grin of a skull; his face was deathly white. 'And so I am lost,' he whispered. 'Forever lost, my son.'

Robert screamed. He would have struggled free, but he was nestled, he realised – as he had been before – upon a gentle curve and swell of lace. He could feel the embrace of bare arms about him, hear a lullaby softly whispered in his ear. 'Mother?' he asked. He almost looked up; but suddenly, from nowhere, there rose a crackling and he felt hot, so hot, as though he were wearing a poisoned shirt of fire . . . and he remembered: his mother was burned. Silently he wept. His tears seemed to hiss and burn upon his cheeks. A hand brushed them away. Robert longed to kiss it, to hold it in his own; but he did not turn. For if it were his mother's, then its flesh would be charred upon the bone, that hand which had always been so beautiful and pale. He moaned; then, louder than before, he called his mother's name.

Dimly, through his fever, he heard Lightborn start to laugh. 'You hear what he calls you? Are you not tempted? It is time perhaps you had a son, Milady.'

'Milady.' Like a drop of water into a waste of flames, the word fell from Lightborn's lips. But who was Milady? Robert struggled to think. The sound of the name was spreading in ripples through his mind. He tried to swim with them, out, out, until they had filled all his thoughts, but then he gave up following, for the ripples were stilled and the sound was lost. On the carriage rumbled, but Robert slept; and for a while, in his oblivion, he lay in peace.

∽◐∾

'ALL THOSE THAT COME TO LONDON ARE EITHER CARRION OR CROWS.'

John Aubrey, *Brief Lives*

His rest did not continue calm for long. The delirium soon returned and, from the margins between sleep and wakefulness, nightmares were bred. Robert imagined he was gazing from the coach. Outside stretched a city of impossible size, a mighty wasteland of dust and noise from which all that was green seemed utterly banished, so that not a tree could be glimpsed, not the barest patch of grass. The narrow streets were shadowed by night; but still, even in the darkest recesses, Robert could see the wild forms of men, some holding torches, all cavorting like the flames of the flambeaux. 'Where are we?' he whispered. 'Are we in Hell?'

Lightborn laughed. 'Very like,' he answered.

But Milady shook her head. 'We are in London,' she said.

'Why do they wave torches?'

'To celebrate the news that the King will return.'

Robert nodded; but as he watched, he knew that she was wrong. For he could make out the revellers now, and recognise them. He was staring at the villagers from Woodton, the same who had watched his mother burn; they were all about him on the streets outside, unmistakable, for cruelty and greed were stamped upon their faces, and murderous intent. They were laughing at him; and Robert knew they were celebrating his parents' deaths. He closed his eyes, but it made no difference. The villagers' faces were still before him, their expressions leering and twisted with hate. 'And yet despite you all,' Robert whispered, 'I shall win back what was lost. I shall be restored to Emily, and see my parents once again.'

Such a vow remained with him, even in the very depths of his fever. He clung to it, although there were times when he believed himself dead and damned in Hell, for he seemed lost amidst horrors too great for a mortal to bear. Yet the worst of it was that he knew he had already borne them; for he was visited by nothing but what he had endured before. Often he would see the villagers again, in a barbarous rout; often he would be with Faustus, riding towards the stones; often he would hear Emily screaming out for help. Sometimes, more rarely, he would see his parents watching him, staring down – his mother a veil of ashes, his father drained white. He would watch their mouths frame wordless commands; but he did not need to hear their words. 'Do not forget, do not forget': the syllables already sounded in his head. Still they echoed; and gradually, from the nightmares, he began to emerge.

One day, he opened his eyes. He could feel a strip of fabric on his brow. It was sodden; but when he moved it the skin beneath was free of sweat, and he knew that his fever had left him at last.

He looked down at the fabric: a square of lace.

'You would not be without it. When I tried to replace it, your fever would grow worse.'

Robert stared round. From the depths of his memory, a word rose. 'Milady.' He whispered it.

She smiled at him. The girl's eyes were as cold and gleaming as before, yet she was also as beautiful; and although he knew he should be afraid of her, Robert found her presence a strange comfort. He became aware that he was lying on a bed, in a small, oak-lined room. He turned back to his companion. 'Where am I?' he asked.

'Safe,' she replied.

Again, he stared into her eyes. This time, he did shiver. Their brightness was like sunlight on a lake of ice. He felt his comfort fade, dissolved into fear. 'Safe from you?' he asked.

Milady's smile remained frozen on her lips. 'Why?' she murmured. 'What do you think I may do?'

'Why' – Robert swallowed – 'drink my blood.'

She stared at him, a frown of fascination creasing her perfect brow. 'Yes,' she said, nodding to herself, 'you are terrified, you truly are.' She paused, as though savouring the realisation. Then she laughed. 'But you have been lying here for many days. Do you not think, if I had wanted to kill you, I would have done so by now?'

Robert frowned, then he inclined his head in acknowledgement. 'But why do you keep me here?' he asked.

Milady shrugged. 'Because otherwise you would have surely died.'

Robert flushed with a deep sense of shame. 'Then I am sorry,' he said, 'to have misjudged you so grievously.' He closed his eyes. Already, he thought, he had betrayed his mother and her gentle faith in the goodness of man. 'For you have been like that Samaritan,' he told the girl, 'who was neighbour unto him that fell among the thieves.' But then an image unbidden came into his mind, of his mother being borne aloft to the stake. 'Where then was the Samaritan?' he murmured, before his voice caught and he choked on his sobs.

Milady stared at him, her surprise apparently intermingled again with fascination. Gently she brushed his tears from his cheeks; then held her fingertip up to the light. 'You are unhappy,' she said, as she inspected it. Suddenly, a look of understanding crossed her face. 'Yes,' she nodded, 'you are unhappy – of course. You have lost people you . . . loved.' She bent forward and kissed Robert softly. Her lips were very cold; despite himself, Robert flinched at their touch.

She looked hurt, but he had not meant to insult her. She raised a hand, to stroke back an errant curl. 'Do you not find me beautiful?' she asked.

Robert swallowed, then spoke the simple truth. 'You are the most beautiful woman I have ever seen.'

She arched an eyebrow. 'Then perhaps we shall make a Cavalier of you indeed, Master Lovelace.'

'Lovelace?' Robert asked.

She smiled faintly. '*Our very sorrows weep, That joys so ripe, so little keep*.' Her last syllable seemed to linger, as she inspected Robert with her unblinking golden stare. 'You have the face of a Cavalier I briefly knew, who bore the same name. And besides . . .' – she shrugged, and gestured to the fabric in his hand – 'I did not know by what else you might rightfully be called.'

'My name is Foxe.'

The lady pulled a face. 'Far too plain for so lovely a boy.'

'Yet it was my father's name.'

'Your father is dead.' She paused, and then her voice softened. 'Is that not so?'

Robert looked away, and did not reply.

Milady watched him. 'If you would fight what has been done to you,' she said suddenly, 'then you cannot remain the child you have been. As Foxe, what are you? Nothing! But as Lovelace . . .' She shook her head; she bent over him again, and stroked his hair so that he stared up from his pillow. 'As Lovelace,' she whispered, 'what worlds of power and pleasure might not be yours!'

'Power?'

Milady nodded. 'Oh, yes. More than you would ever

have imagined possible.' She kissed him on the brow. 'I can swear to that.'

For a moment she stayed close to him, so that her hair brushed his cheek; then she rose and crossed to the door. 'I will have the servant send you food,' she said, 'and after that you must sleep.' But she stared at him in silence for a long while – almost, Robert thought, as his mother might have done, if she were still alive and tending him. Was it really true, he wondered, after Milady had gone, that she might give him the power to return to his home? Was it even possible she possessed such a power? The servant arrived: his flesh was pale, his eyes were dead, just like the soldiers that Faustus had led into Woodton. And Faustus had indeed possessed great powers – terrible powers. Robert took his food. The servant, he realised, did not frighten him at all; rather, he seemed a mark of Milady's good word. Robert finished his meal, then lay and imagined his return to Woodton. Emily would be waiting for him there. Emily was still alive. Such thoughts accompanied him even as he began to sleep. He was soon asleep. For the first time since his fever had begun, his dreams were undisturbed.

But in the morning, he woke to fresh imaginings and doubts. Milady's powers, he wondered – where did they come from? Not from God, he was sure, nor from any source that his parents would have blessed. Faustus, after all, on the ride to the stones, had sought to tempt him with a similar promise; and he had been a demon from the very depths of Hell. ' "Get thee hence, Satan," ' he whispered to himself, as he knelt at his prayers, and heard delicate footsteps climb the stairs to his room. But then, once again, he seemed to see his father drained of his blood before him, and his mother blackened and chained to the stake; and he shook his head in agony. 'Guide me, O Lord,' he prayed, 'for like your prophets of old, I seem lost in the wilderness, and I know not what to do.' But nothing answered him, save the gossamer sound of Milady's footsteps. For a second more, he continued to pray; then he rose and turned to greet her as she stood in the door.

She seemed intrigued to have seen him on his knees, and faintly shocked; but she said nothing. Instead, she laid a great pile of clothes upon his bed and gestured to them: 'I have brought you these.' Robert stared at them, then brushed them with his fingertips and felt a shiver of pleasure. There were silks, and feathers, and yards of lace; he had never dreamed that clothes might be so beautiful and rich. Milady watched his delight eagerly; as before, she seemed to feed off his responses, as though hungry to experience his emotions for herself. She picked up a cloak of deep black velvet and draped it about his shoulders. 'There,' she exclaimed, and clapped her hands. 'Now you are quite the dashing lord.'

Robert threw it off at once, of course. He could see his own clothes, washed and neatly piled on a chair; covering himself behind a sheet, he pulled them on quickly. He had not been his father's son, he thought, to start dressing now like a Cavalier. He explained this to Milady, who seemed barely to believe he might be serious. She picked up a silk coat, and smoothed it against him, studying his expression. 'But you do want it?' she pressed him. She could sense his hesitation, and the gold of her eyes seemed to burn with delight. 'Feel it,' she urged; then suddenly she tossed it aside again and folded him in her arms. 'You must have loved your parents very much,' she breathed, with the same passion with which she had offered him the clothes. She paused, to inspect his expression once again. 'So strong, so simple, so very strange,' she whispered. She kissed him on the lips. 'A mortal's love.'

Then she took his arm. 'At least,' she inquired, as she swept him from the room, 'you have not forbidden yourself to eat?' Robert shook his head. Milady's lips parted in a smile and she touched her teeth, very daintily, with the tip of her tongue.

She led Robert downstairs into a hall, long and low, with red panelled walls. Although it was morning outside, it might just as well have been night, for the windows had been veiled behind thick velvet curtains so that the air in the room seemed very purple and rich. Candles burned softly, spangling the dark. Some were held by statues of boys, laid upon a table in the centre of the room. Robert gazed with wonder at their beauty. The curls of their hair seemed to glide as though in water; about their naked arms, they wore coronets of pearl; only a tiny sprig of an olive-tree, sportfully held, preserved those parts which women love to see. Indeed, their loveliness seemed almost beyond a sculptor's skill; and then a drop of wax fell upon a statue's hand, and Robert saw it flinch, and he realised it was made of flesh and blood like himself. He caught the boy's stare; it seemed drugged, as though veiled across a lotus dream. At once, Robert's wonder was transformed into disgust and he shrank back, hugging himself, lest his own clothes be torn from him and he be placed as a living trophy with the others – or put to uses more terrible yet.

Someone had been watching him, for he suddenly

heard a voice from the far end of the room. 'See how he clutches at his puritan breeches! He is ignorant, and so does not understand that Love is nothing but a naked boy.'

Robert turned to see Lightborn, his shirt opened, lolling at the table with a second man. He swallowed. 'I know,' he said, 'that Ovid claimed Love to be so.'

Lightborn narrowed his eyes. 'Wondrous!' he exclaimed. 'So young to be a scholar, and a rustic too!' He looked across sharply at Milady. 'Yet if he knows this, why does he insist on clinging to his rags?'

'They remind him of his parents,' replied Milady, as though announcing something extraordinary.

'Touching.' Lightborn frowned at her. 'Yet it is scarcely reason enough. Look at him. He is like some religious caterpillar – a blot upon the dark and wondrous beauties of this place. If you truly mean to keep him here, then you must look to him better, Milady.'

'Who is he?' asked Lightborn's companion. 'For all his homespun, he's a pretty-looking whore.'

'He would be,' agreed Lightborn, 'if I were allowed to work on him.'

'No,' said Milady. 'You have sworn it – he is mine.'

Lightborn shrugged. 'As you wish.' He turned to his companion again. 'Charming, Godolphin, is it not? My Lady Helen has adopted a pet. How very like her, to take in a Roundhead, when all the rest of the world is throwing them out.'

Godolphin began to laugh. He collapsed forward suddenly, his whole body shaking, giggling and spitting like a lunatic. Lightborn took him in his arms, and gently pulled him back; Godolphin continued to splutter until silenced by a hand upon his mouth, and then a kiss.

Robert stared, appalled. He had read of such things in the histories of the Romans, of course; but his tutor had told him such abominations never happened now. In life as in Latin, Robert thought, it seemed he was learning more than Mr Yorke.

Still watching, he allowed himself to be guided forward to the table by Milady. There, for a while he was distracted; for he seemed confronted by a very vision of heaven. Roses were strewn across the table, and mounds of food beyond his wildest imaginings. Remembering the meal which his mother had promised him, the goose which Hannah had never cooked, he felt as though he were being taunted by Fate, for there was not only goose before him now but also partridge and quail, fish and pastries, roast meats and fruits. To sit down to it, he vaguely felt, would be a betrayal of the past; yet his hunger was terrible, and he could not restrain himself. Milady watched and encouraged him, her eyes still greedy for the signs of his pleasure, which seemed to fill her with a passionate rapture of her own. But he noted how she barely ate herself; and as he began to satisfy his hunger, he felt once again how alone he was. He wished Emily were with him. Emily had always loved the good things in life – how she would have enjoyed such a feast! But then Robert heard a gasp from the end of the table, and a soft moan. He stared round. Godolphin was lying sprawled back in his chair; Lightborn's face was pressed against his chest, and he appeared to be lapping like a cat drinking milk. Then he paused and glanced up; Robert could see how his lips were smeared with blood, and that Godolphin's body had been patterned with cuts. As Lightborn grinned, and slithered his tongue in and out, Robert looked away.

Perhaps it was best, he thought, that Emily was not there after all.

Yet soon he was longing for her company again. For when the meal was finished Milady led him from the table, out into the streets, and Robert found himself more enraptured than ever – enraptured, and overwhelmed. So this was London! He had come, he was aware, into a place of wonders such as he and Emily had never even dreamed might exist, when they had talked in Woodton of exploring the world. How Emily would have loved to be with him now! For what need was there to explore the world, he thought, when all the world already seemed in London's streets? Sights and sounds, and smells of all kinds; grandeur and squalor; darkness and light. On through the great labyrinth they passed; and with Milady beside him, Robert felt the whole city to be his.

It is Leviathan, he thought, as they paused on London Bridge, a monster of terrible and wondrous size, upon whose back men merely swarm and breed like flies. Yet Milady had tamed the monster, he realised: for beneath her stare it seemed transformed into her plaything, her private toy, and he felt a sudden longing to be like her and share in such a power. He looked up at her. 'Have you always lived here,' he asked, 'to know the streets so well?'

Milady shook her head. She continued to stare into the foam of the river, as it boiled and churned between the arches of the bridge. 'I have not been in London a long while now,' she murmured.

'Then how . . .'

'Once,' she said slowly, 'I knew the city well. Yes, and Lightborn too. But things were very different then.' She glanced towards Southwark, where the bridge met the southern bank of the Thames. 'We have not been back here since.'

'Since what?'

She smiled, and shook her head.

'Will you not tell me?' he pressed.

'One day, perhaps.' She laughed suddenly. 'But I do not believe you are ready for it yet.'

Robert's curiosity was only piqued by this; but Milady's face seemed suddenly frozen and veiled, and he was afraid to ask her more. 'Come,' she said abruptly, 'it is growing dark.' She paused for a moment, and seemed to smell the breeze. 'I have business to attend to, and you – you must sleep. We should return to Pudding Lane.' She began to lead the way back across London Bridge, and Robert followed her, watching as she breathed in deeply again. When he looked up, he saw for the first time that there were two heads, freshly severed, set upon pikes. As they climbed towards their house, Milady paused yet again and, as she sniffed the air, her cheeks grew flushed. There was a cart rumbling past. Robert stared at its load: sacks of entrails from the butchers' shops. But still Milady said nothing; and when they reached the house she left him there alone, to his wonder and his dread. All that solitary night, it seemed, he prayed to God for guidance; the birds began to sing on the eaves outside his room, and the first beams of dawn to steal in through the window; but though he tossed and turned, Robert could hear no answer. He fell asleep at last, exhausted by his doubts; but he had not resolved them. Through his very dreams, the uncertainties echoed: whether his fascination was greater than his fear; whether the promise of great powers was an answer to his prayers, or rather a perilous and most damnable lure.

$$\sim\!\!\circ\!\!\sim$$

'YOU MUST CAST THE SCHOLAR OFF,
AND LEARN TO COURT IT LIKE A GENTLEMAN . . .
YOU MUST BE PROUD, BOLD, PLEASANT, RESOLUTE,
AND NOW AND THEN STAB AS OCCASION SERVES.'
Christopher Marlowe, *Edward II*

He was woken the next morning by a sudden cry. It seemed a woman's, and to come from the hallway downstairs. Robert dressed quickly and crept from his room. The woman was shouting something; she screamed loudly again, and he realised it was a cry not of agony, but of rage. He hurried on down the stairs. As he walked into the hall, he heard laughter – Lightborn's. At the sound of it, the woman screamed at him again.

She was young, and would have been pretty, but her hair was gathered beneath a plain, shapeless cap and her dress was starkly, almost ostentatiously plain. Nevertheless, its cut and fabric were as fine as Milady's, and though she dressed like a Puritan, Robert guessed that the woman must be rich. Lightborn, as before, was lolling in his chair. The woman's face was flushed with anger, Lightborn's perfectly cold. Robert stared at the two of them, then stepped forward. The woman spun round, her face growing even darker at the sight of him. She turned back to Lightborn. 'And do you have so little shame,' she asked, 'that even children are lodged in this dunghill of lusts?'

Lightborn smiled. 'You would do better to ask your husband that, Lady Godolphin, for it is he who has grown so . . . fond . . . of boys.'

She shuddered. 'Where is he, then?' she hissed.

Lightborn shrugged.

Lady Godolphin clenched her fists. 'Please,' she whispered. 'As you are a Christian – return him to me.'

'As I am a Christian?' Lightborn snorted. 'Fawn on me with your morality no longer, Madam. Begone. You are ceasing to amuse.'

'So you will not do as I request?'

Lightborn yawned. 'I will not.'

'I shall send in my men, to ransack this house.'

'Do what you will. But I warn you, Lady Godolphin – the time will come when you repent of these lavish threatenings of yours. Go now, and I may spare you. Bother me further, and – well . . . we shall see.'

Lady Godolphin stood frozen for a second; then her face twisted, and she turned and left the room. Lightborn watched her go. 'These tedious drabs,' he murmured. He looked towards Robert. 'Let her be a warning to you,' he said, 'that you do not continue too long encumbered by religion.'

'But . . .' Robert shook his head in amazement. 'How could you not answer her request? You have stolen her husband.'

'What of it?' Lightborn gestured with a wave of his hand at the hall. 'Would you have us stay in this hovel forever?'

'Hovel? This is no hovel.'

'I tell you, it is. Certainly, compared with where we shall shortly reside.'

'I do not understand you.'

Lightborn grinned. 'Godolphin, my paramour, that bitch's loving husband, is a most wealthy man. I would not otherwise have chosen him. His house is marvellously fine, with carriages and stables and a view across the Park.'

Robert stared at him wide-eyed. 'I still do not understand you,' he whispered.

'Then you are exceedingly slow.'

'You will – what . . .' – Robert swallowed – 'steal it from him?'

'Steal it? Why, no! He will give it to me.' Then Lightborn frowned suddenly. 'But has Milady not told you of the powers we possess?'

Robert stared at him dumbly for a moment. 'She has not said what such powers are,' he said at last. As he spoke, there was a sudden hammering on the door and cries from outside. Lightborn glanced round; his frown began to fade into a smile.

He turned back to Robert. 'Would you care to see what they can perform, then,' he asked, 'our powers?'

Again, there was a violent hammering on the door; and then the sudden splintering of wood.

'Watch,' said Lightborn. He turned, as four men strode into the hall. Heavily built, and armed with clubs, they saw Lightborn and at once began to make towards him. He did not flinch though, but stayed perfectly still, his expression a mixture of relish and contempt, his face as pale and hard as knuckles on a fist. His eyes glittered; and as the men drew near him, so he licked his lips. Suddenly, the men stopped in their tracks; their arms hung useless, and their clubs fell with a clatter from their hands on to the floor. Like birds before a serpent, they stood trapped within Lightborn's gaze.

He turned to Robert. 'Would not a trick like this have served your father well,' he asked, 'when faced by his killers? And might it not serve you, when you seek out your revenge? Observe now, what power I have to rule these fellows' minds.' He turned back to the men. At once, Robert saw how the blood drained from their faces, and their eyeballs rolled as though spun by their fear. They clutched at their heads and fell whimpering to the floor, then whined and retreated like dogs before a whip. Lightborn laughed; the men began to scream. Then Lightborn gestured with his hand, and at once three of them turned and scrabbled from the room. A fourth remained, still cowering on the floor. Lightborn studied him; then he crossed to the table and picked up a knife. He tested its blade on his fingertip; as he did so, the man shuddered and moaned. His face had been sweating like mouldy cheese, and as he stared up at Lightborn he suddenly clutched at his groin. Robert watched the puddle as it formed on the floor, and the smell took him back to the night within the stones.

Lightborn had been watching him quizzically. 'Tell me,' he asked, 'at Stonehenge, did you not similarly be-piss yourself with fear?'

Robert made no reply.

'Yes,' nodded Lightborn, 'I remember the stench from your breeches.' He paused. 'You must have been grievously afraid.' He beckoned Robert forward; despite himself, Robert obeyed. Lightborn studied him. 'What did you see there?' he whispered in his ear. 'Someone who could kill even a creature like myself? That is what you said, is it not? That is what you claimed? Tell me!' He shook Robert suddenly. 'Is that what you saw?'

Robert nodded dumbly.

'I believe you,' said Lightborn, icy cold once again. 'For I smelt it, even above the reek of your piss: dead immortal – a pretty paradox to be hanging in the air. But who could have done it – what order of thing?'

'It was the Devil,' said Robert.

'The Devil!' Lightborn spat.

'I saw its face, it was the Lord of Flies.'

'You saw something else.'

'Then what?'

'Something too great for your own feeble powers, certainly.'

'And too great for yours?'

'That remains to be seen.' Lightborn shrugged. 'But who would have the greater chance against such a creature, do you think, myself – or you?'

Robert bowed his head. He thought of Emily – a prisoner still, or worse, back in Woodton. 'What then must I do, to share in your powers?'

'It is easy.' Lightborn grinned, and stroked the blade of his knife. 'You must surrender a phantom which does not exist.'

'And what is that?'

'Why' – Lightborn's grin grew even broader – 'merely your soul.'

'No!' cried Robert. He shrank back and crossed his hands over his heart.

'You will not be parted from it, then?'

'Not while I hope to see my parents in Heaven.'

Lightborn snorted. 'Heaven, Hell – what are these childish toys?'

Robert stared at him in horror. 'You talk as if there were no God at all.'

Lightborn stared at him wide-eyed; then threw back his

head and laughed more wildly than before.

Robert flushed with sudden anger. What was this strange world he had entered, where such evil could be spoken with such casual ease? More abandoned than ever he felt, more abandoned and alone; and as he shook, so he thought of Emily again, and how she too was alone.

He breathed in hard.

'If my soul is but a phantom,' he asked slowly, 'how then am I to give it to you?'

'Like this,' said Lightborn. He struck, suddenly, at the man by his side. The blade cut deep across the face. 'You see?' he asked, as the man screamed and writhed upon the floor. 'It is really very easy.'

'I cannot do it,' whispered Robert.

'Your parents' ghosts are crying out for vengeance.'

'No. Not at such a price.'

'Are you certain?' Lightborn narrowed his eyes. 'They visit you at night, do they not? I have heard you mutter and cry in your sleep.'

Robert looked away. His mother again, and his father drained white, standing before him, reaching out; Emily, silent, in a soldier's arms.

'The knife.' Lightborn was handing it to him, pressing it into his hand. 'Just one stroke will kill this sorry bag of guts. It is an easy matter. Just a single stroke.'

Robert looked down at the man, who was moaning soundlessly, clutching at his face. His nose had been sliced open, and his left eye seemed put out.

'Do it.' Lightborn's voice was hard and very cold. 'For you shall soon discover how there is no certain pleasure in this tedious world but to witness another person's suffering and pain.'

Robert's knuckles whitened around the handle. He

stared at the man's belly and thought how easy it would be, the work of a second, to slash across it and pull the entrails out. But then, although it was warm in the room, he shivered with the cold; for he was suddenly standing by Wolverton Hall, and Hannah's corpse was lying in the snow, and Mr Webbe was bending over it, and his father too, and he was saying a prayer for the peace of Hannah's soul. 'No,' whispered Robert. 'It is more than I can bear.' He dropped the knife; he covered his eyes; then he stumbled from the room and out into the street.

'A LITTLE ONWARD LEND THY GUIDING HAND
TO THESE DARK STEPS, A LITTLE FURTHER ON . . .'
                              John Milton, *Samson Agonistes*

The city, which only the day before had seemed a paradise of wonders, now seemed a hell, for the streets bore him like the currents of a maelstrom, this way and that, until Robert feared he would be drowned beneath their swirl. Mr Webbe, he remembered, had been once to London and had often told him of what he had seen there: 'Cheats, thefts, murders, lusts, knaves and rogues.' Robert seemed to hear the preacher's voice in his ears; he wept, from homesickness and because Mr Webbe had been right. For everywhere, people stared at him with hatred; a woman, her face encrusted with paint, had even spat at him and pelted him with stones. Robert had fled from her down a broad and dusty street; it had led him at last to a crowded park, in which high ribboned poles had been erected and great bonfires lit. He stared at the sea of faces around him; there were men and women there, young and old, rich and poor, but all seemed greasy and repellent with excitement, and they leered as the villagers of Woodton had leered. 'Please,' Robert asked one man, summoning up his courage, 'what is it that people are celebrating here?'

The man glanced round, and his nose wrinkled as he saw Robert's clothes. 'What has been forbidden these past fifteen years,' he said, 'thanks to your people's prohibition on merriment.'

'My people's?'

'Whose son are you, if not a canting Commonwealth-man's?'

Robert clenched his fists. 'Do not speak of my father,' he answered furiously.

'Why should I not? For he was clearly a fool to let you come to this place, dressed as you are.' The man winked at him. 'I would run, boy,' he sneered. 'For otherwise, such is the mood of the people here, you may be seized upon and tossed into the flames. You would make a merry bonfire to light the King's return.'

Robert choked, and imagined for a moment that he was back on Woodton green. Then he did as the man had advised, and ran. How far, he didn't know; but always in his mind he heard the crackling of flames, and his mother's voice as she was eaten by the fire, her dying promise that they would meet once more in Heaven. And then Robert would look about him in the streets; and think how there was no one in all of London who cared for him; how there was no one but Emily now in all the world.

So should he not return to her at once, he wondered, weak and powerless even as he was? For a moment, he wished he had not turned his back on Lightborn – that he had some powers at least with which to confront the Evil Spirit and, if not to destroy it, then to rescue Emily. He stopped suddenly, and realised he was still as lost as before; he looked about him and saw that he was standing on a street lined with boarded shops. He walked into one of the few which still seemed open; it was a butcher's. Robert remembered the cartloads of offal he had seen in Pudding Lane, and he almost asked for directions there, for he was certain that the butcher would know the way. But he checked himself; and when he asked instead for the Salisbury road, the butcher smiled and nodded, and took him by the arm.

He was led along the street. The butcher was large and bald, and drenched in sweat, but though his grip was very tight, his smile was broad. 'First time in London?' he asked. Robert nodded, and agreed that it was. The butcher's smile widened even more. 'This way,' he said, as he dragged Robert after him down a dark, narrow side-street. A couple of heavy blows, and Robert was lying in the filth. He was vaguely aware that he was being searched; then he felt his hidden purse being found and removed. He tried to protest – that he needed the money, that his parents were dead; but he was silenced by a kick to his stomach, and then to his head. He did not even hear the butcher leave him, but lay where he was, conscious of nothing but the feel of the dirt; slowly he grew aware of his pain, and at last of his despair, and only then did he rise to his feet. He wandered aimlessly, he knew not where. It did not matter; he would never escape. For there was a city his mother had always warned him against, which once entered could never be left. Its name had been Hopelessness; and it was that city's byways he feared he was walking through now.

Robert drifted until it grew dark. He thought vaguely about finding a bed, for his bruises were aching terribly. Then it struck him anew that he had nowhere to go. Passing a church, he pushed at the door; it was locked. He slumped down in the street against its wall and tried to pray, but the words in his ears seemed meaningless noise. Still he tried: 'Guide me, O Lord. Lead me from this place of darkness. Show me a sign.' He waited. Nothing came.

It was growing cold now. He shivered, and wished he had a blanket or a coat. He remembered how he had lain beneath the stars only two weeks before, but that had been with Emily after a stolen swim at midnight, and they had lain on grass together then, not amidst the filth and dust of a street. Robert sighed, and rubbed his eyes. Although it was late, he was not alone. There were other people lying near him, in rags even dirtier and more tattered than his, not only children but adults as well. How long, Robert wondered, had they been without a home? Might he grow a man, and still not have a bed? He sat up suddenly. It could not be possible – *it could not be possible*; but he felt the weight of misery pressing on his chest, and he knew that it was. A week ago, he had had his parents and a home; and now – gone, all gone, and there seemed nothing he could do.

He stared about him hopelessly, and caught the eye of a passing man. 'Please,' he asked. The man nodded and smiled; he crossed to him, bent down and slipped a coin into Robert's hand. 'Thank you,' Robert whispered, 'in the name of Jesus, thank you.' But then he felt the man's fingers exploring his thighs, and he remembered other hands more terrible by far, and he suddenly realised what the coin had been for. 'No!' he screamed. The man backed away, startled; then, as Robert continued to scream, he began to run. Other people were stirring now, blinking sleepily and shouting at Robert to shut his mouth. He fell silent; he hugged himself tightly and fell back to his prayers. But still there was no answer, and the darkness of the street was now silent and profound.

Then suddenly, Robert heard footsteps. He looked round, and could just make out two shadowy forms approaching him along the side of the church. One seemed a boy of about his own height; the other was a man, cloaked and with a hat, gripping his companion's elbow. The boy stopped; at once, the man did too. 'Wait here a moment,' the boy said.

'Do not leave me here,' the man replied, 'for you know that I am helpless.' His voice, though he had whispered, was firm and clear; but the boy ignored him and ran on down the street. He passed Robert; then, on the corner of the church, he stopped and was met from the shadows by two cloaked and hooded men.

'He is back there,' Robert heard the boy whisper. 'You may take him easily, for he is blind and without friends. It seems he has been a very great Commonwealth-man – lead him to the authorities once you have robbed him, and we will doubtless be rewarded for having captured such a traitor.'

'God save the King, then,' answered one of the men. His companion laughed, and then the two of them began to walk down the street to where the blind man stood waiting. Robert ran ahead of them. 'Do you have a weapon?' he whispered in the blind man's ear.

'Who are you?' the man answered.

'There is no time,' Robert hissed. 'Do you have a weapon?'

Expressionlessly, the blind man reached inside his coat and drew out a knife. Robert took it – just in time, for the footpads were almost on to him by now. They caught sight of him, and paused. 'Out of the way,' said one of them. 'This one is ours.'

Robert answered him by pointing the knife at his chest. 'Walk back,' he whispered in the blind man's ear. 'We must reach the high street.' They began slowly to retreat, Robert still pointing the knife at the footpads, who both stood motionless watching him. Suddenly, one of them snarled, then came running forward.

Robert struck him in the thigh, very hard, and the man seemed so surprised that he failed to cry out at first; then, as he collapsed into the dirt, he began to shriek. His companion, blinded by fury, charged down the street; but Robert fought him as though he were every Cavalier in the world, and as he stabbed the man again and again, he imagined it was Faustus, and the thought strengthened his arm. The footpad collapsed and was still; Robert laughed violently, and realised he had been muttering half-formed prayers to himself. He looked about for the treacherous servant boy, but he was nowhere to be seen, so Robert took the blind man's arm and hurried him away. They stumbled through narrow, twisting streets, and all the time Robert was whispering to himself that he had killed a man, that he had shed living blood. He felt no guilt though, only a shuddering exultation, and at last he had to stop, for his legs felt like air and he could not still his hands. He leaned against a wall and breathed in deeply; then he prayed that his parents, watching him from Heaven, would forgive him his sin and wash his stained hands clean.

He had spoken this beneath his breath, but the blind

man, as though reading his thoughts, felt for him and touched him on the arm. 'Do not condemn yourself,' he said. 'The heroic Samson, though he was a prophet of the Lord, thought it no sin to be revenged on his attackers.'

'To be revenged ...' Robert's voice trailed away. He froze for a moment then stared round. The blind man was standing in the street, upright and perfectly still. His skin was very fair and, were it not for his eyes – which rolled as though seeking a light forever lost – Robert might have taken him for a statue set amongst the worthies of some ancient temple, for there was a strength in his expression, and a resolution, which seemed both heroic and strangely remote. He had been a Commonwealth-man, Robert remembered suddenly, and a notorious one; as notorious as his own father, he wondered, who had likewise been hunted and, in the end, put to death? When he took the blind man's arm he felt the familiar roughness of homespun. It almost made him choke. His father's arm, when he had held it, had always felt the same.

'What shall happen to you,' he asked, 'if you are captured?'

The blind man's voice, like his face, betrayed no hint of emotion. 'If I am captured, and then sentenced,' he said, 'I shall be hung and then, while I still breathe, disembowelled. After that, I shall be sawn in four, to serve as a lesson and a wonder to the people.'

'Where do you go now?'

'Into hiding. But my boy has left me. I have been betrayed.'

'I shall guide you.'

'You will risk your life.'

'It is no matter. I could welcome death.'

The blind man frowned, then smiled grimly. ' 'Tis the times' plague,' he muttered, 'when madmen lead the blind.' He felt for Robert's head to stroke his cheek, then tousle his hair. 'If you will take me,' he said, 'I must reach Bartholomew Close.'

'I do not know the way.'

'So your accent betrays. But I am native-born to this city; and though I am blind, I have a sense of the streets. Lead me where I point and, God willing, we shall both be safe.' He began to walk forward where Robert led, then paused a moment. 'I thank you,' he said softly. But he said nothing more; and together, blind man and beggar boy, they walked through the night.

They were not taken by surprise again. Robert led the blind man away from the darkest streets and, though they were passed once by the torches of the watch, they hid in the shadows and were unobserved. By the time they neared St Bartholomew's, the sky was lightening through the clouds to the east, and from the nearby markets rose the hubbub of trade. Robert stared about him, seeing live-stock everywhere – cattle, pigs, sheep; he paused to listen to their noise and breathe in their scents, which seemed to him as sweet as perfumes, for they bore to his nostrils unsummoned memories of home. The blind man turned and brushed his palm against Robert's cheeks. 'You are crying,' he said. He frowned. 'Tell me,' he asked, 'if you are not from London, what cause was it that led you here, so far from your home?'

Robert did not answer. 'We must hurry,' he murmured vaguely, 'it is growing very light.' He began to lead the blind man forward again, stumbling through the straw and slime until they had almost crossed the market place, and were standing by the arch above Bartholomew Close.

Robert looked back at the pens of cattle one last time; and
then suddenly he froze, and shrank against the wall.

'What is it?' the blind man asked. 'Are we discovered?'

Robert swallowed. His throat felt too dry to answer. He
watched as Lightborn and Milady walked together, gliding
past rows of butcher's carcasses as though stepping on
air, their eyes burning, their nostrils wide, scanning the
market place from left to right, and he shuddered as he
realised that they were surely hunting him. He had
learned their secrets, he thought, he had seen too much;
and now Lightborn was regretting he had ever let him go.
Robert glanced down Bartholomew Close. He wondered,
if he ran, whether he would make it unseen; but then he
looked into his charge's sightless eyes, and he realised he
could not abandon him, not so near – and perhaps so far
– from his goal. Robert stared back at the blood-drinkers.
They were standing on the edge of the market place now,
looking all around, and for a moment he thought he was
seen, for Lightborn's eyes seemed to pierce the shadows
of the close; and then he turned, and spoke into Milady's
ear. Robert held his breath; but they did not step towards
him. Instead, they turned and were soon lost amidst the
milling crowds. Disbelievingly, Robert watched them go;
and then he remembered what Lightborn had told him,
that although they could smell the blood of every living
thing, his alone bore not a trace of scent. Robert laughed;
and his companion gripped hold of him, as though
sensing his relief. Still, though, the blind man did not say
a word, not even to ask who the hunters had been, and
his demeanour remained as impassive as before.
Together, they walked down Bartholomew Close.

Halfway down the street, the blind man whispered
directions to his guide. Robert led him to the address,

and knocked quietly on the door. It opened and they slipped inside. A man, his face very pale and drawn, greeted them. 'We were certain you were taken,' he said. 'The militia have been out in force upon the streets.'

'Then we must thank the unceasing gaze of Providence,' the blind man answered, 'and its agent, this boy, who found me and, like a true emissary of God, has guarded me and brought me here to you this night.'

'You only met him this night?' His companion looked appalled. 'But he may betray us . . .'

The blind man cut him off. 'He will not.'

'How can you know?'

'Because . . .' The blind man's eyes rolled; and they seemed suddenly to Robert the index of a great and limitless mind which, without having seen him, could nevertheless see; and without having heard his tale, could still understand. 'Because he is a fugitive,' he whispered, 'like me, from the destruction of our cause and all our hopes.' He reached out for Robert; he stroked his face. Then he turned to the man who had opened the door. 'Now take us, please, to where we may be safe.'

The man led them up a series of stairways to a room at the very top of the house. It was small; but its entrance had been hidden within the opening of a hearth, and Robert prayed that he would be allowed to stay there – he did not think the blood-drinkers would find him in such a place. The man who had led them to the hidden room must have sensed his nervousness, for he patted him on the back. 'Guard your master well,' he ordered. 'He has been a great and loyal servant to the Commonwealth, and I would not see him murdered for his good services.' He crossed to the stairway, then paused by the door. 'I pray you will both be safe here,' he murmured, bowing his head. 'God bless you, Mr Milton.' Then he hurried down the stairs; and Robert and the blind man, whose name he had at last discovered, were left together alone.

For days they hid; then weeks, and then months. There were times when Robert almost wished he had been forced to leave, for Mr Milton's habits were sober and severe: he rose early, and Robert would read to him from the Bible, then from assorted books in his library, in various languages, English, Latin, Italian or Greek. In this way, Robert continued his studies; and he found Mr Milton a more exacting teacher than Mr Yorke had ever been, for the blind man's learning seemed as vast as the ocean, and his scorn of Robert's laziness as cold and profound. Robert soon loathed him; and it would often seem the hours were being drained through a sieve as he sat reading languages he barely understood, his eyes flayed raw by endless blocks of print. Slowest of all were the afternoons; for if Mr Milton's language was harsh, so also was it witty and satirical, but after lunch he would sit alone to write, despite his blindness, and Robert would find himself missing even the abuse. He had been put to the study of Hebrew; and though he discovered he had an aptitude for the language and could soon read it easily enough, he found it easier still to watch the buzzing of flies and to dream, always dream, of the world he had lost, and of where Emily might be.

He rarely spoke to Mr Milton of these thoughts. Once, though, on the day when King Charles entered London and all the city was a din of celebrations, Robert asked his master if he did not feel despair. The blind man answered with a grisly smile. 'Despair like you felt on our first meeting, when you claimed that you were eager for death?'

Robert nodded. 'If you like,' he replied.

'It is true,' Mr Milton admitted, 'that all that I have worked for is collapsed; and indeed, so utter appears the ruin that I have sometimes wondered if the very firmament is not rotten, and the earth's base built on nothing but trash. For it has often seemed to me' – he paused, and stroked his hand across his heart – 'that God has spat in my face.'

There was silence, save for the distant roar of the crowd and then the sound of cannon-fire saluting the King. 'Only sometimes?' Robert asked cautiously.

Mr Milton nodded. 'Indeed. And much less so now.'

'Why?'

'Because I have seen the proof of what God teaches us, that strength shall grow from those who are weak.'

'And what is this proof?'

Mr Milton smiled so faintly that his lips barely moved. 'Why, the proof, Robert – the proof is yourself.'

'Me?' Robert stared at him in astonishment. 'But . . . I don't understand.'

'You continue true to what you have lost.' The blind man sighed, then reached out to brush Robert's arm; when he spoke again, it was with a sudden unexpected urgency and passion. 'Never betray such a resolution,' he begged. 'Swear it. I feel free to ask you such a thing because it is the same lesson which you have taught me. Among so many faithless, you continue faithful – among so many false, you continue unmoved. Do not change the course you have laid out for yourself, Robert, nor swerve from it, however great the sacrifice may be, and however dark the trials.'

'However dark . . .' Robert closed his eyes. He thought he saw Lightborn before him, handing him the knife, pointing to the bloodied, one-eyed man on the floor. '*Do it.*' The words seemed to echo a thousand times, louder and louder, until Robert started as though waking from a dream. He blocked his ears, then stared again into Mr Milton's eyes. 'It is true,' he acknowledged softly, 'I shall not let my parents' dust lie scattered forgotten, nor the face of my friend start to fade from my mind.'

'I know it,' answered Mr Milton. He squeezed Robert's hands. 'And from such an example, I draw strength of my own.'

The memory of such words long endured in Robert's mind – even on the hottest, most stultifying days, when he wished that Hebrew had never been written and he longed for freedom, for his native fields and open skies. Still Robert treasured his master's admiration; for Mr Milton had been the spokesman for his father's great cause, and a worthy one, he thought, the equal in courage and will to Captain Foxe. In darkness the blind man sat, and compassed round with dangers; yet though at any minute there might come the knock upon the door, and then exposure, imprisonment and perhaps a traitor's death, he remained undaunted and his resolution unbowed. Indeed, for all the unease Mr Milton betrayed, he might have been sitting in some college library; for he lived and studied with the utmost calm. Only when writing did he display emotion; for he would sometimes pause and seem oppressed by turbulent thoughts, and when he returned to his manuscript he would scribble fast as though to exorcise some dread. Robert longed to know what the theme might be: it was some poem, he guessed, but when Mr Milton was not working he would keep the papers locked away, and Robert was reluctant to betray his trust. He had asked once, but Mr Milton had merely grunted. Since that time, Robert had kept his curiosity to himself.

In August, as the summer heat mounted, so also did the danger. Once or twice, Robert slipped out on to the streets to see what news and rumours he could scavenge, but he felt no sense of freedom, no thrill of liberation at having escaped from the closeness of the room. For there was a blood-lust abroad, such as he remembered from the village green of Woodton, and he shuddered that the same thirst should be so palpable once again. Towards the end of the month, when it was ordered that Mr Milton's writings be publicly destroyed, Robert wandered through the crowds, scanning the familiar looks of glee on their faces as they watched the hangman stoking his fire, dropping book after book into the smoky flames. To Robert, such destruction seemed blasphemy enough; but as everyone in the crowd was greedily aware, the hangman would soon have more than books on which his art might be displayed. For the time was approaching when the leaders of the Commonwealth were to be officially condemned: fifteen of them, selected by Parliament, would then perish on the scaffold for their treachery to the King. But which fifteen? Robert looked about him again at the eager crowds. He doubted, if Mr Milton were to be named in the list, that he would remain hidden for long. Mobs had a nose for the blood of the condemned, Robert had seen that for himself: victims would always be sniffed out in the end. And if they did come – the soldiers, and the executioners, and the hungry crowds – then he knew what he would do; for he had learned his lesson well. Better to fight than be taken – better to fight and die than be tamely killed. Defending Mr Milton, he thought, he might expiate his guilt: when he had watched, and done nothing, on Woodton's green.

Two days passed at a slow, prickling, crawling thing's pace. Each sound from the street seemed magnified: each cry, each footstep. Sometimes, men would come climbing up the secret stairs: friends of Mr Milton, bringing him the news that there was no news, that Parliament had still not named the fifteen guilty men. Each time, as they approached, Robert would see his master reach for his manuscript and clutch it to his chest, as though it were his child; and Robert found himself wondering all the more what it might be that seemed so precious, and yet so secret too. He dared to ask Mr Milton a second time; but again, his master grunted and gave him his grisly smile. 'In good time,' he answered, 'it may be you will read it, and learn much from what it says.' But he said nothing more; and Robert knew better than to press the matter. He turned back to his studies. He was reading ancient history: the tales of heroes who had avenged terrible wrongs at the cost of everything, even of their lives – sometimes even, Robert thought, of their principles and their souls.

The evening dragged on. Slower and slower, the minutes passed. The news was expected any minute; had been expected, indeed, all that day. Still it did not come. Through the window, Robert watched the sun start to set. He rose and pressed his ear to the door. Silence. 'Sit down,' ordered Mr Milton. His voice was utterly impassive. Wordlessly, Robert shrugged and turned back to his books.

Night came. Robert lit candles. The news would not arrive today, he thought, not now. He felt disappointed. Tomorrow – he would have to brace himself to die tomorrow; he was almost impatient, he realised, for death to arrive. He sighed; and then suddenly, from the street outside, heard a great din of shouting and cheers. He watched Mr Milton tense, then reach across the table for his manuscript. Robert crossed to where his knife was hidden and stood with arm raised, by the side of the door. There was still silence from the house below; and then, rising faintly, came the clattering of footsteps.

Robert raised his arm higher. He glanced back at Mr Milton who was sitting rigidly in his chair, the motionless image of some ancient senator waiting to be struck down by barbarian hordes. The footsteps rose louder. Robert heard the secret doorway in the hearth being forced. Despite himself, he stepped back. There was a sudden silence as the footsteps paused on the stairway outside; then the handle turned; and the door was opened.

Silence again.

'What news?' cried Mr Milton. 'Robert – tell me – who is it there?'

Robert stared at the group of men in the doorway. One of them handed him a sheet of paper. He scanned it. He breathed in deeply; then turned, and placed it in Mr Milton's hands. 'You are safe,' he whispered. 'You are not amongst the fifteen condemned.' He felt light with relief; yet deep inside him, he realised with a sudden shock, there was disappointment too, that he was not to fight and die after all. For his mother's words had lately been always in his thoughts, her vow that she would meet him with his father after death. Yet now, it was clear, he was still lost amidst the moral world; and the way ahead of him seemed darker and more uncertain than before. Where, he wondered, might it lead him now? And what, when he took it, might he find he had become?

∽∾

'O DARK, DARK, DARK, AMID THE BLAZE OF NOON,
IRRECOVERABLY DARK, TOTAL ECLIPSE
WITHOUT ALL HOPE OF DAY!'

John Milton, *Samson Agonistes*

M r Milton too over the next weeks seemed similarly afflicted by doubt. He had emerged from his hiding-place, but he appeared increasingly to brood and be conscious of the worthlessness of things – more, certainly, than he had ever been whilst in fear for his life. He was often insulted on the streets, and he suffered these insults with an impatience he would never have allowed an executioner to glimpse. Robert did his best to defend his master, and would often launch himself recklessly against the blind man's tormentors; but they would merely laugh at him in turn, and his attempts to be martyred were met not with blows, but with jeers. Mr Milton, confronted by such a mixture of indifference and contempt, seemed slowly to sink into misery; and Robert, watching him, became aware how even the most implacable of minds might learn to despair. 'Not me, though,' he prayed. 'O Lord, please, not me.' He began to contemplate schemes for his return to Woodton once again; to yearn for some desperate and terrible measure. But what? Always, his dreams returned to such a question; and always, he shrank from the answer that they gave. For he knew of only one path which might offer him success, and the thought of its course still filled him with dread.

Day by day, though, as he wandered the streets – and almost without his realising it – he grew less careful.

Whereas before he had kept to the margins of crowds, now he mingled with them freely; whereas before he had avoided the scent of blood, now he passed slaughter-houses with only a hurried glance. Yet he was never surprised by Lightborn or Milady; and he began to think that in such a populous city he might roam the streets freely, and still not be found. He started to accompany Mr Milton on ever longer excursions, and to discover that the city, which before had seemed nothing but a wilderness of streets, was not perhaps such a maze after all. He learned where the road to Salisbury began; and he also learned how Pudding Lane could be reached. But though he brooded more and more on what his course of action should be, he continued undecided; and as he pondered, so his carelessness grew.

One fine autumn day, he was walking with Mr Milton along the Mall. From ahead of them, by Charing Cross, there rose a sudden roar. It froze Robert's blood, for it had sounded joyous and cruel, and he had learned to fear such a noise. He tried to continue along the grass; but there was a second cheer and Mr Milton stood suddenly motionless, his fists clenched. 'What do you see?' he whispered. Robert shook his head. 'Am I so weak,' the blind man asked, 'that the workings of evil must be hidden from me?'

'Not hidden,' answered Robert. 'But why stare it in the face?'

'I stare at nothing.' Mr Milton smiled coldly. 'That is your function, Robert. Come. Lead me towards the noise.'

Robert did as he was ordered. 'There is a great crowd,' he murmured, 'and in its centre is a scaffold. A man is upon it, just cut down from a rope.'

'A man?' Mr Milton pressed. 'What man?'

Robert shrugged. 'I do not recognise him.'

'It is Major-General Harrison,' said a jolly-looking bystander. 'One of the fifteen lately condemned to death for treason. Major Harrison is the first to be slain.'

Mr Milton said nothing for some moments. 'Does he go to it bravely?' he whispered at last.

'Oh, yes,' replied the bystander. 'He looks as cheerful as any man could do in his condition.' He was interrupted by a sudden groan, and then loud cries of joy. 'They have cut him open,' continued the bystander helpfully, 'and now his head and his heart are being shown to the people.' He paused, then lowered his voice. 'They say,' he whispered, 'that his wife expects his coming again. They say that he will surely be at the right hand of Christ, so that those who have judged him will be shortly judged themselves.'

Mr Milton's eyes rolled terribly. 'They say that, do they?' He laughed, and not since the night amongst the stones had Robert heard so chilling a sound. 'Then where is Christ now?' the blind man hissed suddenly. 'Where is Christ's judgement here, on earth?' He turned and began to hurry, pushing through the mass of people. Robert had to run after him to take his arm; his master was shaking, he realised. Gradually, as he was led from the crowds, Mr Milton began to compose himself again; but though his calm returned, it seemed as frozen and fierce as his laughter had been. He did not say a word, not as he walked, nor even once he was back in his home. Instead, he went straight to his desk; he unlocked his hidden manuscript. For a long while he sat holding it; then, like the sudden breaking of a tempest, he began to write. Never had Robert seen him compose in such a fury; and when he finally finished, Mr Milton sat as though drained, and almost shocked at himself.

'Tell me,' asked Robert softly, 'what should I do?'

Mr Milton did not seem surprised that the silence had been broken at last. He reached for Robert's hands. 'Whatever must be done.'

'How far should I go?'

'As far as you must.'

Robert paused a while; then he opened his mouth. But Mr Milton, as though sensing the question that was hanging in the air, lifted up his hand. 'As far as you must,' he repeated with emphasis. His blind eyes stared as though endowed with sudden sight; he laid his hands upon Robert's head. 'I shall rest now,' he murmured. 'Do not come with me. It is time for both of us, I think, to find our own way now.'

Robert watched as the blind man went; then slumped in sudden weariness into the empty chair. He realised, looking at the desk, that the manuscript had not been locked away and he stared at the papers with almost superstitious awe. He felt afraid to touch them. But Mr Milton, he thought suddenly, did nothing by accident. Go your own way, he had said. Still, though, the blind man had been the spokesman for the Foxes' cause; and his guidance had always been most precious and wise. Mr Milton had surely understood this himself; why else then would he not have locked the manuscript away? Robert reached out, and took the top page. As he had guessed, it seemed to be a poem. The writing was almost illegible, covered with scrawled corrections and marks; but at the bottom, in a clearer hand, there were lines which had been circled and underlined. Robert touched them: the ink was still fresh. He smoothed the paper back upon the desk, then began to read.

'*What though the field be lost?*' he read. '*All is not lost.*'
He paused, to repeat the phrase beneath his breath. '*All is
not lost.*' He swallowed, then continued. '*The unconquer-
able will,*' he murmured, '*And study of revenge, immortal
hate,*

> *And courage never to submit or yield:*
> *And what is else not to be overcome?*
> *That glory never shall his wrath or might*
> *Extort from me. To bow and sue for grace*
> *With suppliant knee, and deify his power,*
> *That were an ignominy and shame . . .*'

Robert stopped reading. He sat back in his chair, and
the page fell from his numbed fingers to curl on the
floor; but the words he had read from it still seemed to
echo in his mind. Like a trumpet blast they sounded, a
summons to action; and Robert thought how it was said
that the sightless had the powers of prophecy. He remembered now the blind man's first words to him, spoken
after he had slain the footpad. 'Do not condemn yourself,'
Mr Milton had said. 'It is no sin to be revenged on your
attackers.' How much less of a sin, then, Robert thought
to himself, to venture whatever had to be ventured, when
it was the redemption of Emily which was his ultimate
goal. He reached down for the sheet of paper again; he
re-read the lines. 'No sin,' he whispered, 'no sin.' Then he
closed his eyes. He imagined Lightborn was standing
before him, pointing to the wounded man at his feet. He
was handing him the knife. Robert imagined he took it
. . . he imagined he plunged it into the injured man's
face.

He was arrested that same evening. A Sergeant-at-

arms came with a troop of armed men; Robert and his
master were both dragged away. At the jail they were
parted; as Robert was led to his cell, he twisted and called
out to Mr Milton not to fear. He knew why they had been
seized: not on his master's count, but on his own. For
when the troops had arrived, standing by the Sergeant
Robert had recognised Godolphin, Lightborn's lover; and
outside the jail, he had glimpsed the same man again.

But days passed, then weeks, and a couple of months.
Still no one came. Then at last the door was opened, and
Robert heard his name called out. He rose and followed
the gaoler from the cell. Down a long, fetid passageway
he stumbled, then out into the pure air of an open court.
A man in a cloak was waiting there, smoking a pipe. He
turned slowly round, a thin smile lighting his pale face.
'At last,' said Lightborn, 'we meet again.'

Robert blinked. The sun, and Lightborn's eyes, were
too bright for him to bear. 'And my master?' he
stammered. 'Mr Milton – where is he?'

'Released already,' answered Lightborn. 'And let us
hope he remains that way, for – did I not tell you this? – I
was once accounted a poet myself.'

'But why should he not remain released?'

Lightborn blew a ring of smoke from his lips. 'If you
return to him,' he murmured, 'I would not like to vouch
for Mr Milton's fate.'

'What would you have me do, then, sir?'

'Come with me.'

'It needs no threats to persuade me to do that.'

Lightborn narrowed his eyes. 'Indeed?' He rose
and crossed to take Robert's hand, then led him from the
courtyard. 'So I may presume, then, Master Lovelace, that
you will not be running away from us again?'

Robert rubbed his eyes. For the first time, he looked
Lightborn in the face. 'Never,' he whispered. 'Never
again. I have a friend I must rescue – I know what I must
do.'

⚭

'O, WHAT A WORLD OF PROFIT AND DELIGHT,
OF POWER, OF HONOUR, OF OMNIPOTENCE,
IS PROMIS'D . . .'

                              Christopher Marlowe, *Doctor Faustus*

R obert lay in the perfumed waters of the bath-tub. A
circle of drugged eyes surrounded him: Lightborn's
boys, naked save for the paint that gilded their lips and
the pearls about their arms. Their pale hands stroked and
flickered across his limbs. With each caress, Robert felt
the dirt melt away. He knew that with it went his old self,
the old Robert Foxe, lost upon the steam which rose from
the bath and misted the gold of the candle-flames. At
length, he stretched and felt himself utterly cleansed. He
climbed from the bath and the boys began to dry him;
one brought him a pile of clothes which Robert recognised immediately. They were the same Milady had
offered him before: the clothes he had rejected. The boys
began to dress him and this time, Robert did not
complain. He had made his decision: he had pawned his
soul. He was not Robert Foxe, but Robert Lovelace now.

Dressed at last, he paused by the mirror. He barely
recognised the boy he saw reflected there. Would Emily
know him, he wondered. For his blond hair was long
now, and starting to curl. His body was adorned with silk
and lace. At his belt hung a thin, cruel blade – a

Cavalier's sword. Robert rested his hand upon the hilt, then wandered across to the balcony. Below him stretched the darkness of St James's Park. He heard the dim rattling of a carriage's wheels, but from beyond the road, where the tall trees stood dark against the stars, the silence was like ice. Robert knew the rumours, though, that in those groves were practised unspeakable infamies and crimes; and that now he might explore them and not feel afraid. He glanced back at the mirror. Despite himself, he smiled. He had seen how the naked boys shrank back before his gaze, which seemed to fall like a shadow across their lotus dreams. Robert smiled again. All seemed changed. He was now the one who made others afraid.

He left his room, descended the stairs, passed through echoing, endless rooms. He came at last to the hallway, where Godolphin was standing by the doors. At the sight of Robert, he began to shake. He opened the doors, then followed Robert as he passed outside. Together, they began to walk towards the Mall – Godolphin respectfully, at a distance of ten paces. This puzzled Robert; for although Godolphin appeared haggard and desperate, his eyes did not seem drugged, nor his state reduced to the level of those dead slaves Robert had seen before, when they had marched with Faustus upon Woodton green. Yet still, towards a guest in his own house, Godolphin was behaving like a servant; and when Robert turned and tried to ask him why, he cowered like a dog, as though afraid of chastisement from some invisible hand. So Robert walked on in silence; and waited, as Lightborn had instructed him to do, for the distant chimes of midnight to strike.

They sounded at last from across the frost-chilled

stillness of St James's Park. At the same moment, Robert heard the rattle of wheels upon stone; and looking round, he saw a carriage approaching them, of a size and magnificence he would never have thought possible. It halted beside him; and Robert saw that on its side was painted the same coat of arms he recognised from Godolphin's great house. Godolphin himself scurried up to the carriage and opened its door. A pale hand beckoned from the darkness within. 'Come,' Robert heard Lightborn whisper, 'I have prepared you as a surprise for the fondest of your friends.'

Robert climbed inside. Godolphin followed him and shut the door. At once, the carriage jolted and began to move again. Robert was thrown forward. He fell against a dark, muffled form and, as he did so, felt silk beneath his hands. He looked up. Milady's face was shadowed by her travelling hood, but Robert could see two golden eyes, as unblinking as an owl's and, at first, as imperturbable. Then suddenly they blazed molten and, as she lowered her hood, Robert felt consumed by her stare. With a rustling of her skirts, she held him tightly; and for a moment Robert was afraid she would puncture his throat, for her face seemed twisted by frenzy, and her red lips were parted to reveal her perfect white teeth. 'You must never escape,' she hissed, 'never again, never,' and she raised her hands as though to slice him with her nails. But instead, she seized his cheeks and her lips pressed softly on his own. 'You must not . . . you will not . . .' She paused; her pale, perfect face was frozen once again. 'Do not leave me, Lovelace,' she whispered in his ear.

From behind her, Lightborn laughed. 'See how he is dressed! He could no sooner leave than a butterfly could crawl back to its chrysalis.'

'Yes,' nodded Milady, 'how very true.' She angled her head, looking down at Robert's finery. 'You are quite bewitching, Lovelace – as I knew you would be.'

Robert smiled politely. 'Then it is you, Milady, who has cast the spell.'

She raised a thin eyebrow. 'So – growing the gallant already, I see.' She continued to study him, stroking his hair; then clapped her hands in sudden delight and turned back to Lightborn. 'But tell me,' she asked him, 'how was he found?'

'By Godolphin,' answered Lightborn. He stared across at his lover and, as he did so, Godolphin seemed to melt, and he slipped from his seat and crumpled on the floor. Lightborn ignored him; instead he leaned over Robert, whose cheeks he gently stroked. 'For I knew,' he murmured, 'our quarry would surely attend the executions of the Commonwealth-men, seeing that those who were to be killed had once been the leaders of his parents' cause.' He smiled faintly. 'And so indeed it proved.'

Robert forced himself to meet Lightborn's stare; but he could not withstand it and he had to look away, burying his face in Milady's skirts. 'I see, then,' he muttered into the silk, 'that I was easy to read.'

'Oh, exceedingly.' Lightborn's smile broadened. He turned back to Milady. 'These two months we have had him waiting for you, Helen.'

'Two months!' exclaimed Milady. Her brow darkened. She turned to Godolphin and at once he began to hug himself, rocking to and fro as though struggling to keep warm, and muttering with fear.

'He whines worse than ever,' complained Milady, gazing down at Godolphin with distaste. Still he gibbered. Suddenly, she slapped him about the cheek, and the moaning stopped at once. She nudged him with the tip of her shoe. 'Why did you not send for us,' she demanded, 'if you have had him so long?'

'I . . . I . . .' Godolphin stammered, and stopped. He pointed at Lightborn. 'I sent to him,' he gasped at last.

Milady spun round. 'Is this true?'

Lightborn shrugged. 'Be warned,' he told Robert. 'Upset her, and she will pout like a little girl.'

'Lightborn,' demanded Milady impatiently, 'tell me, is it true?'

'We have lately been in Paris, you see,' Lightborn answered, still addressing Robert. 'We had pressing business there. Naturally' – he shrugged – 'the moment I returned, I came straight to your cell and saw that you were freed.'

'But we could have returned long before,' said Milady, 'if only you had informed me. The business was not so pressing.'

'Was it not?' asked Lightborn. 'Was it truly not?' He met Milady's stare, then gestured at Robert. 'It related to him. Why not explain it, Milady, then ask if he agrees?'

Robert stared at her. 'Your business related to me?'

Milady shrugged. 'In a manner, perhaps.'

'What manner?'

A second time she shrugged. 'It was not coincidence,' she murmured at last, 'that we passed Stonehenge at the moment when we did.'

Robert leaned against the table. He felt his heart contract. 'Go on,' he said.

'We had been told that, should we be there on the second day of May, we might see' – she paused – 'a wonder.'

Robert closed his eyes. 'By Faustus?'

'Faustus' – Milady glanced at Lightborn – 'was not his true name.'

'What, then?' Robert whispered. 'What was he called?'

Milady gave a faint, dismissive shrug. 'Something foreign and quite unpronounceable.' Her eyes narrowed slowly. 'We knew him as Tadeus.'

'And who – what – was Tadeus?'

'He had once been a priest, before he grew to be a blood-drinker. When we met him, he was a worshipper of the Evil One and a practiser of the magic arts.'

Lightborn laughed contemptuously. 'Which is to say, he continued what he had been while still a mortal, a superstitious rogue.'

Robert stared at him in surprise. 'But . . . what are you saying? Surely all blood-drinkers practise the magic arts?'

'Why do you think so?'

'Your powers, I have seen them . . .'

Lightborn rolled his eyes. 'And might not a man's powers seem magical to a superstitious dog, or a monkey with religion?'

'So yours . . .' – Robert shook his head – 'I do not understand. You say they are not magical at all?'

'No more than my sight, or my touch, or my smell.'

'Where then do they come from?'

'From the womb of the universe, which is more teeming and fertile than we shall ever understand.'

'But Faustus – Tadeus – his magic was successful. He conjured up the Devil.'

'Or so he claimed.'

'If not the Devil, then what?'

Lightborn shrugged. 'That is what we travelled to Paris to ask.'

'Why? There was someone there who could tell you?'

Lightborn glanced at Milady. 'The woman who first made us the creatures we are.'

Robert stared at them both. Their eyes seemed suddenly impossibly bright. He grew conscious again of Godolphin's faint whimperings; and he wondered if he should not be grovelling on the floor by his side, in the face of beings so dangerous and strange. Yet for a while, he had forgotten they were demons; and that he himself might soon be a creature just like them. 'Who was she, then,' he asked slowly, 'this woman who transformed you?'

Lightborn smiled and looked away, as though reluctant to reply. 'She is known,' he murmured, 'as la Marquise de Mauvissière.'

'And . . .' Robert licked his lips. 'When you spoke to her – what did she know?'

Lightborn glanced out of the window, then he smiled again. 'You shall shortly find out.'

'How?' asked Robert, scrambling to his feet. 'Where are we going?'

Lightborn raised an eyebrow. 'To Mortlake,' he whispered; then glanced out through the window again. The carriage was slowing now; Robert too leaned out. Everything seemed dark. He craned his neck and saw behind them in the distance the spotted blackness of London, piled beneath the stars and the gleaming full moon. The carriage stopped and Robert climbed out. The ground felt boggy underfoot, and he realised he was standing on the bank of the Thames. He looked about. He seemed in open countryside, save for a large ruined building on the river's far bank. Its white brick was pale in the moonlight like bone, and its windows set like sockets in the walls. A single light burned from a room in a tower.

Lightborn led the way towards a waiting boat. 'Come,' he beckoned. 'Madame la Marquise will be growing impatient.'

'She is waiting for us?'

'No,' Lightborn answered. He helped Milady take her place in the boat, then glanced back at Robert with an evil grin. 'She is waiting for you.'

He snapped his fingers. At once Godolphin, who had been sitting hunched by the oars, began to pull on them. Robert lay back in silence. He could feel a terror swelling inside him, such as he had not expected to feel again now that he had agreed to become Robert Lovelace. He gripped the hilt of his sword; tried to remember how he had looked in the mirror; touched the curls in his hair. But with each splash of the oars he felt his unease grow; and when the boat reached the far bank, and he had climbed on to the landing, it was all he could do to continue to the house.

Milady too, to his surprise, appeared almost nervous, for her lips were drawn tight and her delicate nostrils flared. 'It seems much decayed,' she murmured, gazing up at the house.

Lightborn glanced at her. 'Doubtless we shall see it restored soon enough.' He ordered Godolphin to beat a path through the weeds, and began to follow him; then he glanced back. 'It has been almost seventy years, after all.'

Milady sighed, and gathered her cloak about her; then she took Robert's arm. Despite Godolphin's efforts, the approach was still overgrown and, picking his way through the brambles, Robert could see ever more clearly the ruined state of the house ahead of him and its tumbled-down roof. The front door, however, seemed new; and as Lightborn pushed it open, Robert saw the shadows of furniture inside, and tattered hangings on the walls. He glanced up at Milady. She smiled distantly at him; then, still holding his arm, led the way inside.

Robert was reminded at once of Wolverton Hall. There was the same strong smell of droppings and earth, of fungi growing from the dampness on the walls. He followed Lightborn through the hallway, and heard the crunching of snail shells beneath his feet; he looked about him and thought how, if anything, the rooms were in a worse state of disrepair than those he had once explored with Emily. Yet even as he felt the tightness closing about his chest, he realised that there was a difference: for while in Wolverton Hall the decay had seemed bred from the air like some monstrous growth, now, in the rooms he was passing through, the ruin seemed almost fitting, as though it were not decay at all but the building's natural state. Pools of moonlight fell across Robert's path; he stared up, and saw how the roof and ivy formed a single lattice, patterning the thick air with random beams of silver. The lattice, he thought, had the appearance of a cage in which time itself seemed trapped, and rendered still.

He shivered; but forced himself, when Lightborn began to climb a staircase, to follow him up the steps. They were well worn, and seemed to wind on forever: Robert guessed he was climbing to the summit of the tower. At last, when the steps came to an end, he found himself in a small, low-beamed room. A fire burned in a grate, and shadows of flickering orange lit the walls. Robert looked about him; there were books everywhere, on shelves and in crates, or in piles on the floor. They were spread across cushions and rugs, and he was surprised to realise that the room seemed almost comfortable. He walked forward, and saw there were fabulous instruments on low oaken tables: globes, and astrolabes, and what he supposed to be a telescope. He crossed to it. Although he had heard of such a thing from Mr Webbe, he had never, not in his fondest dreams, imagined he might see one for himself. He bent down, and pressed his eye against the telescope's end. At once he saw an orb of impossible brightness, framed against the blue depths of night; and he gasped, that his own mortal eyes should witness such a thing, and behold the beauty of the heavens so close.

'*Notre dame, la lune,*' a woman murmured. Robert turned round in surprise. For the voice had seemed as silver as the globe he had just been studying, as silver and as impossibly remote; and yet both seemed contained in the room – the moon within the glass, the voice within the form of a woman in a chair. She beckoned to Robert; and as he approached her, he saw how her face too seemed silver, as though lit from within. It was not wrinkled; and yet it appeared incredibly ancient, for reasons which he found hard to define. Perhaps it was the thinness of the face and the lips, which seemed expressive of a terrible lassitude; perhaps it was the chill behind her eyes – as cold, Robert thought, as the passage of the years, by which every living thing must be inexorably drained of its warmth and rendered into dust. How many centuries, he wondered, would have had to pass, to transmute the woman's stare into such a thing of ice? And yet her face was still a mortal's: dark-haired, fine-boned; and her dress, though clearly foreign, was nothing strange or antique. Even her face, as she rose to her feet, appeared suddenly to warm with surprise; and Robert imagined he saw, deep within her stare, a gleam of passion and curiosity.

She gestured with her arm towards the telescope.

Robert stared at her uncertainly; then fell to his knees and pressed his eye back to the glass. As he did so, the Marquise bent down close by his side. 'It was once my custom,' she murmured, 'to pray to the moon – to spill beneath her beams a sacrifice of blood – for she was anciently held the protectress of our kind. But now, though . . . well – you have seen her for yourself. Not a goddess – but something more wonderful instead. A new world!' she whispered in sudden rapture. 'Just one amidst an infinite number of such worlds!'

'It is a wondrous sight,' agreed Robert readily.

'But what, do you think, does it teach us?' the Marquise asked. She stole a quick glance towards Lightborn, then turned back to Robert. 'Why,' she nodded, 'that we must have aspiring minds – that our thoughts must move like the tireless spheres themselves, always daring, never content to rest. Do you not agree, Lovelace? That we must always dare?'

Robert stared at her. He frowned; he did not know what to say.

He heard Lightborn laugh, and saw disappointment darken the Marquise's face. 'You are not as eager,' she hissed, 'to brave the unknown, as Lightborn was when I first met with him.'

'Yes,' answered Lightborn, 'but I was then the greater fool.'

Robert glanced round at them both; then returned to the telescope. 'I am not afraid to dare what I must,' he murmured. 'But I would like to know first what you are offering me.'

He heard the Marquise laugh, a chilling and unpleasant sound. 'It may be I am offering you nothing,' she said. 'It may be I am merely advising you how to endure what you have already been given.'

Robert spun round. 'What do you mean?'

Again the Marquise smiled unpleasantly; then she crossed the room to a crate of books. She removed a pile of them. 'I have been so lately arrived,' she muttered, flicking through each one, 'that I have not yet had time to order these ... yes!' Her smile broadened. 'Here it is.' She opened the book, and handed it across. 'Tell me, Lovelace – do you recognise that?'

He stared at the drawing on the page, then closed his eyes. He remembered how the flesh had dribbled from the face on that May Day evening in the ring of stones, dribbled from the new face that was emerging from beneath it. Robert opened his eyes again; saw it, drawn in ink upon the vellum page: that same face, the face of the Evil One, the face that had ... 'No!' Robert flung down the book. He gazed wildly round the room. He stumbled across to Milady, buried his face against her breast; felt her arms clasp him tightly and rock him gently, while her fingers stroked his hair.

'I think we may conclude,' the Marquise murmured, 'that, yes, he does indeed recognise the face.'

Lightborn stooped to pick up the book. He frowned as he studied it. 'Whose is this?' he asked.

'Mine. It was lately written by Tadeus.'

'What is its matter?'

'A true account of that great and mighty spirit by whose power all the universe is upheld and preserved.'

Lightborn snorted.

'If you mock me, Lightborn, then you do not understand. The spirit is risen, and is walking the Earth. Tadeus was successful – what he promised would happen has indeed come to pass.'

Lightborn stared back at her coldly. 'And much good it brought him.'

'I shall be better prepared than he ever was.'

'What? You intend to approach this creature yourself?'

'Why else would I have come back to this benighted isle, where even the blood in the veins tastes overboiled?'

Lightborn shrugged disdainfully. 'I would not recommend it. He will kill you, and your dust will hang in the air like that of Tadeus – which I knew to be there, Madame, for I felt it stinging my nostrils. It is you who does not understand. The creature – the demon – the whatever he is – he possesses the power to destroy our kind.'

'Then think what other powers He may also possess.' The Marquise stared into the flames. 'For do not forget, Lightborn – He is the Prince of Hell, who is God of all this world.'

'And how do you propose to appease this – "God" – of yours?'

The Marquise smiled faintly. She crossed to Robert, where he still lay hugging Milady. 'I shall seek guidance,' she whispered. She reached out to touch Robert and laid the palm of her hand for a moment on his belly. But he flinched, and Milady bent low across his body as though warding away the Marquise, whose smile grew ever broader as she stared at them both. She turned to Lightborn. 'Is it not a charming sight?' she sneered. 'I was not aware that Milady had grown quite so – *maternal* – as this.'

'And why should I not be?' inquired Milady at once. 'Look at him! He is nothing but a child.'

'I think – and you know – he is a great deal more than that.'

Robert frowned. He rose from Milady's lap. 'What do you mean,' he asked, ' "a great deal more"?'

The Marquise glanced a moment at her book, upon the table where Lightborn had placed it; then she took Robert's arm. He struggled to shake himself free, but the Marquise seemed only amused. She crossed to the telescope and, this time, bent down to gaze at it herself. 'I asked you,' she murmured, 'how high you dared to reach, not because I sought to tempt you but because you have already glimpsed the true God, whose very being is as infinite as the universe He made. It may be' – she turned slowly round – 'you are already a part of such infinity.'

'No.' Robert shook his head. 'There is no God but God Almighty.'

'That same God Almighty who permitted your mother to burn, and your father to be drained, drop by drop, of his blood? Might not such a God be better termed the Prince of Hell?'

'No!' cried Robert, trying to block off his ears.

'Do not deny what you know to be the truth. You have gazed upon His face, Lovelace: Satan, the Evil One, the Lord of all the world . . . And yet – and yet – He spared you. Why?'

Robert moaned and shook his head.

The Marquise widened her eyes as she nodded at him. 'He must have had a purpose.'

'No!' cried Robert again. He gazed round in confusion. Milady rose, and crossed to hold him, but the Marquise only smiled. She winked at Milady. 'You know I speak the truth. For why else would He have marked the boy so clearly with His brand?'

'Brand?' whispered Robert.

'Yes,' answered the Marquise, very softly in his ear.

'Which stamps you as the Devil's thing.'

'You may be wrong,' said Milady sullenly, still clasping Robert tightly to herself. 'It may not be the Devil's doing at all.'

'*What* may not be?' cried Robert desperately.

The Marquise angled her head, widened her eyes in mock consternation. 'What?' she exclaimed. 'Has your pretty new stepmother not told you that yet?'

Robert twisted in Milady's arms. He wriggled free, and met her stare. 'Told me what?' he asked.

'How different you are,' whispered the Marquise, 'from every other mortal she has ever known before.'

Milady stared at her with unconcealed anger. 'We had agreed,' she said in a low, thin voice, 'that we would not mention that yet.' Her accent, Robert realised, seemed suddenly altered, less clear-cut, almost common. Lightborn too appeared to have marked the change, for Robert saw him frown, and then cross to Milady and take her gently by the arm. 'I suppose,' he murmured, looking back at the Marquise, 'that when you are preparing to call on the Devil, a broken promise does not amount to very much.'

The Marquise laughed; and then suddenly, her face was as cold and tight as before. With a rustle of her skirts, she crossed to Milady and seized her by her chin. 'It were best,' she hissed into her face, 'that you do not forget where this boy comes from, and whose thing he is. Do not grow too fond, Milady – for he is not, and never can be, yours.'

'Nor yours.'

'Perhaps.' A cold smile returned to the Marquise's lips. 'But at least I am willing to acknowledge that. You have always been foolish, though – always reluctant to admit to what you are.' She began to laugh again; and did not stop, even though Milady seemed ready to strike her.

'Helen.' As Milady raised her hand, Lightborn folded her in his arms. 'It is time that we went.'

The fury was still burning in Milady's eyes but, as he watched, Robert saw the fire grow into ice. 'Yes,' she choked at last. Her accent was now as crystal-cut as before. 'I think you are right.' She turned and, with a sweep of her cloak, began to hurry down the stairs. Lightborn paused by the doorway to offer an ironic bow.

'I shall see you again soon, I hope,' said the Marquise with a wave of her hand. 'All of you.'

'Madame la Marquise.' Lightborn smiled. 'I am confident you will.' Then he turned and, with Robert, followed Milady down the stairs.

∽◦∾

'. . . TAKE A FLIGHT BEYOND MATERIAL SENSE,
DIVE INTO MYSTERIES . . .'
The Earl of Rochester, 'A Satyr Against Mankind'

So icy did Milady's rage seem that, for a long while, as they returned across the Thames and then sat in the carriage, Robert did not dare to speak to her. Instead he stared out, as Milady did, at the dark night; and he wondered what the brand was which she had seen upon him, marking him as different from other mortals – and yet which she and Lightborn had both chosen to conceal. He turned a cold eye upon them. Milady was still gazing fixedly out through the window, but Lightborn met Robert's stare and his thin lips curled.

'I may not be able to read your thoughts,' he said. 'I

can tell what they are, all the same.'

'Answer me, then. Did the Marquise speak the truth when she said I wore the Devil's mark? How much did she know?'

Lightborn shrugged. 'Perhaps nothing.'

'Nothing?'

'What the Marquise truly knows or not is hard to decide.'

'Why?'

'She is glutted with her ambitions.'

'And what are those?'

'Could you not tell?' Lightborn smiled coldly. 'It is her belief that the bounds of the universe may be measured by herself – and that the profoundest secrets of Hell may be revealed.'

Robert closed his eyes. The image of Stonehenge rose before him, encircled by the ring of the dead. 'And have they not been?' he whispered.

Lightborn shrugged again. 'I wonder. Tadeus was much infected by the Marquise's aspirations – and she, certainly, has always promised more than she delivers.'

'What do you mean?'

The smile slowly faded from Lightborn's face. He gazed into the distance of the night. 'It was,' he explained softly, 'no – it is – the Marquise's universal practice to tempt those she feels will be worthy of her powers, by speaking of an unglimpsed world of spirits which the worthy may nevertheless make their own.' He paused for a moment; then the smile, very faintly, returned to his lips. 'It was thus, certainly, that she first captivated me – for I too once had an over-reaching pride. The Marquise would encourage this: whisper to me of a world where knowledge might be infinite, and of the veil that concealed it from mortal sight. Swollen with insolence, and surfeited upon her golden promises, I asked her to rip it from my eyes. She did so. She gave me the gift – the curse – of her state. But it was only when it was too late – when I had become, like her, a drinker of blood – that I found how she had lied.'

'Lied?' Robert stared at him in surprise. 'Yet you have great powers.'

'And no answers.' Lightborn turned to face him. 'For there is no infinite knowledge, despite what Madame la Marquise claims – no – not even once the veil is ripped aside. And so blood-drinkers, like the gullible mortals they had formerly been, are still ravished by necromancy, and dream of piercing the very bounds of Hell. They are fools, of course – they should have learned from their former error that there is no Hell, there is no Devil, there is no Spirit which governs the world. For, in truth, we are ruled by nothing but cruelty and accident, the whims of a godless, pointless universe; and yet they cannot bear to think we should be so alone. Surely, they pray, there is still a Devil in Hell; and surely His power may still be theirs, if only they can find Him – if only another veil be ripped from their eyes.'

'And yet,' Robert murmured, 'Faustus did summon something.' He clasped his stomach; there seemed a numbness deep inside it, as though from where the Marquise had laid the palm of her hand. 'He summoned something; and now – although I cannot glimpse it for myself – it seems I wear that something's mark.'

Milady had been watching him. 'There is no certain proof,' she whispered suddenly, 'that the mark was inflicted by the creature you saw – no certain proof at all.'

'And yet there is something cursed about me? Is it

true, that I am like no other mortal you have known?'

Milady glanced at Godolphin. Immediately he began to twitch and stir, like some sleeping animal suffering bad dreams. 'Like no other mortal,' Milady agreed. Gingerly almost, as though surprised by herself, she reached out to touch Robert. He brushed her hand away. At once she clenched her fingers, very tightly; then slowly, and disbelievingly, she stretched them out again. She laughed faintly as she stared down at her hand. 'See what effect you have on me,' she said. 'Such power' – she glanced back at Godolphin – 'it cannot be a curse. No.' She ran the tips of her fingers along her lip. 'It cannot be a curse.'

Robert could feel now, from the motion of the carriage, that they were passing along paved streets. He glanced out and saw the trees of St James's Park, touched by the first hints of dawn. He looked back at Milady; she was staring at Godolphin, who lay curled and whimpering on the carriage floor. Milady's gaze was unblinking and suddenly very cruel; and her beauty, Robert thought, seemed like that of Medusa, who had appalled those she entranced and chilled them into stone. Godolphin began to slobber over Milady's shoe; she kicked him away, and gripped the side of the carriage, very tight, as she stared out at the Park. Not even as the horses began to slow did she look round again.

Lightborn leaned across to her. 'We are approaching our new home,' he said. 'Are you not interested to see what I have found for us?'

Still she did not look round, not until the carriage had come to a halt. Robert and Lightborn both clambered out, then waited for Milady to descend. 'Well?' Lightborn asked her, gesturing up at Godolphin's mansion. 'What do you think? Do you not wish to drown me with your thanks?'

Milady gazed up wordlessly, then she walked towards the main door. Godolphin scurried to open it for her. Still wordlessly, she walked through into the hallway, and on into the dining room. She gazed around her again. 'It has,' she said at last, 'opportunities.'

'I am glad,' said Lightborn, with a short bow. 'Perhaps now, then, you will cease this pettish humour of yours.'

Milady did not reply. She continued to stare about her. 'And all this' – she said at last, fixing her gaze on Godolphin – 'was his?'

'You know,' answered Lightborn, 'that I always choose my lovers well.'

'He has signed it over?'

'He has.'

'So he who had so much now has nothing – and of his own free will.' She looked at Robert. 'Do you see,' she whispered, 'to what baseness mortality may easily be brought?'

Robert frowned. 'What do you mean, Milady?' he asked her very slowly.

She made no answer but crossed to Godolphin, her heels clicking on the marble floor. He cringed and moaned beneath her stare, his wails growing more and more desperate, as he began to wet the hem of her dress with his kisses and his tears. Milady endured them for a while; then she sighed at last with disgust, and looked away. 'Throw him out,' she told Lightborn. 'He stinks of his madness.'

'No!' Godolphin's cry rose and fell on an aching, rending sob. 'No!' he wailed again, scrabbling towards Lightborn, seizing his hand and kissing it desperately. 'Not away,' he cried, 'not from you, you promised me, please!'

Lightborn shrugged. 'But Milady will not have you, you see.'

'No, no, please!' Godolphin stared frantically round at Milady, who was seating herself upon a chair, watching him. But though her red lips were parted, she said not a thing; and she concentrated instead upon smoothing out her skirts, then beckoning to Robert to sit by her side.

Lightborn took Godolphin by the hair and began to drag him across to the door. Godolphin seemed barely to have sufficient breath to bring up his sobs; yet still he pleaded to be allowed to stay. 'Anything,' he wailed, 'anything, I will give you anything.'

Lightborn laughed. 'But you have nothing now to give.'

Godolphin's words were lost on another heaving sob.

'Except . . .' – Lightborn suddenly paused and frowned – 'except for your wife.'

Godolphin's sobs fell silent; he gazed up at Lightborn with his mouth open wide.

Lightborn bent down close by his face. 'Where has she fled?'

Godolphin stammered something meaningless.

'I swore,' said Lightborn, his eyes glinting, 'I would be even with the bitch. Well?' He gestured towards the door. 'You heard my terms. Go and fetch her from her hideaway. Then I may consider permitting you to continue here.' He glanced across at Milady. 'We shall be needing a footman, after all.'

Robert stared at him in disbelief. 'You cannot send him like a beggar from his own home.'

'I shall do what I please,' Lightborn answered coldly. 'You are forgetting – it is not his but my home now.' He glanced down at Godolphin again. 'Well?' He gestured towards the door again. 'Go! Fetch me the whore.'

Godolphin shuddered; for a moment a look of confusion and doubt crossed his face, but then he rose to his feet and stumbled from the room. Robert heard his footsteps echoing across the hall; then the front door was slammed, and there was silence again.

'What will you do,' Robert asked, crossing to face Lightborn, 'if he brings you back his wife?'

'Milady!' Lightborn called out in a weary tone. 'I believe your pet is turning Christian again.'

'What will you do?' Robert demanded, raising his voice.

Lightborn grinned. 'Get her to love me – that will be quite revenge enough.'

'What do you mean?'

'You have truly not guessed?'

'Lightborn!' Milady had risen from her chair.

'It is too late now,' he answered. 'He may as well know.'

'Know what?' Robert asked.

'Why – that like the sun, the love of my kind dazzles all those who gaze upon it. To be straight' – Lightborn stared deep into Robert's eyes – 'it reduces them to madness.' His grin broadened. 'Such, without fail, is the fate of all those we love.'

'All?'

'All,' whispered Lightborn. 'All – save only you.'

Robert stared round at Milady, who stood where she had risen – face frozen, eyes unreadable; then back at the door through which Godolphin had just left. He began to run after him, calling his name, through the house and out on to the Mall, but the street was empty and, though Robert gazed up and down it, he could see no trace of the ruined man. He stared into the wilderness of the Park. Godolphin must have vanished into that, he thought. Robert saw that there were carriages lined along its margin, and then watched as two men stumbled out from the trees, arm-in-arm, both laughing. One was fumbling with his breeches. They both clambered into a carriage which at once, with the crack of a whip, began to pull away. Robert watched it leave, then stared back into the Park's darkness. It remained impenetrable, despite the rising sun to the east. He wondered if he dared to enter such a darkness. He wondered, if he did, what he might discover there; what might happen to him.

'How can you know,' he asked aloud, 'I shall not grow like Godolphin?'

'I cannot.'

Robert turned round. Milady was standing behind him, two or three paces away. She did not attempt to draw nearer.

'It seems, then,' said Robert with a low laugh, 'that I am trapped between two possible, unenviable fates. Either I shall end such a ... thing ... as Godolphin is become; or you will love me without destroying me, in which case I can be certain that I am branded with the Devil's mark.'

Very faintly, she inclined her head. 'But I do not say it is the Devil's.'

'Why would it not be?'

'For the same reason that I do not believe my love will destroy you.'

'Tell me, then.'

Milady parted her lips, as though to speak; then she paused and shook her head. 'I think ... no.' She half-laughed, and shook her head again. 'You cannot understand,' she murmured. 'But tonight ... all the Marquise said ... it was the thought, Lovelace – the thought – of losing you ...'

'But why should you care,' he asked, 'who has everything else?'

'The ...' A look of blank misery swept across her face. 'The *loneliness*,' she whispered at last, as though confessing some terrible sin.

Robert stared at her and, for the first time ever, he realised that she was reluctant to meet his eye. 'Tell me,' he said, more softly than before.

'It is not true,' said Milady, after another long pause, 'that *all* mortals must be destroyed by our love. There are those ... the children of my kind ... who can endure our love, and not be driven mad ...' She shrugged faintly. 'And so – of course – they are highly prized.'

'Then why have you not sought out one of those?'

Still Milady would not meet his stare. 'They are hard to come by,' she said shortly. 'But even they ...'

'Yes?'

'Even they ...' Now Milady did look up. Her eyes, Robert saw, were gleaming; her red lips parted. 'They do not compare,' she said in a sudden rush, 'with you. For with you – how can you understand? – but it is as though ... as though I am no longer a blood-drinker at all. I feel mortal. I cannot read your mind; but your emotions – I feel aware of them. Your fears, your passions, your joys ...' She paused again, stretched out her hand. 'I had forgotten,' she whispered, 'how it felt to be human. But Lovelace, my dear ...' She touched his hand with her fingertips. 'Can you ... do you ... please' – she swallowed – 'understand?'

Robert turned from her. For long moments, he stared again into the darkness of the Park. 'In truth,' he said at last, 'whether I do or not, I have little choice.' He reached without looking back for her hand; felt it touch his. 'How could I leave you, Milady,' he asked, 'who rescued me from the stones, and who has been ever since, now that my parents are no more, like a sister – no – like a mother to me?'

She made no answer. But she dared to reach for his arms; dared to hold him; and for a long while – Robert could not tell how long – she stood embracing him.

'There is another thing,' he murmured.

'Indeed?' she inquired.

'Whether I am marked by the Devil, or no . . .'

'Yes?'

'I must return one day to Woodton. For I would, if I could, destroy the Spirit of Darkness. And even if I prove too feeble for such a task – there is a girl . . . a friend – I would rescue from there . . .'

Milady seemed to start. Robert gazed into her eyes; but her stare appeared suddenly blank and cold.

'Milady?' He swallowed. 'Please.' Tenderly, he reached down to hold her hand. 'You must not think me ungrateful. For what hope do I have of redeeming my friend, save with you, and all your powers by my side?'

Milady smiled at him crookedly a moment. 'What hope indeed?' she murmured at last. Then she began to walk with him from the Mall; began to walk into the Park, into the darkness of the trees. Soon they were swallowed; and as the shade closed about him, Robert felt suddenly what it meant to be certain at last that he would one day go home.

'WHAT HATH NIGHT TO DO WITH SLEEP?'

John Milton, *Comus*

It appealed to Lightborn, a few days later, to reveal something more of what his powers might perform – for he was enraged, as he exclaimed suddenly, by Robert's 'sickly Christian taint'. He held his nose, as though sickened; then leaned across. 'Could you remember, do you think,' he asked, 'where that butcher had his shop, who attacked you and stole all your money?'

It was late, and very cold. They had just been to a play: the first that Robert had ever seen. His mind was still reeling from the strange conjunction of new experiences and sights: not just the drama itself, with its powdered actresses, and verses, and golden sets, but the audience too amidst which they had sat – ladies in silks and satin masks, rakes in magnificent, curling wigs. Robert remembered how he had gazed down from his box at the stinking, yowling pit; and he thought how pleasant it was to have money and power, which could offer such a sight, pleasant like the warmth of drink in his veins, pleasant like the carriage which now kept him from the rain. Robert had never understood before what the temptation of wealth might be, for to his parents it had been nothing, and this had protected him from learning it for himself. Nor would he ever have done, he consoled himself, had he not needed to return to Woodton; and as he thought this, he was relieved, that his sin was not so great.

Lightborn leaned across, and waved a hand before his eyes. 'The butcher,' he repeated. 'Do you know where he lives?'

Robert started, then he licked his lips. For no reason that he could explain, he had felt a rush of something light and golden in his stomach. He turned back to look through the carriage window, at the rain-blotted streets outside. They had entered Drury Lane. 'It is not far,' he said slowly. He pointed. 'Up there towards the church.'

Lightborn grinned, and leaned out from the window to shout instructions. The carriage turned and rumbled into the high street of St Giles, then through streets ever more narrow and squalid, until at last they were in the heart of Whetstone Park. Robert pointed to a row of mean, boarded shops. 'There,' he said. 'That is where he lives.'

The carriage halted. Robert swung open the door. Outside the street seemed deserted even of beggars and whores, so bitter was the night. Rain was thudding down into the mud, and a moaning wind brought a stench of rotting thatch. Robert shivered, and turned back to look at his companions. 'What do you intend to do with him?' he asked.

Milady smiled. Then she tied her black vizard about her face again, so that her delicate throat seemed even more white by the contrast. 'I do not think,' she said, 'that you should witness this yet.'

Robert nodded wordlessly, watching Milady as she rose to her feet. And then, although he could not see her cheeks, he knew that they were flushing; and he saw how her golden eyes were aflame. Again, he felt the rush of lightness in his stomach, and a whisper of something like breath along his arms. He leaned back, and pressed himself against the padding of his seat; he breathed in deeply, to try to stop the lightness from spreading further through his blood.

Milady brushed past him. But as she did so, Robert

saw how she caught a scent on the wind, and then there was the lightness again, flickering through all his limbs, and he was rising after her, out of the carriage and into the rain, for even as the lightness made his head seem to spin, so it also seemed to promise something wonderful and strange, and he could not bear to allow it to fade. Milady had turned to face him; he knew, beneath her vizard, she would be looking startled. Then she reached out to touch him; and he saw, through the slit of her mask, her ruby lips smile.

'What do you feel?' she asked, clutching him to her.

'I . . . I don't know,' he replied. 'But whatever it may be, it is wonderful.'

There was a sound of a door creaking open. Robert turned and looked. The butcher was standing there, bleary-eyed, and as fat as before.

'I am sorry,' said Lightborn, 'to have aroused you so late, but your name was given to us as someone who might provide us with some sustenance.'

The butcher stammered and bowed.

'You see,' Lightborn continued, 'our need is grown quite consuming.'

'What would you have, then?' the butcher asked.

Lightborn grinned. 'Oh – something rare, I thought.'

He beckoned the butcher to follow him, and began to lead the way along the muddy road. The butcher, like a dumb thing, shambled after him. As Milady took his hand, Robert felt his head spin again, and he struggled to repress the lightness in his stomach – although he did not want to, he realised, for with each breath he took his nerves were tingling with unspeakable delight. He imagined he was flowing with the rush of the pleasure, as though he were weightless and borne on golden air.

'Down here,' he whispered in Lightborn's ear, 'this was where he took me.' He led the way into the tiny alley, stepping across an open midden, slipping in the mud as the darkness grew more close; but still the lightness was beating through his veins, faster and faster now, so that he could not help but laugh, for even the stench in his nostrils was rippling his blood, like the whisper of a breeze across the strings of a lute.

The butcher stopped, afraid now; suddenly, he broke and tried to run. But he too slipped and then Milady was upon him, slicing at his throat with a pearl-handled knife, while Lightborn gnawed at the wrists with his naked teeth. At the first gushing of blood, Robert thought he would be sick, for the pleasure was so dizzying that he grew terribly afraid, and full of horror at the new experience he had discovered, unable to believe such sensations were his own. But then he mastered the pleasure; and he realised that nothing, nothing he had ever known, was the equal of this joy which seemed to hollow out his guts. He knelt down beside Milady. She had torn off her mask: her cheeks were hectic, her eyes aflame, and her bright lips the brighter for their damp scarlet gleam. She laughed, and squeezed his hand, and as she did so Robert felt a wash of love for her, his companion in so dark and secret a pleasure which he might never otherwise have learned to feel. For a moment, it was true, he wondered from where it came; for as Milady lapped at the butcher's torn throat, he felt a sudden revulsion at the sight of her drinking blood, which he knew must be the source of her pleasure at least, even though he had not tasted a drop. But then the rush of his own ecstasy bore him up once again; and so he closed his eyes, and leaned back against the wall, and surrendered to the mysterious joy.

They left the butcher's corpse by the midden, a smeared mess amidst the filth of intestine and skin. The rain was still drizzling but, as Robert breathed in the damp night air, it seemed full of energy and light. In the carriage, Lightborn held Milady in his arms. He was still panting deeply; his eyes seemed almost red. He began to caress Milady's breasts, then to kiss her with that same urgent, gulping greed with which he had fed from the butcher's wounds. Milady moaned at the touch of his lips on her bare skin. The smell of her perfume hung sweet and sharp in the air, as she arched her back and stretched out her arms. At the same moment, Robert imagined he saw a thousand points of light burning like stars; and he reached down to his breeches. He laughed with a wild, exultant hysteria; he touched himself. Again, the lights. 'What is happening?' he cried. 'How can I feel like this?'

When the carriage stopped, he almost slumped out through the door. He stared around hungrily. The street was empty – and then he thought of the Park. He began to hurry towards it; but Milady reached out and held him by the arm. 'No,' she whispered. She seemed barely able to speak, struggling to control her breath, as though too deep a gulp of air might unchannel the flood of that pleasure which Robert could see in her eyes, and in the flush that had spread like a dawn upon her cheeks. He followed her.

Already, from the rooms inside the mansion, Lightborn had begun to fashion a pleasure-house. Upon the walls were tapestries, and friezes made of crystal, crafted from a thousand gleaming colours, in which the gods might be seen in sundry animal forms, committing riots and fantastical rapes. Candles lit the air with sparks of living fire; and two boys dressed as goat-footed satyrs

stood ready in attendance, holding fans of curling,
painted plumes. Lightborn beckoned them to stand
behind him as he lolled upon a sofa; then, as Milady
joined him, he rang a silver bell. At once, as though he
had been lurking in the shadows waiting for the summons, Godolphin appeared in the doorway, dressed in
the livery his own lackeys had once worn. 'The surprise,'
Lightborn whispered hoarsely, 'bring it, man, bring it.'
Godolphin bowed, and retreated.

Lightborn stared at Robert with a heart-stopping smile.
'I have,' he murmured, 'a great delicacy for you.' He
paused suddenly, and seemed to gasp; he reached for
Milady, kissing her as though only the touch of her
breath could supply him with his own, and then he broke
and turned to smile at Robert again. 'I thought,' he said
in a silken, mocking tone, 'for your first time, to share
with you in your sin, you might prefer a suitably puritan
whore.'

He gestured with his arm. Robert turned to see
Godolphin pulling on a chain and, behind it, on wheels, a
plain metal cage. As it emerged from the darkness,
Robert saw a human form crouching behind the bars,
huddled like a beast in its furthermost corner.

'She thinks she is too fine,' laughed Lightborn, 'but
the bitch shall soon learn her new profession.' He
clapped his hands. 'Well, Godolphin – show Lovelace his
whore.'

Godolphin bowed, and unlocked the cage. With a
single, brutal pull on her hair, he dragged the woman
out, then stood over her as she cowered upon the floor.

'Look at me,' Lightborn whispered. 'Look into my
eyes.'

Slowly, reluctantly, the woman raised her head. Robert

stretched his hand down to his breeches again. What had Lightborn meant, he wondered, by calling her a puritan? For her hair had been dyed yellow, and teased into curls; her face was brightly painted; she wore a bright, low-cut dress, such as only the cheapest whore would ever think to wear. But then, as he studied her, she began to sob a prayer; and Robert's eyes widened in sudden disbelief. 'Why,' he exclaimed, turning to Lightborn, 'it is Lady Godolphin, is it not?'

There was an explosion of laughter from Lightborn and Milady. 'What think you?' asked Lightborn. 'Will the bitch serve?'

'I . . .' Robert swallowed; he stared at her again, and knew that she would – knew that he wanted her, there, on the floor. He clenched his fists. The lightness in his stomach was hollowing him again. 'She does not . . .' he murmured faintly. He shook his head. 'I cannot . . .' His voice trailed away.

Milady glanced at Lightborn. He nodded, and again ordered the woman to stare into his eyes. She screamed as she did so; then the cry froze upon her lips, and she began to lick them, very slowly, as her limbs and body writhed. 'See,' exclaimed Milady, 'the wanton gleam in her eye! The harlot goes to it now!' She clapped her hands with delight; she turned to kiss Lightborn and fold him in her arms. Robert watched them briefly, then felt naked arms embracing him in turn. He looked round. Soft, moist lips met his own; thighs closed about his hips, and began to grind. 'Here,' he heard murmured in his ears; and then Lightborn was leading him across towards the sofa. The lightness in his blood seemed to give Robert strength: he lowered his burden on to the cushions, then joined her as she lay there with arms outstretched for him, his whore. For a second he broke from kissing her, and glanced round: Lightborn and Milady were watching him from the darkness, phantom shapes marked only by their eyes which glittered like burning jewels, impossibly bright. And then they were gone, and Robert looked down again; and as he touched the woman's flesh, the lightness in his blood rose and broke across the world

❧

'I'LL PLUNGE INTO A SEA OF MY DESIRES
AND QUENCH MY FEVER, THOUGH I DROWN MY FAME,
AND TEAR UP PLEASURE BY THE ROOTS. NO MATTER
THOUGH IT NEVER GROW AGAIN.'

The Earl of Rochester, Valentinian

His guilt, when he woke to it, made Robert leap at once to his feet. The woman stirred, and reached out sleepily for him. He glanced back down at her. Her scent was heavy with honeyed sweat; her face smeared with paint; her limbs bare of her prostitute's rags. He felt the sudden lightness again, and he had to force himself to brush her fingers from his thighs. Hurriedly, he wrapped a cloak about himself. As he left the room, he did not look round.

He found Milady seated by a fire in her chamber, gazing into the softly-burning flames, a bottle of red wine and a goblet by her feet. She seemed lost in some private ecstasy; and only when his shadow fell across her did she stir and glance up. She smiled with lazy pleasure as she reached for him. 'Was it not magical?' she whispered. 'For Lovelace – Lovelace – I felt it all.'

'Felt what?' asked Robert coldly.

Milady smiled again, and hooded her eyes. 'How can you ask?' She pulled him down and, despite himself, Robert laid his head upon her lap. 'Not for a long time,' she murmured, 'not since – oh, many, many years – have I known such wanton delights as I shared with Lightborn today. For it was you, Lovelace, your sporting, which served – as it were – to whet my own.'

'How is that possible?' Robert asked.

Milady shrugged faintly. 'I have told you – by some strange transfusion, I can share in your emotions and all your delights.'

'And I, it would seem, can share in some of yours.'

There was a brief silence. Milady bent and reached for the goblet by her feet. She sipped from it; and, very faintly, Robert felt the hollowing in his stomach which the night before had presaged the killing of the butcher.

He stared down at the bottle. 'It is blood?' he asked.

Milady inclined her head. 'Compounded with claret. The best. Haut Brion.'

Robert gazed from her lap into the pattern of the flames. 'Will I,' he asked softly, 'when I become a creature like you, always feel a pleasure like I knew last night?'

'Doubtless,' replied Milady, stroking his hair. 'Indeed, it will surely be the greater, for there is nothing to compare with the actual taste of blood.' She paused, then murmured in his ear. 'Did it terrify you?'

'Yes,' said Robert. 'As much as, last night, it ravished me as well.'

'Do you want it again?'

'Yes,' said Robert at last.

'What will you do?'

'I shall wait.'

'Until what?'

'Until I am ready to return to Woodton, and seek Emily's escape.' He looked up at Milady. 'For I do not look to grow a blood-drinker for the pleasures it may bring, but for the powers alone.'

'Of course.'

'It is the truth.'

Milady smiled. 'Yet you did not play the puritan upon the sofa last night.'

Robert shook his head. 'It is no sin to enjoy the pleasures which God has given us – but only to reach after more . . . and to seize from others what is theirs alone to give.'

Milady frowned. 'What do you mean?' she asked him sharply.

'It was wrong, what we did to Lady Godolphin.'

Her golden eyes widened in puzzlement. 'Why?'

'Why, Milady? Why? It was a rape.'

'She went to it willingly enough.'

'You know full well that at first she did not.'

Milady studied him, puzzlement and fascination mingled in her expression. She shrugged at last, and took another sip of wine. 'Then what would you have us do?'

'She must be sent with all honour – yes, and with money too – to a place where she may resume her former life, for we have done her much wrong.'

Milady arched a thin eyebrow, and smiled as she shook her head. 'Lightborn will not like this.'

'No – for he can enjoy no pleasure unless it has some shade of cruelty to it. But you must persuade him, Milady.'

She shrugged faintly. 'You know, sweet Lovelace, that I ever do as you request.'

And so she did; and Lady Godolphin was indeed sent away. Naturally, Milady had been correct that Lightborn would not be pleased; and his fury against Robert was contemptuous and cold. But Robert was not afraid: he knew that Milady continued his protectress, who was the only being in creation Lightborn loved, the only being he would not willingly hurt. But for all his mistress's power over him, Lightborn did not surrender easily; and he grew all the more determined to teach Robert the ways of god-lessness, so that the canker of religion might not infect his house any more. 'For I am a lord of the living and the dead,' he muttered, 'a creature of dreadful powers – and I shall not be preached at.' Instead, he began to grow a preacher himself. He would insist, with many fluent arguments, that religion had no purpose but to keep fools in awe, and that all who thought otherwise were hypo-critical asses. He would sometimes light his pipe with strips torn from a Bible and, surrounded by his boys, would describe how St John had been the lover of Christ, and used him as the sinners of Sodom might have done. Then Lightborn would gesture towards the Bible and invite Robert to light his own pipe with it, since he had surely proved how it was nothing but a record of bugbears and hobgoblins, and jugglers' tricks. When Robert refused, as he always did, Lightborn would sigh piously, look to Milady and shake his head. 'And yet this is the same godly youth who watched you and I tear a fellow Christian to shreds, and then stained this room with the heat of his lusts, which he inflicted upon a woman quite as holy as himself. Lord!' – he would raise his eyes up to the roof – 'what hypocrites these Christians must be!'

Robert would ignore such taunts; but he felt their

sting, and the truth of their charge. He remembered what he had sworn to Milady: that he would not witness the drinking of blood until he was ready to drink it himself; and he struggled hard to keep to this vow. He was helped, in the beginning, by his need to master the arts which he would require for his return to Woodton. His lessons in horsemanship were resumed, and soon taken to a level where he had far surpassed his teachers; likewise in the use of weapons, of daggers and pistols, and every kind of sword. It was with the blade that Milady had first given him, however, that Robert grew most brilliant; and he came to love it as though it were almost an extension of himself. Yet sometimes he would find he was afraid to handle the sword; for it was cruel and deadly and, when it flickered through the air, he could imagine what it might mean to be as cruel and deadly himself.

In his blackest and most secret thoughts, however, Robert began to think he might almost welcome such a fate. For the more he practised, and the more dangerous he became, so also, upon the passage of the years, the more did he find himself growing tortured by his vow. He would always know when Lightborn and Milady had fed, for their eyes would spark and their very flesh gleam, and they would brush past him laughing, arm-in-arm, as though drunk. Robert could not then endure to continue in the house, for he knew that if he did he might hear their pleasuring, which would fill him with a strange and tormenting jealousy, and darken his already dark and fierce desires. He would walk instead through the streets, or through the groves of the Park, half-tempted to spill some obscure person's blood in the hope that he too might grow ravished by its scent.

Then one day, in the Park, he surprised a couple of

footpads who had seized a lady and were holding her at knifepoint, forcing her to hand them her jewellery and purse. Robert alerted the footpads to his presence with a cough; and then, in the fight which ensued, ran them both through the heart. He sniffed the blade, but he felt nothing at all; and he wished that Milady might have sniffed it in his place. But he did not take it back to her: he wiped the blade clean, and kept true to his vow. Instead, to keep the pangs of desire at bay, he took to having women in their homes or in brothels, in the streets or in the Park – wherever, in short, Fate might give him the chance. Nor was Fate chary; for Robert was young, and handsome, and rich. With the help of such advantages, and his own gnawing appetite, he had soon grown, before he was barely seventeen, a most practised and accomplished libertine.

And with practise, at length, came a refinement of his tastes. He was fortunate in the woman he had rescued in the Park, for she had been an attendant to Lady Castlemaine, most lovely and notorious of all the mistresses of the King. Having gained his reputation for gallantry, Robert was soon an object of considerable interest; and it was not long before he began to grow flattered, during the fashionable hours for a stroll through the Park, by the coy attentions of the very best sort. At first, it was true, his admirers seemed almost reticent; and Robert, who often had Milady on his arm, realised they had mistaken her for a rival for his heart. But such a consideration did not concern his conquests for long; and when they discovered that Milady, far from seeming jealous, appeared almost to draw pleasure from their coquetries, they redoubled their oglings and flutterings. Promises were whispered; assignations made; and

Robert soon found that he had an open invitation to the Court.

He had often wondered, in his darker imaginings, what lay within the sprawl of Whitehall Palace. It stood heaped at the southernmost end of the Park, a jumbled mess of buildings and styles which had always seemed to Robert – passing beneath the shadow of its outer walls, and remembering his father's mortal hatred of kings – to possess the outlines of some structure of Hell. Feeling his parents' eyes to be upon him, it took Robert a long while before he could summon the resolve to pass inside it; and he was only persuaded in the end by Milady, who appeared eager to witness its secrets for herself. Lightborn, however, refused to go, muttering that he would not crook the knee to the flummeries of a king, nor to any mortal; and Robert himself, as he passed with Milady through the Palace gates, felt a chill about his heart, as though he might expect to see the Devil at any moment. It was very cold, just a few days after Christmas, and thoughts of the Devil were much on Robert's mind. But then, as they walked along the Privy Gallery, they suddenly passed by the King himself; and Robert – who had witnessed the blank stare of evil before, and under-stood its look – knew at once that Charles Stuart was no demon, nor risen up from Hell. His Majesty was sur-rounded by a carpet of small dogs; and yet their yapping was nothing compared with that of two women, both wondrous beauties, who were standing on either side of him screaming abuse. One Robert recognised: she was Lady Castlemaine, the mistress who had first invited him to her apartments in the Court. Her rival was just as lovely, but icy-faced and very young. The King was smiling disengagedly; he began to fiddle with his gloves.

The dogs whined and yelped. The ladies screamed on.

'It is said that cunts, like oysters upon rocks, fix upon the King, that they may conjure up pearls.'

Robert looked round. Two young men were standing by the Gallery wall, both dressed as he was in the height of fashion: one tubby and jovial-looking, the other tall with refined, handsome looks. It was the second man who had spoken; and Robert was struck by the contrast with the matter of his words – for as his voice had been haunting, so also was his face. His eyes were hooded and his lips soft and sensual; and yet there appeared something almost innocent in his expression, like a rebel angel undefaced by his fall. His beauty, it struck Robert, seemed almost like Milady's; and then he saw how the young man was studying her, as though with the same thought. Milady met his eye, and smiled, and arched her brow. The young man struggled to meet her stare: for a while he succeeded, then at last he looked away.

Milady continued to observe him. Slowly, she lowered the hood back from her hair. 'What is it, then,' she asked softly, 'which those two ladies are seeking to conjure from the King?'

'Why,' the young man replied coldly, 'that quintessence of all earthly ambitions – a place in a carriage.'

Milady narrowed her eyes. 'I do not understand.'

'It has been lately delivered,' explained the second young man, 'as a gift to the King. Such is its magnificence that they who ride in it cannot help but be observed. The quarrel, therefore, is who shall ride in it first?'

'A pretty issue,' said the first man, gazing back at the ladies, 'when the two of them are nothing but flesh upon bones.'

'Are not we all?' Milady asked.

The young man smiled faintly, then bowed his head. 'Doubtless you, Madame, would know that better than myself.'

Milady's golden eyes grew wide with puzzlement. There was a silence: the young man met her stare again, and his lips curled faintly, but then, as she seemed about to speak to him, he turned round suddenly. There had been a scream. The younger of the two ladies kicked at the dogs; then she screamed again, and ran down the Gallery. The young man sighed wearily. 'Is that not ever the way?' he asked. 'Weigh a virgin and a whore, and who shall win out?'

'Why,' asked Robert, as the lady ran past them, 'what do you mean?'

The young man smiled slyly. 'Miss Stewart, whom you just saw pass by, has been denying herself to the royal prick – and what cannot be had is ever most desired. Yet it would seem, in the final reckoning, that not even the promise of her jewel was sufficient to gain her the prize.'

Robert gazed at Lady Castlemaine, as she walked from the Gallery by the side of the King. 'What then did she possess,' he asked, 'which might rival what Miss Stewart had to offer to the King?'

'Nothing,' answered the young man, 'but merely a threat.'

'A threat?'

'Why, did you not observe how the whore is pregnant? She has been menacing, if she is not given her way, to miscarry the child.' His face grew suddenly cold, and his smile seemed a miraculous compound of pity and spite. 'It is said,' he whispered in Robert's ear, 'that full forty men a day are provided for my Lady Castlemaine, and yet that still, like a bitch, she wags her tail for more. What think you, sir? Could that possibly be true?' His smile broadened; yet Robert was suddenly aware of a terrible emptiness behind it, bred of weariness, and disgust, and satiation. There was scorn in it too, he realised, directed at himself; and he felt, with a strange and unexpected dizziness, how loathsome flesh was, how rotten and sweet. He flushed at the thought of his coming tryst with Lady Castlemaine; of coupling with her – a squirming dog upon a bitch.

He did not say another word until the young man and his companion had both bowed to them and left. 'Who was he?' he murmured to Milady, then shuddered, for the disgust he had felt still lingered in his thoughts, like a sickly mildew that would not be purged. 'He seemed almost to be a creature like yourself, for it suddenly struck me that I was sharing in his thoughts.'

'Yes,' answered Milady, 'and they appeared most bitter and exhausted, strange in one so young.' She paused, and pursed her lips. 'Yet he is certainly a mortal.' She took Robert's arm, and he saw how her features were alert with interest. 'I wonder what his history might be.'

'You have no idea?'

She shrugged. 'I do not have the experience to say. We should perhaps discover the Marquise, and ask for her advice.'

Robert smiled coldly. 'I was not aware you were seeing her.'

Milady shrugged noncommittally. 'It would not require us to visit her at her home. We shall soon discover her here at the Court.'

'At the Court? The Marquise?'

'She has a cousin, I believe, a Miss Elizabeth Malet, newly arrived here in London from the country.'

Again, Robert stared at her in disbelief. 'A cousin?' he exclaimed.

'Well, in truth, I believe her to be a great-great-granddaughter, but there are difficulties in acknowledging the truth of such a state.'

'The Marquise was married?'

'Many times, I believe. But once in London, on her last sojourn here, yes.'

Robert shook his head, half-baffled, half-surprised. 'And so what is this – "cousin" – doing at the Court?'

'Why, what do you think? Attempting to discover a husband for herself.'

Robert shrugged. 'I had not realised the Marquise was so . . . family inclined.'

'Why should she not be?' Milady answered sharply. She frowned as she met Robert's stare, then looked away. 'They share each other's blood, after all.'

Such an explanation struck Robert as barely convincing. But Milady appeared unwilling to say any more; and her silence, as they walked on through the endless corridors and halls, appeared to Robert strangely bruised and withdrawn. He wondered what she might be hiding from him; and he grew disturbed at the memory of secrets she had held from him before, and the manner in which they had at length been exposed. When they discovered Miss Malet at last, however, the Marquise was not with her, nor expected for a while. 'You may discover her,' said Miss Malet, 'at the Queen's masquerade – to be held on Twelfth Night, in three days' time – but of course, you will already know that for yourselves. Madame has assured me – most determinedly, I might add – of her intention to be there; and so she surely shall, for we are lately become the very closest of friends!' She clapped her hands together. 'Why,' she exclaimed, 'it will be my first royal ball!' Robert smiled. Miss Malet was no older, he guessed, than he was himself, young and pretty, with long golden hair. She reminded him somewhat of Emily – or rather, of Emily as he had imagined she might seem now. 'May I count upon your own presence at the masquerade?' Miss Malet inquired. Robert bowed and assured her, as he left, that she could.

He resumed his wanderings with Milady through the palace. Robert could almost believe they might never escape it, for the corridors seemed like a mighty labyrinth, conjured perhaps by some sorcerer, in which those who were lost would grow dizzied by the pleasures, the gaming and the drinking, which filled every hall, so that soon they would forget they had ever thought to leave. And who could blame them, he thought, as he gazed at the beauty of the ladies and the rakes, at the brushing of silk upon silk, lace on lace, lips on lips – why indeed should anyone want to leave? 'And yet I do,' he thought suddenly, 'and I do not know why.' He glanced at Milady, feeling again the sense of some secret come between them, some shadow of discontent. Yet that was not all: for there was a dullness even worse than the discontent. How feeble his sensations had begun to seem; how pallid and drained. He remembered the young man, and the strange disgust he had evoked within him. Robert rubbed his eyes. The disgust, like some drought, still seemed to linger, so that when he gazed upon the pleasures and delights of the palace he felt no joy in them, but only a parched and blasted boredom which seemed to gasp for rain from a burning, empty sky.

'Where then relief?' Robert asked himself. He could not endure to continue with Milady, for he knew of only one certain answer to such a question, and her presence was tempting him to cast his vow aside, to seek the answer out. He could tell, as they parted, that she would soon be hunting; for the sight of others' appetites always served to rouse her own, and he could see in her eyes the familiar hungry gleam. He felt, in his own stomach, the sudden tingling of gold; and the temptation to go with her grew almost too strong. With an effort, he fought it back; but the lightness persisted, even after Milady had departed, and he felt again how dull all things had grown in comparison with its touch.

Robert attempted to drown the lightness beneath drink; and when that failed, to gamble it away. He had soon lost several bags of coins, and the lightness was now starting to prickle in his stomach. He gambled more; he lost more coins; still the prickle burned and, veiled by guts, would not be scratched. Robert recalled his tryst with Lady Castlemaine; he hurried to her quarters. Once arrived, he sought to vent the pain upon her, upon the fabulous beauty of her soft and welcoming flesh, as though the ravening itch might be spewed out from his prick. At last, when his stomach seemed as empty as his ballocks had become, he imagined that the prickling might be gone; and that without the prickling, he might finally find some rest.

Robert fell asleep; he began to dream. He imagined he was walking through St James's Park. He recognised the path: it was where he had first walked with Lady Castlemaine; but the trees which lined the way along either side seemed to be bending and seeking for him, like monstrous creatures with a thousand necks, for on the end of every branch was a ravening mouth, and Robert saw how they were cunts, open wide and lined with teeth. He tried to fend their searching jaws away; he began to run, and then he saw a grove ahead of him, and in it was Lady Castlemaine, her legs open wide, waiting to be serviced by a line of hard-pricked men, and yet she was all-devouring and could not be full-gorged, although a vast meal of slime was soon flowing out from between her thighs, seeping down the path and rising in a flood. Robert struggled to escape it; but he began to choke, as the slime filled his nostrils and oozed down his throat.

He woke with a violent start. He staggered from Lady Castlemaine's side and, reaching for a wine bottle, gulped the contents down. But the taste and scent of his dream still seemed to linger, as the sense of disgust had done the day before; and Robert found himself wondering all the more who the young man had been, who seemed capable of inspiring such loathsome phantoms of ennui. He was determined now to search him out, to discover what it was which had infected him so. For it appalled Robert to think that the phantoms might return again, and that his pleasures be forever loaded with disgust; and so he decided to accept – what he had first resolved to refuse – Miss Malet's invitation to the masquerade; for he knew that he would surely find the young man there.

And so it was that, when the time came, Robert passed into Whitehall with Milady on his arm – a guest at His

Majesty's Twelfth Night ball. He prayed as he did so that
his father's spirit might forgive him.

∾◌∾

'. . . NOW CONSCIENCE WAKES DESPAIR
THAT SLUMBERED, WAKES THE BITTER MEMORY
OF WHAT HE WAS, WHAT IS, AND WHAT MUST BE
WORSE . . .'

John Milton, *Paradise Lost*

Arriving in the Banqueting House, Robert despaired
at first of recognising anyone. The ball was a
fabulous swirl of colours – of feathers, and masks, and
impossible wigs – beneath which the presence of those
who wore them seemed lost, dissolved utterly into their
outward display. But then suddenly Milady pointed with
her fan. 'Is that not the strange man we met before?' she
asked. Robert turned, and looked. The young man was
seated amidst a crowd of his fellows. His mask had been
torn away, and he already seemed drunk; he spoke into
the ear of his companion, the tubby, jovial-faced man he
had been with before, and then both men burst out
laughing. Robert left Milady, and began to approach
them. As he did so, he realised that all the rakes had
turned and were watching him. The young man was
saying something to them, and Robert thought that he
caught the name of Lady Castlemaine. There was another
explosion of laughter, and he blushed beneath his mask.
He stood frozen for a moment; but the rakes continued to
stare at him, and the young man said something else
which provoked a further roar. Robert could feel his
blush burning him; he clenched his fists and turned

away. Once he glanced back; and again there was laughter, and toasts, and ribald shouts.

'Does he mock you on my account, poor sprig?' Robert looked round, to find Lady Castlemaine beside him. She too was unmasked, not surprisingly, Robert thought: for she was far too vain to cover her face.

He pointed to the young man. 'Who is he?' he asked.

'My Lord of Rochester,' Lady Castlemaine replied, 'and, to my shame, my cousin.'

'Your shame?'

'Oh, yes.' Lady Castlemaine sighed and raised her eyes. 'He has only been arrived from France these past two weeks, and yet already he is accounted a most notorious rake.'

'I am sure Your Ladyship's name for virtue will not be spotted by his crimes.'

Lady Castlemaine laughed prettily. 'Let us trust not.' She tossed back her head; and then suddenly froze. 'And yet even as we speak on that same topic of virtue, I fear the King may be in danger of falling for its show.' As though drawing a dagger, she rasped out her fan. 'You must excuse me, Lovelace.' She brushed quickly past him, and began to glide across the hall.

Robert watched her as she went; then he saw what it was which had alarmed her. The King was kneeling, his hand upon his heart – appealing, so it seemed, to a lady on a chair. The lady herself was masked; but Robert recognised the breasts and perfect figure of Miss Stewart.

'Poor prince, he is governed by his prick and must follow where it leads, for it is proud and peremptory, and shall not be gainsaid.'

Robert glanced round. Lord Rochester was standing by his side.

'What man would not follow his prick,' asked Robert coldly, 'if it led to such delights?'

'As what?' Lord Rochester laughed. 'As Lady Castlemaine perhaps?'

'It is surely my sacred duty,' answered Robert, 'to go wheresoever my sovereign shall lead.'

'Then is His Majesty blessed indeed, to have the loyalty of so many members of his Court.' Lord Rochester laughed again drunkenly. His eyes, Robert could see, were glassy; yet suddenly, as he leaned forward, his face appeared to grow mobile and alert and Robert imagined that he saw, beneath the glassiness of his stare, a passionate and terrible lucidity. 'If I mocked you before,' he whispered, 'I trust you will understand, it was only to mock what is mortal in myself.'

'But I do not understand,' answered Robert. 'Who in all this assembly is not guilty of such a fault?'

'Who indeed?' Lord Rochester smiled. 'This is truly a much-fucking Court. Yet I think you do understand me when I say that there are creatures here with more – immortal – desires.' He shivered, and grinned, and lifted his glass; and Robert looked towards where he was raising his toast. He saw Milady: she was attendant upon a plump and very drunk young rake; her eyes, through her mask, seemed like golden fire. Lord Rochester cocked an eyebrow at Robert, and half-curled his lips. 'I think,' he murmured, 'that your lady's conquest will soon be found dead, mysteriously murdered or floating drowned upon the Thames.'

Robert stared at him, appalled. 'How do you know of such things?' he whispered at last.

'I might very well ask the same question of you.'

'I . . .' Robert swallowed, and turned away. 'It is a

strange story,' he said at last.

'*Mais d'accord.* How so?'

Robert did not answer; he continued to watch Milady and the rake. Again, he felt the stirring of gold within his guts. 'I feel ...' he murmured; then staggered and breathed in sharply, as pleasure in a rush licked like fire through his blood. 'I feel it,' he gasped, 'without drinking, the delight ...'

'What, it is striking you now?'

Robert nodded.

Lord Rochester seized him by the arm. 'And how is it?' he asked eagerly. 'The pleasure – you must tell me – how does it feel?'

Robert closed his eyes. 'It is paradise,' he said. 'There is nothing in all the world which can compare.'

'What – not even my Lady Castlemaine?'

Robert smiled, and shook his head.

'Aye,' nodded Rochester. 'And yet still you seek to flee from such pleasures to her cunt.'

'Would not you?' asked Robert.

Lord Rochester stared at Milady, then emptied his glass with a single sudden gulp. 'I do not know,' he said at last. 'For I begin to fear I am more in love with pleasure than my happiness.'

'Not every delight need endanger it.'

Lord Rochester laughed contemptuously. 'Ay, but every delight does which is worth the possessing. I do not willingly blacken my soul, sir – and yet so polluted has it already grown that I find the greater the pleasure, the more terrible must be the sin. If you doubt me, consider your lady once again. Or better ...' – he paused, and his grin seemed suddenly set like a skull's – 'observe the Marquise de Mauvissière.'

'What,' Robert asked, 'she is here?'

Lord Rochester gestured with a wave of his hand.

Robert looked, and caught a sudden glimpse of the Marquise through the swirling, dancing throngs. He pushed his way forward, to observe her more closely. He saw how she was seated by Miss Malet in the corner of the gallery, whispering something urgent in her ear, as though offering her cousin a warning or advice – the very picture of a courtly chaperone. But then suddenly, as Robert watched her, the Marquise's face appeared to darken; her lips parted as though with hunger, and an unspeakable greed seemed to glitter in her eyes. She swayed, as though dizzied by her passions, and steadied her hands upon Miss Malet's breasts. She squeezed them very gently; then stretched out her fingers, as though they were claws.

'Christ's blood,' said the tubby man, Lord Rochester's friend, who had wandered across to join them both, 'yonder is a lady with a passionate nature.'

'Very true, Savile,' Lord Rochester grinned. 'Very true.'

Robert stared at the Marquise as she seemed almost to swoon with her desire. 'What might be the cause of so terrible a passion?' he whispered.

The tubby man, Savile, stared at him with a puzzled look. 'Is it not clear?' he asked. 'Her sensibility is in favour of the fairer sex.' But Lord Rochester's surprise seemed even deeper still. 'The cause?' he whispered into Robert's ear. 'Do you truly not know?'

'No,' answered Robert, 'and I grow weary that such secrets are still hidden from me.'

'Then come,' said Lord Rochester, 'and find out the cause for yourself.' He led Robert by the arm, across to where the Marquise and Miss Malet were sitting.

Robert watched how the Marquise leaned her cheek upon Miss Malet's shoulder, and breathed in her scent. At once she writhed, and her eyes began to roll; and then Robert too breathed in, and heard himself gasp. 'No.' Yet he did not mean it; for he imagined he was soaring with his blood into the air, leaving his body and becoming liquid gold. He was made of a thousand, thousand fiery sparks; and each spark gave him pleasure such as he had never known before. He longed to scream. Was there a point, he wondered, where delight began to hurt, for it was too sweet, too sweet, the sweetest of pains, he would be melted before it, be dissolved into the air . . .

Yet he had not been, Robert realised, as he was carried from the ball and then outside into the bitter winter air. He shook his head, and looked about him. He was standing on a flight of steps, above a boat which was rocking on the river's choppy waves. He was being supported on either side, he discovered, by Savile and Lord Rochester. 'What happened?' he mumbled. 'Where are we going?'

'You swooned,' answered Lord Rochester, 'from the excess of your pleasure. And we are going upon the river, that you may have the purgative of the cold.'

Savile laughed cheerily, and nudged him in the ribs. 'I do not know what you have been drinking,' he said, 'but I should like to sample it for myself, for I have never seen such a look of pure delight as when you grinned back there, and your legs went down.' He winked, and raised up a bottle of wine. 'A plague on this stuff, it is good only to make piss.'

'Then you are most fortunate, sir,' whispered Robert, 'that it is good for nothing worse.' But Savile did not hear him, although Lord Rochester did for he turned and laid a

finger on his lips. With Savile's help, he began to guide
Robert down the steps, and when they had reached the
boat Robert lay for a while in silence upon the cushions,
still feeling the ripples of gold flowing out through his
blood. 'My God,' he whispered at last, into Lord
Rochester's ear. 'My God, my God.'

Lord Rochester turned, and gently took him in his
arms. 'So you had truly not been told?' he whispered
back.

'Told?'

'You know.'

'Tell me.'

Lord Rochester shrugged faintly, and paused to
arrange the lace upon his cuffs. 'You must know, then,'
he murmured at last, 'that to blood-drinkers, descendants
of their own kind have magical properties. For example –
they can be loved by a blood-drinker, and yet not be
driven mad by it. This, as you can doubtless understand,
makes them highly prized . . .'

Robert nodded faintly. He remembered Milady telling
him of such a breed; and yet she had not described it
fully, not admitted what it was . . .

'However,' Lord Rochester continued, 'they rarely
survive to be loved for very long. For it is their misfortune
that they possess this quality above all others – that their
blood, to the blood-drinker who is their relative, is the
sweetest, the most fortifying, the most intoxicating
draught of all.'

Robert shook his head in mute horror and misery.

Lord Rochester nuzzled him. 'So tell me,' he whispered with sudden eagerness. 'The feeling . . . the
pleasure . . . was it as wondrous to feel as it appeared?'

Robert sighed, long and deeply, as though the

sensation now clotting in his veins might be brought up on his breath. But still it lingered; and so he trailed his fingers through the icy waves to reassure himself that a world of everyday senses still existed, a world in which water continued to be cold. He shivered, gratified, then hugged himself. He gazed at the Palace as it receded down the Thames; and at once felt the darkness shadow him again. Turning, he stared out at the vast wilderness of London; then up at the stars in the freezing winter sky. The darkness was everywhere; the darkness was deep inside himself. He could feel it, as he had done before when the butcher had been slain, burning his soul. He reached for Savile's bottle and began to drink. But the wine did not extinguish, only served to stoke the flames. Robert moaned and shuddered, as he gazed at the bank and the whores who stood dotted by the river steps. 'Let us land,' he muttered faintly, 'we must . . . let us land.'

Savile grinned and nodded, and shouted orders to the boatman. They glided up beside Milford Stairs. 'Dirty Lane!' Savile shouted as he staggered from the boat. '*En avant*!' He began to lead the way, weaving arm-in-arm with Lord Rochester, while Robert followed, not saying a word, his mind an inferno of wretchedness and lust. 'Whores!' cried Savile, as he swayed along the frozen streets. 'Must have whores!' He turned into Dirty Lane, pushed open a brothel door and gazed about him, mouth flapping open and shut like a fish's. 'Twatscour the crowd of them!' he giggled suddenly; then fell flat on his face. Lord Rochester stepped over him. 'I do not wish to have to choose,' he told the madam. 'Send up four of your best, and we shall have 'em every one.'

A long while it took Robert, longer than before, to purge the thrill of blood from himself and become master

of his own desires once again. Yet even then, as he lay
among the sodden sheets and knew himself drained, the
idea of what he had felt at the Banqueting House still
remained with him: a terrible, tempting, predatory idea.
He shuddered, and ordered his prostitutes away, for he
had been thinking of Emily and could not bear to remember her as he lay amidst such company. 'I am lost,' he
said, gazing at the roof, 'lost without hope of guidance.'

Lord Rochester glanced round. He was still whoring.
His expression was distant; for all the pleasure it
betrayed, he might have been practising his fencing
strokes. 'I am bored by this fucking,' he murmured in
French. 'I would sooner, I think, hear your story of your
life.'

'Cannot you do both?'

Lord Rochester smiled. 'A fine suggestion.'

Robert rolled across the bed. He began his tale. By the
time he had finished it, his eyes were moist with tears.
'You see, my Lord,' he said, as he wiped them away, 'what
a hypocrite I am, that I weep for my parents and for my
childhood friend, yet am grown such a fiend.'

'You are not yet a blood-drinker.'

'Not yet,' murmured Robert softly. 'Not yet, not yet.'

'And would not ever be it seems.' Lord Rochester
paused. 'Your friend – Mistress Vaughan – she is still
alive?'

'So I hope.'

'And yet to win her, you think you must become a
blood-drinker yourself?'

Robert shrugged.

'Aye,' nodded Lord Rochester, almost as though to
himself, 'it is a fearful choice.' He lay for a moment,
numbed by the thought; then shuddered. 'For it

must ever be our hope, as we stumble through the gloom of life's night, that there is indeed somewhere light – a sun – a God.' He sighed, and lifted up his face to gaze into the candle-flames. 'And so it is,' he whispered. 'I will help you as I can. For in the choice confronting you – I find the image of one I must also one day make.'

Robert gazed at him intently; but before he could speak, Lord Rochester had raised a hand. 'A minute,' he apologised; and did not continue until he had finished with his whore, and pushed her aside. 'Yes,' he nodded, as he began to dress, 'I too have been offered the gift you wish to spurn – and the doubt it fills you with, has filled my thoughts as well.'

'How was it, then, you met with a blood-drinker?' Robert asked.

'Upon my travels.' But Lord Rochester did not elaborate, buckling on his sword instead, and leading the way down the stairs. He paused by the door to toss the madam some coins. He gestured towards Savile, who lay snoring on a couch. 'See that he is returned home.' He left two further coins upon the table, then passed into the street.

'Should we not see him home ourselves?' Robert asked.

'We have more pressing business.'

'Why, what would you do?'

'Seek a resolution, perhaps, that you need not have the choice between failing your parents' memory, or growing a drinker of your unborn children's blood.'

'You do not understand. There is no resolution.'

Lord Rochester raised his hand. 'Come,' he said, 'there will be time enough to discuss these matters on the way. Yet I believe, in your case, that there may be hope after all. For you are not yet like me, whose every pleasure seems jaded and flat. You might still be content with the ... simple ... things in life.'

Robert remembered his dream of Lady Castlemaine. He shrugged faintly. 'I feel my delight in them already start to fade.'

'Then there is all the more urgency that you find an abiding happiness before you kill the prospect dead. You must leave London at once – you must redeem Mistress Vaughan.' As he said this, Lord Rochester gazed around impatiently. They had returned to the Milford Stairs, where the boat they had arrived in was still bobbing upon the tide. Lord Rochester approached the boatman; he whispered in his ear, then took his place upon the cushions in the prow. Robert joined him. At the same moment, the boatman shouted orders: the moorings were slipped; the boat drifted out into the darkness of the Thames. 'Mortlake!' Lord Rochester directed. He turned back to Robert. 'For who better to direct you on your journey than *Madame la Marquise*!' As he spoke, the boat began to turn; and the oarsmen to strain as they rowed against the tide.

'THE FASHION HAS EVER BEEN, FOR OLD WOMEN AND MAIDS TO
TELL FABULOUS STORIES AT THE NIGHT-TIME, OF SPRIGHTS AND
WALKING OF GHOSTS.'
John Aubrey, *The Natural History of Wiltshire*

The militiaman stirred and rose from his fire. As he did so, there was a crackling of sparks, so that he almost sat down beside it again, convinced that it must have been the spitting he had heard; for he could not imagine who might be abroad at such an ungodly hour, in such weather, and upon such a lonely and ill-omened road. But he supposed it was his duty to make certain; and so he reached for his sword. He swung open the stable door. He could make out nothing through the gale-lashed sleet. He shuddered. It was on just such a night as this before, he thought, that the dead man had been seen; and he would not be surprised, so terrible was the storm, to see any number of demons risen from their graves.

Reluctantly, he gathered his cloak about him, then slithered down the muddy bank to where the barricades had been raised. Again he peered into the darkness, and again could see nothing but the icy rain. He turned, about to hurry back to his shelter, when he heard a sudden splashing from the road ahead. 'Who goes there?' he shouted, his voice raw and hoarse with fear and the cold.

The splashing was unmistakable now: someone – or something – was approaching through the mud.

The militiaman cowered behind the barricade, his sword shaking as he held it aloft. He could see a form through the sleet now, and then a second – horsemen, cloaked and hooded against the screaming of the gale. The first reined in his horse by the barricade; and the militiaman, gazing up in terror, could see nothing of his face but the gleaming of his eyes.

The horseman leaned forward in his saddle. 'Raise the barrier,' he commanded, 'we wish to pass.'

The voice had seemed young, and the militiaman felt some of his courage return. He tightened his grip around the hilt of his sword. 'There has been plague in the village,' he announced.

'Plague?' The horseman seemed to frown. 'Is it abated now?'

'Praise be to God, it does appear to be dying.'

'Then let us pass.'

'I have my orders not to allow anyone through.'

The horseman turned in his saddle and glanced at his companion, who had ridden up to join him at the barricade. 'We are seeking shelter.' A woman's voice. The militiaman stared up at her in surprise. Her eyes were brighter and colder than her companion's, and even the pallor of her face appeared to gleam like snow. 'Do not hinder us,' she whispered. She paused. 'It would not be wise.'

Bitter the storm had been all night, and icy the wind; but the militiaman had not imagined that his blood might feel so frozen until that moment, so deathly seemed her voice. Despite himself, he lowered his sword. 'I shall have to inform my commanding officer,' he muttered as he began to fumble with the lock on the barricade.

'Do as you must,' the woman said.

The militiaman shuddered again beneath her stare, and hurried to swing open the gates. He paused as the horsemen prepared to ride through. 'There is a dead man abroad,' he stammered suddenly. 'The man who brought the plague, he has risen from his grave.'

The riders glanced at each other. 'This report is certain?' the young man asked.

The militiaman choked back his emotions, and nodded violently. 'My friend was on duty last night. He was surprised by the man, attacked, and is even now grievous sick. You may discover your own fate if you wish to seek my friend out, for he lies confined to his room in the village ahead. But if you know what is best for you, you will leave here now and never come back.'

The two travellers did not reply, but shook out their reins, and began to continue along the track which led into the village. The militiaman watched them until they had been swallowed again by the sleet; then he turned and began slithering in the opposite direction, happy for the chance to seek his officers out.

'This is truly all the food you have?' Robert asked.

The tiny servant girl shook, and wrung her hands. 'I am sorry, sir,' she stammered, 'but we have had no travellers here, not since the plague was arrived. And we had no men in the fields to gather the corn, and all the shepherds are dead, and all the herdsmen too . . .' Her voice trailed away.

Robert studied her. She seemed as bare of flesh as the plate of bones was before him. He reached out to calm the writhing of her hands; they felt impossibly thin. 'It is no matter,' he said. 'Please . . .' He pushed the plate forward. 'Eat it yourself.'

The girl stared at him uncertainly while, from beside him, his companion snorted. Robert turned to face her. 'You have no objection, I assume, Madame – seeing as how you refreshed yourself – what? – no more than two hours ago.'

The Marquise smiled faintly. 'No objection at all,' she murmured. She watched as the girl, hesitantly at first and then with increasing desperation, sucked on the bones. 'It is best, after all, she be fattened up.'

At the same moment there came the sudden sound of hooves from the yard outside, and the jingling of spurs. The girl wiped at her mouth and rose hurriedly to her feet. She stared nervously at the door as the sound of footsteps began to splash towards it through the mud. 'These past months,' she whispered, 'we have had no travellers, and now all this number on the single night . . .' She scurried across the room, but before she could reach the door it was swung open by a man with an upraised sword, and a cloth bound fast across his nostrils and mouth.

The stranger bowed to the Marquise. 'Madam.' Then to Robert. 'Sir. You will oblige me, please, by rising to your feet and going promptly on your way.'

The Marquise remained perfectly still; Robert, however, slowly pushed back his chair and rose to his feet. 'Why,' he asked, after a pause, 'do you not recognise me, Colonel Sexton?'

The Colonel narrowed his eyes, then took a step forward. 'In the name of our dear Saviour,' he whispered, lowering both the cloth and his sword, 'it is not . . . it cannot be . . . not John Foxe's boy?'

Robert inclined his head. 'The very same,' he replied.

'But . . .' Colonel Sexton studied him more closely, then shook his head. 'You are wondrously changed.'

'You, however, I perceive, are not.'

The Colonel gazed down at his militiaman's sash. 'It is true,' he nodded wryly, 'I have survived in my post, despite the restoration of His Majesty.'

'I am very glad to hear it. My father did not.'

'No.' Colonel Sexton bowed his head. 'He was one of the first to die, I believe, of the plague?'

'Plague?' Robert asked, startled.

'When it first broke out in Woodton.'

'Who told you such a thing?'

'Why, Sir Henry Vaughan.'

Robert smiled grimly. 'Did he indeed?'

'What, you mean . . . he did not tell the truth?'

Robert did not answer. 'The plague?' he asked, after a pause. 'When is it supposed to have arrived?'

'It was brought by that foreigner, Faustus, or so I was told – from Bohemia. So it would have been in Woodton – oh – these past four years.'

'And you are certain it was plague?'

Colonel Sexton frowned with puzzlement. 'I have not been into the village myself, it is true, for there is a quarantine practised there – set in place by request of Sir Henry. But I see no reason why it would not be the plague.'

'Was there any proof given of it?'

'Indeed, yes.' Colonel Sexton lowered himself on to the bench and, as he did so, instinctively raised the cloth up to his mouth. 'Some months ago,' he said, in a low, urgent voice, 'a man escaped Woodton, and fled as far as here. He never travelled further, for he was laid low, and soon all this village too was infected by his sickness. And that is why – with all respect – I must ask you to leave, for if you do not I shall be compelled to include you in the quarantine.'

'We have a pass,' said Robert, reaching inside his cloak.

Colonel Sexton took it; his frown deepened as he studied it. 'It is signed in the name of the King,' he said. He tossed it back across the table. 'I am certain your father would have been very pleased, Robert, to know in what high circles you would grow up to mix.'

Robert smiled faintly, but did not reply.

'Very well,' said Colonel Sexton, rising again to his feet, 'since I cannot prevent you, you may continue on your way. But I would advise you not to linger here for long, nor to visit Woodton. The plague, it would seem, is not finished yet.'

'One of your own soldiers, I believe, fell sick with it last night?'

'As you say,' nodded the Colonel, pausing by the door, 'one of my own soldiers.'

'And is it true,' asked Robert, 'that he saw that man from Woodton, who first brought the plague here?'

Colonel Sexton paused. 'That man has long been dead,' he replied at length.

'Your soldiers told me he had been seen risen from his grave.'

'My soldiers have been on duty in this place of death too long.'

'You do not believe their testimony, then?'

Colonel Sexton swung open the door. He stood for a moment in silence, then inclined his head. 'Goodnight, my boy,' he said. 'Madam.' He turned, and left; and his footsteps were soon lost upon the screaming of the wind. There was a brief splashing of horse's hooves – and then nothing but the gale and the drumming of the sleet.

'This vile weather,' shivered the Marquise. 'Who would be out on such a night?'

'Who, indeed? Only monsters and ghouls.'

The Marquise smiled faintly as she rose to her feet. 'I shall not be long.'

Robert nodded. 'I shall wait for you in our room.' He watched the Marquise glide out into the yard; then he rose and asked the servant girl to lead him to his bed. She nodded wordlessly. Her arms were shaking, Robert saw, as she lifted up the torch and began to creep like a mouse along a dark, unlit corridor. He wondered what was scaring her; but then he looked about him and realised that the girl had been speaking the simple truth, that the inn must indeed have been empty for months. Cobwebs hung everywhere, compounded with the mould; doors were bolted and boarded across; many of the floorboards were rotten through. 'I have given you the only fit room,' said the servant girl timidly as she climbed up the stairs. 'It looks out over the yard. That way you may see if anyone . . .' Her voice, as it always seemed ready to do, trailed away. She paused by a door. It was shiny with rottenness. The room beyond it too smelt strongly of mould, but the bed had been prepared and the sheets looked clean; and Robert had been riding since early that day.

'Will it serve, sir?'

Robert nodded. He reached into his purse, and tossed the servant girl a coin. For he did not doubt that he had, as she had claimed, the best room in the inn.

The girl took the coin. She curtsied, and turned, then

lingered by the door. 'The . . . the . . .'

Robert looked up at her. 'Yes?' he asked. 'You have something to say?'

The girl swallowed and tried to speak again. 'The man . . .' she stammered at last. 'The man . . . who had the plague . . . he *is* risen from the dead. The Colonel – he would not admit it . . . but it is true . . . I saw him . . .' She shuddered, and rocked herself to and fro. 'I saw him last night.'

'Where?'

'He was in the yard.'

'Might you not have been mistaken?'

'No, no . . . I knew him. His face . . . I saw it, it . . . it . . . *gleamed*.'

Suddenly she began to sob. Robert crossed to her, and took her bony body in his arms. He thought it would fall to pieces, so thin and fragile it seemed. 'I wish . . .' the maid gasped, 'I wish . . . I could leave this place.' Then she broke from his arms, and turned, and ran. He heard her footsteps clattering down the stairs.

Robert continued motionless until they had faded quite away, and there was no sound at all save that of the gale. He frowned, then crossed to a window, and unbolted the shutters. A gust of icy rain was swept into his face. He sheltered his eyes, then leaned out to survey the yard. It seemed empty: a quagmire of water and mud. Beyond it, he could just make out the shadow of the church, half-veiled behind the storm-swept yews of the graveyard. He stared as hard as he could, but could make out none of the graves themselves. He wondered if one of them might truly be empty. He gazed around the yard again; then closed the shutters. There was still no sound but that of the wind. Robert stood frozen a moment, then

he drew out his sword. He laid it beside him as he retired
to his bed.

❧

'. . . CHAOS, THAT REIGNS HERE
IN DOUBLE NIGHT OF DARKNESS, AND OF SHADES . . .'
                                John Milton, *Comus*

R obert slept badly. He dreamed that spiders, black-
spotted and filled with poison, were scuttling over
him, breeding and spreading until all the room was submerged beneath their webs, and he could no longer
breathe, so heavy was their weight. He awoke in a sweat;
and as he did so, thought he heard footsteps from the
yard outside. He hurried to the window, and unbolted it
again; but the yard still seemed empty and so, after a
lengthy wait, Robert returned to his bed. He closed his
eyes; but he could not be certain now whether he was
sleeping or awake. For he imagined he heard footsteps on
the stairway outside, and then a scrabbling at the door;
yet when he crossed to open it, there was no one to be
seen. Rats, Robert thought, falling back into his bed; and
then gradually there were rats all about him, with
sharp-pointed, envenomed teeth, and they were breeding
just as the spiders had done – and Robert knew it was a
dream, even as he felt their weight pressing down upon
his chest. He struggled for breath, and opened his eyes.
At the same moment, there came the sound of footsteps
in the yard. This time, Robert was certain he had heard
them; and then suddenly, from downstairs, there rose a
girl's piercing scream.

Robert grabbed his cloak and sword. He sped from the

room, and as he hurried down the stairs he heard a second, longer scream. 'No!' the girl shrieked. 'No!'; and then she spoke a word that Robert was certain he must have misheard. He flung open the door which led into the dining hall. The tiny servant girl was cowering in the corner of the room, an expression of numbed terror on her face, her finger pointing at the doorway to the yard. The door itself was swinging in the gale and, as he looked at it, Robert saw how its lock had been smashed. He crossed to it, he stared out into the night. The sleet had grown thicker, and he could see nothing at all beyond a couple of feet. He turned back to the servant girl, who was still cowering in the corner, the look of horror frozen on her face. Robert crossed to her. 'What was it?' he asked her gently. 'For I believe that I must have misheard your cry.'

She gazed up at him. 'You did not,' she whispered at last.

Robert breathed in deeply. He bent down, and took her hands.

'My father ...' She swallowed, and stopped. 'He has been dead this half year. Dead of the plague.'

Robert rocked her in his arms. 'Are you certain, then,' he whispered, 'that it was indeed your father whom you saw?'

'He looked,' she whispered, 'just as when I buried him.'

Robert stared at her a moment more; then rose to his feet again. He handed the girl his dagger. 'Secure the door,' he told her, 'as well as you can. Let no one in. *No one.*' He took her by the arm, and led her across to the hearth. 'Light a fire, and stay by it. Do not leave it on any account. Do you promise me?'

The girl nodded dumbly. Robert smiled at her with a show of confidence he did not truly feel; then turned, and hurried outside. As he entered the yard, he heard the door slam shut behind him and bolts being drawn. He paused for a second, then began to splash his way across the yard. The mud sucked like a glue on his feet, and soon his boots were so clogged that he could barely lift them forward. He stopped to clean them; and as he bent down to scrape the mud off his heel, he thought he saw a sudden gleam of something moving through the rain. He pointed his sword, then slowly crept forward. There was a low stone wall running ahead of him. Robert reached it, and peered over its top. He could just make out a jumble of graves through the rain, with the yews beyond them, and the squat form of the church. He stared about him, then pulled himself up to the top of the wall. He could see now that one of the graves had been desecrated: soil had been scattered in mounds around the headstone, and the coffin half-dragged up from the excavated trench. Robert jumped from the wall; he crossed to the grave. The coffin-lid had been smashed open; the coffin itself was empty, and the trench was too, save for muddied, sodden strips of winding sheet. Robert frowned. He bent forward, and studied the headstone. As he had suspected, the date on it was recent. The cause of death was given – the plague.

Suddenly, Robert heard a splashing from behind him and, before he could turn round, felt hands about his neck. He swung back his elbow; he felt it hit something soft, and then he was wriggling and twisting free. He spun round. There was a dark form standing above him. Robert stabbed with his sword, but his assailant was already fleeing through the graves, its arm across its eyes.

As he staggered to his feet, the creature paused once and stared back at him. Its face was a corpse's, stupid and rotted, with yellow eyes which seemed utterly dead. It might have been one of the soldiers, Robert thought, who had marched on Woodton at Faustus' back, save that the gleam of its skin seemed blackened with spots, and he supposed such sores were the mark of the plague. The creature turned again, as though afraid to be watched, and vanished into the darkness. Robert stumbled and slipped across the graves, but when he reached the place where he had last seen the creature, there was nothing but a bog of jumbled footprints. He cursed, and followed what appeared to be the freshest track. It led him to the yews. Their shelter was dank and dripping, but he welcomed it nevertheless. As he looked about him, the darkness seemed even more pitch than before. Robert crept onwards. He could see a light now, and it took him a moment to realise that it was coming from the inn. He bent forward further, and strained to see the door.

Then he felt a hand again, this time on his shoulder. 'It is bolted,' said a voice, 'for I only just now tried to enter there myself.'

Slowly, Robert turned to look round.

A figure, black-hooded, was standing behind him. Her face was pale like that of a moon feebly shining through the clouds.

'Milady,' he whispered.

She lowered her hood. He saw, beneath her cloak, that she wore a man's riding habit. She had put her hair up, with only a single curl escaping across her cheek, so that her beautiful face, like her costume, might seem more like a boy's. It was also hard, and very cold.

'Why have you pursued me?' he asked.

'Why did you abandon me?' she replied.

'I discovered . . .' – Robert licked his lips – 'the nature of the Marquise's interest in Miss Malet – the attraction that a bloodline has to your kind.'

'What of it?' Milady shrugged faintly. 'I would have told you myself in due time.'

'I do not believe you,' said Robert, after a moment's pause. 'For you knew, once I learned of it, that I would never persist with my intention to grow into a creature like yourself.' He smiled coldly. 'And so it has turned out.'

'And yet you fled to the Marquise?' Milady stared at him in disbelief; and Robert thought he saw, mingled in her expression, pain as well. He brushed past her, though, and did not meet her eye. 'We do not have time to stand here,' he said. 'Did you not see the creature I was pursuing?'

'Creature?' asked Milady. 'I saw no creature.'

Robert glanced back at her with a frown. 'Is it not one of your powers, that you can sense such things?'

She stared about the graveyard, and her nostrils flared. 'It may be,' she said at length, 'that the gale is too strong.'

'The Marquise's powers, though, would not be so feeble as yours?'

'Feeble?' echoed Milady bitterly. 'What is this, Lovelace, that you reproach me for being weak in those very qualities which have also made you hate me?'

Robert continued to walk forward. 'I did not say,' he murmured, without looking round, 'that I hated you.'

'Why then did you flee me?'

'Because . . .'

Milady seized Robert's arm and forced him to stop.

'Because . . .' he said again, and at last he met her eye, 'so far from hating you, Milady . . .'

'Yes?' she asked. Her eyes seemed bright with anger now. She reached for Robert's face; she dug her nails into his cheeks. 'Yes?' she hissed again. 'So far from hating me – what?'

Robert looked past her at the sleet-pounded graves. 'We do not have the time for this,' he said, trying to shrug off her grip. 'There is a deadly danger abroad.'

Milady's fingernails gouged even deeper into his cheeks. 'Then I am all the more insulted, that you did not ask me to share it with you.'

'How could I have done?' cried Robert. 'I knew, after what I discovered at the ball, that to grow a creature like you is to be worse than damned. At least I might be confident with the Marquise, that she would never succeed in persuading me to enter such a Hell.'

'Why not, Lovelace?'

'You know why not.'

'I want you to tell me. I want – I need – to hear it from your lips.'

'Because the Marquise ...' Robert paused; he pulled Milady's hands from his face, and turned away to stare at the church. 'Because the Marquise means nothing to me.'

Milady breathed in deeply.

'That is why,' said Robert distantly, 'I was persuaded to ask for her help by my Lord of Rochester, who also, it seems, knows something of a blood-drinker's love, how overwhelming – how dangerous – how tempting it can be. For he himself, he told me, was once offered what you have offered me.'

Milady nodded to herself. 'Yes,' she murmured, 'then that might explain it, the strangeness in him that I felt ...' She looked up sharply. 'Who was it,' she asked, 'who gave him such a chance?'

'He did not tell me the name. A Turk, I believe, whom my Lord Rochester had met upon the road during the course of his travels. And it was by means of this Turk that he also met the Marquise, for he had been given a letter of introduction to her. He therefore knew of her interests, and her powers. He took me to her, that night after the Palace masquerade. And so it was that we have travelled here together – the Marquise and I – alone.'

'With the intention, I presume, of seeking your revenge?'

'Of course,' said Robert sharply.

'Against a spirit whom the Marquise believes to be divine?' Milady laughed. 'And have you told her, Lovelace, that it is your ambition to destroy this god of hers?'

Robert shrugged. 'She is not interested in my motives. She cares only that I was spared – that I wear, in her own phrase, the stamp of the Devil – for she believes that it marks me as somehow his creature: that I am suited to guide her, and lead her before him.'

'And is that not what you may indeed achieve?'

'So I must hope. For we both need each other. Our motives may be different – but our object is the same.'

Milady smiled, and shook her head in mocking disbelief.

'What else could I have done?' asked Robert in sudden anger. 'For I am mortal; whereas she is a creature of terrible powers. I need her help. I had no other choice.'

'No other choice?'

Robert met her stare; he did not reply.

Milady paused. 'And when you both reach your object,' she asked at length, 'what then?' She paused a second time; and the mocking smile began to fade from her lips. 'But I am feeble, of course,' she whispered with sudden bitterness, 'compared to the Marquise.'

Robert gazed at her for a moment, then sighed and turned away. As he did so, Milady reached out and laid her hands upon his cheeks again, so that he had no choice but to stare back into her eyes. They were glittering brightly – with anger, Robert thought, until she leaned across and spoke into his ear. 'Lovelace.' Her voice seemed not angry at all, but urgent, almost sad. 'Why do you fear me?' she whispered. 'Can you not understand?'

'Understand?'

'Why, yes.' She smiled. 'That it is as a mortal I shall ever love you best.' Milady continued to hold him for a moment; then kissed him suddenly on the brow and turned away. She gazed about her and shivered, as though only now made aware of the pounding of the rain, still beating upon the branches of the yew trees overhead. She raised her hood, and turned back to Robert. 'If you want my help, then you have only to ask. Otherwise I shall leave you at once. Decide, Lovelace. Decide it now.'

He stood frozen for a moment. Her stare was golden and very deep; he imagined he would sink into it, as he had done that first time, when he had lain upon her lap and felt her cool hand on his brow, that time in the carriage, leaving the stones. He stared into the darkness; then shook his head suddenly, and crossed to her. 'I saw a corpse,' he said. He took her arm. 'A corpse, out there somewhere, risen from the dead.'

Milady nodded faintly. 'Then I should be able to discover it.' She stepped forward from the yews. She sniffed the wind; she frowned, and shook her head. Robert joined her and suddenly saw, ahead of him, a second empty grave. He pointed; then, as he walked forward to inspect it, discovered a third and began to run.

There were emptied graves all around him, all about the church. He gazed with horror at the shattered coffins, at the shreds of winding cloth flapping in the gale.

Milady tensed suddenly.

'What is it?' Robert asked. 'Is something there?'

Milady angled her head. Still breathing in the gale, she crossed to the wall, and then walked along its side as far as the gate. She turned back to Robert. 'The Marquise,' she whispered, 'where did she go?'

'To seek out a restorative, after our long journey.'

'Then I dread to think . . .' She smelt the air again. 'Quick!'

Robert stared at her in surprise, but Milady did not pause to explain. Instead, she led the way beneath the church porch and then out towards the inn yard. There was a sudden sound of something splashing through mud. 'There!' cried Milady. She pointed, and Robert saw a dead thing, and then another, both slouching along the side of the churchyard wall. Their eyes were gleaming; and behind their blackened, shredded lips, broken teeth were bared in a snarl. Then one of them was suddenly upon him; and Robert thought, as the weight of the creature knocked him to the ground, how impossibly fast it had moved. But he had only a second to make such a reflection, for the creature's jaws were opened wide now and its yellow saliva was dripping on his face, blinding him for a moment so that he could only smell, not see, its hungry, searching mouth. Its breath was diseased, foul with rottonness and mud; and Robert put up a hand to ward it away. He touched the thing's face, gripping it tightly, until the flesh seemed to ooze beneath his fingers; but he could not halt its descent, and its weight pushed his arm ever back into the mud. He blinked desperately, and opened his eyes to find he was staring straight into the creature's own. The gleam of their hunger was terrible now; and yet, as Robert looked, so the fire seemed to fade, and then suddenly the eyes were stilled, frozen cold and dead. Robert felt the creature's grip slacken about his throat. He struggled free; and as he did so, he remembered how the other dead thing, in the graveyard, had also cowered before his gaze. Robert rose to his feet and, pulling out his sword, stabbed down hard into the creature's chest. It writhed and screamed, and tried to crawl away. He stabbed down again, and this time felt his sword puncture something soft and engorged. A black liquid bubbled up from the wound. It slipped thickly across the creature's chest, and ebbed into the mud.

'You have found its heart. It is over now.'

Robert turned. Milady was standing beside him. Her cloak was torn; her hair dishevelled and streaming in the wind. With one hand, she smoothed back her tresses; with the other, gestured at a second body lying in the mud. Robert crossed to it. He recognised the bejewelled hilt of Milady's dagger, protruding from the creature's chest. He bent down and drew it out, then cleaned it on his cloak and handed it back to her. As though distracted, she ran her thumb along the blade. 'At first,' she murmured distantly, 'he would not obey me.' She gathered her cloak about her, and stared down at the corpse. 'It was very' – she raised an eyebrow – 'very strange.'

'It is unusual,' Robert asked, 'that these dead things do not obey your commands?'

Milady nodded. 'It is an unparalleled event. Why, Lovelace, do you remain such a leveller that you have not yet understood the nature of the world? Have you not witnessed for yourself how the greater rules the lesser, the master the slave, in a chain of being that extends without end?' Her eyes glittered, though whether with mockery or earnestness, Robert could not be sure. 'This creature' – she nudged the corpse with her toe – 'should have cowered before my merest glance.' She paused. 'Yet he did not.' She started suddenly, gazing towards the stables. 'And so it is, I am afraid for the Marquise.'

She delayed no further, but hurried at once across the yard. There was something lying by the stable door. Milady bent down beside it; Robert joined her where the Marquise was slumped, eyes closed, body twisted, on the straw. Milady pulled out her dagger from her cloak, then drew the blade across her wrist. A delicate line of blood welled up from the cut; she held the wound to the Marquise's lips. 'She is drinking,' she nodded to herself. The Marquise stirred, and moaned. Suddenly she bent double; she clutched at the straw, then moaned again as she began to vomit. She muttered something unintelligible; then bent over again. Her vomit, as it dribbled across the straw, was viscous and black; like the blood, Robert thought, which had risen from the dead thing's punctured heart.

'What was it?' Milady whispered. 'What did you drink?'

'The blood,' gasped the Marquise. 'I do not know how, but it is venomous.'

'What!' Milady exclaimed. 'You did not drink from those risen things?'

The Marquise retched again; then nodded faintly. 'I would not have done,' she gasped, 'save that I was curious, for when I met with the creatures they would not at first obey my commands, and so I wished to taste them, to make certain what kind of thing they were. See!' She held up her hand. In the darkness, Robert could see faint pock-marks, disfiguring the marble whiteness of the skin. 'The blood sprayed me,' whispered the Marquise, 'when I cut through their throats, and its touch burned like quicksilver.'

Milady was gazing at her in astonishment. 'So you have never met with their breed before?' she asked. 'You do not know how it is that they are risen from their graves?'

The Marquise reached for Milady's wrist, and licked at it again. 'Tadeus spoke of such creatures,' she said at last, 'which he had seen infesting a village in Bohemia.'

'And where had they come from?' Robert asked.

'Tadeus claimed' – the Marquise pursed her thin lips – 'that they had been imbued with the breath of the Evil One.'

'And was he right?' Milady asked.

The Marquise waved with her hand. 'You have seen the creatures out there.'

'Then the man . . .' – Robert swallowed – 'the man with the plague who came from my village . . .'

'Was no man,' answered the Marquise. 'Nor, though they may once have been, are the other creatures now risen from their graves.' She struggled to her feet. 'We must destroy them,' she whispered hoarsely. 'For they are dangerous and strange; and their numbers, I fear, are growing all the time.'

At that very moment there rose a noise like that of fists hammering on wood, and a distant shriek. The hammering came again and Robert, who had walked out from the stable, pointed to the inn. 'I left a girl inside there,' he said. He narrowed his eyes. The storm was fading now, and dark forms could just be made out through the haze of the drizzle. Several were gathered around the inn door; others had climbed the roof, and could be seen crawling like slugs towards the shuttered windows. Robert began to run across the yard. There was a sudden splintering, and the door was left hanging from a single hinge. Robert heard a sobbing wail from inside; the creatures were starting to pass through the doorway. 'No!' he cried out. 'No!' The creatures turned at his scream, then they froze. Robert glanced back; the Marquise and Milady were both by his side, and for a moment he thought it was they, mistresses of the night, who must have petrified the dead things so; but then he took a step forward and, as he saw the creatures shrink and bow their heads, he realised with a shock that they were cowering before himself.

He glanced back again. The Marquise was frowning now; but her eyes, as she watched him, appeared eager and bright, as though with suspicions either roused or confirmed. Robert wondered what she might be thinking; but before he could ask, there came another scream, desperate now, from beyond the door, and he spun round and drew out his sword. He ran through the mud towards the crowd of the dead. They gibbered softly, and fell back before him, covering their eyes with their blackened, rotting hands.

Robert reached the shattered door, and ran inside; as he did so, he heard a cry from the far end of the room. The servant girl was crouching there, by the side of the fire, just as he had ordered her to do; and three of the dead things, in a ring, were watching her. One of them had been creeping forward; it tensed, then leapt. The girl stared at it dumbly, too terrified to shriek, even as it seized her by the throat and began to squeeze. 'No,' she choked suddenly, 'no, please, please – Father.' Then her eyes widened; she had seen Robert. 'Father!' she cried again, despairingly now, as the creature stiffened and then staggered, run through by Robert's sword. It turned and reached out, as though to throttle its attacker; but it met Robert's stare and staggered again, backwards, into the hearth. Immediately, it was enveloped by fire. The flames spread across the creature as though its skin had been coated in pitch; and within seconds its body was a twisting, writhing torch. The creature tried to scream; but its lips and mouth, and all its flesh were melting fast, and no sound came forth but a soft, hissing sigh. It stumbled forward; then began to collapse into a bubbling soup, so that soon its human form had been utterly lost, and there was nothing left but a sticky pool of guts, which hissed and turned to steam as it spread across the floor.

'Excellently done,' smiled the Marquise. She brushed Robert aside, and seized a burning log from the fireplace. She held it before her as though it were a poisonous snake; and as she advanced on them, the two remaining creatures began to whimper and grow maddened, for they were trapped against the wall. A single touch: the flames enclosed them both; the flesh, as before, began to melt across the flagstones. The Marquise smiled thinly. 'It has ever been the surest way,' she nodded, 'and the easiest, to dispose of such trash.' She glanced out of the window. A pale light was dawning, through the drizzle. 'Come,' she said. 'This is a business we must finish, before we continue on our way.'

She asked the servant girl for tapers and lamps, which she ordered to be lit. When they had been prepared, she led the way outside. The yard was empty. Robert stared about him in despair, but the Marquise smiled, and gestured towards the eastern sky, where streaks of orange and pink were breaking through the cloud. 'These creatures, it would seem, are not so deadly that they relish the day.' She narrowed her eyes as she stared at the graveyard. 'It would have made our task harder, had it not been so.'

The Marquise led the way across to the church, then paused as she stared about her at the graves. 'Here,' she said, pointing, and crossing to one where the coffin had been smashed. A creature lay curled up in the grave, half-covered by soil but still scrabbling at the trench's sides, so that more earth might fall and conceal him wholly from the light. The Marquise lit a taper; then bent down, and seized the creature's wrist. As though its fingers were trails of gunpowder, she touched each one; then rose to her feet to watch her handiwork. The melting flesh bubbled and oozed up through the soil. 'See how it is mingled with the mud,' the Marquise whispered, 'to form a single compound of liquid dust.' She gazed about her. 'Soon, all this place will be thick with such a slime.' She brought a scented cloth up to her nose; then crossed with her lantern to a second grave.

As she had promised, the business was soon finished. Within the hour, three cloaked and hooded horsemen were passing the barricades, taking the road which led towards Woodton and leaving behind them a village calm like death. A stench, greasy and charred, hung above the grave-yard; but nothing moved there, nor disturbed the foggy air.

⤫⦿⤬

'. . . SIGHTS OF WOE,
REGIONS OF SORROW, DOLEFUL SHADES, WHERE PEACE
AND REST CAN NEVER DWELL, HOPE NEVER COMES
THAT COMES TO ALL.'

John Milton, Paradise Lost

'It was on this same spot,' said Robert. He stood frozen in the shadow of the giant stone and seemed almost to hear, in the icy stillness, the imagined creaking of a rope in a breeze, the dripping of blood upon a risen, monstrous form . . . He shuddered, and looked about him. 'And yet now,' he said loudly, 'there is nothing here.'

'Nothing?' murmured the Marquise.

'Nothing.' Robert crossed back to his horse. He did not mention the fear in his stomach, faint but inexpressibly sweet, which had touched him the moment he entered Stonehenge. He glanced at Milady. She was twisting a bracelet round and round her wrist; while beside her, the Marquise sat rigidly still. Both, Robert thought with a shock, appeared as unsettled as himself, and he wondered what they knew, or might have sensed, to make them so; for he had never imagined that either might grow afraid.

He spurred his horse forward, not wanting to linger among the stones, not now, not so close to journey's end. Emily. *Emily.* But though he sought to fill his mind with memories of his friend, the terror in his stomach did not fade, and as he approached the wood beyond which Woodton lay, the bare winter trees, and the darkness of their shadows, filled him with foreboding, so that he could barely hold the reins in his hands, and he had to pause, to steady his grip. The Marquise and Milady both halted beside him. All three gazed in silence at the road ahead, as it passed into the wood and was lost amidst the fog.

'I hid amongst those trees once,' said Robert, 'from a horseman swathed in black, whose face was so dreadful it still haunts my dreams.' He rode slowly forward, until he could feel the first damp shadow of a bough overhead. He shivered, and halted again. 'What will we find there,' he whispered, 'beyond the trees?'

The Marquise glanced at him sharply. 'You are the one who has seen Him risen.'

'You still affirm, then, it was indeed the Evil One?'

'Evil?' The Marquise smiled contemptuously. 'There is nothing good or evil, but terror makes it so.'

'Yes, and I remember that Faustus argued the same. But he was rendered into dust for all that, and lost upon the wind.'

'Faustus knew much – but he did not know all.'

'And you – can you be so certain that you do?'

The Marquise stared distantly ahead. 'I do not know all,' she acknowledged at last, 'for if I did, then I would be like a god myself, and not need to continue along this road. Yet what I do know, I trust, will be sufficient to guard us and spare us from the fate of Tadeus.'

'Tell me, then,' said Robert, 'for I would not have any more secrets kept from me.'

The Marquise shook her head. 'What I *can* reveal is of no matter now – and what I *need* to reveal, I do not yet know.' She formed her thin lips into an icy smile. 'I am sorry.' Then she spurred her horse forward, and was lost almost at once amidst the fog and the trees. Robert glanced at Milady; she smiled back faintly at him, then she too began to ride into the wood. Still he sat frozen in his saddle. He could feel his fear now risen in a sweat upon his brow: clammy and grey, like the dripping fog. He wiped at it with his hand; sat frozen for a moment more; then shook out his reins and began along the track.

At first all seemed still, and he imagined he was entering that kingdom of the dead, black with mists and formless wraiths, of which he had read in the legends of the Ancients. He remembered the night when Hannah's body had been found; and how he had imagined then that

Hell was formed not of flames, but of ice. Who was to say he had been wrong, he thought – and that he was not indeed on the road to Hell now? Then suddenly, from ahead of him, there rose a muffled voice; and Robert felt a shiver of relief for, although it had sounded contemptuous and angry, it had seemed mortal at least. A militia post, he decided, remembering the guard from the night before. He felt within his cloak for the royal pass. He could see figures ahead of him now, and a barrier – not makeshift as the one the previous night had been, but tall and fortified with brambles and stakes. It did not just block the path, he realised, but formed a stockade for as far as he could see. He wheeled in his horse, and stared up at the gate. Four soldiers were standing along its top. One of them was shouting at the Marquise to go away. Robert recognised the man at once: Elijah Brockman, one of Sir Henry's labourers, whom Emily had once seen at Wolverton Hall. As Robert inspected him, he realised with a shock that Elijah was not dressed as a militiaman at all, but in strange, rusted armour and tattered, rotting clothes. Robert had not seen such a uniform for a long while – not since that May Day all those years before, when soldiers had marched on Woodton and guarded the pyre where his mother had been burned.

'And yet,' he thought aloud, narrowing his eyes, 'they do not seem like the dead.'

The Marquise glanced at him. 'Nor are they,' she replied.

'Then what?'

'Mortals – mortals all. The merest trash.' She turned round, and gazed up at the guards. They were all shouting at her now, laughing and yelling abuse. One of them picked up a stone and flung it at her. The Marquise held up an arm to ward it away; and at once the soldiers fell deathly quiet; their faces grew white, their weapons clattered to the floor. The Marquise inclined her head, and the soldiers immediately scurried from their post. Robert heard the scraping of metal bolts; and then the two wooden gates were swung apart. The Marquise rode slowly through the gap. As she did so, she turned in her saddle and beckoned to the men. Like whipped school-children, they gathered about her, their eyes bright with fear. 'Now,' the Marquise purred, outstaring each guard in turn, 'tell me what your business is, locking honest travellers out?'

'Orders,' stammered Elijah. 'We ain't got no choice.' He turned to his comrades and appealed for support. They all began to shout at once. The Marquise raised a hand; silence was restored immediately. She pointed at Elijah with her riding crop. 'You,' she said. 'Whose orders?' She waited. She slashed, suddenly, with her whip across his cheek. As Elijah grovelled in the mud, she leaned from her saddle and whispered in his ear. 'I said, whose orders?'

'I . . .' Elijah licked his lips. 'Him,' he said at last, very suddenly. '*Him.*'

The Marquise smiled seraphically. 'And does – *He* – give you his orders himself? Can you lead me to *Him*?'

At this question, the soldiers' faces grew even paler than before. They stammered meaninglessly, as though filled with terror at the very idea.

The Marquise's smile grew all the broader. 'Your officer, then,' she asked. 'You do have one, I presume? Someone who receives – *His* – commands, and passes them on to you?'

'Oh, yes, yes,' the soldiers cried out at once.

'Very well.' The Marquise pointed her crop at Elijah again. 'Lead us to him. And the rest of you – you have orders – see you obey them well.'

She glanced round at her companions, and nodded; then spurred her horse forward as Elijah led the way. Robert and Milady followed her, riding side by side along the track. They wound through the trees; then emerged into the open; and before them stretched the plain again, and through the fog the first faint outline of the village. Robert trotted forward slowly. He had imagined the view had been forever branded on his memory; yet now he saw Woodton again, he barely recognised it. The fields all around it were charred; the buildings he could see appeared roofless and collapsed; the whole scene was one of the utmost desolation. He would have thought the village had indeed been wiped out by the plague – as Colonel Sexton had claimed – save that on the margins of the wood, and in the blackened fields, gangs of labourers were at work, lines of shivering, bone-thin slaves. Robert gazed at them closely: certainly, they did not seem infected with plague; nor indeed like the creatures of the previous night. But they were all shackled; and as they toiled, women and children as well as men, they would be struck by the whips of well-fed guards, uniformed just as the sentries had been. Robert sat frozen on his horse, staring in horror as a young girl was lashed until she cried, and fell motionless, and still she was lashed.

'Tell me,' he asked, beckoning Elijah, 'what has happened to Emily Vaughan?'

'Emily . . .' The soldier blanched. 'Why, sir' – he frowned, and narrowed his eyes – 'do you know of her?'

'Where is she?'

Elijah laughed suddenly, a cracked and mocking noise.

'There are those as can answer that much better than myself.' He laughed again, then spurred his horse along the road into the village.

Robert pursued him. 'What did you mean by that?' he cried angrily, seizing Elijah's reins.

The soldier stared back, his blackened teeth set in a grin, as though trying to restrain not mirth, but stupid fear. 'I'm just doing like what she told me to,' he shouted, waving at the Marquise. 'Taking you to my officer.' His grin faded suddenly. 'Ask him, if you want, about Emily Vaughan.'

Numbly, Robert let go of Elijah's reins. They were entering the village now. Robert glanced at the houses on either side of the road. Nettles filled their floors; their wooden beams were slimy with mould; brambles had covered what tumbled stones remained. Nor was abandonment the only mark of desolation, for often the ruin had been more deliberate. The trees which had lined the village road had all been sawn down, and their stumps painted with bitumen; and it took Robert a moment – gazing about him, wondering what was wrong – to realise that the very church was gone. He left the main road; galloped down the bank to where the church-yard had been. There was nothing left of it but shattered headstones and weeds; while on the ruins of the church itself he saw a gang of slaves working – tearing at piles of stone with their raw hands, or carrying and scattering the rubble across the fields. Many of the labourers Robert recognised. One of them was Jonas, Elijah's father. Yet a guard stood over him, brandishing a whip, wearing the uniform which Elijah too wore; and Robert wondered how it could be, that father and son were separated so.

He rode slowly back to rejoin his companions, who

were waiting for him on the village green. He shuddered to be approaching the place and Milady, seeing him come, rode across to him and reached out to touch his hand. Robert barely felt her; for he was imagining suddenly that he was surrounded by screaming faces, and that in the corner of the green two stakes had been prepared.

'Lovelace.' Milady touched his hand again.

Robert started. He rubbed his eyes. There were no stakes after all. But he realised that of all the places in Woodton, the green itself appeared unchanged, as though in memory of the decision that the villagers had made there, of the bargain they had struck. Robert wheeled his horse round slowly. He stared at where his parents' house had once stood. Not a trace remained of it: not a grass-covered mound, not a single brick. Instead, three gallows had been placed upon the site; and from each one, a gibbet filled with bones and dried guts swung.

'You should never have come back, Robert Foxe.'

Robert turned round in surprise.

Elijah laughed at him mirthlessly. 'Aye,' he nodded, 'I guessed it were you – for all you've grown a Cavalier. Well – it will not help you.' He nodded towards the gibbets. 'He has ever hated your family's memory, terrible he has, worse even than death.'

'He?'

'Aye,' Elijah nodded. He pointed, then cackled. 'Why, who did you think my officer was?'

Robert stared; then slowly followed Elijah as he led the way again along the road. But he had no need of a guide now: not along a path he knew so well. The Vaughans' house soon began to emerge from the fog. Robert observed that it still appeared well-maintained: its roof had not collapsed, and there were lights gleaming from inside its windows. Elijah swung down from his horse, and led the way in through the main door. The house, Robert thought as he followed inside, appeared much changed: not like a residence at all but rather like the Council Hall, where his father had worked. As Elijah paused by a door, Robert asked him to explain. 'We all live here now,' Elijah answered. ' 'Tis one of the rewards for the duties we perform.'

'And the others?' Robert asked. 'Your father, for instance? Where does he live?'

Elijah scowled, but did not reply. Instead he swung open the door, and stood aside. At the same moment, from the room beyond, there came a bellowed shout of indignation; and then, as Milady and the Marquise both glided inside, a sudden deathly silence. 'Ask him,' whispered Elijah in Robert's ear; then he turned, and was gone, and Robert passed through the doorway.

Sir Henry Vaughan was standing frozen by his desk, trapped within the glitter of Milady's stare. As Robert entered the room, he clenched his fists, and wrenched his gaze away; he turned to the newcomer; and as he did so his face, already pale, grew white. 'Ro ... Robert?' A muscle in his forehead pulsed, and the skin about his lips appeared a sickly blue.

'Where is Emily?' Robert asked softly.

Sir Henry staggered backwards against his desk. 'She ... she is dead,' he stammered.

'How?'

'We ...' He swallowed. 'There are ... rebels ... escaped – in the woods. She ... they killed her.'

'Why?'

Sir Henry paused. 'For food, no doubt.'

'You mean . . . ?'

Sir Henry licked his lips, and stared out of the window at the rubble-strewn fields. 'Food in Woodton is in very short supply.'

Robert gazed at him in horror and disbelief. Slowly, he crossed the room. 'What is this enclosure of Death you have fashioned here?' he whispered. He shuddered; and suddenly all the world appeared to swim, as he reached for Sir Henry's throat and flung him back against his desk. 'Tell me!' he shouted. 'What is happening here? Why are you making a Hell of this place, a pit of desolation, which was once where I lived, and all I loved?'

'Lovelace.'

Robert felt a cool touch upon his cheek and glanced round. Milady was standing beside him. She took him by the arm. 'Leave him,' she whispered. She nodded; and Robert watched the Marquise approach Sir Henry, raise his chin with her fingertip. She stared into his eyes for a long while, watching him shiver and almost melt with his fear. 'You know,' she whispered, 'who it is we wish to see.'

Sir Henry shook his head slowly. 'No!' he wailed. 'Please, please, no!'

'Have you seen Him yourself?' the Marquise asked, ignoring his appeal.

'I . . .'

The Marquise waited. Suddenly, her eyes appeared to blaze: Sir Henry sank to his knees, clutching his head and moaning like an animal seized in a snare. The Marquise nudged him with the tip of her riding boot. 'I asked you,' she hissed softly, 'a simple question.'

'I have not seen Him,' Sir Henry whispered back. 'Or rather. . .' He swallowed. 'It is hard to explain . . .'

'Nor is that surprising,' nodded the Marquise, 'for you are mortal. Go on.'

'I approach Him, but . . . I sense, I don't see Him . . . And that is how I know,' he added weakly, 'what His orders are.'

'Where does this happen?'

Sir Henry closed his eyes, and gestured with his hand.

'Wolverton Hall,' said Robert slowly, gazing out of the window at which Sir Henry had pointed, at the fog-drenched horizon.

'Is he right?' the Marquise asked.

Sir Henry nodded almost imperceptibly.

'Take us there.'

He began to moan and shudder again, and once more he was trapped within the Marquise's stare. 'Please,' he whispered. 'The danger . . .'

'And must not there be danger in every great undertaking?' The Marquise's eyes gleamed triumphantly. She nodded towards the door. 'I gave you an order. *Take us there at once!*'

∽∾

'ADDERS AND SERPENTS, LET ME BREATHE A WHILE!
UGLY HELL, GAPE NOT! COME NOT, LUCIFER!'
                    Christopher Marlowe, *Doctor Faustus*

Robert had not required Sir Henry to show him the way. Instead, he had hurried at once from the room. He mounted his horse and began to gallop through the ruined village, up the track which led back to the wood. Only at the point where the two paths separated – the one heading onwards into the trees, the other turning left towards Wolverton Hall – did he wheel in his horse, lost in sudden, unbidden thought. He remembered how he and Emily had once stood on the very same spot, gazing at the sinking sun, wondering if they dared to pursue the hoofmarks in the snow. There was no sun now, only grey, dripping mist; and no Emily. Robert glanced round. Sir Henry was approaching along the village road. He turned his face away, rather than meet Robert's stare.

'Who was it killed her?' Robert asked, crossing to join him so that they were riding side by side.

'How should I know?' muttered Sir Henry. 'There are many rebels abroad.'

'What – those who would not be slaves?'

For the first time, Sir Henry dared to turn and meet his stare. Anger and fear passed like clouds across his face. 'You do not understand,' he whispered at last.

'No,' said Robert. He stared out at the blackened fields, and the lines of scarecrow slaves. 'I do not.'

'There was – there is – no other way.'

'How can you pretend that?'

'I have done what I had to do, to protect those I could.'

'By turning their home into a wasteland of despair?'

'Listen to me,' Sir Henry lowered his voice and, as he leaned sideways in his saddle, Robert realised for the first time how haggardly the flesh hung upon his face, how weary his expression seemed, how haunted his eyes. 'We have no provisions here,' he whispered, 'no food of our own, for the fields have been sown with rubble and salt. What we are given to eat is provided by the . . . "grace" . . . of Wolverton Hall. We must therefore labour as we are commanded to do, for if we do not, then all of us shall starve, and though you may think we are thin now, soon we would be skeletons, and all this place a wilderness of bones.'

'Yet you, I see, are not as weak as your slaves.'

Sir Henry sighed. 'I have told you – we must each labour in the tasks we have been given.'

'And you – and Elijah – and all your men ... your tasks have been to chain and beat your neighbours, then?'

Sir Henry rubbed a weary hand across his eyes. 'I was instructed, when the new order of things was established here, to arm and privilege the strongest amongst us, so that they might supervise what had to be done.'

'To supervise?' Robert shook his head. 'Yet I saw a guard flog a girl across her shoulders until she lay in the mud.'

'It may be,' said Sir Henry slowly, gazing into the fog, 'that the evil we do is devouring our souls.'

'It may be indeed,' said Robert. He shook his head, and almost laughed with despair. 'And yet cannot evil be fought against?' he asked. 'Cannot even the most corrupted souls be saved?'

Sir Henry made no reply.

'Escape, at least!' cried Robert. 'Cast off the chains, unbolt the stockade gates, leave this Hell behind!'

'We cannot.'

Robert stared at him in silence for a very long while. 'I do not understand,' he said at last.

'No,' answered Sir Henry. He stared ahead of him; and his face grew twisted and pinched as he raised a hand to his mouth. 'As I told you,' he whispered, 'I am afraid you do not.'

He spurred his horse forward suddenly. Robert, staring after him, saw the first faint silhouette of Wolverton Hall; and then, on the icy breeeze, smelt a terrible stench, so strong that he swayed and thought that he would faint. As Sir Henry had done, he raised a hand to his nose; but the stench seemed to burn his nostrils, and to settle in his guts in a haze of venom which could not be coughed up, however much he tried. He could see now – built around the wall that bounded the gardens of the house – a vast expanse of rotting wooden shacks; and it was these, he supposed, which were breeding the stench. It was a compound, Robert thought, of every loathsome thing, of rottonness, vomit, excrement and fear; and he knew, without repeating the question he had put to Elijah, that he had discovered where the villagers of Woodton now lived.

Sir Henry confirmed him in his supposition. 'You see now,' he said, still clutching a hand across his mouth, 'why men will consent to brandish a whip and beat their fellows, for this is the alternative to the barracks in my house, a sty in which the weak and sick must surely die.' He gestured with his hand; and Robert saw, lying in an open yard, shivering bodies barely clothed in rags, huddled amidst the frozen ordure. 'But there are children . . .' Robert whispered. He swung down from his horse; he began to pick his way towards them. As he did so he saw, smeared with filth amidst the mud and rotten straw, what appeared to be a glimmer of gold. He bent down and picked up a bracelet of jewels, then stared about him, and saw wealth littered everywhere.

'What is this,' he cried, 'that riches should lie scattered in the midst of such poverty?'

'Why,' smiled Sir Henry grimly, 'can you not guess? That is the gold with which Faustus bought the village, to secure the death of your mother at the stake.' He laughed violently as he watched Robert fling the necklace back into the mud; then began to choke. ' "Neither cast ye your pearls before swine"!' he cried. He choked again, the laughter suddenly dead on his lips, and turned in his saddle. A bell had started to clang from beyond the wall. 'For know ye not,' Sir Henry whispered, 'swine want only their swill.' He bowed his head. 'Only their swill.'

The bell continued to toll. The bodies in the mud had begun to stir, some staggering to their feet, some crawling through the filth, some barely able to move at all.

'What is this?' asked the Marquise. 'To what are they being summoned?'

'To their feeding time.' Sir Henry pointed at the gateway which led into the Hall. Robert gasped; and even Milady and the Marquise, he saw, seemed to shrink in their saddles. For two creatures of the kind which he had destroyed the night before were emerging from the gateway; and yet, for reasons which Robert found hard to explain, they seemed in every way a thousand times more loathsome and frightful. He remembered what his father had told him of the monsters discovered in the cellars of the Hall, which had crawled in the darkness like maggots in raw meat; and he supposed he was seeing the same creatures now, emerged into the day. They were carrying a large pail, which they raised and then emptied out across the mud. Robert saw that Sir Henry had been speaking only the truth when he had called the food swill; yet the crowds of the sick reached out for the husks and vegetable tops, and fought over them, as though they had been the finest delicacies.

'But there is not nearly sufficient for them all,' Robert exclaimed, as the fighting grew worse and the liquid swill began to drain into the mud.

'They have not worked,' said Sir Henry shortly.

'But they are sick.'

'Yes, and will soon be worse.'

'But see' – Robert pointed – 'there are those too weak to seize a single scrap.'

'And there are those,' Milady murmured, 'who never shall.'

Robert looked, and saw a body lying face down in the mud: a tiny child. The dead things were crossing to it; they began to shred flesh from the bones with a heavy knife; and secrete their pickings in bags about their necks. 'No!' cried Sir Henry desperately, as Robert drew his sword. 'Do not approach them!' Robert ignored the appeal. The creatures looked up: they both hissed and bared their fangs, and Robert had to look away, for their breath was foul with a stench of rotten meat. Then he stared at them again, and raised up his sword, for he could see how they were crouching like wolves about to leap. But as they met his gaze, they suddenly shrank; and their fat, soft lips seemed almost to smile. Robert stabbed once, then twice: they both fell back. Down and down he plunged, trying to find their hearts; but no blood rose up; and the creatures began to stir again, and their fingers to twitch. They opened their eyes, and Robert saw that the smiles were still upon their lips. They dragged themselves through the mud as far as the wall, then rose slowly to their feet. They gazed about them, eyes gleaming, and smiled at Robert one final time; then they turned and walked slowly back through the gateway.

'Pursue them,' cried the Marquise, 'for it must have been one of their breed which infected the village where we stayed last night. Who can say, then, where they might not lead us to now?' She spurred her horse forward and, as he followed her, Robert found himself crossing the lawn where Hannah's body had been found, and his father and Mr Webbe had knelt together in the snow. What an eternity of horrors, Robert thought, had rolled past since then; and he gripped his sword the tighter, resolved afresh to be revenged or to die in the attempt. He stared ahead at the Hall's dark windows, and its rotted door. His companions were dismounting by the steps which led up to it, but Robert did not wait for them, for the dead things were already entering the Hall and, as he pursued them as far as the door, Robert felt the sudden touch of fear again – a shiver in his stomach which spilled out through his blood and brushed his nerves as did the sweetest pleasures. He paused on the top step; gazed into the waiting blackness beyond. There was a gleam of pale flesh, moving away, and then it was gone, swallowed by the shadows. Robert felt the shiver again, still spreading outwards but thicker and darker now, like clotted blood. He turned round to search for a lantern. Sir Henry had brought one with him, but, as he lit it with a shaking hand, he sank to his knees and began to shudder all the more. 'Please,' he stammered, appealing to the Marquise. 'Please.' But she laughed, and pointed to the blackness of the Hall; and Robert, running down the steps, seized the lantern and hurried back to the door. He raised the lantern; he walked into the Hall. At once his fear seemed a thousand times worse, as though bred from the close and foul-smelling air. As Robert looked about him, he could see nothing at all beyond the lantern's weak light; but from the distance he heard soft retreating footsteps, and then what seemed to be a distant cry.

'Not him,' Sir Henry begged suddenly, pointing at Robert. 'Do not permit him to come with us.'

The Marquise stared at him, intrigued, and raised an eyebrow. 'Why?'

Sir Henry's eyes darted to and fro, bright with a

desperate, hunted fear. 'It . . .' He swallowed; and at the same moment, from the depths of the house, there came a second faint cry, a long, soft sobbing moan. 'It is not safe,' Sir Henry began again, loudly, as though to blot out the noise. 'If dangerous for you, then how much more so for him.'

He stopped talking, and Robert listened to the darkness. 'What was that cry we heard?' he asked.

Sir Henry swallowed, and paused, as though preparing to lie. 'I do not know,' he said at last.

'I think you do.' A cold, sick suspicion was forming in Robert's guts.

'Why, Lovelace,' asked Milady, a faint frown on her brow, 'what do you mean?'

Robert raised the lantern, and gazed down the long dark corridor from where the cries had seemed to come. 'I dread to say it.' He began to walk, then to run along the corridor. The Marquise followed him; she seized his arm and pulled him back, her face gleaming from the shadows like pale fire. 'Be prepared, Lovelace,' she hissed. 'For you cannot begin to understand what it is we now approach. Beyond lie the Gates of Death, and that veil which must be parted if we are to gaze, as we hope, upon the sacred Mysteries of the world. We shall not be like that bold Roman, who entered the Holy of Holies of Jehovah and found nothing – for nothing must always come of nothing. Of the true God, however, in His sanctuary, much may be expected. And so again, I warn you to be prepared.'

'I thank you, Madame.' Robert pulled her hand from his arm. 'But you forget – I have already gazed upon the face of your god.'

'Yes,' nodded the Marquise. 'And have not yet understood what it was that you saw.'

Robert frowned at her for a moment; then shrugged impatiently, and turned again. There came a sudden soft moan from the darkness ahead, and though it faded as fast as it had risen, there lingered a sound of something being slapped. Robert began to hurry again along the corridor. Ahead of him, he saw a sudden glimmer of white; he raised his lantern; he saw a creature of the kind he had been pursuing, bloated and soft, lying in a pool of something sticky on the floor. At first, Robert thought the liquid must be blood; but then he bent over to inspect it more closely, and almost gagged, for it seemed from its stench to be a compound of sweat and semen, yet touched with the rotten, damp odour of the grave, which Robert remembered all too well from the previous night. He dared to feel the creature's naked flesh: it too was sticky, and Robert realised that the liquid was oozing from its pores, so that the whole corridor, as far as he could see, appeared to glisten with it. There were more pale bodies lying in the darkness ahead, and piles of earth heaped against the walls. Robert walked forward; and he saw that the earth was littered with dried chunks of flesh. He remembered what he had seen outside the gate – the bodies in the mud and the creatures with their knives – and he had to lean against the wall, to try and calm his guts.

'There is worse,' whispered Sir Henry. He nodded slowly, and took the lantern from Robert's hand; closing his eyes, he seemed to mutter a prayer. Then he walked forward, but slowly, for there were more creatures now, lying in their sticky pools of filth; and the way across their bodies was a hard one to pick.

He paused at last beside an open door. 'This was lately Sir Charles' library,' he murmured, staring through the doorway at the room beyond. 'Twice I have come here, to learn the will of the new master of the Hall – but never unsummoned. Are you certain, then, that you dare to proceed?'

He was staring at Robert, who answered him by seizing the lantern again, then pushing past the Marquise and through the open door. As he did so, he heard the slapping noise, and a moan of despair very close, so that he knew he had discovered the source of the cries. He raised the lantern; he stared about him.

As in the corridor, mud and litter were piled across the floor. Human bodies, their limbs bound fast, lay twisted amidst the rubbish. They were naked and pale, with barely the strength to moan, or even to stare up, although they blinked and struggled to look away, for the light of the lantern was burning their eyes. All of them, Robert saw, were smeared with silver filth, the same as had glistened in the corridor outside, so that they seemed imprisoned within a cocoon of the stuff, helpless to shrink from those who would feed upon them. For, like monstrous grubs, their pale bodies swollen and suffused with pink, dead things were drinking from their mortal hosts; and sometimes as they drank, their moist lips would slap. One paused in its meal, its mouth still sucking as though the fetid air were blood; it rolled from its prey; then lay bloated in the mud.

Robert and Milady both looked away; but the Marquise studied the creature with fascination. 'It would seem, then,' she murmured, 'that this breed of thing need not always kill its meal but, like the leech, is content to preserve its host alive. Do you observe it, Milady?' Milady did not reply. The Marquise smiled faintly, and turned round to Sir Henry. 'These people here,' she asked, 'how long can they endure being fed upon like this?'

Sir Henry had closed his eyes. 'A year,' he said slowly. He swallowed. 'Yes, a year, maybe two.'

Robert stared at him with an ugly frown; then gazed around the room, holding the lantern aloft. A woman began to scream as the light fell on her face, and her fingers started to twitch helplessly. Robert crossed to her. Two of the creatures were feeding on her, one on either flank. He kicked them both; they fell off at once, as though over-engorged. The woman still screamed; Robert bent down beside her but, though she could not endure to open her eyes, she screamed all the more, her words violent and meaningless. With a shock, he realised that he knew her. 'Why,' he exclaimed, 'this is Mary Brockman, Jonas' wife. Does he know that she is here?'

Sir Henry did not reply.

Robert rose and crossed to him, the suspicion he had felt before now growing into terrible certainty. 'Does he know,' he asked again, 'that his wife is here?' He drew his sword; he pointed it at Sir Henry's throat. 'Tell me. *Does he know?*'

'Answer him,' whispered Milady. She froze him in her stare, and Sir Henry's eyes began to bulge with the effort of resisting her command. But he could not maintain his defiance, and he writhed as the words at last came out. 'Yes,' he moaned, '*yes!* Jonas knows his wife is here.'

'And how did that come to be?' Robert asked. 'Did he surrender her himself?'

'Please!' wailed Sir Henry, twisting his hands as though trying to cleanse them. 'We had no choice.'

'No choice but to do what, Sir Henry?'

'It was for the best,' he stammered, nodding violently, 'the only way we could hope to survive. Not just us – but all the village. For otherwise, we knew, we would all have been destroyed.'

'Unless?' Robert asked.

'Unless all of us – that is – the members of the guard . . .'

'*Unless?*'

'Unless . . .' Sir Henry swallowed. 'Unless we surrendered a person we loved . . .'

Robert breathed in deeply; but the filthy air only made him feel more sick. His arm shaking, he lowered his sword. 'And you as well?' he whispered. 'You did what was asked?'

Sir Henry wiped his hand across his forehead. His hair and beard were matted with sweat, and his eyes more desperate than they had ever been. 'Not all of us,' he said at last. 'But for each man who refused, ten were tortured – tortured to death – before their friends and their family on the village green.' He turned aside; like Robert, he gasped for air; and as he fell upon his hands and knees, he began to retch. 'Please!' he shrieked. 'Please! We did it for the best!'

Robert studied him for a moment; he did not raise his sword. 'Where is she?' he asked, his voice perfectly calm.

Sir Henry stared up at him; he did not reply.

Robert studied him a moment more, then turned in a frenzy of fury and despair. He crossed to the darkest end of the room, shining the lantern into the shadows, inspecting each face he discovered there. But it was in vain; and so he began to hurry this way and that across the floor, still holding up the lantern, until he had reached the opposite wall and had looked in the face of every person in the room. 'Not here,' he whispered. 'Pray God then she is dead.' He turned round. 'Your own daughter, Sir Henry. Pray God that she is dead!'

Sir Henry made no reply. Like a lunatic, he was rolling his head round and round, as though his skull were a censer, and his memories smoke which might be dispersed and lost upon the air; yet his eyes betrayed him, that he would never forget. Slowly, he pointed at the room's darkest corner. Robert turned again and stared; then he held up his lantern. Dimly, he made out an open door.

He crossed to it, but the Marquise was faster. He followed her through. There was a narrow passage ahead, a second doorway, and then steps. Robert watched as the Marquise began to hurry down them; he paused at their summit and felt a blast of something terrible, as though the waiting darkness were a mighty wind, loathsome with the stench and evil of Hell. As he took a step down, it seemed a struggle merely to command his limbs. He could feel the terror in his stomach singing to him now, singing and clawing at the very same time, so that as he continued to descend, disgust and pleasure were insensibly mixed, and his stomach seemed made of liquid air. He clutched at it suddenly, and leaned against the wall. 'What is happening?' he moaned. For the pleasure was so painful, he thought it would rip apart his guts and send them spilling down the stairs. He laughed at an idea so grotesque; then doubled up again, still laughing wildly, as he sobbed at the pain.

'You have a pretty humour, Lovelace, to smile in the very entrails of Hell.'

He felt Milady's hand against his cheek, and glanced up at her. She too was smiling, yet it only made her loveliness seem all the more deathly – for her face, Robert realised, was icy with fear, so that he reached up, despite himself, to hold her hand and comfort her. Her smile broadened, and she looked away as though ashamed to have her terror glimpsed. 'We must leave,' she murmured urgently. 'The dead things behind us are stirring, and if they seal the doorway, we shall never escape. Wait here.' She stared into the darkness. 'I must search for the Marquise.'

She brushed past Robert; and as she did so, he struggled to his feet. She glanced round, and shook her head; but still he tottered, hands on stomach, down the steps. 'I must see . . .' he whispered. He swallowed. 'I must find . . .'

Robert felt another sudden stab of pain from deep inside himself, searing and delicious, so that he half-screamed, half-moaned. He lost his footing; he stumbled to the foot of the steps. The light in his lantern began to flicker and fade; he cupped it nervously, and watched with relief as the light was preserved. Then he raised the lantern high. Ahead of him was an archway; everything beyond it seemed to swim before his gaze. He barely felt conscious of his own thoughts any more, for he seemed possessed by the mingled pleasure and pain which was beating now with the rhythm of his heart. The very darkness seemed red; and as he passed through the archway, it pulsed, and shimmered, and flooded his mind. Then he was flowing with it, as though drawn on a tide across the floor, towards a second archway, and beyond it a blackness which could not be pierced. The Marquise was standing before this impenetrable gloom, her arms upraised, a look of rapture and triumph on her face. She was chanting in a language Robert had never heard before; and with each word, the blackness seemed to swirl, and thicken, and form itself anew. As it did so, Robert felt himself drawn ever closer to it; for though the pain in his stomach grew worse with each step, so also, entwined with it, the pleasure grew as well. The source of both seemed to lie in the blackness, as though Robert himself were a part of it now, his profoundest emotions absorbed into its depths. Waiting for him there, he could sense a mystery of wondrous and awful power, and he longed to behold it with all of his soul.

Suddenly, though, as he walked towards the blackness, he grew aware of something holding him back. He turned. A lady – a girl – had taken his arm. She was of a terrible beauty – her long hair streaming as though in a gale, her face lit silver, her eyes gleaming gold. Robert tried to shrug her away, for the blackness was waiting, and the mystery it held; but still she kept hold of him and, though he could hear nothing at all but the pulsing of the dark, her lips were moving as though fashioning words. He frowned. Milady. That was her name. He had known her once, long, long before. But what was anything compared with the blackness ahead? He turned again, for its tide was sucking him implacably now, sucking on his stomach and the agony and pleasure which were intermingled there. But still Milady held him; and when he glanced back at her angrily, to beat her away, he saw that she was pointing, and despite himself he looked.

Dead things, in the vaulted darkness all about him. Soft, white, writhing things, feeding on a carpet of human flesh. At once, the pounding of the darkness was gone; and with it, as well, the desire for revelation. Robert felt nothing in his stomach now but a freezing, heavy sickness, which seemed to stir and twist as the dead creatures moved, as though all of them were ruled by a single mind; and then he shuddered, for he knew that they were. The Marquise was still chanting. 'No!' Robert screamed. 'No!'; but just as he had ignored Milady before, so now the Marquise was deaf to him. The darkness beyond her was growing ever thicker; and Robert turned at once and plunged amidst the dead things, for he dreaded to think how little time there might be. Yet it was all he could do to continue with his search, for he would sooner have waded through a flood of eager worms; and he felt ready to faint at the thought of being chained for years in such a place.'Emily!' he cried out. 'Emily!'; before the syllables stung his eyes and were silenced in his throat.

He found her at last. She lay beneath two bloated, pink-touched things, which Robert knocked off from her as though they were ticks. He could not see her face through his tears; could not see, only feel, how thin her body was. He clasped her in his arms. She stank of the silver filth which caked her; yet to Robert, kissing her tangled hair, she smelt more lovely than the perfumes of the Indies. He tried to sever her bonds. He could not grip his knife's handle, nor see the blade through his tears. Suddenly, he felt it being taken from him; the bonds were cut. 'Bring her,' Milady ordered, 'and with all your speed.' She pointed; and Robert wiped at his eyes. He saw, all around them, how the dead things were stirring and rising to their feet. 'The lantern!' Milady cried. She ripped a strip of cloth from her cloak, then lit it; she flourished it in the face of the nearest creature. But the flames did not catch; they hissed, then died; and still the creatures rose and, as they massed, drew in close.

Robert gathered Emily in his arms. As he rose to his feet, the dead things seemed to freeze, then to squeak and moan. He took a step forward; the ranks before him seemed to ripple and sway. Three or four had gathered by the archway which led out to the steps; Robert took a second pace towards them; as the others had done, they shuffled and moved back.

'Madame!' Milady screamed. 'Madame, come quickly!'
Robert glanced behind him. The Marquise was on her

knees. The darkness beyond her was flickering now, as though it were a tempest of fire; dimly, in its very heart, a form could be seen: a figure rising from the blackest flames.

'Madame!'

The Marquise screamed suddenly. The darkness was rolling from the figure in the flames. Robert stared into its face. Its lips parted, they formed a smile.

The Marquise shrieked again. She raised an arm across her eyes and twisted backwards, staggering blindly into Milady's arms. Her flesh seemed hideously withered to the bone; and, staring at her hair, Robert saw that it was white. 'Quick!' he screamed. 'In the name of God, run!' He stumbled through the archway, then paused to wait for Milady and the Marquise to pass by. As they did so, he glanced back. The darkness in the far cellar was as it had been before; no face, no form could be made out now. The dead things, however, still crouched, burning-eyed; and their teeth were bared in cruel, mocking smiles. What their amusement portended, Robert did not pause to think; he knew only, as he climbed with Emily up the steps, that whatever it was, it seemed to have been the cause of their escape.

∼⚭∼

'THOU ART MY WAY; I WANDER IF THOU FLY;
THOU ART MY LIGHT; IF HID, HOW BLIND AM I.
THOU ART MY LIFE; IF THOU WITHDRAW'ST, I DIE.'

                                        The Earl of Rochester, Poem

They were not pursued; and the puzzle of their escape, once they had left Woodton far behind them and reached the comfort of a tavern in Salisbury, continued to trouble Robert. Yet he had Emily; not only in his arms but filling all his thoughts, so that his forebodings were banished to the margins of his mind. He clasped her tightly to him, carried her up to her room. She seemed lost in troubled dreams; yet soon, Robert prayed, she would emerge from them forever – if only she might be well . . . if only all might turn out well . . .

He stood by the bed; laid Emily gently down, still wrapped in the cloak with which he had covered her before. 'So soft a resting place,' he murmured, kneeling by her side, 'you should have had these past two years.' How frail she seemed, how pinched and white; and yet for all that, touched with her old loveliness which her health would surely restore to fullest bloom. Robert laid his ear upon her breast, to listen to the beating of her heart; he stroked back her hair; then kissed her, very gently, as he had last done five years before.

'What a pretty vision! Yet it might seem more poetic still, if only you would wash away her stink.'

Robert stared up. Milady was watching him from the far shadows of the room. She had unpinned her hair and cast off her riding habit, so that through her thin shirt he could make out the swell of her breasts.

'You are right,' he said. 'Send for hot water.'

Milady plucked at an imaginary skirt. 'Yes, sir,' she sneered, 'of course, sir, at once.'

'Please,' said Robert. 'Let us not quarrel.'

'Then do not command me as though I were a chambermaid.'

'I am sorry.' Robert gestured with helpless frustration at Emily. 'I am much distracted.'

Milady paused, then took a step towards the bed. 'How is she faring?'

Robert shrugged helplessly again. 'How can any of us know?' He watched Milady, to see if she might contradict him, might offer him a cure; but she only nodded slowly and turned away again.

'Please.' Robert rounded the bed. Milady seemed almost to flinch as he took her by the arm. 'Please,' he begged again, 'I could not endure it, after these five years apart, if she were now to die and be snatched away a second time.'

'Five years!' exclaimed Milady with a flat-toned contempt. 'You think that a long time to be alone?'

'Will you not help me?'

'I am surprised you should think I could. Have not your years of lovelorn anguish taught you this, that I am a creature who gives not life, but only death?'

'Not true. For what was it, if not life, you gave to me?'

'I gave you what I could, Lovelace.' She paused, and glanced down at Emily. 'Nothing more.' She turned again, and crossed to the doorway. 'I am sorry.'

Robert followed her out. 'The Marquise, then.' He hurried after Milady along the passage. 'She is rich in knowledge. It may be she can help?'

Milady glanced round, and smiled mockingly.

'She is not yet recovered, then?'

Milady opened a door, and gestured at Robert to pass inside. 'See her for yourself.'

Robert crossed to the bed in the centre of the room. It had been veiled; he parted one of the curtains, and stared down. The Marquise lay motionless save for the twitching of the fingers on one of her hands, snatching endlessly at the edge of her sheet. Her flesh was hideously withered and lined; her hair white, and thin across her scalp; her whole body shrunken, so that she sat hunched in her bed like an ancient monkey. Even her eyes seemed muddied and dull, the window on to unutterable fears, and Robert could barely endure to meet their gaze. 'What did she see,' he whispered, 'in that blackness she conjured, to fill her with such horror?'

'What indeed? Only think – *la grande Marquise* – reduced to such a state.'

Robert glanced round at her startled, for Milady's voice had seemed suddenly much sharper, much more common – as it had seemed once before, when she and the Marquise had quarrelled upon his first visit to Mortlake. But Milady herself appeared unaware that her accent might have slipped; and Robert was careful to veil his surprise. He turned back to the Marquise. 'Will she emerge from her sickness soon, do you think?'

'Who am I to say?' Milady shrugged daintily. 'It is the Marquise herself who is best qualified to answer such a question.'

'All the more regrettable, then, that she is unable to.' Robert knelt down by her side. He tried to calm the ceaseless twitching of her fingers at the sheet, but they would not be stilled; and although he forced himself to meet her stare, the Marquise continued to gaze as though into a terrible desolation. 'What might she not tell us?' Robert whispered. 'There is so much she has chosen to conceal. How little we know – and how far we have to go.' He sighed, and rose to his feet. 'Pray she recovers – and recovers very soon.'

Yet it was Emily who emerged from her sickness the faster. For long days after their arrival in London, Robert would sit by her side and tend to her, as her fever began to burn away and her strength to return. Once or twice she would open her eyes, and seem to recognise him; and then one day at last, she whispered his name. 'Robert.' She smiled weakly. 'So you remembered your vow.'

'Vow?'

'Yes.' She stared at him as her smile began to fade, and her eyes to grow glazed. 'That we would never be parted,' she murmured at last. 'You promised me . . .' She swallowed. 'That day when my mother was killed – you promised . . .' She turned away and laid her cheek upon the pillow; Robert thought she was falling back into sleep. But as he rose to his feet, she gazed up at him again and reached for his hand. She squeezed it with all the strength she could muster. 'I never forgot,' she whispered. 'All that time . . .' She sank back upon her pillow. 'Never forgot . . .'

She closed her eyes, and said no more. But her sleep did not seem feverish that night; and the following morning, when she woke, she was able to sit up in her bed and to talk more fully. The next day she was able to stand; and the next to be dressed and to leave her room. Robert led her to a balcony. She stood there a long while, gazing at the Park, and the spires and towers beyond. Robert remembered how, all those years before, he had longed for her to share his first wonder at the vision of London; and now she was sharing her first wonder with him. 'So many people,' she whispered, 'so free, all so alive.' Then she turned; and as Robert walked through the mansion by her side, still she gazed about her with undisguised awe. 'What a wondrous place!' she exclaimed at last. 'And yet this is your home? This is where you live?'

'And you as well, I trust.'

'How is it possible, Robert, that you have come into such a place?'

'I share it with a lady and a gentleman. The lady – you wear her dress – she is a kind and generous friend.'

Emily stared down at the satin of her skirts, and the froths of lace across her arms. 'She must be generous indeed,' she nodded, 'to have given me such clothes.'

'Then come,' said Robert. He took her by the hand. 'Let me take you to meet her. For there is no one I love in all this world but you and Milady.'

He found her at table with Lightborn, and Robert began to approach her; yet at the sight of Milady, Emily suddenly flinched, and Robert had to pull her forward as though she were a bashful child. He saw how Lightborn grinned; and how Milady herself sat perfectly frozen, then looked away. Robert glanced back at Emily: her lips were parted in horror, her eyes staring wide. 'Please,' Robert whispered despairingly. 'Do not be afraid. For she has been like a second mother to me.'

'A mother!' exclaimed Lightborn, overhearing him. 'Did you catch that, Milady?'

Milady turned round slowly, but did not reply. Her stare was even more icy than it had been before. Lightborn's grin broadened. 'Both the ladies seem passing shy,' he said. 'Yet who can be surprised? For it is always an awkward occasion, is it not, when a son introduces a beloved to his mother?'

He raised his glass in a mocking toast. No one joined him. 'Wine?' he asked Robert, offering him a bottle of the deepest red. 'Thank you,' said Robert, 'but I would prefer the white.' He reached for the bottle and poured out a glass. No one else spoke. Neither Lightborn nor Milady were eating; and though the banquet was sumptuous, Emily only picked at her food. Robert was glad when Milady made her excuses, and when Lightborn followed her and left them alone. Still Emily did not speak, save to ask if she might not leave the house and have her first walk through the London streets. Robert agreed with all readiness. 'For here, dearest Emily, lest you forget, you are no prisoner, but may do as you wish.' Emily stared at him strangely, but still kept quiet. Only when they had left the house behind, and passed some distance along the Mall, did she turn to him at last.

She held him by his cheeks, and stared a long while into his eyes. At last, her face lightened. 'I prayed it was not possible,' she whispered, 'that you had become one of them.'

'One of them?'

'You know.'

Robert paused, and shook his head. 'They are not as Faustus was.'

'They kill, though, do they not?'

This time, Robert did not answer. Emily turned from him, and gazed out at the trees. A soft, silver drizzle was falling. She bent back her head, to feel it against her cheeks. How long was it, Robert wondered, since she had last stood in the rain? He watched her as she closed her eyes. He could not tell, such was the drizzle, whether there were tears mingling with the drops on her face. For a long while, she said nothing more; then at last she opened her eyes again. 'I cannot . . .' she whispered, 'I cannot endure . . .' She paused, and shivered; she took Robert's arm. Her stare, though, was distant, still into the rain. 'I cannot endure,' she said simply, 'to be near to them.'

Robert shook his head. 'Yet she is kind,' he insisted. 'She will do you no harm.'

'You cannot know that,' answered Emily. She clung to

him fiercely, and at last met his stare. 'I know what it means,' she whispered, 'to have my blood desired. And I tell you again – I will not go near your friends.'

Nor did she. Robert persuaded her to continue in Godolphin's mansion; but she would not talk, nor eat, nor be in the same room with Milady, and Milady for her part seemed content to stay away. Yet even when she and Lightborn were both absent from the house, Emily would continue nervous and upset; for she found in the eyes of Godolphin and the other creatures there a constant reminder of what she had been, reflections of her own former suffering and state. To escape them, she would dress in breeches and walk, always walk, through the London streets, or across the fields and hills that stretched beyond the city. Robert was happy to accompany her; for such expeditions reminded him of their childhood exploits, and of a time when all had seemed innocence. Only in the evenings would he share with Emily more worldly pleasures; for it was then that he would show her what London had to offer, masques at the palace, theatres and balls, an endless, giddying swirl of delights, so that caught up upon it there would be no time to think, no time to remember. Yet in the very centre of the whirlpool, Emily herself remained the one fixed point: an opening on to a world of lost happiness, and a promise, it seemed, of happiness yet to come.

That he might not lose such a hope became Robert's single passion. Increasingly, he came to share in Emily's fears, and to welcome Milady's absence from his life. He began to wonder if Emily had not been right, that they should leave Godolphin's house; perhaps leave London altogether and travel the world, as they had always promised each other they would do when they had gazed at the stars as children in Woodton, and dreamed of all the wonders which lay beneath the sky. But still Robert could not bring himself to go, to abandon Milady yet again. He continued to live under the same roof, and Emily with him; and all the time, his fears and his dreams grew the more.

It was Lord Rochester, in the end, who decided him. They met by chance one night at the Theatre Royal. Savile was there too – and it was he who first observed Robert and Emily. He cried out drunkenly, and came lurching from his box to join them. He studied Emily greedily, then nudged Robert in the ribs. 'That's a fine little baggage you have there,' he whispered loudly. 'Damn the whore, but I love 'em demure.'

'I assure you, sir,' answered Robert furiously, 'that this lady is no whore.' He reached for his sword; but as he did so felt his arm being seized, and when he looked round saw Lord Rochester standing by his side. He too was studying Emily – not with lust, however, but with something almost like recognition. He bowed to her politely. 'You are newly arrived from the country, my Lady?'

Emily laughed shortly. 'I am afraid to answer you, sir, lest my accent should betray me even more than looks.'

'The freshness of them both, my Lady, does you nothing but credit.' Lord Rochester bowed to her again, then turned aside to Robert. 'Am I to presume, Lovelace, that your charming companion is Mistress Vaughan?'

'The very same, my Lord.'

'I am gratified to hear it.' A smile curved his heavy lips. 'You may remember, when last we spoke, I promised you the chance of a resolution such as this. For a source of certain joy is all we need in this world, if we are not to be the playthings of eternal restlessness.'

'As you see, my Lord, I now possess such a source.'

'And the Marquise?' Lord Rochester lowered his voice. 'Did she also obtain what she had desired?'

Robert smiled grimly. 'I see, then, that you have not heard.'

A shadow of surprise seemed to pass across Lord Rochester's face. 'Christ's wounds,' he murmured, 'she has not been injured?'

'Grievously,' answered Robert. 'Although as to her present condition, I could not comment, for I have not been with her now for several weeks.'

'Most wise of you.' Lord Rochester stood frozen for a moment, lost in thought. 'If you should see her,' he said at length, 'you might mention to her that I have in my possession *mummia*.'

'*Mummia*?' Robert asked, frowning.

'You remember – I spoke to you before of the Turk, with whom I met upon my travels. It was he . . . but no.' Lord Rochester shook his head. 'This should no longer be your affair.' He glanced at Emily; then laid his hand on Robert's shoulder and drew him away. 'Will you be advised by me, Lovelace?' he whispered in his ear.

'You know, my Lord, that I have been so before.'

'Very good. Then take Mistress Vaughan, and leave your blood-drinking friends behind, and go, go anywhere you may not be found. You have seized a fragment from the wreckage of your life. Cling to it, Lovelace. Do not seek to enter the maelstrom again. I speak as someone who is trapped in it myself.'

'But . . .'

'Will you do as I advise?'

Robert stood in silence for a moment, gazing at Emily. Then he crossed to her, and took her by the arm. 'Come,'

he whispered. 'We have a journey ahead of us.' He bowed
to Savile; then more fully, as he passed him, to Lord
Rochester. He left the box; and, as he descended through
the crowds, felt Lord Rochester's eyes upon them, until
they had reached the exit and passed into the street.

He told Emily, as they travelled back in the coach, that
they would be leaving the next day. She stared at him in
surprise for a moment; then kissed him silently and
passionately. Robert saw the silver of tears in her eyes,
and she clung to him throughout the journey back. Once
arrived, he escorted her to her chamber; then went to
discover Milady. He found her, as he had once before, the
morning after his first taste of love, curled by a fire with
wine in her hand. Then, as she had stared up at him, her
eyes had been filled with a soft and lazy ecstasy, such as
he would never forget; but now they seemed dulled and
desolate. She gestured to him to sit by her side and
Robert did so; he allowed her to reach out and gently
stroke his cheek.

'Are you leaving?'

Robert nodded.

Milady continued to stroke his cheek. 'You no longer
have any need of me, then,' she murmured at last.

'Do not say that, Milady, for you know it is untrue.' He
paused. 'But you will also know, Emily can never be at
peace here.'

'Will you marry her, Lovelace, be wedded in a church?'

'Yes,' said Robert slowly. 'I wish to marry her.'

Milady laughed bitterly. 'And so you have come to me
for my blessing, as though I were indeed your mother?'

'Who else should I ask for her blessing and her love, if
not that woman who, Emily aside, is dearer to me than all
the world?' Robert rose to his feet. He took Milady's

hand, and kissed it. 'If you love me,' he whispered, 'then pray for my happiness.' He crossed to the doorway. 'Goodnight, Milady.' Then he turned and hurried away down the passage; and left Milady alone with her wine by the fire.

∽

'THIS DAY, MUCH AGAINST MY WILL, I DID IN DRURY LANE SEE TWO OR THREE HOUSES MARKED WITH A RED CROSS UPON THE DOORS, AND "LORD HAVE MERCY UPON US!" WRIT THERE WHICH WAS A SAD SIGHT TO ME, BEING THE FIRST OF THAT KIND THAT TO MY REMEMBRANCE I EVER SAW.'

Samuel Pepys, *Diaries*

Robert retired at once to bed, but sleep would not come. Instead he felt a terrible restlessness, though whether with delight or dread he could not be sure. At length, he surrendered to it and crossed to his balcony. For a long while he stood staring out at the night, at the trees in the Park as they were swept by the wind; and then, as though on some sudden presentiment, he left his balcony and hurried to Emily's room. Not since she had been sick had he entered it at night; but now the door, which she usually locked, was open wide, and so he passed inside. She was sitting up in her bed. 'So you too,' she whispered, 'could not sleep.'

Robert went to her. Emily stared at him a moment, then stretched out a finger and slipped off a ring. She gave it to him: 'Put it on.' Robert did so. 'There,' she whispered. 'Will such a wedding suffice?' She smiled, and kissed him, as Robert took her in his arms. 'For did not Mr Webbe tell us once that it is not a priest who creates man and wife, but their own love only?' Again, she kissed him. 'And thus it is, that I answer myself.'

It was only later, as she lay pillowed upon his chest, that Robert first observed the marks: two of them, violent red dots, upon the otherwise pale skin of Emily's back. Immediately, Robert froze; and Emily, feeling him tense, lifted her face and stared at him sleepily. 'What is it?' she murmured.

Robert answered her by touching the marks. 'Can you feel them?' he asked.

Emily frowned. She twisted, and brushed them with her fingertips. 'They must be insect bites,' she said.

'They are not . . .' – Robert paused and shrugged – 'old wounds, perhaps, which you have somehow disturbed?'

Emily stared at him. 'It may be,' she said at last. She touched them again, then shook her head. 'Yet they do not feel as though they are. They feel somehow . . . more fresh.' She smiled faintly at Robert. 'So what else can they be, but insect bites?'

She embraced him again, and curled up in sleep; and Robert thought – listening to the soft rhythm of her breath, feeling how calmly she lay upon his chest – that she was surely right, that there was nothing to fear. Gradually, he too began to drift into sleep; and then suddenly he was awake again, for Emily seemed in the grip of a nightmare, tossing violently and moaning as she slept. The sheets were sodden and, as Emily shivered, the sweat glistened on her skin. The two marks on her back seemed even redder than before; and when Robert touched them again, she screamed and jerked awake. Her shivering was terrible now. She stared at Robert as if she did not recognise him at all; then she doubled over, and began to vomit on the floor.

Robert sped to find Milady. He discovered her still by the fire. 'Have you been feeding on her?' he cried.

Milady stared up at him, baffled. 'You are raving, Lovelace.'

'The marks on her back – was it Lightborn or yourself?' Still Milady stared at him, puzzled; so Robert seized her by the arm and pulled her after him. As she began to understand his accusations, so also she began to reject them indignantly; and Robert believed her. 'Lightborn, then,' he exclaimed. 'It must have been him.'

Milady shook her head. 'Lightborn has been preying in Deptford these past two nights.'

Robert realised, to his surprise, that he felt sick with disappointment. He had wanted it to be Milady – had wanted it to be something he might seek to prevent. 'It may be nothing but a fever, then,' he said. He had paused outside Emily's chamber; Milady glanced at him, her face like a mask. 'Let us find out,' she replied.

But Emily was gone. The bed was empty, stripped of all its sheets, and the door which led out towards the stairway had been unlocked. Robert ran across to it; he went through on to the stairs and he saw, dropped at their base, one of the sheets. At the same moment, from the direction of the hall, there came the sound of a door slamming; and he ran as fast as he could down the stairs. But he was too late to catch up with Emily; for though he followed her through the main door out on to the street, when he looked up and down it the Mall appeared empty, and the Park as well, for as far as he could see. Milady joined him as he stood peering vainly on its edge. 'This city is a cruel place,' she murmured, 'in which to lose one you love.' She took him by the arm. 'We should start our search without delay.'

They had no luck all that morning. Then, in the late afternoon, they discovered a beggar-man who had seen a girl swathed in sheets, crouched shivering in a doorway at the end of Drury Lane. They journeyed there at once; and found others too who remembered having seen her. Emily's trail led towards St Giles, into the very stinking heart of the rookeries; and Robert, remembering the butcher who had robbed him there, began to fear the worst. Yet still the trail led on; and for as long as it did so, Robert knew that hope remained.

At length, pointed towards the church, they found a large crowd gathered in front of it. Everyone was gazing up at the sky; some were screaming and moaning, others in tears. They appeared to be listening to someone's cries; and then, as Robert drew closer, he knew whose they were.

'It is an angel clothed in white!' Emily was shrieking. 'Burning, deathly white!'

Robert pushed forward and saw that Emily, like the crowd about her, was gazing at the sky. Her sheets were torn and muddy, like funeral clothes; her face was blotched with spots and sores. 'Do you see him?' she sobbed. 'How he wields a fiery sword in his hand, now waving it – and now brandishing it over his head!' The crowd surged and moaned, and shaded their eyes. Robert stepped forward, and took Emily in his arms; she was shivering, and her skin felt burning hot. 'Woe!' she cried. 'Woe, for all London must be destroyed!'

The crowd parted as Robert led her through, as though in dread of her; and yet even once she was past them, they continued to stare into the sky and to sob and moan. Emily too was muttering to herself, and seemed not to recognise Robert at all. He could see now how the spots had spread across her neck. He glanced at Milady – afraid to speak, to ask her what she thought. But all the time, he was remembering Colonel Sexton's warning, and wondering if perhaps it had not been true: that Woodton had indeed been a place of pestilence; that with all its other sufferings, the village had been infected with a terrible sickness too. Even as he thought this, he heard a sudden shriek from a window above. A woman appeared at it; her face too was covered with spots, violent and red, encircled by blue. 'Oh, Death!' she cried. 'Death, Death!' From behind her there rose a wailing like a suffering child's.

Emily was returned to her bed. Day after day she would scream in her delirium, as though the pain she felt were boiling her alive. It was now April. Robert would leave her windows open, so that she might be cooled by the breezes; and from the distant spire of the church of St Giles a perpetual tolling would carry, echoing across a frightening, mournful stillness. Yet weeks passed, and still Robert refused to admit that Emily might die; for he had learned that the sick in St Giles were expiring within days of their infection, while Emily, for all her suffering, still clung feverishly to life. Then at last, one morning, he discovered swellings in her groin and under her arms. They were tumour-like and black; and it was impossible for him any longer to deny the name of her disease. Yet still Robert refused to utter it, or even to hear it said, as though by banishing the word he might banish the possibility of Emily's death; and it was Lightborn who finally spoke the dread name first. 'The plague is spread beyond St Giles,' he said that same night. 'It is officially confirmed, and indeed, I have just come from Long Acre and seen, painted upon all the doors, red crosses and a mewling prayer for help. "Lord have mercy upon us," they scrawl.' Lightborn laughed derisively. 'It is not the Lord who will save anyone, but only ourselves.' He beckoned to Godolphin, who was standing in attendance with a bottle of wine. He was shivering, Robert saw, and a violent sweat was glistening across his brow. 'Turn around,' Lightborn ordered; then reached for a knife and ripped the livery off Godolphin's back. 'There,' he said, pointing. 'He has the spots. Out, Godolphin, out you go – I will not have you here to infect my sweet boys.' He turned to Robert. 'Your whore upstairs as well. It is certain now that she has the buboes? Well – she wanted to leave us, and so indeed she shall.'

'But she is too sick to be moved,' cried Robert in fury.

Lightborn shrugged. 'What should I care?' he asked. 'I have told you, Lovelace – the bitch must go.'

Milady reached out and laid a hand upon Robert's arm. 'We shall take her to our house in Pudding Lane. It is not prettily furnished – but I doubt she is in a humour to be much concerned by that.' She turned to Godolphin. 'Order the carriage prepared and its curtains drawn. We shall drive through the meanest streets, where we shall not be seen.' She paused, then frowned as she saw spots upon his neck. 'It were best, I think, you come with us as well.'

All was soon prepared. Already, the plague's hold upon Godolphin was gripping him so rapidly that he could barely stay upright in his place; while Emily, who seemed unaware that she had even been moved, was laid out full-length on the opposite seat. Robert sat with her, to wash her brow, and to calm her when she sobbed or cried out with her pain. Once, so piercing were her screams that Robert glanced out through the curtain, to ensure she had not been heard. But no one in the street had even glanced round: all were walking very fast, with cloths about their mouths or their faces to the ground. Upon almost every door they passed, it seemed, red crosses had appeared; as though the very city were a trunk of mortality over which the crosses were spreading like monstrous spots.

Yet beyond St Giles the marks of plague were few, and in the City itself the crowds on the streets seemed as bustling as ever, as though the darkness of St Giles had risen in a strange and far-off world. For all that, once the carriage had halted by the house in Pudding Lane, Robert and Milady did their best to make certain they were not being watched, as they helped Godolphin from the carriage, and then in through the house's front door. As Emily was transported in turn, they were careful to ensure that she was covered by a sheet, so that not a trace of her skin could be seen; for it was rumoured – so Lightborn had reported – that infected dwellings were being locked up and guarded for forty days; and Robert had no wish to be immured inside the house. For, as he agreed with Milady, standing by Emily in the bare and echoing dining hall, there was a mystery to the plague, and its sudden appearance in London, which neither of them had chosen to speak of before; and which might need all their time and energies to solve.

Robert bent down by Emily's side. He clasped a hand to his nose, for her sweat stank like poison; and when he touched her face, its flesh seemed putrid. 'How like those risen dead she seems, whom we saw in the village where the plague had struck.'

Milady nodded. 'Exceedingly like.' She turned and crossed to the window; gazed at the streets and the traffic outside. 'Half of that village, it appeared, had been wiped out,' she murmured. 'And now the same plague is here. What a freight of death will there not be, in a city so mighty and populous as this?'

'It is possible,' answered Robert slowly, 'that it is not the same sickness – that it was not Emily who brought it here after all.'

'All things are possible.' Still Milady stared out through the window at the streets. Robert watched her for a moment, then turned back to Emily. He bent down to kiss her on her blackened lips; she moaned with pain as he did so and, gazing into her eyes, he saw a stare of unutterable horror. It seemed very like that of the Marquise, which he had gazed into as she lay on her bed in the inn; and suddenly, Robert was struck by a remembrance.

'All things are possible,' he echoed Milady, rising to his feet. He crossed to her. 'What do you know of a medicine named *mummia*?'

'*Mummia*?' Milady frowned. 'Why, what should it be?'

'My Lord Rochester mentioned it when I told him that the Marquise had been struck down.'

Milady shook her head. 'I have never heard of such a thing.'

Robert gazed towards Emily, where she lay sobbing on her bed. 'Yet if my Lord Rochester were right, and it were indeed a cure . . .'

'Yes, Lovelace, but still, it would not serve for her.'

'Would it not, though?' asked Robert. He crossed to Emily. He raised a curl of her hair, and kissed it softly; then glanced back at Milady. 'For the Marquise was brought low by what she saw in the vault – the very same vault from which Emily was brought. Yes,' he nodded, 'yes, and now I remember! When I rode that day with Sir

Henry, I asked him why he kept the guards upon the
barricades and did not allow the villagers the chance to
escape. He answered me that I did not understand; and
then rode on, and would not say more. It may be that he,
who had been the spokesman for Wolverton Hall, had
indeed learned its secrets better than we knew.'

'What secret – that those who left the village bore the
plague germ in their blood?'

Robert nodded. 'For just as the dead thing bore it to
the village where we stayed, now Emily has brought it in
her own veins to London.' He laughed harshly with
sudden despair. 'Or so at least I find I must hope – for
what other chance of a cure does she have?' He glanced
across at Emily as she began suddenly to shriek again,
scratching at her buboes as though to gouge them from
her flesh.

'She does not have long,' Milady murmured. 'Her
sweat smells of death.'

'And yet how long she has already endured,' answered
Robert, as he knelt by Emily's side.

'A great length,' agreed Milady, 'such as might indeed
mark her out as infected by a strange and monstrous
spirit, for her agony has been a cruel and lingering one.
So come.' She raised her hood, and took his arm. 'You
must seek out Lord Rochester and his *mummia* at once.'

Robert gazed down despairingly at Emily. 'I cannot
leave her.'

'You must. For whatever this *mummia* may be, I doubt
Lord Rochester will surrender it into a servant's hands.'

'He would surrender it to you.'

'Yes, but I must go to Mortlake. For it may be that
Madame has already been cured and, should you not be
able to discover Lord Rochester, then she will be your one

remaining chance. Lovelace!' She tugged on his arm.

But Robert shrugged her away, and bent down again to embrace Emily. In his arms, she paused in her screams; she opened her eyes and, for the briefest of moments, Robert thought that she smiled, and recognised him. But he could not be certain, for her lips were too rotted, her eyes too hectic; and so he kissed her, then released her, and hurried from the room. In the doorway, he glanced fleetingly back. The light was fading and he could see nothing on the bed but a curled-up silhouette, the sheets wrapped round it sodden with sweat, so that the body seemed already swathed in funeral clothes. Robert swallowed, then turned and did not look round again. He followed Milady out into the street.

The carriage drove them together to Milford Stairs. Milady embarked there for the journey upriver to Mortlake; and as she parted from Robert, she squeezed his hand and whispered in his ear that all would soon be well. But he could not believe her; for he remembered how Lord Rochester had once promised him the same, when they too had left for Mortlake from Milford Stairs; and how that promise had led him to Wolverton Hall. And now Emily was dying, and maybe all of London with her too. Desperately, Robert urged the driver on; and yet he felt in his soul that he was wasting his breath – that hope, along with Emily, was already dead.

As they drew closer to Whitehall, the traffic grew worse, and by Charing Cross the roads seemed impassable. The carriages were painted on their sides with coats of arms, and Robert wondered if they bore noblemen already fleeing the early rumours of the plague. He abandoned his own carriage at the end of the Strand, and passed through the traffic to the Palace on foot. Beyond the Holbein Gate there seemed an even greater hubbub, for war had been lately declared against the Dutch, and officials and secretaries were scurrying wildly about, brandishing papers, discussing the news. But Robert also observed servants loading trunks and piles of clothes; and saw how some of the courtiers' rooms appeared deserted. He could not believe that Lord Rochester himself might have fled; but he was not in the Palace and, although Robert pressed his servants, they swore they did not know where their master might be found.

In the end, he had no choice but to return to his carriage. 'Pudding Lane,' he cried, 'with all the speed you can!' His former ambitions – that Lord Rochester be found, that Emily be saved – now seemed nothing but the merest phantoms of air; and indeed, the great castle of his hopes had collapsed into nothing but the wish that he might find Emily still alive. He gripped his carriage's side, and prayed as desperately as he had ever prayed before. Yet as they drove into the City, the traffic barely thinned; and Robert saw, leaning from the carriage, how lanterns in windows were already heralding the dusk. He had been absent, he realised, for several hours: time for more than the light of day to fade.

As they turned into Pudding Lane at last, Robert craned out desperately from his carriage window. Immediately, he felt a sudden sickness parch him from his stomach to his throat. For two guards were standing by the house; and as he leapt from the carriage, he saw that the front door had been padlocked and nailed up with boards. A red cross had been painted over it, and a prayer for the Lord's mercy; but Robert doubted that prayers would be of much assistance now.

He crossed to one of the watchmen. 'Was she dead?'

he asked. 'The girl here – was she dead?'

The man stared back at him nervously. 'You knew her?'

Robert nodded, struck suddenly dumb; and at once the watchman stepped back.

'Please,' said Robert. 'I must know.'

The watchman swallowed. Fear and sympathy seemed mingled on his face. 'There were shrieks heard,' he said at last, 'and they must have been her dying ones because, when we went in, the girl was done for. There's a man still alive there, though he won't be for long. If you want to give us money, we can see he still gets food.'

Numbly, Robert felt in his purse and drew out some coins. He stared up at the window of the dining hall. 'Is she still in there now?' he asked.

The man stared at him in surprise. 'God bless you, no!' he exclaimed. 'She was taken for burial immediately.'

'Where to?'

'Not about here, it won't be, they don't want the plague dead staying round here.'

'Then where?'

'Not my problem, burying the dead.' He shrugged. 'She'll have been taken to St Giles.'

'When?'

The watchman shrugged a second time. 'I don't know. Not long ago.'

Robert stared at him a moment more; then turned, and cried out in anguish, 'St Giles!' He ran, the carriage already moving, and took his seat. As he did so, he almost felt like laughing in despair, for he realised how wrong he had been before, when he had believed that his ambitions had sunk as far as they could go. For now his only wish was that he might see Emily dead, just once, so that dirt might not cover her forever unseen, that her grave not lie unmarked and unhallowed by his mourning.

He leaned from the window again. They were making better speed now than they had done before, and the streets were already narrowing and growing darker as they entered the slums that stood about St Giles. Everywhere Robert looked he saw the blight of the plague. Houses stood boarded-up or tenantless; filth was piled high in neglected alleyways; the very air seemed stagnant and heavy with abandonment. Shrieks might sometimes be heard, and cries of distress, echoing through the silence from opened windows; but there was no one abroad, save only the watchmen on guard by red-marked doors. Robert peered in vain for a glimpse of the plague cart: the stillness of death seemed absolute.

Then suddenly, just as Robert was preparing to abandon his search, his nostrils were struck by a loathsome stench; and, at the same moment, he heard the distant rumbling of wheels. He ordered his carriage to halt; he clambered out; following the sound of the wheels down a side-alley, and on through a maze of squalid, winding streets. At last he saw the cart ahead of him, half-way down an alley leading on towards the church. Men were crying out to the windows above them, asking for the dead; or they were gathering coffins and naked bodies which had been laid out in the street.

Robert cried out to the men to halt, but they paid him no attention, for they could hear nothing above their own cries and the creaking of their cart. He ran down the street. As he drew nearer to the cart, he caught a glimpse of its load – the bodies lit white and ghostly by the torches, and piled almost to overflowing in a jumbled, stinking mess. Robert held his hand up to his mouth; then clambered up on to the back of the cart. Desperately, he began to rummage through the carcasses. The driver turned round and shouted at him to stop. Robert drew out his sword and pointed it at the man. 'I am looking for a girl, brought to you this evening from a house in the City. Do you remember such a corpse?'

The driver goggled at him, terrified, then shook his head. 'None from the City.'

'Then where would she be?'

'She was brought to St Giles?'

'So I was told.'

The driver stammered something, and pointed, then suddenly grinned terribly. 'I will show you.' He twisted round and shook out his reins; the cart rumbled forward along the street, and then away from the houses into the open ground before the church. The driver pointed again. 'There,' he yelled. His eyes narrowed as he stared at the ring on Robert's finger. 'Your wife will be in there.'

Slowly, Robert climbed down from the back of the cart. The stench he had smelt earlier was overpowering now. It rose from a mighty pit, dug out from the churchyard and lit a hellish orange by a ring of blazing fires. Unsteadily, Robert walked forward. Ahead of him there lay a multitude of corpses, spread out across the pit, and in places piled so high that they reached up to the rim. Where they did so, labourers were busy covering them with soil; but the task was urgent and the layer very thin. Robert watched the men work; then heard a yelled command and turned round. The driver was readying his cart to dispose of its load. A second order was shouted and corpses began to be dragged from the cart; they slithered and bounced until they came to rest in the pit. Robert watched as more were slung into their grave; but he did not see Emily, although he waited until the cart had been emptied. When all was finished, he slowly bent down. He picked up a handful of soil. He tossed it out in an arc across the pit; then he turned and left, past the fires, into the dark.

∽◌∾

'MUCH WINE HAD PASSED WITH GRAVE DISCOURSE
OF WHO FUCKS WHO AND WHO DOES WORSE . . .'
   The Earl of Rochester, 'A Ramble in St James's Park'

'They were no students of human nature', announced Savile, 'who closed those places in London where a man may have his fun. For I declare, I have never been fonder of my pleasures than in this time of plague.'

'To Death, then,' answered Lord Rochester, raising a bottle. 'Our sweet lady Death.' He kissed the bottle softly, then glanced at Robert. 'Why, Lovelace,' he asked, 'will you not join us in our toast?'

'Death is no lady,' answered Robert coldly, 'but only a skipping whore, for her kiss is diseased and rots away the flesh.'

'God's wounds, Lovelace . . .' Savile frowned at him glassily. 'You were not so dark-humoured earlier this night. Why, you have fucked so hard that all of Greenwich must be sore.'

'Do you think,' answered Robert, 'that because a man sweats and grunts upon some whore, he is made merry by it?'

'So I had always understood.'

'Then you understood falsely. For he may fuck, and drink, and play the rake, and yet hope for nothing in the end save only to forget.'

Savile pulled a face. 'And what was your success in attaining such a goal?'

Robert did not answer immediately, but rose and crossed to the tavern window. He stared out at the Thames, following with his gaze its sweep towards the sea. On the eastern horizon, a forest of masts could now be clearly made out – the fleet for the war; and beyond it, the first faint golden haze of dawn. 'Just as the sun unpurples the night,' Robert murmured, 'so the passage of hours bleeds my oblivion away.' He turned round again. 'And I am left to contemplate instead the mournful truth, that remembrance is the worse for having briefly been forgot.'

Lord Rochester stared up at him intently. 'Such regret is ever the fruit of our pleasures.' He smiled and, leaning back against a sleeping whore's thigh, began to stroke the curve of her belly. 'For despair is a bastard bred upon desire, that most notorious suicide, which ever feeds upon itself and at length, over-surfeited, expires.'

Robert turned away again, for he was reminded by Lord Rochester's words of his dream of Lady Castlemaine, which he had long sought to forget. 'Yet by the same token,' he said softly, 'the progeny of despair must in turn be desire.'

'Indeed,' Lord Rochester agreed. 'And it is thus that a debauchee is so rapidly maimed, for his mind, host to such an endless cycle of procreation, must perforce grow dulled by it. Unless, of course . . .' – he drained his bottle suddenly in a single draught, then tossed it aside – 'he can discover a fresh and unsampled object of desire.'

Savile grunted. 'Unsampled, my Lord? You, certainly, will find that pressing hard.'

Lord Rochester glanced fleetingly at Robert, but did not reply.

Savile grunted again, and staggered to his feet. 'God be my witness, I am content with fucking whores.' He stared about him blearily. 'Montagu.' He nudged a body sprawled beside him on the floor. 'What do you say? Are you content with fucking whores?'

Montagu half-opened one eye. 'What,' he muttered, 'you would have me do it now?' He groaned, and turned away again; and Lord Rochester laughed contemptuously. 'Thus is my case proven, when even so prodigious a fornicator as Montagu is rendered impotent and stale.'

'Not so,' answered Savile, 'for it proves merely that pleasure comes in many different forms. After exertion, rest – after whoring, sleep.' He tore down a wall-hanging, to cover Montagu; then curled up himself beneath a cloth from a bench. 'And so to both of you,' he nodded, 'a very good night.'

'And now he will snore like a pig,' said Lord Rochester, 'and I shall not be able to join him in sleep, and thus he will serve to prove my case after all.' He stared up at Robert. 'What now, Lovelace? Will you return with me to London?'

Robert shook his head. He paused by a mirror to arrange his wig, then reached for his cloak and sword. 'I must go,' he said, pausing by the door. 'I have business in Deptford.'

'Deptford?' Lord Rochester sat up, intrigued. 'That is an ugly place for so pretty a gentleman as yourself.'

'Yet it is favoured by those much prettier than myself.'

'Indeed?' Lord Rochester jumped to his feet. 'You are meeting with Milady?'

Robert nodded.

'What does she do there?'

'She – and Lightborn too . . .' – he shrugged – 'they have both been always strangely drawn to Deptford.'

'And yet perhaps,' said Lord Rochester, 'it is not so strange. For doubtless, just as Greenwich is full of plague-fleeing whores, so Deptford is crowded with sailors from the war, who will be drunk and therefore all the easier prey.'

'Doubtless.'

'And what is your business there, Lovelace, so early with Milady?'

'Nothing of any great moment.'

'Tell me.'

'Why' – Robert's smile was crooked – 'we have an abduction to plan.'

He turned, and said no more, but clattered down the stairs. He began to hurry along the river front, but Lord Rochester pursued him and seized him by the arm. 'You cannot, Lovelace, like some prick-teasing jade, arouse me in that way and then leave me unfulfilled.'

'And I must answer you, my Lord, as any teasing jade would, that I have another and more pressing assignment than with you.'

'And I must answer you in turn, Lovelace, that I treat all jilting flirts – thus.' As he spoke, Lord Rochester tightened his grip, so that Robert, although he struggled briefly, could not break free. 'Now,' said Lord Rochester, 'let us continue on to Deptford.' He led the way forward, as though Robert were a lady to be escorted on his arm. 'Tell me, then,' he inquired with perfect civility, 'who is this victim you will be abducting tonight?'

Robert walked in icy silence for a minute. 'A lady,' he said at last.

'Do I know her?'

Robert smiled grimly. 'Indeed, we have already discussed her at length.'

'Then I doubt she is a lady.'

'I can assure you that she is.'

'What are her qualities?'

'Unspottable virtue, inestimable wealth ... and the very best' – Robert smiled – 'the very *bluest* of blood.'

Lord Rochester's eyes narrowed. 'She has a pedigree, then?'

'Indeed, my Lord – such as to a connoisseur is more priceless than gold.'

Lord Rochester released his grip, and walked on in silence for a few more paces. 'Am I to presume, then,' he asked at length, 'that it is your intention to abduct Miss Malet?'

Robert did not meet his stare. 'You are shrewd, my Lord.'

'A deed to be performed, no doubt, at the request of the Marquise?'

'We must, if we are to show a true Christian spirit, be obedient to the desires of the feeble and the sick.'

'Yet I gave her the *mummia*. She is risen from her bed.'

'Yes, but still withered and lined, too weak to leave her house, still less to hunt her prey. She believes that Miss Malet may serve as a ... restorative.'

Lord Rochester paused in his walk, and studied Robert with a quizzical frown. 'I do not understand,' he murmured. 'I had thought your principles too generous and just to contemplate such a deed.'

'My principles are fast becoming subject to necessity.'

'A fashionable avowal.'

'Yet it was not fashion which has taught me, but rather dread of walking into the same ambush twice. For before, my Lord, when I travelled to Woodton, I was like those

Cavaliers my father had fought against, who would charge without heed or care and be defeated easily. So I must grow a wiser and more subtle general, one who studies an enemy as deeply as he can.' Robert paused. 'The Marquise has held back a great deal from me, concerning the Spirit whom it is now my one ambition to destroy.'

'And she will tell you what she knows, if you will only kill Miss Malet?'

'It is not I who will kill her.'

'Spoken like a true and honest hypocrite!'

Robert smiled grimly. 'I had not realised your own morals were so scrupulous either, my Lord. But since you seem resolved to play the preacher with me, let me tell you that my conscience is easily salved by the thought that, if I kidnap Miss Malet, it may well be that all London shall be saved.'

'A high and soaring claim, Lovelace.'

'It affords me no joy that I can justify it. For did you not understand, my Lord, that when I brought Miss Vaughan to London I also brought the plague? If it is to be fought against, then I must first know what the taint was in Emily's blood. Such a task is made all the more difficult, by the fact that I . . . that her body . . . that her corpse has not been found . . .'

He fell into a sudden silence; and Lord Rochester, inspecting him, shook his head. 'Is it not possible, Lovelace, that your judgement on this matter has been influenced by your grief?'

'Grief?' Lovelace's face grew strangely twisted; then he started to laugh. 'But I feel no grief at all. Indeed, I feel nothing whatever. My heart is as dead as stone. No, my Lord – let us talk no more of this.' He broke free, and continued hurriedly on his way; and Lord Rochester, shrugging faintly, followed him along the path.

They had arrived at Deptford Creek by now; and London could be seen clearly ahead of them, vivid against a relentless, blinding blue sky. There seemed no clue at such a distance of its agony; save that on the Thames, the traffic was becalmed and still, as though unwilling to approach the death-infected city.

'How can you be certain,' asked Lord Rochester slowly, 'that the Marquise is indeed the best qualified to help you?'

'I cannot be certain. But what choice do I have?'

'What choice indeed?' Lord Rochester smiled distantly, then glanced at the wherries gathered at the head of the Creek. 'I should hire a boatman here,' he said, as he crossed over the footbridge which led to Deptford Strand. He glanced up at the wharves, then again across at London. 'Anywhere else,' he murmured, 'the boatmen will be hard to persuade.'

'So you will not come to meet with Milady?'

'I would not like to intrude,' Lord Rochester answered, walking on towards the wharves. Then he paused suddenly, and glanced back. 'Yet I find it strange,' he murmured, 'that Milady should help you at all.'

'Why?'

'Surely she would like to keep Miss Malet for herself?'

'Keep her?' Robert frowned. 'I do not understand.'

'Do you not remember what I told you, when we rode upon the Thames, that blood-drinkers may love the descendants of their own kind, and yet not drive them mad? Surely Milady would welcome such a prize?'

'But she has no need of it,' answered Robert. He

smiled, and turned to stare across at Deptford Strand. As he did so, he felt the faintest tingling of gold within his blood, and his smile grew broader with the lightness in his veins. 'Why do you think that she has fostered me?'

Lord Rochester studied him for a long while; then answered his smile. 'Do you sense her now?' he whispered. 'Her pleasure in blood?'

Robert breathed in deeply. 'Very distantly,' he answered. He smiled again, and closed his eyes.

'And it is as lovely as ever? As rich as before?'

Robert opened his eyes again, but he could not stop smiling. Lord Rochester, who had been studying him intently, bowed with just the faintest inclination of his head; then he climbed down the steps and boarded a boat. 'So you are determined,' he cried up suddenly, 'that it will be tonight?'

'Tonight,' Robert answered. He paused. 'By Charing Cross. For she dines with Miss Stewart, and will be abroad very late.' Then, not wanting to say any more, Robert turned and hurried away along the wharves. The pleasure in his veins was growing stronger with each step. Ahead of him, before the Navy yards, a line of mean streets ran up from the Thames, and he knew that Milady was on one of them. He found the street; it was lined with storehouses and ugly-looking taverns, of the kind in which sailors might grow so drunk that they would then collapse and lie snoring in the mud – easy pickings indeed. As Robert walked along, the pleasure grew almost unendurable. Then he saw her at the very top of the street, staring up at a large, substantial house – very old, Robert guessed, and facing out on to the Green beyond Deptford Strand. He wondered what Milady's interest in it could be. Perhaps it was to one of its rooms, he guessed, that she had taken the sailor whose blood was now flowing like gold in her veins.

He touched her shoulder. When she turned round, startled, her face wore none of the lazy passion he had been expecting to see; instead, it seemed desolate, almost wild with strange grief. 'Lovelace. Dearest Lovelace. Let me hold you.' But she said nothing more; and when she broke away at last, her expression had faded and seemed icy once again. Robert wanted to ask her what it was that she had seen or experienced that night, to affect her so; but her stare was forbidding, and his questions were frozen stillborn upon his tongue. Then she smiled suddenly and gave him a kiss, almost skittishly, as though stealing it like a lovesick girl. 'Why should I be dread,' she whispered, 'for so long as I have you?' She took his arm. 'Come.' She began to lead him back down the street towards the wharves. 'We have an abduction to prepare.'

❧

'ABOUT 18, HE STOLE HIS LADY, ELIZABETH MALET, A DAUGHTER AND HEIR, A GREAT FORTUNE; FOR WHICH I REMEMBER I SAW HIM A PRISONER IN THE TOWER . . .'

John Aubrey, *Brief Lives*

It was as the carriage was rumbling out from Whitehall Palace that Robert felt the pistol being placed against his head. He turned round very slowly. 'You are changing the plot, my Lord,' he murmured. 'It is not I, but Miss Malet, who is to be abducted tonight.'

'And so she shall be, for I have need of her myself.' Lord Rochester grinned. 'Request Milady to do nothing foolish, if you please. None of her tricks.'

Robert paused. He heard the pistol being cocked; he looked across at Milady. She was watching him and Lord Rochester together, her golden eyes calm and utterly opaque. Robert nodded to her; she continued to stare a moment more, then slowly turned in her saddle. At the same moment, a group of horsemen rode out from the shadows to take their places in a half-ring by the entrance to the Strand. They all wore masks; and as the carriage turned into Charing Cross, so they drew out their swords.

'No time to waste,' Lord Rochester whispered. 'Request Miss Malet to step out from her coach.'

Robert glanced round. The pistol was still cocked, and aimed at his head. Lord Rochester gestured with it; Robert pulled up his mask, and cantered forward. The carriage had already been stopped. He dismounted, and approached the door; as he swung it open, he was greeted by cries of mingled outrage and fear.

He ignored them; and politely requested Miss Malet to step outside.

'Damn you to Hell!' bellowed an old man, whom Robert guessed to be her guardian. 'What do you mean to do with her, you villain?'

'I?' answered Robert. 'Be thankful that I can do nothing at all.'

Miss Malet stared up at him wide-eyed. 'Then for whom are you working?' she whispered.

Robert paused. 'One who, I believe, will do you no harm.'

'What is his purpose?'

'His purpose?' Robert took Miss Malet's hand; he helped her from the coach, then across the street to where a second carriage stood. 'Why,' he whispered suddenly in her ear, 'I believe that he intends to make you his wife.' Then he stepped back, as a footman slammed the door and the carriage began to rumble down the street. The horsemen rode with it; but Lord Rochester himself still remained by Charing Cross, until the carriage had vanished and could be heard no more. Then he waved cheerily in turn to Robert and Milady. 'Present my regrets to the Marquise,' he cried. He wheeled his horse round, and galloped hard in the opposite direction to the coach. Onlookers had been gathering all the time; as Lord Rochester left Charing Cross, so the cry went up that he had been the abductor, and horsemen from the Palace were soon pursuing him hard. As Robert watched them go, Milady shook her head. 'It will be the most notorious scandal for many a year,' she whispered. 'There will be no chance now that Miss Malet can be seized again and made to disappear.'

'And that,' Robert answered, 'was surely his Lordship's aim.'

'He is a most fearless villain. Would you have me kill him?'

Robert paused; then shook his head.

Milady leaned back in her saddle, and arched an eyebrow. 'You seem passing cool, Lovelace, considering the man has just lost you the Marquise's good will, and doubtless much more.'

'Doubtless,' nodded Robert slowly. 'Yet I wonder, all the same, whether he might not have something to offer in return.'

'Why?' Milady stared at him, intrigued. 'What might he know, that the Marquise does not?'

Robert shrugged; then smiled, as more horsemen

galloped past them in pursuit. 'Well – it seems I shall soon have the chance to ask him. For whatever other plans his Lordship may have had, he was clearly determined to be easily captured.'

And so it proved. Robert had no problems in keeping abreast of the news for, as Milady had anticipated, the attempted abduction was indeed the scandal of the hour, and in the midst of war and gathering plague, the Court found it hard to talk of any other matter. Lord Rochester had been taken; he was being brought back to London; he was being sent to the Tower. The King, it was whispered delightedly, was in the most furious rage. Who knew what the errant Earl's fate might not be? Robert too wondered about this; but he doubted it was the King whom Lord Rochester had to dread. A visit to the Marquise confirmed this supposition; for the theft of Miss Malet had flung her into a rage more deadly by far than that of any king. She answered Robert's pleas with an icy contempt, and spoke only to damn Lord Rochester to Hell. 'I shall teach him the meaning of suffering,' she hissed, 'for believe me . . .' – she reached up to touch her lined and withered face – 'I have a far deeper knowledge now of what it can be.'

Robert sent this warning in a note to Lord Rochester; and waited for a reply. For a while, he thought that it might never come; but then at last he was delivered a pass, signed 'R.', to the Tower. Robert left at once. Journeying through London, he could see everywhere the encroaching marks of the plague. By now, the red crosses had spread far beyond St Giles, and beneath the burning blue sky the whole city reeked, as though of mortality and fear. Once Robert caught a glimpse of a plague cart; and he paused, and bowed his head to offer a prayer for

Emily's soul. Then he swore with sudden fury – for he knew that the time for prayer was long since passed. He hurried on to the Tower, where he was shown to Lord Rochester's quarters. He barely dealt with courtesies; for he was growing desperate and impatient, and he had a pressing demand to make.

Lord Rochester answered it with his usual lazy smile. 'I only wish that I knew my own intentions,' he murmured, 'as well as you appear to do.'

'Come, my Lord,' said Robert impatiently, 'you owe it to me not to make sport of my request.'

'Owe it to you?' The smile grew colder. 'But you are bitterly mistaken, Lovelace. I owe you nothing at all.'

'Indeed? Yet you know what you did to my hopes, when you stole Miss Malet.'

'You wanted her stolen. Why, you told me the very place and the time.'

Robert did not answer this. Instead, he turned and looked away. 'Yet you would not have taken her,' he said slowly, 'had you not desired her for a reason of your own. We both know, my Lord, what that reason must be.'

There was a lengthly silence. 'I am still not decided,' said Lord Rochester at last.

'Yet you are very nearly.' Robert turned round again to face him. 'And when you are resolved – I would like to come with you to meet with your Turk.'

'My Turk, Lovelace?'

'Was that not how you described him to me? The Turk you met with upon your grand tour of Europe? The Turk who taught you all the mysteries you know. The Turk who has offered you a strange and deadly gift. I must meet with him, my Lord. I must find out what he knows.'

'And what makes you think he would know anything at all?'

'From whom else could you have obtained the *mummia*? Why, not even the Marquise had heard of it before. And yet it salved the evil which had struck her in the vaults – the evil which no one else knows how to confront. I would learn, my Lord, what that evil truly is. For I fear – I very much fear – I am somehow infected by it; that I wear, as the Marquise has put it, the Devil's brand.'

Lord Rochester stared at Robert in silence, his lips half-curved between a frown and a smile.

Robert waited a moment; then brought his fist suddenly crashing down upon the table. 'Tell me!'

'Why should I?'

'Because I must know what I am . . .' – Robert paused, and swallowed – 'and what I might become.' He swallowed again, to compose himself. 'Please, my Lord. Please. I have no other hope.'

Slowly, Lord Rochester rose and crossed to the window of his room. 'There is a problem,' he murmured at length, gazing out at the sky. 'The Turk – the Pasha – he is in Amsterdam.'

'What is he doing there?'

'We had arranged – a while ago – to meet there, at a place that was of mutual convenience.' Lord Rochester paused, then gestured at the distant masts on the Thames. 'Unfortunately,' he murmured, 'it is rather less so at present – now that His Majesty's Navy has imposed its blockade.'

'Why then do you not arrange to meet in some other town?'

'The Pasha is . . . unwilling . . . to leave Amsterdam.'

'Why?'

'He is . . . unwilling.' Lord Rochester paused, and did not expand. Instead, he leaned out through the window and angled his head, as though listening for something faint on the wind. 'There,' he said suddenly.

'What?'

Lord Rochester smiled. 'A possible solution to our problem.'

Robert joined him at the window; and then he heard it, a muffled, far-away boom. He frowned. 'Cannon-fire?' he asked.

Lord Rochester nodded. 'There is a battle begun against the Dutch on the Channel. I have written to the King – and will shortly join the fleet.' He leaned out further and breathed in the air. 'What do you say, Lovelace?' he asked. 'Will you come with me to war?'

Robert stared at him impatiently. 'There must be an easier way . . .'

'No,' said Lord Rochester. 'For I must, before I dive into mysteries which would forever deprive me of mortality, be confident that I wish to bid farewell to Death, the certainty of which is all that makes us human.' He turned to Robert. 'Do you still believe,' he asked suddenly, 'that you will meet with your parents in the bosom of Heaven, and that all your mortal suffering will there be washed away?'

'It surprises me,' replied Robert at length, 'to hear you ask such a question.'

'Does it?' Lord Rochester laughed hollowly. 'And yet all men would have faith, if only they dared. For without faith, what is left us? A world whose belly is a bag of turds, her cunt a common shore, a stinking compound of shit and slime. It must suck us down, Lovelace, it must drown us . . .' He paused, to gaze out again at the burning sky. 'Save that still hope lingers, the hope which lies in Death . . .'

Robert did not answer. He was remembering his mother's dying cry, her promise that they would meet again beyond the Celestial Gates. He had not heard it so clearly for a very long while.

It would still speak to him, unbidden, in the days and weeks which followed. Lord Rochester, as he had claimed he would be, was soon released from the Tower; he journeyed with Robert to the east coast; and from there they both took ship to join with the fleet. Even upon the waves, though, the cry would still echo in Robert's mind, and he almost wished that it would not surprise him so insistently; for he knew that it affected his will, and clouded his resolve to seek out his revenge.

Lord Rochester, however, was in a death-haunted humour; and he would not leave the topic of the after-life alone. The closer that the English fleet drew to the Dutch, the more urgent grew his meditations, as though he were desperate to believe that doubt might be something like the sea, boundless and ever-flowing, upon which he might be borne forever, away from his meeting with the Turk in Amsterdam. 'And yet in truth', he muttered one night, 'I find it hard to conjure up any doubt at all. For reason and experience both suggest the same truth, that we are bundles of sensations, mere matter, nothing more. There is no life beyond death – but merely annihilation.'

One of his companions in the cabin shook his head. 'Do not say so,' he muttered fearfully. 'For tomorrow it may be we shall fight, and I feel it strongly in my soul that I am fated to die.'

Lord Rochester stared at him, intrigued. 'Why, Wyndham,' he asked, 'do you truly believe that your soul, if you are killed, will survive your mortal dust?'

'I trust so, yes.'

'And yet still you dread to die?'

Wyndham shivered. 'Let us not talk of this matter any further,' he said. He reached for the swaying lantern overhead, and guarded the flame with his hands, as though in doing so he was keeping watch upon his life. Lord Rochester grinned. He turned to Montagu, who had come with him and Robert aboard the same ship. 'What do you say?' Rochester asked his friend. 'Do you agree with Wyndham, that our religion speaks the truth, and that death is but a portal on to a fresh and wondrous state?'

Montagu frowned, and did not answer the question. 'I feel it too,' he murmured slowly, as though with sudden surprise. 'I feel that I shall die.'

Wyndham gazed at him wide-eyed. 'It cannot be,' he whispered.

'And yet if it should be true?' Lord Rochester pressed. 'If you should both die, what then?'

Montagu frowned at him. 'I do not understand.'

'I must know,' whispered Lord Rochester, leaning forward. 'And so would we all.'

'Know what?' asked Wyndham, licking his lips.

'The truth of what awaits us.'

'What do you propose?'

'That we enter into a solemn vow. All of us, together, now at this moment.'

'What are we to promise?'

'That tomorrow, should any of us die, we shall appear to the others and give notice of the future state . . .'

Rochester paused. 'Or prove, by our non-appearance, that it does not exist at all.'

Montagu glanced at Wyndham, then laughed harshly. 'I shall consent to no such thing.'

For a while, Wyndham stayed frozen, gazing at the lantern as it swung back and forth with the rolling of the ship. Then at last he closed his eyes, and nodded slowly.

At once, Lord Rochester reached for their hands. 'Swear it,' he whispered. 'Swear it upon the dearest proofs of our religion. Swear to return if it is true, that there is indeed an after-life, a state beyond death.' When all was finished Lord Rochester lay back, as though after a furious bout of pleasure, and smiled. 'And now,' he murmured, 'we must wait and see. It will prove, I think, a most valuable experiment.'

The next day, battle was joined. Robert, standing with his companions on the deck of their ship, followed the progress of the engagement; and he soon realised that he was watching a disastrous defeat. For the English ships were cramped and could barely move, so that they became sitting targets for the Dutch guns; the shrieking of the gale was soon mingled with that of the injured and the dying, and the waves were flecked with bobbing corpses. Yet Robert and his companions, and their entire ship, were barely fired upon; and indeed, when the battle was finished and the English fleet withdrawn, it was discovered that only four men out of the hundreds on board had been killed. Of these four, two had been Montagu and Wyndham. They had been hit by the same cannon ball, so that they had been reduced to a mingled mess of limbs and guts right by the side of Lord Rochester, splashing across his cloak. He had gazed down at their corpses for a moment; and then turned to

Robert, a single eyebrow raised. 'Now,' he had murmured, 'let us wait and see.'

They did so for the next two nights. Robert would pace the decks, gazing out at the storm-lashed waves or up at the sky, as though expecting to see the spirit of the dead upon the gale, but there was nothing borne to him on the winds, save only plumes of spray; and he knew that the ghost would not appear. It was true, he wondered what Lord Rochester might have seen; but he could not ask, for his Lordship was away on secret business with the Admiral, and it was not until three days after Montagu's and Wyndham's deaths that he finally reappeared. He stood framed in the cabin doorway for a long while, as he met Robert's stare; then he laughed suddenly and shook his head. 'It has often been said,' he proclaimed, 'that the truth best lies in silence – and now Wyndham has proved that it is so indeed.'

Robert crossed to him. 'You are decided, then?'

Lord Rochester narrowed his eyes, and did not answer at once. 'We have been much exercised the past days,' he murmured at length, 'with how best to deal with these mud-dwelling Dutch. It has been suggested that we do not yet have the ships to whip them as they deserve. It has been suggested that what we need is a little more time – that we should negotiate a holding truce – have talks, perhaps, or talks about talks. All in the utmost secrecy, of course.'

Robert nodded slowly. 'The utmost – of course.'

'I have volunteered myself in the service of such a plan, and have taken the liberty, Lovelace, of volunteering your own name as well. I trust you are agreeable.'

'What would I not do in the service of my King?'

'Your loyalty does you credit.' Lord Rochester nodded

curtly. 'Very well. We shall leave tonight on a small, swift vessel, in conditions, as I have mentioned, of the utmost secrecy. We shall set sail for Holland, and when we arrive we shall approach the Stadholder of the Dutch Republic.'

'And where, my Lord, is the Stadholder to be found?'

'Why, Lovelace, it is hard to be certain. Indeed, it is possible – no, likely – that we shall not be able to discover him at all.'

'That would be a great tragedy.'

'An exceeding one.'

'Yet we should not permit our fear of failure to blunt our resolve.'

'We most certainly should not.'

'For who knows what other fruits our journey may not bear?'

'A most positive attitude. Who can know indeed?' Lord Rochester smiled suddenly. 'And so prepare yourself, Lovelace. Let us delay no more. We leave within the hour for Amsterdam.'

∽◌∼

'. . . SOARING PIERCE
THE FLAMING LIMITS OF THE UNIVERSE,
SEARCH HEAVEN AND HELL, FIND OUT WHAT'S ACTED THERE,
AND GIVE THE WORLD TRUE GROUNDS OF HOPE AND FEAR . . .'
        The Earl of Rochester, 'A Satyr Against Mankind'

'It is fitting,' said Robert, 'for a man who would soar high above his own mortal baseness, that you are come to Amsterdam, where so many wonders and riches are raised upon such shit.'

'It is indeed,' nodded Lord Rochester, 'a veritable

blood-drinker of a city.' He paused, and gazed about him. 'I do not wonder the Pasha is come here to recover.'

'Recover?' asked Robert.

Lord Rochester stared at him sharply. 'Did I not mention,' he murmured, 'that the Pasha has been sick?'

'You did not.'

Lord Rochester shrugged faintly. 'Then that was most remiss of me.' But he said no more and instead leaned back in the boat, trailing his fingers through the water as though lost in contemplation. Robert turned from him to stare ahead again. For a long while, the nearer the boat had drawn to Amsterdam, the less he had been able to see of the city, for his view had been obscured by a great forest of shipping which made those of London seem the merest woods, so vast was its extent. For all that it was night, Robert could still hear a babel of cries and orders being shouted from the docks; and on the faint summer breeze there were borne to him a thousand different smells, perfumes and spices from every corner of the globe. Mingled with them all, though, was the native scent of mud, growing steadily stronger as the docks were left behind and the boat began to pull into a network of canals. Away from the harbour front, the water seemed thicker and the darkness more profound, as though they were passing, Robert thought suddenly, into the very body of the city, and were afloat upon its blood. He glanced round again at his companion. Lord Rochester was leaning forward now, his expression tense and alert. He spoke something to the oarsmen; then pointed ahead towards the canal's right bank. Robert too gazed ahead. He could see now how the bank was lined with buildings of extraordinary magnificence, warehouses and private homes, their ornate gables etched against the stars, their fronts freshly painted, so that their gleam in the dark was like that of pale flesh. Robert remembered the bodies in Wolverton Hall, and shivered, despite the prickling heat. He drew a cloak about him, and stared ahead again with redoubled dread and hope. Only one of the houses on the canal seemed derelict, its ruin all the more evident for the splendour of its neighbours; and it did not surprise him to see that the boat was veering slowly towards it. There were steps, greasy with weeds, which led down to the water; the boat drifted slowly to a halt, and was moored by their side; and then Robert followed Lord Rochester up on to the bank.

The door of the house opened as the two men approached it. Lord Rochester passed inside; Robert followed him. There was no sign of the servant who must have opened the door, nor any sound, and Robert would have guessed the entire house to be empty save that along the walls great torches had been lit, burning with heatless, ash-white flames. The scene they illuminated was one of magnificent desolation, a room which stretched so far back that it was lost in darkness, and contained nothing at all but bare boards, and a single staircase sweeping upwards until it too, like the room, was lost in the dark. Lord Rochester crossed to it, his footsteps echoing through the vast stillness, and began to climb the steps. Robert paused a moment before following; for he realised, gazing about him, that the proportions of the room were impossibly large. He stared after his companion, whose form was already fading into the darkness; then began to follow him up the stairway, up and up. At length he paused a moment more, and gazed back down the stairs at the room he had left. It seemed even vaster and emptier than it had done from the floor, and Robert rubbed his eyes and shook his head, for he dreaded to think what place he had entered. Yet it was too late to turn; and so he stumbled on upwards until suddenly, through the shadows, he saw a wall ahead of him, and an open door. Lord Rochester was walking through it. Robert clutched at the crucifix he wore about his neck; then he began to hurry. He approached the doorway, he passed through it . . . At once, as he did so, he was doubled up with pain, such as he had not felt since the passageways of Wolverton Hall.

He fell to the ground, clawing at his stomach as though the agony were something he might tear out with his hands. So searing was it that he was rendered unconscious of all that was about him; but dimly, through the mists of pain, he heard a haunting, silver-toned voice. 'The medicine. Give it to him. Quick.' He felt himself being held in someone's arms; and then a bottle was placed between his lips. He swallowed. An acrid, burning liquid scalded his throat. He swallowed again, trying not to choke; and felt the pain in his guts gradually starting to grow numb.

'It seems,' said the voice, 'we share a linked ailment, you and I.'

Robert stared about him. He was in a room with its windows open to the stars. It was airy and large, but not impossibly so, and it was as though – he thought – having passed through the door, he had returned to the everyday world. Yet the fittings of the room, when he stared at them more closely, seemed exotic and strange: there were cushions piled everywhere, and thick patterned rugs; jewelled and golden censers filled with burning incense; no furniture at all save for low, silk-lined couches. On one of these a man lay hunched, his body twisted as though in terrible pain, so that he seemed barely able to move; and Robert knew, as he walked round to face him, that this could only be the Pasha. For his eyes were a blood-drinker's, incandescent and profound, and his skin gleamed like silk illumined from inside; but stretched tight, very tight, across the contours of his bones. He would have been handsome had his face not been so haggard, and so deathly pale that he scarcely seemed a Turk; yet still, intermingled with his suffering, were the marks of wisdom and incalculable age, so that Robert, kneeling by the Pasha's side, felt he was in the presence of some mighty angel, fallen from Heaven but still stamped with the greatness of his former state.

'Not an angel,' murmured the Pasha, 'but only a man, many years – centuries – a millennium ago.'

Robert gazed at him in shock, then narrowed his eyes. 'You can read my thoughts?' he asked. 'And yet I had thought my mind was closed to your breed?'

The Pasha smiled faintly. 'As I told you, we are linked by a common suffering – and also, it would seem, by something more as well.'

'Then tell me ...' Robert stared at him in sudden, desperate hope. 'Tell me what it is ... tell me what you know ...'

'First ...' The Pasha's voice seemed hoarse with pain, and it faded away upon a rattle of breath. He struggled to reach for a tall, fluted bottle; but his arm was too weak, and Lord Rochester had to pick it up for him. It contained a black, viscous liquid, which Robert recognised from its smell as the liquid he had been given when he had entered the room. Like a priest with a goblet of communion wine, Lord Rochester raised the bottle to the Pasha's lips, and tipped it gently as the Pasha began to drink.

'It must be a wondrous medicine,' said Robert, watching as the Pasha appeared to revive, 'to cure us both with such rapid ease.'

'As wondrous,' Lord Rochester answered, 'as it is also secret and rare. And yet I have spoken of it to you before, Lovelace, for this is that same *mummia* which I gave to the Marquise.'

Robert gazed at the liquid in fascination. 'And what is it,' he murmured, 'which can have such effect?'

Lord Rochester smiled at him coldly, and gestured towards some bottles gathered by the wall. Robert crossed to them. Each one was filled with a clear, thick substance; and in each was suspended a part of some limb. Robert knelt down by the nearest bottle. It contained a hand, so black and shrivelled that it seemed almost a claw, floating ponderously in the liquid like some blind, sea-bred thing.

'It is crushed,' said the Pasha, 'and mingled with wine, that it may be consumed more easily and the taste be concealed.'

'And . . .' – Robert stared again in disgust at the floating hand – 'and these are severed from the corpses of your victims?'

The Pasha shook his head. 'If only they were,' he answered, 'it would save much effort and expense, for indeed, there is nothing in the world so valuable nor so difficult to find.'

'What marks them, then, to render them so priceless?'

The Pasha smiled. 'You intrude upon dark and ancient mysteries, my friend.'

'Intrude?' Robert laughed balefully. 'No. I have long been lost amidst them.'

The Pasha's thin smile broadened. He picked up the bottle of liquid by his side and, raising it to the moonlight, gazed at it a while. 'I call it *mummia*,' he murmured at last, 'for that is the name by which it must be ordered, when I speak to the merchants who bring it to me here from the tombs of Egypt. For you should know, Lovelace, that it was the practice of the ancients to embalm their dead – and that these dead are plundered, and hawked in the Cairo bazaars, to be used in medicines or worn as idle charms. So it is easy enough for me to have them bought – and yet in truth, for my purposes, barely one in an infinitude of such corpses ever serves.'

'Why, sir,' asked Robert, 'what qualities do you require them to possess, which are so hard to discover?'

'A secret long sunk into dust, abandoned within temples lost beneath the sands and forgotten, forgotten, these many centuries now. In Egypt it was guarded, and Ur, and Hindustan, where bodies may still be found and dragged from mouldy graves. The ancient Hindoos called such corpses *Raktavija* – "seed-blood" – a fitting name, Lovelace, for the blood-line was fostered and protected by the priests from generation to generation, so that each parent's blood served to seed that of the child. The lines are long dead now; yet they were royal, and so their tombs may sometimes be discovered undisturbed, and traded to those who can comprehend their worth.' The Pasha gestured towards the windows, and the great host of masts stretching far out from the docks. 'And that is why,' he whispered, 'I wait in Amsterdam, the great market of the world, where everything and anything may be purchased in the end.'

Robert sat in silence, gazing at the row of bottles and their sticks of withered flesh; then he turned again, to stare into the Pasha's pain-haunted eyes. 'And for what purpose,' he whispered slowly, 'was this "seed-blood" bred?'

'To serve as a charm, and an antidote.'

'Against what?'

'Can you not guess?'

'Tell me.'

The Pasha sighed, and for a long while gazed in silence through the window at the moon. 'He has had many titles,' he murmured at last. 'Seth, he was named by the ancient priests, the spirit of darkness which haunted the deserts and rose upon the burning winds of the night. Azrael, we Muslims call him now, the angel of death. Your own religion too has its names for him; you do not require me to repeat them all to you.'

'And so he is indeed, then ...' – Robert swallowed, and hugged himself – 'he is indeed whom the Marquise claimed him to be?'

'The Prince of Hell?' The Pasha smiled and shrugged. 'It is true, he bears his own hell with him, for he is evil, Lovelace, and deadly, almost beyond comprehension. And yet ...' – the Pasha paused, his smile still lingering faintly on his lips – 'we must trust he is no god.'

'What reasons do you have for saying that?'

The Pasha pointed to the *mummia*. 'Would a god be kept at bay by a sludge of flesh and wine?'

Robert gazed at him with sudden, feverish hope. 'And what else?' he whispered. 'There must be more. Please – I have to know – for I am sworn to destroy him.'

The Pasha met his eyes for a moment; then he began to laugh and Robert felt a flush of mingled anger and despair. 'My ambition, then, is so contemptible?' he asked.

'Not contemptible,' answered the Pasha, 'but over-reaching, perhaps.' He reached for a knife, then parted his robe to expose his naked chest. He sliced the blade across his rib-cage and a thin liquid, so watery that it was almost clear of red, dribbled down his side. 'My blood,' the Pasha whispered, 'was once ruby-thick and rich without price, for I was – I am – the greatest of my kind. And yet see!' He touched his wound and raised his finger to the stars. 'I was grievously wounded,' he whispered distantly, as though to himself. He glanced at Lord Rochester. 'You remember, my Lord, when you discovered me upon the road – was I not almost a corpse?'

Lord Rochester inclined his head. 'You were indeed,' he answered, 'a thing of skin and bone.'

The Pasha smiled bitterly as he dabbed his finger into his blood again, and held it back up to the stars. 'I too,' he murmured, 'like you, Lovelace, have sought to overthrow Azrael – even, as you can see, to the very point of death. And yet for a while, since I had emerged alive from our great fight – albeit only barely – I had hoped it was my enemy who must have died instead.' He licked his finger-tip thoughtfully. 'And then Lord Rochester wrote to me. He told me the news of his meeting with you.'

He paused, and his eyes began to widen. They were blazing; and Robert felt them suddenly searching deep into his thoughts, as though his mind were a darkness being scanned by lanterns. He saw, unbidden, his mother consumed by the dancing flames; his father swaying as the rope swung in the breeze, to and fro beneath the lintel of the stones, to and fro, as the blood dripped slowly down; and then suddenly, Robert cried out and held his arm across his eyes, for he imagined that a hellish figure was rising before him, its form emerging from beneath its melted shell of flesh, and that it was searching for him, reaching for him, freezing him to death. He screamed. . . . he could feel the pain in his stomach again, like a spitting shard of ice; and then the bottle, as before, being placed against his lips.

He drank the *mummia* and the pain began to fade, but it still lingered in his blood like the echo of a chill. He opened his eyes. Lord Rochester was kneeling by his side, and the Pasha's stare was hooded once again.

Robert rose to his feet.

'You are leaving us?' the Pasha murmured.

'If there is no hope,' answered Robert, 'then I see no purpose in remaining here.'

'I did not say there was no hope.'

'You acknowledged it yourself, that he cannot be destroyed.'

The Pasha shrugged faintly. 'Not destroyed, perhaps. But injured, Lovelace, injured almost to destruction.'

'No.' Robert shook his head violently. 'I saw him amidst the stones; he was recovered, restored. Whatever wounds you once inflicted, they are now wholly cured.'

'Not wholly – not yet.'

'I tell you, I saw him.'

'And I tell you that if he were not still wounded, then all of your country, and far beyond its shores, would already have been drowned under oceans of blood, and survivors would be gazing upon the slaughter and saying that the time of universal desolation had arrived, that the Apocalypse was come. So please – take your seat.' The Pasha gestured with his hand; and as he did so, he gasped and seemed seized again by pain. 'I have much to tell you.' Then he doubled up in agony, and could say nothing more until he had been given the bottle of *mummia* again and had drained it to the dregs.

He lay back at last, and closed his eyes. Silence filled the room, heavy like the perfume of the incense clouds.

'There is no weakness,' the Pasha murmured at last, 'but to cringe and despair because one thinks oneself weak. For so long as one's will is undefeated one is strong, for so long as the desire for revenge still endures. You see me, Lovelace' – he parted his robe, and gestured to his wound – 'I do not talk from ignorance. For it may be that as mortals are to my breed, the sport of our humours and appetites, so we are to beings higher than us – yet still, it would be the basest of abdications not to believe that I might surpass them in the end and, in doing so, achieve much good – much good . . .'

As he said this, the gleam in his eyes began to cloud, and his voice trailed away into silence again. Robert leaned forward and licked his lips. 'What beings are they, then,' he whispered, 'who are mightier than you?'

'I cannot be certain,' the Pasha answered, 'whether they even exist, for it may be that even Azrael was once just a creature like myself, and that the rumours, the whispers, of these beings I have heard were nothing but the echoes of my own thoughts and fears.'

'Yet you do not believe so?' Lord Rochester asked.

The Pasha shook his head. 'Whatever they may be – angels, demons, the deposed ancient gods – I have no choice but to trust they may be found, for with their wisdom, their powers, what might I not do? I might escape my thirst for blood. I might love, and not destroy the minds of those I love. I might gain the strength – who knows? – even to defeat Azrael, and destroy him forever.' He smiled faintly at Robert. 'A worthy prize,' he whispered, 'would you not say?'

Robert sat frozen. 'And are you any nearer,' he asked slowly, 'to gaining it for yourself?'

Still the Pasha smiled. 'It may be,' he whispered.

The silence suddenly seemed paralysing. Robert forced himself to part his lips, to speak. 'No more secrets,' he whispered. 'Tell me all! Please.'

The Pasha stirred painfully, propping up a cushion so that he might rest his head; then he gathered his cloak about him and, so doing, began to tell his tale.

∽○○∽

'BUT MOST OF ALL, RABBI LOEW FEARED THE PRIEST TADEUS, WHO HATED THE JEWS, AND WAS A DEVOTEE OF THE MAGICAL ARTS . . .'

Traditional Jewish Folktale

'I t happened,' the Pasha said, 'in the latter years of the previous century, that I was the guest in Paris of the Marquise de Mauvissière. We had been – I will not say friends – but occasional partners, perhaps, in a common quest to penetrate the mysteries of our nature. The Marquise was not then what she has since become, a slave to her own superstitions, for her studies were yet to lead her to her present belief that there is a Prince of Hell who is the God of all the world – and so we were able to imagine that our interests might be shared. It was in such a spirit that the Marquise told me of reports she had received from Tadeus, a priest of a bold and ambitious character, whom she had chosen not long before to make a creature like ourselves. This Tadeus had been writing to her from his native Bohemia, describing strange plagues and rumours abroad in the countryside – but darkly, as though reluctant to specify what such rumours might be. I was not greatly intrigued. As I have said, the man had once been a priest – it had ever been his work to forge mysteries out of nothingness. Yet for all that, since I was planning to return to the East and would have to pass through Bohemia, I determined I would turn aside on my journey and pay a visit on him, to see if his dark hints might be anything more.'

The Pasha paused, and seemed to fall into silence. But though his lips no longer moved, Robert could still hear his words – sounding, he imagined, from the depths of his own brain. 'Tadeus had written,' Robert heard the Pasha seem to say, 'from a place named Melnik, to the north of Prague. I arrived there at length one winter afternoon.' At once, Robert saw in his mind an image of the place: there was a castle and a church on the edge of a great cliff, and a mean village straggling down the side of the hill. A strange aura of suffering and desolation seemed to hang in the air, and Robert sensed at once that it was touched by some great evil. He blinked and rubbed his eyes; and when he opened them again, it was to see the Pasha gazing as though into the distance.

'I approached the church.' The Pasha spoke, as before, without moving his lips. 'I could see that the doorway to the crypt was open, and I heard a strange noise, like that of things being scraped, rising from the depths beyond. I dismounted from my horse and passed into the crypt. From ahead of me, I could see the glimmer of something pale; and then I realised, as I descended the steps, that the crypt was filled with skeletons, so that it was almost overflowing with skulls and jumbled bones. Two groups of men were camped in the ossuary, and it was they who were making the scraping sounds, for they had great piles of corpses next to them and were shredding the flesh, so that the bones would be clean.'

'What were they doing?' Robert asked.

The Pasha smiled faintly. 'Naturally,' he answered, 'I asked them that at once. They seemed half-crazed by fear, as well they might have been, and scarcely able to talk. I beckoned a man from the first group to me. As he rose nervously to his feet, I saw that he was wearing a Jew's yellow hat. I gazed at him in astonishment, wondering what he could be doing in such a place of death, so far from the ghetto and in a Christian church. When I asked him, he stammered that he and his fellows were working to the orders of their Rabbi in Prague; and then, as though terrified that I might not believe him, he turned to the second group of men and appealed for confirmation. None of them answered; but I knew the man had been telling the truth, for I could see now that the second group were local peasants, who would never have allowed Jews into their church without a previous specific command. So I crossed to them, and asked them in turn who had given them their instructions. The nearest man swallowed, then whispered, "Father Tadeus." I nodded, and asked him where the Father might be found. At this, the peasants and Jews alike glanced at each other nervously; then one of the peasants spoke a village's name. "But the plague there has been more deadly than anywhere else," he cried. "Do not approach it, for it is stamped with the Devil's mark!" His warning intrigued me; and I asked him if the bones he was perched upon were those of other victims of the plague. He nodded; and at once both groups of men began to redouble their work. For, as one of the Jews explained, the bones had to be cleansed of corrupted flesh, so that the plague might not spread and infect all the world.

'I wondered what his Rabbi had told him, to make him dread such a cataclysm, and to believe it might be stopped by shredding flesh from victims' bones; and even more, I wondered what the Rabbi's business could have been with a Christian priest – and a blood-drinker at that. I knew, though, that Tadeus was the best man to answer such questions; and so I left the church and set off to discover him. The journey was not far; yet it was a difficult one, for whenever I would ask for directions, people would shake their heads and look away, or seem never to have heard of the village at all. Nor, I was soon to realise, had they necessarily been lying; for when I finally found myself approaching the place, I discovered that the road was overgrown, as though it had been abandoned for many, many years.' He paused; and Robert imagined he saw a scene of desolation before him such as he recognised at once. 'Nothing stirred,' the Pasha murmured, 'not even an animal, not even a bird among the trees; and around the village itself there was a ring of stakes, and then a mighty wall, as though it had been built to keep the world away.'

'And those inside the village as slaves,' Robert said. 'For I witnessed the same when I journeyed to Woodton – overgrown roads, and a wall around the village.'

The Pasha gazed at him unblinkingly. 'So Lord Rochester has told me,' he said. He stirred, and leaned forward from his couch. 'Listen, then,' he hissed. 'Learn what Woodton's fate may be. I discovered no village left beyond the wall – nothing but a wasteland of rubble and ash. Half-rotted corpses were strewn across the fields. There was a castle still standing; but as I rode towards it, I felt that aura of stillness, of evil and death, which I had first sensed in the church at Melnik, and which was now unbearably strong, as though I had reached the very heart of a spreading ring of darkness. I passed into the castle.

At once, I felt a terror such as I had not known for many, many years – for centuries, perhaps. But it does not require me to conjure it for you, Lovelace; for I know that you have felt such a terror yourself.'

Robert nodded without answering, then breathed in deeply. 'And in the castle?' he whispered. 'What did you discover?'

'It was empty. Whatever had been there was gone without trace – and yet as I was to discover, it could only recently have left.' The Pasha paused; then smiled coldly. 'As I rose from the place,' he continued, 'I met with Tadeus. He, like me, had been drawn to the village, suspecting that it might have held some mystery; and indeed, he had attempted to reach it only a few weeks before. On that occasion, though, he told me, he had been unable to find it – for the village and its castle had been accounted as lost.'

'*Lost?*' Lord Rochester frowned. 'What do you mean?'

The Pasha shrugged faintly. 'That it had vanished from the face of the countryside.'

'How was that possible?'

The Pasha shrugged again. 'The roads which had once led there could no longer be found. It was as though the village itself had dissolved into air.'

'Yet when I went to Woodton,' said Robert in puzzlement, 'I had no difficulty discovering it.'

'Yes.' The Pasha narrowed his eyes. 'You had no difficulty. But had the Marquise approached the village, and you not been with her – what then, do you think? Would she have been able to discover it for herself?'

Robert shook his head. 'What are you saying?' he asked.

The Pasha paused. He glanced at the *mummia*, then

up again into Robert's eyes. 'We know,' he said slowly, 'from sundry proofs, that you are not like other mortals, that you are somehow marked. You are surely not so fearful, Lovelace, as to deny that to yourself?'

Robert sat frozen. He could feel the chill in his stomach again. He clenched his fists, and stroked the knuckles along the curve of his lips.

'Why else,' the Pasha continued in a low and deathly murmur, 'would I be speaking to you now? For it is not my custom to discuss things in this manner with mortals, as though the world were a corpse laid out in a lecture hall and I some doctor, slicing and skinning its surface away, exposing the filaments of mystery underneath, which run so deep that even I cannot see where all of them may lead.'

'You cannot see . . .' Robert frowned; then shook his head. 'What does that mean, then, in plain language? That you cannot tell me what this mark is, which you say has been stamped upon me? That you cannot tell what it might signify or portend?'

The Pasha did not answer.

Robert rose slowly from his seat.

'What we do not know,' the Pasha whispered, 'we must attempt to discover.'

Robert spun round, his face contorted with frustration and contempt. 'How?' he cried. 'If you do not know, what chance can there be?'

'None at all,' answered the Pasha, 'if you do not have the patience and the courage to sit still, and listen to those secrets which I can reveal. I have told you, Lovelace – and feel too weak to waste my breath on saying it again – that though the danger is terrible, a faint hope still remains.'

He gestured to the place beside him. Robert stared at the Pasha a moment in silence; then crossed to the cushions, and lay down. He breathed in deeply. 'You spoke of secrets.'

'As Tadeus did to me, amidst the blasted fields where the village had once stood – of the proofs of a great and deadly mystery.'

'And what were these proofs?'

The Pasha smiled coldly. 'Perhaps you are not as ignorant as you fear, Lovelace – for I am certain they will already be familiar to you. The plague Tadeus had already mentioned, in his letters to the Marquise. But he told me also of a breed of the risen dead – more virulent even than the plague itself, and resistant to all his powers of command. He had traced the origin of both to the ruined village and could no longer doubt, now that he had penetrated at last to its heart, that it had indeed been the seat of some monstrous evil; perhaps, he whispered in my ear, of the Anti-Christ himself. I scoffed at this; but Tadeus shook his head, and half-smiled. He knew that I was an infidel, he sneered; but one did not need to be a Christian to recognise the evil. Why, he told me, even in the Ghetto there were rumours abroad; and it had been a Rabbi who had suggested how the evil might be fought.

'This intrigued me; for I remembered the Jews in the crypt, and how they had claimed to be working for a Rabbi in Prague. Tadeus confirmed that this had been the very same man: Rabbi Jehuda Loew ben Bezalel. I asked him how they had met. Tadeus answered that it had been in a plague-stricken village, where Rabbi Loew had been seeking, like Tadeus himself, to discover the origin of the sickness, and of the risen dead. I was astonished by this and asked if Rabbi Loew was a blood-drinker himself, to know of such things. Tadeus shook his head. "But he is a great and learned magician," he replied, "wise in every branch of human knowledge, and perhaps in that which is not human too. For it is whispered in the Ghetto that he is the master of the science of the hidden name of God; and that the past and the future are open books to him. I can almost believe it; for how else did he know that the plague could be halted, and the dead preserved peaceful in their graves, by stripping the bones of all those who had died? I trust that explains, Your Excellency, the sight you discovered in the church at Melnik. And it is clear that the plague is already cured, and that the Evil Spirit, whatever else it may be, does not possess that power of Ezekiel's God to raise up dry bones, and give them back their breath. For instead, the bones in Melnik rest where they are stacked; and so it is that a deadly peril has been averted".'

Robert shook his head. 'But I do not understand. Why would Tadeus be pleased to see such a danger stopped?'

'He had not yet succumbed to his ambitions and grown a worshipper of Evil.' The Pasha curled back his lips in a mocking smile. 'How else would he have been able to work with Rabbi Loew, who was only a mortal and, worse than that, a Jew? Yet I could tell that Tadeus' admiration was suffused with envy; and that he not only resented the Rabbi's learning but desired it for himself. He had tried to conceal this from me at first; yet the nearer we drew to Prague – where Tadeus had a home, and had suggested we should stay – so the more naked his jealousy became. He took me that night, when we had arrived in the city, to a narrow, winding lane in the shadow of the Castle, where the tiny houses were barely a shoulder's width apart and the scent of strange distillations hung heavy in the air. Tadeus gazed about him with contempt; then up at the massive darkness of the Castle. "There is a new Emperor come to Prague," he whispered, "who has gathered alchemists here to spin moonbeams into gold, and to provide him with the powers of the philosopher's stone. For the Emperor has been startled, it is said, by strange rumours of disaster, glimpsed in melancholy dreams or foretold by portents of fire in the sky – and so he has turned for comfort to the hidden arts. He is right to do so, of course; for how else is the evil now abroad to be confronted? Yet what a fool he is as well, to have gathered his pack of charlatans here when the true magic" – he gestured – "lies out there."

'I looked. We had descended the narrow lane by now, and from where we were standing the whole of Prague was spread out before us. Beyond the river, cramped within a wall, was a labyrinth of dilapidated buildings and streets, dense and misshapen, like the city of a dream. Tadeus was pointing at it. "It has ever been said," he whispered, "that the Ghetto is a place of potent witchcraft." His eyes narrowed as he turned to face me. "What is the source, do you think, of the Rabbi's secret powers?"

'I continued to stare out at the Ghetto. "You have told me of no powers," I murmured, "only of learning."

' "And is learning not power?"

'I smiled. "If you are so eager, Tadeus, to possess it, why do you not enter his mind and drain it from his thoughts?"

' "I have already tried," answered Tadeus.

'I stared at him in surprise. "And what did you find?"

' "All night in his dreams I wrestled with him – and like that angel who fought with Jacob by the ford, I could not prevail." He paused. "You," he whispered suddenly, "you are the greatest of our kind. You could break the Jew."

DELIVER US FROM EVIL

' "Why should I wish to?" I murmured.

' "Because I believe he is the tool of the infernal spirit."

'I frowned. "And yet he was the one who caused the plague to be halted."

' "A trick, Your Excellency, a trick. You do not know these Jews as I do. We must break him soon before his powers grow too great. For with the Evil One's strength, what may not he try?"

'I could sense how desperate his eagerness was. I nodded, very faintly. "Soon, then," I agreed. "I will visit him soon."

'I left Tadeus, and hunted all that night. Returned to his house, I felt strangely tired; and for the first time in a long while, I fell asleep.' The Pasha paused and closed his eyes; and at the same moment Robert saw a strange scene before him, like the landscape of a dream. There was a great and empty plain. All was still on it save for a single figure, just a pinprick in the distance but walking towards him; and with each step that he took, Robert was filled with strange dread. Nearer and nearer the figure drew, staff in his hand. He was cloaked, Robert could see now, and wore a hood pulled down close across his face. More than anything in the world, Robert wanted to see what was hidden underneath it – what his face might be like. He was almost by Robert's side now; as he raised a hand to the edge of his hood, Robert could feel, with a burning certainty, that there was some great and wondrous mystery about to be revealed. He began to pull the hood back. Robert started, and reached forward to seize it for himself. At the very same moment, the dream seemed to fade; and the Pasha opened his eyes. He breathed in deeply. 'And thus it was for me,' he murmured. 'I found myself awake.'

He stirred, and sat up more fully. 'I rose at once from

my bed,' he continued. 'I must have slept all day, for it was already night again and the streets outside were empty and still. I left the house; yet the dream still seemed to be with me, so that I almost wondered, walking through Prague, whether I had ever woken up at all. By the Charles Bridge, I paused for a moment and gazed across the river at the Ghetto walls. The towers and the roofs of the houses were so twisted that I thought again how like buildings in a dream they appeared. I walked on to the bridge, to cross towards them. As I did so, I felt a sudden shiver of something sweet and unexpected, like a ripple of silver passing through my blood. I looked towards the far end of the bridge. It was empty – save for a single figure approaching me. As he had done in my dream, he wore a cloak and a hood. He held a staff in his hand; and as he drew nearer, I could see that his shoulders seemed stooped, as though with great fatigue. I stayed frozen where I was. As he came level with me, so he lifted his hand. He seized the edge of his hood; and as he drew it back, I knew that this was real, that I was not still asleep. And yet his face might indeed have been a vision in a dream, for it was unearthly and terrible, stranger than any I had ever beheld, so that I was filled at once with a mixture of repugnance and awe. He was not a creature like myself, of that I was certain, for his eyes were far brighter than my own, and impossibly deep; and although his face wore no wrinkles, he seemed fabulously old, ancient beyond measure – but how I knew this to be so, I could not explain. The wanderer glanced at me piercingly, not pausing in his walk; then he passed me by. I stood frozen where I was, watching him as he left the bridge; and then I started suddenly and sought to pursue him. But he was already vanished, and the empty streets mocked me, echoing my cries.

'I turned, and resumed my former journey. I crossed the bridge, and then, beyond the Ghetto wall, found myself lost amidst narrow, filthy alleyways, crooked with old houses and teetering galleries. As though it were a whirl-pool, I allowed the Ghetto to sweep me along, bearing me always into its heart, until I found myself in the shadow of a blackened, triangular wall; and I knew I had arrived at the synagogue. The windows seemed dark; but having passed into the hall, I could make out the glimmer of a single light falling in a wan beam from the room beyond. Noiselessly, I glided through the doorway.' He paused, and Robert saw the scene before him. There was a room of stone and wood, very like a chapel. It was empty, save for a single figure at the far end of the room, seated in a tall chair marked by a star above which the oil lamp was flickering dully. The man wore a long black beard and the robes of a Rabbi; and he held a book, clasped tightly, open on his lap. His eyes, though, were hooded, as though he were scanning the depths of distant thoughts.

'He did not look up,' the Pasha said, 'until my shadow was upon him. His face, as he raised it, seemed bled of all emotion. "This soon?" he whispered.

' "Why?" I answered. "You have been expecting me?"

'The Rabbi studied me more closely. "I have been warned to expect Samael, the venomous beast . . . *Havya besha* . . ." His voice trailed away. "But you are not he." He reached up to touch my cheek; he stared into my eyes. "So you are a blood-sucker, then, like Father Tadeus." He sighed. "Are you come like he did, to pilfer my dreams?"

' "He failed."

' "And would you do any better?" The Rabbi rose to his feet. "For be warned, demon – you are standing in the presence of the mysteries of God."

'I smiled. I widened my eyes. Then suddenly, as though stabbing him, I seized him in my mind. He fought hard, very hard; but he could not resist me, for my strength was too great, and I felt him start to weaken until his thoughts lay naked before my gaze. I knew, then, that Tadeus had been lying to me, that Rabbi Loew had bartered nothing to the Spirit of Darkness but was a brave, and learned, and fearless man. Like a huntsman freeing a bird from a trap, I released him from my hold. He stared at me wordlessly, and did not move, save to tighten his grip upon the sides of his book.

' "Who was it," I murmured, "who warned you to expect the Angel of Darkness?"

'The Rabbi frowned. "Why bother to request what you can take from me by force?"

' "Because I met in my dreams, and just now upon the bridge, a man with a face as ageless as time."

'The Rabbi continued to stand motionless, his eyes closed as though in prayer. "And why should this man," he asked at length, "have served to stay your hand?"

' "Because I am a great and mighty spirit," I answered, "and yet the man on the bridge was one mightier than myself – and I have known such a being only once before. That was in the deserts of Egypt, when I met with Lilith, the harlot-princess – and ceased to be a mortal. So be warned, Rabbi. If I spare you" – I smiled distantly – "it is because you remind me of the man I used to be."

'The Rabbi met my stare. "The spirit you met with . . . you need have no fear of him on my account, for he will do me no harm. He is known as the guardian of the chosen of God."

' "And is that why he has come to you? In answer to some danger?"

' "Can you not answer that yourself?" The Rabbi smiled faintly. "For he came to you as well."

'I took a step forward and leaned very close to the Rabbi's cheek, so that his beard brushed my own. "Who was he?" I whispered.

'The Rabbi paused, then hugged his book to his chest. "If I tell you his business with me," he said, "I would betray his trust, and my own chances of success."

' "Success, Rabbi? Success in what?"

'He shook his head, and sat down once more.

'I gazed at him a long while; and then at his book. I turned at last and walked from him, into the blackness at the far end of the room. By the doorway, though, I paused and turned again. The Rabbi still sat frozen; and his skin, lit by the lantern's wash, seemed to gleam like pale gold. "My name is Vakhel Pasha," I cried. "Should you need me, send for me at Constantinople. You will discover me there." I bowed my head, then turned. "*Shalom*, Rabbi Loew."

'He did not answer me; but I trusted – and dreaded – that in due time, he would.'

∽∾∽

'THERE, IN A QUARRY OF CLAY, RABBI LOEW MEASURED OUT THE FIGURE OF A MAN, AND DREW HIS FACE IN THE DIRT, AND HIS ARMS AND LEGS, IN THE WAY THAT A MAN MIGHT LIE ON HIS BACK. AND THEN HE CIRCLED THE GOLEM ROUND SIX TIMES . . .'

Traditional Jewish Folktale

The Pasha paused, and stirred uneasily.

'And what then?' Robert asked. 'Did he come for you?'

'I heard nothing from anyone,' the Pasha replied, 'save only Tadeus. As he had done to the Marquise, he sent news of dark rumours and celestial signs, portents of some looming apocalypse.'

'Signs?' Robert frowned.

'In one letter,' the Pasha answered, 'he wrote of reports of the Wandering Jew, who had mocked Christ on His way to Golgotha, and been sentenced for the crime to eternal restlessness. I remembered the figure I had seen upon the bridge, the sense I had felt of his incalculable age, barely veiled behind his unwrinkled flesh; and I wished that Tadeus had written his letter in more detail. But I did not reply to him and demand a full account, for I knew that he was greedy for my knowledge, just as he had been greedy for Rabbi Loew's. Of the Rabbi himself, Tadeus wrote very little. One rumour, though, he did mention: that the Rabbi had created a monster made from clay, to serve him as a slave in his infernal practices. The monster lived, it was said, in the synagogue attic; and bore upon its forehead the Devil's mark.

'But Tadeus did not mention the monster again, nor Rabbi Loew; and his letters grew gradually briefer, and then stopped altogether. I received little other news, although once or twice I met with spies returned from Prague, reporting to the Sultan on the state of his enemy. One of these remembered Rabbi Loew: it was said he had been granted an audience with Emperor Rudolf – unheard-of honour for a Jew! – and that the two men had spoken alone for an hour. It was rumoured, the spy added, that the Rabbi had told the Emperor of a terrible secret; although what the secret was, no two sources could agree.

'The years passed; I heard no more of Rabbi Loew; and

I supposed, in the end, that he must have died. But then one day, as I sat in my palace above the Golden Horn, I was delivered a book hand-written in Hebrew; and when I opened the pages, I discovered a flower. It was very delicate and dry; and around its stem a shred of silk had been tied, with the promise inscribed, that "the grass withereth, the flower fadeth: but the word of God shall stand forever." I laid the flower gently aside, and began to read the book. It had clearly been inscribed by Rabbi Loew himself; for it told of great and terrible secrets such as only the most elect of the learned might have known. Once before, the Rabbi wrote, there had been a killing time, foretold by infallible signs; and these signs had been read by the *Tannaim*, the teachers of tradition, who had understood the language of the book of the universe. They had seen written in this script of things the coming destruction, when all of the world was to be drowned beneath blood, and the Spirit of Evil would raise its temple amidst the carnage. Yet they had also read, even as Jerusalem was being destroyed and the temple of the Lord was crumbling into ash, that the world itself might still be preserved; that the Spirit of Evil might be drawn out with a hook. But they did not know how this was to be done; for only the Lord may bind Leviathan, and the secret of His wisdom was hidden from them. And it was then that a Wanderer had appeared, as ancient as the first of the sons of Adam; and he bore the secret with him, of how the Beast might be bound . . .

'At this point the account broke off – and it was on the blank facing page that the flower had been pressed. I left Constantinople that same night, and rode like the breath of wind towards Prague. The city, when I arrived there, seemed filled with signs of discord and coming war, for there were soldiers everywhere, and mobs seething with hatred, milling through the streets or gathered on the squares. Only in the Ghetto did all seem quiet; yet the stillness was that of melancholy, and the calm appeared imbued with mourning and dread. I prayed that I was not too late, and quickened my pace towards the Synagogue. When I arrived, I asked for Rabbi Loew. He was not there, I was told; for he was very sick. I would find him in his house, past the Synagogue itself.

'He was lying in his bed, his children and grandchildren gathered all about him. As I entered the room, they shrank from me, as though I were an emissary of Death; but the Rabbi whispered to them all to leave us alone, and they obeyed him, though with silent reluctance in their eyes. I crossed to the Rabbi. His beard was now the purest silver, and he seemed so weak that he could barely stir; but his voice, when he spoke, was as clear as I remembered it. He asked me to sit by his side. I did so, and placed the flower he had sent me back in his hand; then laid the book upon his lap. I opened it at the blank page. "It is the lesson of your Scriptures," I told him, "that those whose curiosities are tempted will always succumb."

'The Rabbi smiled faintly. "I trust you will forgive me. But I had to be certain you would come to me at once. I am very near death."

' "Tell me, then, why you delayed your summons for so long?"

'A look of the profoundest melancholy crossed the Rabbi's face. "Because it was only recently," he whispered, "that my failure became clear."

' "Your failure?" I stared at him coldly. "So you have summoned me here to be – what? – your heir in some mission I do not understand?"

'The Rabbi waved his hand to and fro in a faint gesture of reconciliation. "I will reveal all I can, so you will then understand."

' "Yet I am a demon," I whispered. "You have said so yourself."

' "A demon?" The Rabbi waved his hand again. "It is said in the secret writings that not even the demons are absolutely cursed. And so I believe, Vakhel Pasha. For why else would he have come to you as well as to me?"

' "He? The Wanderer?" I narrowed my eyes. "Tell me, then, Rabbi – tell me who he was."

'The Rabbi smiled faintly, and seemed to gaze far away. "In the most secret writings of Judah the Pious," he murmured at length, "I have found the assertion that the Wanderer is Cain, still a fugitive and vagabond, eternally seeking to expiate his sin. But I have seen him, I have stared into his eyes . . ." He looked up to meet my own gaze. "I do not believe he had ever been a man."

'I leaned forward. "What, then?" I whispered. "What did you see?"

' "He appeared to me," the Rabbi answered, "as though from nowhere – as it had been written in the secret texts that he would. He gave me a book. I opened it. The script was like nothing I had ever seen before. 'How shall I read this?' I cried out to him. He gave me no answer, but only smiled, so that I felt like covering my face with my hands, for his silence seemed too great for mortal eyes to endure. But still I dared to look at him, and to speak a second time. 'Samael,' I asked, 'the venomous beast – how am I to defeat him?' Again, the Wanderer smiled; and then he turned, and went, and I was left alone. But the book was still in my hands; and when I studied its secret script again, I knew that the Wanderer had been Raziel, the angel of all that is hidden, who watches with a jealous eye over the mysteries of God. And it was as I was thinking this, and clutching the book, that you" – he smiled at me – "appeared before my seat."

' "And the book," I whispered slowly. "What did it reveal?"

' "Its meaning continued a mystery to me. I would study it for hours in the Synagogue each day, and each day I would imagine that I had mastered it, that I had finally understood its script – and yet in truth, my understanding was like a pebble flicked by a child, skimming across the words as though they were water and never coming to any certain rest. Years passed. I began to despair. I still studied the book as diligently as I had ever done; but I was afraid now that I might not be worthy of its mysteries. Then one hot afternoon, as I sat alone at my work, I was interrupted by my granddaughter. She had been told that she was not to disturb me; but she was very young, and she had picked a bunch of flowers which she wanted to give to me. I scolded her gently, but I took her gift; and when she had gone, I found that I could no longer study the book, but only gaze at the flowers. The Ghetto is a place of dust and stone; nothing grows here, save for weeds in the cemetery; and the flowers, delicate mementoes of some countryside verge, struck me with the force of a revelation, something wondrous and strange which I had almost forgotten. I found I was gazing at the traceries of the tiny petals as though they, not the book, contained all the mystery; for they seemed to form the language of the universe. Suddenly, I could sense a sublime meaning in everything. I reached for the book and found that I could read the script in that as well. The whole world seemed contained within it: the past and the future; where I sat, and beyond. Yes, I thought, the book is indeed a lake, its surface as calm and silver as a mirror; and now at last, I can pass beneath its surface . . ."

'The Rabbi paused; then muttered a faint prayer under his breath. "How shall I describe," he whispered, "what cannot be described? For the book, like the law of God, is many things. It is a collection of words, to be read and comprehended. Yet it has a meaning too which is more, much more, than the value of its words; as though the text were a body and its truth a soul, greater by far than the matter which contains it. And it is fitting I should describe the book in such a way; for its secrets are those of creation: of the spirit of Yahweh, who breathed into the motionless Adam, and made life out of dust. Without such breath, what is any man? Imperfect. Unfinished. A rough lump of clay . . ." The Rabbi paused, then breathed softly on the back of his hand. "A man," he whispered slowly, "might mould an image of himself – but he cannot give it life. It would continue as nothing but a compound of dirt – for it would lack *neshumah*, the spirit of God. A deadly prison, then, deadly and dull – if a spirit were somehow to be trapped within its clay . . ."

'I gazed at the Rabbi and could see, reflected in his eyes, the pale glitter of my own. "You formed it, then?" I whispered slowly. "You formed such a . . . ?"

' "*Golem*." The word seemed to linger in the air. The Rabbi shuddered suddenly and his voice, when he spoke again, was hoarse and low. 'I determined, yes, to form a *golem*. But not at once – not until all was ready – for there were other mysteries I still had to fathom. I have said that the book was like the surface of a lake, through which one passed as one studied its words. And indeed, I might have thought that I had plunged into water, for golden currents would swim before my eyes, and eddies of strange light; and yet in truth, I was seeing things not less, but more clearly than before, for my gaze, I supposed, was become like an angel's – like that, perhaps, of Raziel himself. I could see lines and beams, some lesser, some greater, but all endowed with celestial power; and I felt, as I passed through them, that such power might be my own. Yet I was afraid to dye my thoughts in their light, for they were part, I knew, of a secret architecture by means of which the universe itself was maintained – and I dreaded to trespass on the mysteries of God. But I also knew that I could not wait for long; for sometimes, borne upon the beams, I would catch a faint sense of evil, of a darkness corrupting and muddying the light; and I would remember that the Angel of Evil was still abroad. And as I delayed – so the darkness ever seemed to grow."

' "So tell me," I whispered. "Tell me what you did."

'The Rabbi stared at me strangely, for my eagerness must have appeared hectic in my eyes; and for a moment he fell silent, as though suddenly afraid of my designs. I pressed him again; he smiled very faintly, then began to tell me of a man named Dr Dee. It may stir your sensibilities, sirs, to know that this Dee was an Englishman, one of the hundreds of alchemists gathered in Prague, all buzzing about the Emperor like flies above meat. Yet Dr Dee himself was not merely a charlatan but also a learned and brilliant man, the master of many branches of knowledge – one of which especially served to interest Rabbi Loew. For Dr Dee had written of immortal and invisible beams, which were possessed of a sacred and miraculous power. It was the argument of the Doctor that in his own native land the ancient priests had built temples along the line of such beams; and so the Rabbi wondered if the same might not have occurred in Bohemia. It was with such a hope that he approached Dr Dee and, having sworn him to silence, revealed to him the secret of his book.

'He knew that he had taken a risk; and so indeed it proved: for Dr Dee could not resist the temptation laid so suddenly before him. Unbeknown to Rabbi Loew, he began to copy out the text of the book, and then, when he had completed it, fled from Bohemia back to England. Yet Rabbi Loew was not too concerned; for he doubted that Dr Dee, even if he had succeeded in copying the text correctly, would ever succeed in reading it; for he had not been able to do so before, not even with the help of Rabbi Loew himself. What the Doctor had succeeded in discovering, however, written in ancient texts, had been the tradition of an ancient line of sacred power passing through the heart of Prague, through the very centre of the Charles Bridge itself; and although Dr Dee himself was fled, the fruits of his research had been left behind. So the Rabbi went with his book to the edge of the bridge. He began to read the script, and to pass into the world of mystery it revealed. And he saw then that Dr Dee had been right: that the bridge was crossed by a mighty stream of energy, so pure that it could barely be glimpsed at all, and of a power such as he had never experienced before. As the Rabbi stood in the wash of its flow, he knew that it offered him the best chance he would have.

'He followed the line beyond the bounds of Prague, to a quarry on the bank of the River Vltava. That afternoon, he bathed himself; then recited passages from the Kabbalah, and the one-hundred-and-nineteenth Psalm.

As night began to fall, he swathed himself in a hood of purest white; then, carrying a torch, returned to the quarry. He knelt by the river bank, where the clay was thickest; and began to form a human shape, three cubits long, laid out in the heart of the great line of power. When it was completed, Rabbi Loew rose again to his feet. He began to read from his book, circling the figure of the *golem* as he did so, feeling himself melt all the time into the power. He could see the line more clearly now, a whirlwind of dark fire touched with brightness about its edge, and with amber in its heart; and now it was the world beyond which instead seemed indistinct and faint. Still the Rabbi continued circling the *golem*, reading from the book; and the amber grew brighter, so that he could see nothing else beyond it. By the sixth circuit, all the darkness had been consumed; the amber was blazing in a mighty wall of fire, and the Rabbi cried out, for he seemed diffused into the flames and the infinite points of life that they cast; and then he laughed, and understood – that he was now the light.

'He stopped reading and dropped the book. It cast out waves of colour. He looked around. The world was all about him again, but strangely, like a rainbow's reflection cast upon a stream. Yet the Rabbi could control it: could make it obey the slightest ripple of his thoughts. He gazed along the line of power, still blazing but with the form of liquid crystal now; and the Rabbi could see where it led, for mile after mile, so that vast distances seemed to shrink into nothing. He thought of the Evil One – of Samael, the Venomous Beast. Nothing appeared. It was not possible, the Rabbi thought, to imagine its appearance – to imagine the face of the enemy of God. So he traced in his mind, as though it were wet sand, the letters of its name; and as he did so, he gazed into the depths of the line.

'Suddenly, in its very heart, he could make out a mannikin, a tiny silhouette. It appeared to be struggling; but the Rabbi fixed it with his stare and would not let it go. Nearer and nearer it drew, borne upon the line of power; and the Rabbi saw, to his horror, how it was staining the crystal of the blaze with its darkness, so that he, who was the light, could feel his own power start to fade. But he did not release the figure – not even though there was a coldness now reaching deep into his bones, and the darkness was screaming like a gale through his thoughts. More and more pitch it grew; and then suddenly the Rabbi could see nothing at all. He stood frozen. The gale faded away, and the silence seemed so icy that it made the Rabbi scream. Still he was answered by silence; and then suddenly the figure was before him, a monstrous size, a compound of shadow save for the furnace of its eyes. It reached for the Rabbi and twisted back his head; then lowered its jaws towards the side of his neck. The Rabbi cried out a prayer. It had no effect. Despairingly, he gazed down at the ground where he could see the book, its pages open. The Rabbi read them, a secret incantation; and as he did so, the darkness was streaked again with light. He repeated the incantation, and the creature staggered as though suddenly wounded. Yet it did not release its grip, but with a shriek of mingled agony and rage flung the Rabbi down into the mud. Its jaws were still apart; as they drew near to his throat again, the Rabbi could feel the drip of its saliva. He twisted his head round desperately, trying to sink deeper into the mud; and as he did so he saw, upon the bank, a host of swaying flowers. The image of his granddaughter – all

those years before, holding up a bunch of flowers to him
– filled his mind; and he recalled how surprised by joy he
had been, tracing the beauty of each tiny petal.

'At the same moment as he remembered this, he
heard the creature scream; not with hatred now, but with
a desperate pain. The Rabbi could feel it shuddering, and
then releasing its grip upon his arms. He twisted, rolling
away across the mud, so that he came to rest amidst the
flowers. He turned and looked back towards the creature.
It was writhing and shrieking as though consumed by the
light. The Rabbi turned again and reached for the flowers;
he picked a bunch and held them to his nose; he breathed
in their scent. And all the time he was thinking –
thinking of the secret magic in the book, by the power of
which the Beast was to be bound. He raised his eyes
again; he crossed towards the creature. Still he could
make out nothing of it save for its silhouette; but then, as
he seized it in the toils of his thought, he saw its darkness
start to glisten and he realised that the creature was
sweating out its blood. He gazed down at the model of
the *golem*. Blood, in a thick rain, was falling on to it. And
all the while the creature was shrieking, as its limbs and
body continued to wither, and its blood was drunk by the
greedy clay. The Rabbi reached down for the book and
then, still clutching the flowers in his other hand, he read
out the secret incantation once again. Like the breath of a
wind trapped within a house, the creature's scream rose
and then faded into silence; its skin and bones collapsed
into dust, and the clay of the *golem* glistened with damp.

'The Rabbi bent down beside it; then from within his
robes he drew out a single strip of parchment. It had
Hebrew letters inscribed upon it – the *shem hamephorash*,
the secret name of God. He placed it within the *golem*'s

open mouth; and the clay figure writhed, and bucked, and then was still, as the dampness faded and the clay was baked hard. The Rabbi turned to the dust of bone and skin behind him, and buried it deep within the mud; then he left the quarry and began the walk back to Prague, still with the book and the bunch of flowers in his hands. Once returned to the Ghetto, he ordered four of his followers to fetch the *golem* and place it in the attic of the Synagogue. No one saw them as they went about their task; and once the *golem* had been carefully hidden beneath prayer shawls and books, the Rabbi ordered the door to be boarded up. He then issued the sternest prohibition, forbidding anyone to pass into the room; for it contained, like the Temple, the mysteries of God.'

'And as is ever the way,' Lord Rochester drawled, 'someone disobeyed him?' He smiled lazily. 'For mortal flesh exists to break such commands.'

'That may be,' answered the Pasha, 'and yet still, the Rabbi was no fool. For he was reluctant to see the *golem* buried away from his watchful eye; and he knew that, even lifeless, the terror it inspired was deterrence enough. Only the violence of the Christians could have endangered its hiding place, and it was for that reason that the Rabbi had requested his audience with the Emperor. He revealed to him, during their secret conference, the truth of the *golem*; and Emperor Rudolf, a man much troubled by presentiments of evil magic and war, believed the Rabbi's story. He granted the Jews of Prague his personal protection, and then demanded to see the *golem* for himself. Despite the Rabbi's best efforts to dissuade him, the Emperor would not be denied; and so it was that one night, Rudolf arrived in disguise at the Synagogue, climbed the stairs and ordered the doorway to the attic to be opened. He then passed inside, and for a long while gazed down at the face of the *golem*. When he left the attic at last, he ordered that the door be boarded again, but even more securely than before; otherwise, though, he said not a word. From that moment on, the Emperor was rarely seen abroad again. It was said that his melancholy had devoured his senses; that he was raging mad; that he was dead. The Rabbi, hearing such rumours, would sometimes glance up at the single attic window and pray, deep, deep in his heart, that he had done things for the best. Sometimes too, when he sat in his study, he would glance at a bunch of flowers in a vase, to make certain that their petals were not losing their bloom. For ever since that night in the quarry by the river, the flowers had not faded but had remained as fresh as when the Rabbi plucked them first.'

'And yet they did fade in the end?' Robert whispered.

'It was one of the bunch he had chosen to send me – pressed inside his book.'

'What had happened?'

'The Rabbi was never certain. He had discovered the flowers withered in his study; he had hurried to the attic; he had found the boards across the doorway smashed from inside.'

'And the *golem*?'

The Pasha smiled thinly. 'Vanished, of course.'

'It was Faustus?' Robert whispered. 'Tadeus?'

The Pasha shrugged very faintly. 'The Rabbi thought not – for he believed the fault to have been his own.'

'How?'

'He told me a story, that night when I sat with him, and had asked him myself to explain such a claim. He told me of Aher, famous in the Talmud for his evil, who had once been Elisha ben Abua – the most learned of all the teachers of Israel. But Elisha had journeyed too far into the garden of knowledge and his curiosity, like Eve's, soon grew fatal. He betrayed his faith, he followed evil – for there are mysteries too dangerous for the mortal mind to glimpse. It was the dread of Rabbi Loew that he too had beheld such mysteries, when he had dared to enter the book of Raziel and invoke its power.'

Robert frowned. 'But what had been his sin?'

'Arrogance. The arrogance which had led him to keep the *golem* in the Synagogue, and not smash it into pieces and scatter the dust upon the winds. "For I could not believe," he told me, "that the secret would be kept, the danger restrained, unless I watched over it myself. And now" – he raised the withered flower up from the book – "you can see how my pride has reaped its own reward. The *golem* is shattered; the *shem* spat out; the Beast is broken free of its bonds . . ."

'And was he right?' Robert asked. 'Had the Spirit's evil been too great for the clay?'

'So it seemed,' the Pasha answered. 'For as the Rabbi warned me, its strength would be undimmed – grown indeed . . .' – he paused – 'and it was . . . it was. . .'

Lord Rochester leaned forward. 'You read the book, then?' he whispered. 'You passed into the world that its pages opened up?'

The Pasha sat in silence for a long while. 'That same night,' he said at last, 'as the Rabbi read the book – so I read his mind. It was thus I was able to understand the script.'

Robert breathed in deeply. 'And what did you see?'

'Many things.' The Pasha hooded his eyes, as though gazing into the depths of his memories. 'Many things.'

He swallowed; then opened his eyes once again. 'As I said,' he murmured, 'the Rabbi had been right – the creature was stronger than it had ever been. For it fed upon the evil which it also served to breed; so that I began to fear that all the world would be destroyed, and it would reign across a universal wilderness of death. Long I pursued it, as ruin was brought to Prague, and then to Bohemia, and then far, far beyond – and still I could not find it, nor bring it to the struggle. Years passed. The land was fertilised with bones and charred by war, so that civilisation lay choked beneath weeds and wolves returned to the emptied villages; and still I pursued it, still I hunted the Beast. I began to close on it; yet its strength now was deadly, and I feared to draw near. Yet I knew that I would certainly perish if I did not, along with all the world; and in the end, I did it, I met with him . . .

'Of our struggle' – the Pasha paused – 'I do not wish to speak. The night of that memory is too deadly to recall. Yet I had hoped, in the end, that the creature was slain, for I saw his blood swallowed by the *golem* clay. I did not then repeat the Rabbi's mistake – I shattered the figure and scattered the dust, so that it mingled with the mud on the Vltava's bank. And it was only then, when my victory – as I thought – was complete, that I could feel how deadly my own pain now was. I resolved to journey to Paris, to seek out the Marquise and rest a while with her; but my wounds would not permit me to travel so far. I collapsed upon the road and, in my fever, lost all sense of time. Years and years I must have lain in the mud, rotten with sickness; and it was only good fortune which brought me here at last.' He reached out for Lord Rochester's hand, and brushed it softly; then he glanced back at Robert. 'For it was my Lord Rochester,' he murmured, 'who discovered me, and helped to set me on my way – as I had known he would – for I had seen it all before. . .'

'Seen?' Robert frowned. 'I do not understand.'

The Pasha tightened his grip on Rochester's hand. 'In the world of the book,' he whispered, 'time itself, it appears, can sometimes be warped. The past – the future – both can be glimpsed. There is not much I remember of the things that I saw but I suddenly recalled, when I met with Lord Rochester, that I had seen myself crippled and rotting in mud before, and I knew – I cannot say how – but I knew that my saviour was to be an English poet and lord. And so indeed Lord Rochester proved; for the visions of the book, it would appear, do not lie. That is how I can be certain . . .' – he paused, and struggled to rise to his feet – 'that is how I know . . .' He swallowed, then took a pace forward. As he staggered, he clawed at Lord Rochester, pulling him down so that the two of them fell together to the floor, the Pasha straddling Lord Rochester's chest. He bent forward and kissed Lord Rochester softly on his lips. 'That is how I know,' he whispered, 'that he is the one.'

Lord Rochester smiled. He reached up to stroke the Pasha's thin cheeks; then he pulled him down and kissed him, urgently now. At length, the Pasha broke away and sat, eyes closed, gulping down air.

'The one?' Robert asked slowly.

The Pasha unhooded his stare. 'Who will fight and destroy Azrael forever.'

'It can indeed be done, then – for all that you failed?'

'Failed?' The Pasha's eyes gleamed. 'You are harsh, Lovelace.'

'And yet you did fail.'

The Pasha smiled coldly. 'This time there will be no Tadeus to rescue the Spirit from its prison of dust.'

'How did he do it?'

'That must be discovered.'

'And the book – the Rabbi's book – where is that?'

'That too must be found. And soon. For as long as the creature continues in your village, it remains enfeebled, it is still drawing strength. But once it leaves . . .' His voice trailed away.

Robert shook his head; for he remembered the shadow rising up in Stonehenge, remembered the Hell revealed by its eyes, remembered the ice . . . What hope against such a power? What hope, especially, for a mortal like himself? He shook his head again. He could feel the Pasha's stare reaching deep into his thoughts and he clutched at his head, to try to keep it out. 'No,' he cried suddenly. 'No! I do not want it, no!'

'Are you certain?' the Pasha murmured. His eyes were undimmed, and pity and contempt were mingled in their stare. 'Perhaps not yet, Lovelace,' he mocked, 'not quite yet . . . But remember' – he smiled – 'you can hide nothing from me. I think – very soon – you will ask for it . . . yes.' The sibilant lingered, a serpentine hiss; and then, as it faded, so too did his smile. The Pasha stretched out his arms; and his expression was suddenly a terrible one – haughty and fierce, and yet shaded by woe. 'It would make no difference,' he murmured, 'if you were to desire it after all. For I am weak . . . too weak – and my blood is too thin to be shared with more than one.' He pulled at Lord Rochester's shirt, ripping it open so that the chest was exposed. Very gently, with his nail, he drew a thin, ruby line. Then he paused and glanced up at

Robert once again. 'Go with Lord Rochester,' he ordered. 'Discover all you can. And, Lovelace . . .' – he smiled – 'I wish you all luck.'

Robert could hear a pounding now, deep all around him, like that of a heart. At the same moment, his every sensation was touched by gold, sweet, sweet, inexpressibly sweet; even the stabbing he could feel in his guts. He heard a scream; and simultaneously, the delight and the pain both thudded in his ears, and the whole room seemed to quiver and grow shadowed by red. The screaming rose again – but strangely altered from before, so that it seemed almost a cry of ecstasy. Robert stared across at where Lord Rochester lay, spread out beneath the Pasha who was crouched upon his body like a ravening beast, tearing and lapping at the naked chest, until all the flesh had been stripped away, and the heart lay exposed beneath the open ribs. It was still twitching, but very faintly now; and the slow, soft thud of its beat emptied Robert's mind, so that nothing remained but golden pleasure and the pain. The heart stopped; and the agony in Robert's stomach was now unbearable. He waited, desperately, for the heartbeat which he knew was bound to come; and then it rose, very slowly – a blood-drinker's beat. Again it sounded; and Robert knew for certain now that it was Lord Rochester's heart, reborn, remade. Once more; and the gold and the red were starting to fade into black. Lord Rochester was stirring now, and rising to his feet, besmeared with gore; but Robert could barely make him out. The mists were closing in; the pain in his stomach was unbearable now. On the quickening ripple of Rochester's heart, it stabbed deeper and deeper; until at last all was black; and Robert felt nothing any more.

❧❧

'SHALL I MAKE SPIRITS FETCH ME WHAT I PLEASE,
RESOLVE ME OF ALL AMBIGUITIES,
PERFORM WHAT DESPERATE ENTERPRISE I WILL?'
                    Christopher Marlowe, *Doctor Faustus*

It was not until a week later, when he was approaching
Deptford, that Robert remembered where he had
heard of Dr Dee before. The meeting his father had held
in the house of . . . Robert closed his eyes. Mr Aubrey –
that had been his name. The same man who had
discovered Mr Yorke's corpse had also been the one who
had talked of Dr Dee. Robert struggled to think why. His
recollection was very faint. It had been cold, kneeling on
the frozen ground, ear pressed to the window-pane; he
found it hard to remember much else. But *something*
important had been discussed that day – something just
beyond his memory . . .

Robert might almost have stopped wondering about it,
save that he was struck by a sudden line of thought. His
father's business with Mr Aubrey, he knew, had been
related to the series of murders – a series committed in
the shadow of ancient sites. Robert remembered what the
Pasha had said of Dr Dee: that he had believed in the
existence of invisible beams, along which the pagan
priests had built their temples. Might such a beam have
linked the murders as well? Might they have been
committed to invoke its hidden power? Robert decided
that his father must have at least suspected such a link –
for he had been expecting the murders at Old Sarum and
Stonehenge. Who else would he have consulted on such a
business if not Mr Aubrey, the Wiltshire antiquarian?

And if that had been the case – then what else might Mr Aubrey not also have known?

So intrigued was Robert by the implications of this question, that he determined to leave for Wiltshire at once. But it did not take him long to realise that such a resolution might present him with difficulties. Disembarked at Deptford, he hurried to the waterfront, only to discover that the wharves were almost empty; and it was only by paying an extortionate fee that he was able to hire a boat at all. Even then, despite the thought of the money he was charging, the riverman's face continued blank with fear; and the nearer they drew to London, so the more he seemed to shake. Soon Robert could hear a great roaring coming from the river ahead. It was the rapids, he realised, tumbling through the arches of London Bridge – a sound he would normally never have expected to hear, not above the deafening tumult of the city. And it was only then that he became aware how still London was, hunched like some stricken animal upon the bank, motionless in the agonies of death. Upon the docks and in the streets, not a soul seemed abroad; and nothing disturbed the silence, save the occasional distant shriek.

Landed at Botolph's Wharf, Robert found the air loathsome with a sweet, rotten stench which grew ever heavier as he left the Thames behind. Knowing that to search for a hackney would be useless, he began to hurry through the deserted streets, handkerchief tightly pressed to his nose. The scenes of desolation which he remembered from St Giles were now to be found spread all across the city, for like some noxious red weed, crosses marked almost every door, and coffins and bodies lay piled amidst the rubbish. Of those still living, there was barely any sign; and grass was peering through the cobblestones. All of London seemed abandoned to death – and if London now, Robert thought, then perhaps soon all the world.

He continued as far as Hyde Park; and was not greatly surprised to discover a makeshift military camp barring the road which led to the west. He approached the barriers, nevertheless; but when the soldiers learned of his intended journey, they shook their heads and laughed in his face. For the King, they told him, was now in residence in Salisbury; and refugees from London were not greatly welcome. Robert damned Lord Rochester under his breath. If only he had been in London, there would have been no problem, for he would surely then have had access to a pass. But Lord Rochester, having had no wish to lose his place at the Court, was still with the navy; although he had sworn, when they parted in Amsterdam, that he would return to dry land as soon as he could. Robert gazed in frustration at the barricades. Not soon enough, he thought. He gazed back at London, as still and deathly as a corpse laid in its tomb. Not nearly soon enough.

Yet even as he cursed himself for having ever returned to the city, he was reminded of the reason he had chosen to come back. He turned again and left the barricades, heading towards the silence and rotten stench of the city. St James's Park, lately the haunt of fine ladies and wits, now lay abandoned to weeds; and not a single horseman was abroad upon the Mall. Even Godolphin's house, although there was no red cross daubed upon its side, seemed infected by the air of desolation; and as Robert passed inside, he grew suddenly afraid that Milady too had fled. Yet he could not believe it; for what business was it of a blood-drinker to escape a place of death? He called out her name. Nothing answered him, save a prickling silence, and the dance of dust motes caught in the light. Robert called out again. Still silence. He began to run down the corridors, crying out Milady's name all the time and recognising, in his own voice, the tightening accent of desperation.

'She is sick.'

Robert paused on the stairs. Lightborn was standing at their top.

'Sick?' Robert stared up at him in horror. 'How do you mean, sick?'

'She has been a foolish girl, and drunk infected blood. For the plague in these mortals is like poison to us.'

'When did she drink it?'

'Weeks ago. Indeed, Lovelace – it was when you went away, for she was then much distracted.' He smiled faintly, but his stare seemed to harden and grow as distant and cruel as it had ever been. 'You should hurry to her. It may be you will serve to lighten her spirits.' His smile began to fade. 'For she has spoken of you much, in her delirium.'

Robert hurried at once to her room: Milady lay curled up like a kitten in the darkness of a far corner; and the gleam of her skin was a deathly white. As he knelt down beside her, she struggled to rise up, whispering something very fast. She swallowed, and gripped his hands; then suddenly seemed to recognise his face. 'Lovelace!' She kissed him, and the touch of her lips was scorchingly hot. Then she slumped back and lay as she had done before, in a soft, shuddering ball. Her shift clung fast to the sweat on her skin, and Robert realised with a shock how slight she had grown.

She moaned suddenly, and parted her lips like a baby

eager for milk. Robert glanced round to see Lightborn now standing just behind him. 'See', he whispered, 'how she licks her lips – and yet it serves her nothing, for her tongue is withered and as dry as sand.'

Robert gazed at Milady in despair and remembered, just a few months before, how he had gazed down at Emily in the same way. 'She is not . . . not in danger?' he asked.

'Who is to say?' Lightborn shrugged. 'It is certain that I have never heard of such a thing before, that blood be made dangerous to our taste by disease.'

'What then must be done?'

Lightborn grinned. 'What do you think? She must be given fresh sustenance. And so it is that all this time, while you have been away upon your travels, I have been feeding her.' He seized Robert's arm suddenly, and his voice became a hiss. 'What do you say, Lovelace? Do you dare to serve her as I have done?'

Robert did not answer, but stared at Milady and closed his eyes.

'Do not tell me, Lovelace, you are still the thing of your mewling conscience?' Lightborn laughed derisively. 'Why, man, it is no worse than feeding rats to a serpent.'

'I was not in the habit,' Robert answered, 'of keeping serpents as pets.'

'A pity.' Lightborn gazed down again at Milady. 'For it might then have taught you that even the deadliest of creatures deserve sometimes to be loved.'

Robert stared round at him with sudden fury. 'Do not mock me, Lightborn, for you know that I love her – that I love her full well.'

'Then prove it,' Lightborn whispered. He tightened his grip on Robert's arm. 'Prove it to me now.'

They went out that same night. Lightborn led the way through the darkening streets, towards the distant flickering of mighty fires. As they drew nearer to the source of the flames, so the sweetness in the air grew ever thicker and the sound of shrieks and sobs more widespread. 'London's flesh is rotting upon its bones,' Lightborn whispered. 'If it were not for the danger of infection from the blood, I could truly love this time. For see, how Death with its greedy talons tears out the city's heart.' He rounded a corner, and gestured with his arm; and Robert saw, stretching before him, a pit of the kind he had seen in St Giles – but ten times as vast, so that gazing at the multitude of corpses it contained, their rottenness lit by a circle of great fires, he could well believe that the time of the Apocalypse was near. He remembered what the Pasha had told him, of how the plague in Bohemia had been halted by stripping off flesh from the bones. No such solution would be possible now, he thought, as he stared about; for he seemed to be witnessing the common grave of man.

Lightborn, however, appeared perfectly unconcerned; and indeed, as Robert watched him, he jumped into the pit. Robert could see now that there were other people amidst the carcasses, wailing as they clung to the corpses of their loved ones, or searching through the putrid jumble, just as Robert remembered he had once done himself. Lightborn approached these people one by one; he would whisper to them, then nick them very gently and taste their blood upon his fingertip. At length, he scrambled out from the pit once again, and hurried back to Robert. 'I have convinced these fools I am a physician,' he whispered, 'with an infallible medicine for preventing the plague. Play your part well, Lovelace. Tell them it is true.'

He nodded and turned. A woman and a couple of men had now gathered behind him, their eyes red and crazed by grief. 'Your medicine,' the woman cried, 'will it serve to cure my child?'

'Without doubt,' Lightborn answered. He gestured to Robert. 'For you see how healthy it has kept my good friend. Tell them, Lovelace. Tell them it is so.'

Robert paused. He stared at the wretched woman, her face contorted with mingled misery and hope. 'Six children I had,' she cried, 'and now only one. Tell me, please, sir, tell me you can help!'

Still Robert paused. He closed his eyes and saw at once the image of Milady, curled up on her cushions; then he imagined her disease-rotted, and tossed into the pit. He nodded. 'Yes,' he said slowly, as he met the woman's eyes. 'Yes. I swear it, the medicine will surely cure your child.'

Lightborn grinned. 'Very good,' he whispered. 'Done like the most nonchalant of hypocrites.' He then took Robert's arm, and began to lead the way. Returned home, he passed through the house and up the stairs, as far as the doorway to Milady's room. 'In there,' he whispered, 'you will discover the end to all your miseries.' The woman gazed at him wildly, then ran into the room. The two men followed. Robert heard the faint thumping of their footsteps across the carpets, and then silence. 'Let us go and see,' Lightborn whispered, taking Robert's arm. 'Make certain that Milady is taking her medicine.'

Robert passed inside. The two men were standing frozen, hands clutched to their heads and eyes bulging, as though paralysed by the dread of some nightmare, while the woman was moaning, sunk upon her knees. Milady was gazing at her intently; no longer curled up, she still seemed like a cat but now alert and bright-eyed, observing her prey. She darted suddenly, and Robert saw that she held a dagger in her hand. The tip of the blade caught the woman's throat, and a shower of rubies arced out from the wound. Milady moaned with pleasure as they fell upon her face: one drop she licked, and tasted with her tongue; the others she rubbed and stroked into her skin. Then she embraced the woman and began to lap, eyes closed, from the wound to her throat. The blood was seeping out now in a slow, heavy stream and, as Milady felt it start to stain her shift, so she gasped with rapture and writhed up and down, until her breasts and stomach were sticky with gore. When she gazed up at last, her eyes seemed drugged with a lazy, clotted pleasure. 'Better now,' she whispered. 'Yes, I feel – better.'

She gulped hard, as though struggling to hold back the flood of her ecstasy, then gazed across the room. As she did so, a shadow of horror passed across her face, and she pointed at Robert. 'You promised, Lightborn . . . Not him . . . Not like this . . .'

Lightborn smiled mockingly. 'But it was Lovelace, Milady, who helped to bring you this medicine.'

'No . . .' Milady shook her head faintly, then clasped her breasts and rubbed them softly, seeming to lose herself as she stroked her fingers through the blood. Delicately, she dabbed at one of them with her tongue. 'Not like this,' she gasped again; and she tensed her whole body, as though fighting back her pleasure. But her victims were already kneeling down before her: bending back their heads, exposing their throats. 'You promised . . . no.' Then she slashed with her knife. Her eyes seemed an inferno of gold, and her teeth like delicate razors of pearl. She bit, and drank, and gasped in rapture as before. 'No, no,' she still moaned as she started to writhe; but she was lost in her pleasure now, and her faint sobs died away.

Yet in truth, Robert was already as unconscious of Milady as she was of him. For with the onset of her pleasure had begun the rippling of his own, and with the pleasure so also the agony had come. Worse than ever it seemed, rising up from the depths of his stomach as though there were something trying to gnaw its way out; and it was all he could do, before he was lost to the dizzying red swirl of his pain, to scream at Lightborn to search through his coat. Then everything was mist; and not until he felt the bottle being forced between his teeth, and the foul taste of *mummia* burning his throat, did he open his eyes again. Lightborn was staring down at him. 'Lord,' he sighed, 'sickness everywhere. How tedious it grows.'

Weakly, Robert staggered to his feet. He gazed around him. The three corpses were piled in a twisted sprawl, while Milady lay curled asleep amidst her cushions. Robert crossed to her. The sickly gleam had faded from her skin, and both her cheeks and lips seemed rosy once again. A faint smile of satiation curved her mouth, so that her expression, composed as it was in the calm of deep slumber, nevertheless seemed dangerous and cruel. Robert felt dizzied by it – and by the beauty which it somehow served to heighten. He felt a faint rush lightening his veins and, at the same moment, the gnawing in his stomach. Seizing the *mummia* he took a hurried gulp.

Lightborn stared at him intrigued. 'What is that stuff?' he asked.

'The same medicine my Lord Rochester gave to the Marquise.'

'You have more of it?'

'Following me in my trunk. It should be here within the day.'

Lightborn nodded slowly. 'Clearly, then,' he murmured, 'your travels have not passed without success.' He struggled to compose himself, but could not conceal the sudden glint of eagerness in his eyes. 'Tell me, Lovelace. Tell me what you found.'

Robert began his account and found himself wondering, as he did so, what the nature of Lightborn's interest might be. For although he was sitting perfectly still, Lightborn could not disguise his excitement; and as he listened to the story of Rabbi Loew, he gave up even the attempt. 'And the book,' he whispered, at the end of the tale, 'where is the book now?'

'Lost,' Robert answered. 'For when the Pasha woke from his struggles, it was nowhere to be found.'

Lightborn nodded to himself, then slouched back in thought. 'You are aware, of course,' he murmured at length, 'that the Marquise's present home was once Dr Dee's?'

Robert stared at him in astonishment. 'No,' he answered slowly, 'I was not aware of that.' He paused as a host of dark speculations suddenly darkened his mind. 'Did the Marquise – did you – did you know Dr Dee?'

Lightborn smiled faintly. 'He was a most celebrated man.'

'And his copy . . . his transcription . . . of Rabbi Loew's book?'

Lightborn's smile faded, and his gaze grew distant once again. 'Doubtless,' he asked at length, 'the *mummia* arriving from Amsterdam – it is intended for the Marquise?'

'Some of it, yes.'

'Then I suggest, when you make your journey to Mortlake, that you direct your questioning to her.'

'So I shall,' Robert answered, 'when I visit her. But I was intending first to attempt Milady's cure.'

'With the *mummia*?' Lightborn frowned. 'Why should it work on her?'

'Because it appears to counter the poison of the Spirit of Death. The plague in Milady's veins – it was brought originally from Woodton, so might the *mummia* not serve to cure her sickness too?'

Lightborn stared at him in silence for a moment then he shrugged faintly and rose to his feet. 'Let us hope you are right.' He crossed to the door; then paused and turned. 'And while you tend to Milady,' he said, his smile suddenly very cruel, 'why not direct your questioning to her?'

He left before Robert could ask him any more, and was gone from the house as though vanished into air. Robert was left alone with Milady; and for the next couple of days nothing disturbed them, save for the arrival from the docks of the travelling trunk. Within it were several flasks of *mummia*, one of which Robert used to tend to Milady; and as he did so, he could almost see the sickness being purged from her veins. By the time that Lightborn reappeared, with further garnerings from the plague pits in tow, Milady had grown well enough to rise from her cushions and to request Robert not to watch her as she drank. For her thirst and pleasure seemed intermingled with guilt, such as he had never seen in her before; and he wondered, as he left her, what its origin could be.

Soon, though, with health came her composure once again; and on the night when she first left her room and hunted for herself, Robert chose to tell her of his travels, and then to ask her what she knew of Dr Dee. She stared at him strangely. 'Why?' she murmured. 'What has Lightborn told you?'

'Nothing, save to imply that you once knew him – and perhaps as well that you knew of his book.'

Milady began to play with her curls, sweeping them backwards off her naked shoulders. 'Then I shall not deny it,' she murmured at last.

'Why did you not tell me?'

'You never asked.'

Robert gazed at her in frustration. 'You surprise me, Milady.'

'Indeed?'

'Surely you can see how important the book might be?'

She shook her head. 'It is no longer in Mortlake. Why do you think the Marquise has been living there, if not to ransack every corner and lift up every board? However' – she tossed out her curls again – 'if you do not trust me, Lovelace, you should ask the Marquise yourself.'

At once, Robert reached out to hold Milady's slim hand. 'Please. You know it is not a question of that – only of my desperation to rediscover the book.'

Milady laughed. 'And you think you are the only one, Lovelace, to feel such a desperation?'

Robert frowned at her and she laughed again; then she rose to her feet, still holding his hand. 'We should go,' she said. 'It is time we took the Pasha's gift to the Marquise. And on the way – I shall tell you what I can of the book, and of Dr Dee.'

'ALL MY PAST LIFE IS MINE NO MORE;
   THE FLYING HOURS ARE GONE
LIKE TRANSITORY DREAMS GIVEN O'ER,
WHOSE IMAGES ARE KEPT IN STORE
    BY MEMORY ALONE.'

The Earl of Rochester, Song

They left in the coach-and-six. The few people on the streets gazed at them in amazement, and Robert wondered when the last nobleman's carriage had been seen abroad in London. By the camp in Hyde Park, it slowed down briefly, but a single glance into Milady's eyes was sufficient to persuade the guards to raise their barriers; and the coach continued on its way towards Mortlake. Milady leaned out from the window to make certain of their progress, then sat back again in her seat; but she had begun to fidget and could not compose herself. Robert remembered how uneasy she had been before, on their very first journey to visit the Marquise; and he wondered what memories the Mortlake house aroused.

'I was never closely acquainted with Dr Dee,' Milady said suddenly. Her voice seemed altered, almost imperceptibly so: yet it was clear to Robert, who knew her so well, that her accent had indeed slipped, as it had once or twice slipped before. 'It was Lightborn who mingled in such circles,' she continued, 'and had done for several years before I met him, so that he had grown a friend of heretics and spies – a dangerous man. That was why I loved him – for I was very young – and he seemed to promise me a world of infinite excitement.' Milady paused, and laughed bitterly. 'Infinite indeed!'

'How had you met him?' Robert asked.

'In a Southwark tavern,' she answered, 'or a brothel, I should say – for I was far from being titled Milady then. My mother had been a whore. She had died when I was very young. The mistress of the brothel, rather than throwing me out into the streets, had kept me to wait upon the other whores, to scrub their rooms and mend their clothes. I had thought she did this out of love for my mother – and it was only later that I realised what her true motive was. I . . .' Milady paused, and flicked out her fan; she raised it to her face, as though to cool the flush that had risen in her cheeks. 'I shall never forget,' she continued at last, 'the first time. I was not even certain what was happening to me. I was only a child. I had not appreciated, for all that I had lived my life in a brothel, the tastes – the strange tastes – that some men can have . . .'

Robert gazed into the deep gold of her eyes. They were perfectly clear now, but he remembered how there had been tears in them before – that first time he saw them, when she nursed him in her lap as they rode from Stonehenge – and he felt a sudden sense of shame that he had never once thought to ask her since why she had cried. Yet even now, gazing at her, he could not believe it, that Milady, the beautiful, wondrous Milady, could have truly understood what it was that he had suffered . . .

She smiled at him quizzically. 'You find it so hard to imagine?' she asked, as though reading his thoughts. She reached across to hold his hand. 'When I was a tiny child,' she laughed, as though almost in tears, 'I could never believe that the whores had once been children too.'

Robert nodded slowly. 'And so it has been with me,' he whispered, 'looking at you.' And so it was even now, he realised suddenly; for still he could not imagine Milady as a mortal, despite what she had told him, for she was too altered, too remote from what she had been, for him to glimpse the little girl in her face. He leaned forward, and clasped her other hand. 'What happened, then?' he asked her. 'How did things change?'

'Lightborn,' she answered distantly, 'came one evening with friends. I had not seen him before – as I was later to discover, his tastes did not run greatly to girls. He had come to the brothel, I suppose, merely for a drink. It was I who served it to him. And yet something – I saw it in his eye – something about me interested him. It may be that he saw the child's face beneath my woman's paint, and was intrigued by it, for he was ever a connoisseur of suffering, and my fear and shame must have been clear to such a man. But whatever the reason . . . he came back the next night, and the night after that, and then the following day he took me from the brothel. He was a poet, he explained to me; and was staging an entertainment in the house of a patron. I was to play the role of Venus. I asked him why he had chosen me. He kissed my hand, then answered me without any apparent mockery, that my beauty made me worthy to play the Goddess of Love – for I had the face and the form of a true immortal.

'I learned my lines, and played my role; and when it was finished, I was taken back to the brothel. The following week Lightborn came for me again. This time I was to play Hero, a lovesick Grecian maid. I had thought that he would laugh as he told me this, that he had cast a whore in a virgin's part; but again he did nothing but kiss my hand – and I felt what it might be not to be despised, and beaten and forced. This time, when the masque was finished, I did not return to the brothel but was taken by Lightborn back to his own rooms. He told me that I was now to work for him. I knew that he must have paid for me; and indeed, I served him with an almost slave-like devotion, for he was never cruel to me, never vicious; and although he would sometimes kiss me and caress me through my gown, he never forced his attentions any further. I continued to perform in his various masques; and sometimes, too, I would play a quite different part. For it increasingly pleased Lightborn to have me accompany him even to those houses where he was not to stage his entertainments; and in such gatherings, I learned to behave as though I were his mistress or wife, for he would settle me upon his lap and, as he talked, he would play with my curls or follow with his finger the curve of my face.'

'And it was at such a gathering,' Robert asked, 'that you met with Dr Dee?'

Milady nodded. 'Yes – and with the Marquise as well – in the very house we are coming to now. There was much discussion that night of perilous matters – of magic, of spirits, of selling one's soul. Lightborn in particular seemed obsessed by immortality; by the delights it could offer – and also the threats. For it was loneliness he spoke of most – of being immortal and loveless, eternally alone. I suddenly realised that he was not jesting, as was his usual custom, but truly believed that he might indeed never die; and I felt my blood run cold, as I wondered what my own role in such a fantasy was to be. I shrank, and tried to slip from Lightborn's arms; but he would not let me go, and he stared into my eyes for a long while and said nothing at all. Then at last I felt him shudder; and he

whispered in my ear that I should not be afraid, that he
would remain a mortal and be tempted no more. And
indeed, I was to discover later that the Marquise had
offered to transform him that very same night; and he
had done as he had promised me, and refused her gift.'

'What altered, then?' Robert asked. 'For something
must have done.'

'A great reckoning,' Milady smiled, 'in a little room.'

'A reckoning?'

Milady nodded slowly and glanced out through the
window. The carriage was slowing now; as it juddered to
a halt, she sat perfectly still, gazing at the silver of the
moon upon the Thames. 'It happened that same day,' she
said at last. 'He had been cold with me during all the
journey back from Mortlake – brooding, and distant, and
contemptuous – as though it had been my fault he had
chosen to reject the Marquise. Returned to his rooms, he
ordered me to prepare his trunk, for he was leaving, he
told me, the next day for France – and leaving alone.

'He did not tell me what his business was – but I
already knew. I have mentioned that Lightborn mingled
with spies; not surprisingly – for I had soon come to
realise that he had been one himself. It was not only his
muse which his patrons had been sponsoring, for many
times – while I had been performing in his masques,
reciting his lines – he had been busy with less elevated
matters. And that was how I knew that a fresh plot had
been brewing – and that Lightborn, having abandoned
his dream of immortality, was now preparing to abandon
me as well.

'He had slept briefly on our return, then left that same
morning. Some hours later there came a servant from
Deptford, ordering me to deliver up the trunk. There was

no other message – no token, no farewell. So I sent the trunk – and went with it myself. We were delivered together to a tavern on the Green. You have seen it for yourself. Lightborn was upstairs there in a private room, with three other men. There were maps and papers spread across a table, and I knew the men at once to be notorious spies. Their business together was clear enough; but there were bottles as well as maps upon the table, and all of the men seemed ragingly drunk. Their eyes had lit up as I entered the room; and one of them leered and rose to his feet. He tried to grab me by my arm, but he missed and staggered, and then Lightborn pushed him backwards so that he fell against the wall. Lightborn kicked him hard, and smashed his head against the floor; then he turned back to me. "It is too late now," he whispered. His voice was angry and slurred. "For do not forget, Helen – it was you who persuaded me – you who looked at me with terror in your eyes, so that I might see what would greet me in every human stare, should I not flee, flee, flee my own desires across the world. So leave me, Helen, lest you tempt me to prove my own maxim true – *that will in us is overruled by fate.*"

'I stood frozen, paralysed by the force of his despair. And then suddenly, I felt someone seizing me by my hair and pulling me backwards. I screamed and, as I twisted, saw my former assailant risen to his feet. He had a dagger in his hand, which he held up to my throat. I kicked him as hard as I could; and as he cried out, I broke free of his grasp. I saw Lightborn reaching to the table for his own knife, but he was too late, for even as he lunged across the room his adversary struck at him, and I heard Lightborn scream as he fell to the floor – and then there was silence, and the whole room was still.

'Lightborn screamed again – a terrible, wailing curse. I ran to him, and cradled him in my arms. The dagger had entered his skull above the eye; and watery blood was seeping down his face. "The book . . ." he whispered. Then he shrieked again, and his eyes began to glaze. "The book . . . Mortlake . . ." His voice trailed away and I felt him slump in my arms.

'The three other men were all standing frozen in dumb horror. I ordered them to lift Lightborn and cover him with a sheet; then to carry him down to the river-front. So great was their terror and shock that they obeyed me without question; and so it was that I soon found myself, Lightborn in my arms, being rowed back down the Thames – back towards the house we had left that very night. I had not understood Lightborn's mention of "the book"; but I remembered his belief in the chance of immortality – and I found myself praying that we would discover it after all.'

'And your prayer was answered.'

Milady's lips twisted into a faint smile. 'In a manner of speaking.'

'How do you mean?'

She gazed through her window for a moment; then swung open the door and stepped out delicately on to the bank. Robert joined her, but she did not look round at him, staring instead across the river at the house. 'The Marquise had gone,' she said, 'when we arrived at last. There was only Dr Dee.' She laughed softly. 'He was not best pleased; he kept telling me to leave him alone, to take Lightborn away. He did not want a murdered spy found in his house.'

'And the book? What about that?'

'Of course, I asked for it as soon as I could. Dr Dee fell

silent for a moment. Then he shook his head and said it
wouldn't help. The cipher still eluded him; he could not
read the script. By now I was in despair. I knew that
Lightborn was very near death. I asked Dr Dee to bring
out the book; he did so. For a minute he flicked through
the pages, shaking his head; then at last he sighed and
slammed it shut again. Lightborn moaned, a terrible,
dying sound. I reached for the book myself. Why, I didn't
know – for I had never learned to read. I opened it, and I
found . . .' She reached for Robert's hand. 'Lovelace . . . I
found . . . I found that I could read it, after all.'

'You?' Robert stared at her in consternation. 'But . . .'
He shook his head. 'How?'

'It was not . . .' – Milady narrowed her eyes – 'not that
I was reading it – rather . . . that the script was reading
me. How can I describe it? – no – I can't – for it cannot
be described. It was as though . . . as though I had passed
into a different world where everything was water –
which I could ripple and disturb.' She bowed her head.
'Strange,' she whispered. 'Deadly strange.'

'Deadly?' Robert frowned. 'Yet its power – you used it,
surely, to save Lightborn's life?'

'He did not die, if that is what you mean.'

'He awoke recovered?'

'Save for the scar.'

'And the book? Milady – what happened to the book?'

She smiled distantly. 'I was never able to read it again.'

'How do you mean?'

'The script . . . when I looked at it again – the next day,
and the day after that – I found that it meant nothing to
me – just a jumble of swirls and scrawls upon a page.'

'How was that possible?'

Milady gave a delicate shrug. 'And yet,' she whispered

suddenly, 'I could not regret it. For just as Lightborn had been snatched from the very gates of death, so I too . . .' – she swallowed – 'so I too had been changed.'

She paused; and her voice, so lovely and haunting, had sounded for a moment so sweet with pain as well that Robert reached for her at once, and clasped her tightly in his arms. 'Changed?' he whispered in Milady's ear. 'How do you mean?'

She shook her head dumbly, continuing to stare across the river; then turned at last, and buried her face against Robert's chest. 'I was no longer,' she whispered, 'the person I had been. What else can I say? My innocence, perhaps – it was that which had been purged. For I had felt what it might be to soar beyond the bounds of mortal knowledge, to grow the mistress of forbidden sensations and dreams. Lightborn's yearnings had mingled with my own. We had braved the shadow of Death together; and we were – we are – indissolubly bound.'

She breathed in deeply, pulling down hard on the edge of his cloak; then turned suddenly and broke from his hold. She spoke an order to the coachman, who hurried down towards a boat moored amidst the rushes, and sat ready with the oars. Milady took her own place in the prow, where Robert joined her, and the two of them then lay back in silence as the boat pulled out into the silver-flowing Thames.

'And the Marquise?' Robert whispered at length, gazing round at the house. 'When did she . . .'

'Make us into creatures like herself?' Milady hugged herself. 'Very soon afterwards. It was not difficult for Lightborn to persuade his superiors to pretend that he was dead. It offered him the perfect cover for his mission – except, of course, that he never followed it through. We travelled as far as Paris, and met the Marquise there. The result?' She smiled, and reached up to touch the diamonds in her ears. 'I became a lady – my Lady of the Dead.'

'And the book?' Robert pressed. 'Did you tell the Marquise you had read it? Did you tell her what it had done?'

Milady's smile broadened. 'Why do you think she is searching for it now?'

'And what do you think? Might it still be found?'

Milady shrugged. 'I ordered Dr Dee, before we left, to have it burned; for I knew it to be a thing of danger – and tempting, oh, so tempting. That was why I could never have destroyed it myself. And what I felt . . .' – she paused – 'maybe Dr Dee felt as well.' She smiled distantly. 'But do not ask me, Lovelace – ask yourself instead. What would you have done? Would you have destroyed such an instrument of promise? Look into your own soul.'

Her eyes glittered, as though tempting him to answer. Robert was relieved when there came a sudden bump from behind them, as the prow of the boat drifted up against the bank. He clambered out, then offered Milady his arm; and together they climbed in silence to the house. But by the doorway she paused suddenly, and reached up to Robert's ear. 'Sweet Lovelace,' she whispered, 'you must be very careful now. Do not trust the Marquise. For remember – if she discovers that you want the secret book too, she will look on you not as an ally, but as a foe.'

In the hours that followed, Robert was careful to heed Milady's warning. He found the Marquise still as shrivelled and lined as she had been before: her skin yellow, her hair dirty white and clumped in sparse tufts across her chin and oozing scalp. Only in her stare did she seem recovered, for her eyes were no longer glazed, but darted and flickered like the tongue of a snake; so that even as she sat hunched in her chair, she gave the impression of a ceaseless, ravenous mobility.

Robert gave her the flasks of *mummia*. The Marquise poured herself a glass, and drained it in a single gulp; then stared at Robert intently, suspicion and interest intermingled in her eyes. 'Report to me, then,' she said at length, 'how the Pasha fares, and the stories he had to tell.' Robert did so. The Marquise sat with hands folded, listening intently, probing with occasional deftly-aimed questions, until at last Robert's narrative drew to a close and she nodded, as though in satisfaction. 'You will understand, then,' she whispered hoarsely, 'my own interest in this book. For many years, while the original lay in the Pasha's hands, I was content to wait – for one does not lightly provoke the Pasha's wrath. But now he is . . . weakened.' She smiled horribly, and touched her withered face. 'My own need too, you will see, has grown somewhat. So I would hope – I would trust – you will bear my interest in mind.'

Robert rose to his feet, and bowed. 'Of course, Madame.'

The Marquise curled back her lips, baring her jagged teeth in a smile. 'Naturally,' she continued, 'I would not like you to think that I suggest that as a threat. *Quid pro quo*, Lovelace – a favour will earn a favour; help will earn help.'

Robert stared at her in surprise. 'Help, Madame?' He narrowed his eyes. 'Help with what?'

She laughed. 'Bring me the book, Lovelace, and then you will find out.'

'Even the shyest of prick-teasers, Madame, know that temptation must be seasoned with a glimpse of naked flesh.'

The Marquise's eyes glittered as she studied him; then she nodded shortly. '*Ma chère*,' she whispered, beckoning to Milady. 'I gather you have lately been sick with plague-stained blood?'

'Yes,' Milady frowned, 'thank you, but I am quite recovered now.'

'What was it cured you?' the Marquise asked. She tapped the bottle of *mummia*. 'Might it have been this?'

Milady's frown deepened. 'Yes, but . . .'

'Fascinating.' The Marquise hissed out the word. '*Fascinating*.' She grinned horribly. 'So it would seem that Tadeus' argument was indeed correct.'

Robert felt a shadow fall across his heart at the very mention of Tadeus' name. 'Tell me,' he whispered, 'what this argument was.'

The Marquise's grin grew thinner. 'The fruit of his observations and experiences in Bohemia. It is contained in this volume, which he presented as a token of his respect to myself.' Reaching for a book from the table by her chair, she flicked through the pages. 'Remember this?' she asked. She turned the book round. There was a drawing in ink upon the page; Robert did indeed remember it, for the Marquise had shown it to him once before. Now as then, it served to chill his blood. It was a drawing of the Evil One – of Azrael.

'So you see,' the Marquise hissed, closing the book again and putting it aside, 'there are books of secrets that I already possess.' She glanced at it again; then reached out to touch and stroke Robert's stomach. 'If you would share it with me, Lovelace – you know what you must do.'

Robert gazed at her in silence, then brushed at her hand to remove it from his stomach. 'It might concentrate my mind,' he said at length, 'to have just a hint of what the secret might be.'

'A terrible one.'

'You astonish me,' replied Robert coldly. 'Surely you can tell me something more than that?'

'I could – but I choose not to.' The Marquise suddenly pulled away her shawl to reveal the low-cut gown beneath, and her withered, shrunken breasts. 'My flesh, alas, is not as ripe as it once was. But I trust you will agree – I can still tease a prick.'

'Indeed, Madame, you can.' Robert gazed at her a moment more, then bowed and turned away. 'Indeed you can.'

He might almost have told the Marquise, he decided later, had she not shown him her dried-grape dugs. He glanced across at Milady where she lay in the boat, and gently, through her cloak, kissed her perfect breasts; then began to confide in her instead. For he had suddenly been struck, he told her, as they had climbed up together from the river to the Marquise's house, by the memory of how he had done the same thing many years before – of how he had climbed through Mr Aubrey's garden in Broadchalke, up towards his house. And at the same moment as he had recalled this, Robert went on, he had also remembered something else – something which in Deptford had remained just a haze. Mr Aubrey opening a book. Pages written in a meaningless script. And a dim memory of Mr Aubrey's boast – that the book had once belonged to Dr Dee.

'SON OF A WHORE, GOD DAMN YOU, CAN YOU TELL
A PEERLESS PEER THE READIEST WAY TO HELL? . . .
THE READIEST WAY TO HELL? COME QUICK . . .'
                    The Earl of Rochester, 'To the Postboy'

Robert and Milady left the next night, and travelled
hard along the dusty road to Salisbury. They had no
difficulty in entering the city, for they discovered that the
King had long since grown bored and left for Oxford,
taking all his court with him. Nor, it soon appeared, was
he alone in having uprooted himself; for on their arrival
in Broadchalke, they discovered Mr Aubrey's house
empty, and were informed by a servant that he was
abroad on his travels.

'Travels?' Robert asked, in a fury of disappointment.
'Travels where?'

The servant shrugged. 'Anywhere. Everywhere. For he
is researching for his books, and in such a mood he is
never to be found.'

Robert stared about him in frustration. The shelves, he
noticed, had been emptied. He asked the man where all
the books had gone.

'They have been packed away and sent to London, for
Mr Aubrey is seeking to sell this place. His fortunes have
lately been much reduced.'

'Where in London?'

The servant shrugged disinterestedly: he didn't know.
Milady took Robert's arm; then she stared at the servant,
whose face at once turned pale. His eyes bulged; he
staggered, and had to lean against a table to support
himself. 'You understand, then?' Milady murmured at

last. 'You will have him contact us as soon as he returns?'

The man nodded dumbly.

'Good,' Milady purred. She paused, then slipped a coin out from her purse. 'He may write to us in Oxford,' she nodded, dropping the coin on to the floor. 'To Robert Lovelace; address – the Court.'

They travelled to Oxford in the hope of discovering Lord Rochester there. 'For it were best,' Milady said, 'since he is the Pasha's chosen heir, that we tell him of our search for Mr Aubrey's book. Who else is there, who might have the power to read it? And indeed Lord Rochester will need to, if he is to journey to Woodton and yet have hope of a return.' She said this as they rode along the track beside Stonehenge; and both she and Robert glanced towards the trees. But nothing stirred beyond them, and they quickened their pace and left the scene behind.

Arrived in Oxford, they discovered that Lord Rochester had indeed returned from the fleet, and was now the toast and talk of the Court. For as Savile explained to Robert one evening, his friend had grown a thousand times more dissolute than he had been before the war; and yet before the war, he had already been a most notorious rake. 'And so it is,' Savile belched, 'that the courtiers say that though the Dutch be dull, yet they are the midwives to wit. For the more intemperate Lord Rochester becomes, the more his blood is inflamed; and the more his blood is inflamed, the more his wit seems to grow. It is my favourite sport at present to make my Lord drunk, purely for the pleasure of seeing how wild he can become, and what riots he will lead.'

Robert smiled; for he doubted it was wine which served to fuel Lord Rochester's humours. And Lord

Rochester himself, when they met, confirmed his suspicions readily enough. 'Blood!' he proclaimed. 'It is the finest pleasure known to spirit or flesh. And yet, Lovelace, see . . .' He raised up his glass; then stroked his crotch. 'It is the property of this most exquisite of delights, that it does not diminish but serves to fuel all other pleasures too. I had grown afraid, before our visit to Amsterdam, that my appetites had been forever sated; and yet now they are restored to me, and they are more violent and ravenous than they ever were before.'

'Overjoyed for you, my Lord – overjoyed, I am sure.'

Lord Rochester narrowed his eyes. 'What, Lovelace,' he murmured, 'not jealous, I hope?'

'I would never be jealous of you, my Lord – for I have some knowledge of what you must soon confront.'

'Yes,' said Lord Rochester with a sudden iciness. 'Naturally you do.' He rose to his feet abruptly, and called to the servant for his cloak. While it was fastened he continued silent, then glanced again, as though in passing, at Robert. 'You will inform me when this man, this Mr Aubrey, is found?'

'Naturally, my Lord.'

'Very good.' Lord Rochester crossed to the door, then paused again. 'Oh – and Lovelace – in the meantime – it were best you kept yourself away from me.'

'Indeed?' Robert stared at him in startled anger. 'For what reason, may I ask?'

Lord Rochester yawned. 'Because you remind me of matters other than my pleasures. I have not had my sensations restored to me, to have them blunted by your gallows talk.' He paused a moment more, daring Robert to challenge him; and indeed, without thinking, Robert half-drew his sword. But Rochester only smiled, and shook his head; and Robert, flushing, dropped the blade back in its sheath. He continued frozen for several minutes after Lord Rochester had gone; then tried in vain all that night to drown his fury with drink.

Milady, when he told her later, did not seem surprised. 'For this quickening of sensations is common to us all, when we first develop our yearning for blood – all the world seems made for our pleasure. And yet it does not persist.' She paused; and Robert saw, gazing into her eyes, a sudden bleakness, like that of the passing of the years, borne upon time as desert sands are borne on winds. He kissed her on her cheek, and smiled to see it bloom a sudden crimson. She glanced round at him, then lowered her eyes. 'Do as Lord Rochester has ordered you,' she murmured. 'For as I have said – his present humour will not endure for long.' She sighed, and reached for a goblet of wine; she drained it in a single, disinterested gulp, then dropped it on the floor and stared at Robert once again. With her finger, she traced the curve of his lips. 'For the time will soon come,' she whispered, 'when his pleasures are as rare, and therefore prized, as mine are now. And then he, like me, sweet Lovelace, will be yours.'

Robert smiled at her, and kissed her hand; and for a moment almost believed her compliment. Of course, in his heart he knew that Milady's nature was unchanged, that she was far too deadly and wondrous to be anyone's – that a wolf, however docile, must always be a wolf; and indeed that same night, as he pretended to sleep, he heard her rise and slip into the streets. But he was not surprised now, as he had been before, that she desired to prey alone; for he could see how it had become her most pleasing fantasy – that she was a mortal like himself, that she did not drink blood, that she was not compelled to kill. And Robert, as he sought to share in the pretence, found that it came easily; for it brought back life to the faded ghosts of memory – to that lost world of friendship he had once shared with Emily. He had not understood before, he realised, how achingly he had missed it; but now, as it returned . . . now he understood. It surprised him, his joy: that Milady, who had once been his almost-mother, was now his almost-sister, his almost-Emily, instead.

Almost – because at the same time, she was becoming something more. It did not require poetry now to instruct Robert in the nature of love; yet the sense of surprise was almost as great as when he had first read Ovid, and closed his eyes, and found that he was dreaming of kissing Emily's lips. Almost-sister – and something more; and Robert felt again, as he had done all those years before, the delicious thrill of guilt that someone so close should seem so suddenly tantalising, so infinite and strange. He realised how coarse his pleasures must have grown, that it should surprise him how desire might seem more pleasurable than climax in some whore – as though his yearning were suddenly too precious to be fulfilled; even, he thought, to be spoken of at all. For although Milady, like him, appeared perfectly aware of their new game, she too seemed unwilling to acknowledge its existence, so that not even the rules of their courtship were defined, but evolved instead unacknowledged and unsaid, in response to the silent patterns of their love, which now teased and delighted Robert's every thought. For although the pleasures they gave him were delicate, yet they were also unexpectedly, painfully rich: the scent of perfume on Milady's arm; the way a curl might break free and fall

across her cheek; laughter, then a sudden silent meeting
of their eyes. And it was under such influences that
Robert found all else fading from his mind: the weight of
despair, and foreboding, and dread; and he began to
imagine it might never return.

Then, one night, he received an urgent message from
Milady, asking him to come to her. They met beneath the
Oxford stars; and as he kissed her, he felt her lips part
and her tongue touch his. But she broke away again
suddenly, and gazed down at the ground; and Robert
laughed to see her looking so coy, as though she were
some virtuous innocent. He reached after her; but she
pushed him away; then pulled out a letter from between
her breasts. She smoothed it out. 'Mr Aubrey,' she said,
'has written at last. He is travelling to London. He has
given us here – see, Lovelace – his address.'

Robert took the letter and inspected it. 'Why,' he
exclaimed, 'what a goose-chase we have had! He is
staying on the Strand.'

Milady nodded. 'And so we must discover Lord
Rochester, and leave for London at once.' She took the letter
back, then turned and began to hurry away. Robert followed
her: he seized her arm; he tried to kiss her again. But again
she broke away and, as she looked round, Robert saw that
her eyes were aflame like sun on ice. 'You surprise me, sir,'
she hissed. 'I had thought your resolution stronger, than to
permit you at such a moment to think only of your prick, as
though you were no better than some rutting dog.' She
turned again, and ran along the road; and as Robert
recovered from his shock, and began to pursue her, he saw
her pass through the doorway of a tavern and disappear.

Following her through the door, he caught a glimpse
of her across a crowded, smoke-thick room, being led up

a stairway by a nervous-looking maid. Robert pushed his way through the crowds, then ran up the stairs; and on the landing at the top he saw the maid unlock a door. Her hand was shaking; and as the door swung open, she cowered back. Milady brushed past her; and Robert, following, saw Lord Rochester on a bed entwined with four naked, red-daubed whores. There were empty bottles scattered everywhere, and Robert saw that their rims were caked with dry blood. Lord Rochester was laughing violently; he reached for a further bottle by his side, then slowly poured its contents over each pair of breasts, so that they gleamed with blood as though made sleek with crimson oil. 'Faster,' Lord Rochester gasped suddenly, 'faster!' His eyes began to roll, his fingers to clench and, reaching for one of the girls, he gripped her so tightly that she started to scream, and Robert saw blood, yet more blood, trickling down her arms, seeping out from under Lord Rochester's fingernails. He too was screaming now as he pulled the girl down closer; he began to suck and lick greedily at the blood on her breasts. Then he reached for another bottle, and drained it in one gulp; his whole body bucked – it writhed and thrashed, then at last lay spent. The girls too lay utterly still; and the silence was sticky with the scent of sweat and blood.

'Get out,' Milady screamed suddenly. 'Get out!' The whores stirred and rose lazily; but as they met Milady's stare, their expressions were bled white and, reaching for their dresses, they stumbled from the room. Milady crossed to Lord Rochester; she tossed him his shirt. 'You too, my Lord. We have urgent business ahead.'

Lord Rochester raised an eyebrow, but otherwise did not stir. 'You forget, Milady – I am no longer a mortal, to be bent to your will.'

'A letter from Mr Aubrey has arrived.'

Not a flicker of interest crossed Lord Rochester's face. 'Indeed,' he continued, as though not having heard her at all, 'it is I who am properly your master now.' He met her stare; and Robert saw how Milady's face seemed suddenly to freeze. Lord Rochester smiled cruelly. 'You have inter-rupted me, Milady, in the course of my pleasures. You have sent my whores away. I might rightfully bid you to serve me in their place. Might I not, Milady? Might I not make you be my whore? You have had practice enough, of that I am certain.'

Milady clenched her fists; then, with a visible effort to contain her fury, she turned away. 'It is precisely because you have inherited the Pasha's powers,' she whispered, 'that you must come with us now, to discover the book and see if you can read it.'

Lord Rochester yawned. 'I am not in the mood.'

Robert stepped forward to join Milady. He was clutching at his stomach; for his pain had returned, borne on the wings of Lord Rochester's pleasure. 'And yet you know,' he said coldly, 'that time is running out.'

'Let it.' Lord Rochester yawned again. 'For as I have just said, Signor Devilfuck – *I am not in the mood.*' He stretched; then sighed, as though the tedium of the business had grown suddenly too oppressive to endure. 'You go to London,' he ordered. 'Discover the book. Keep it for me there. The plague, it is said, is dying out, and the Court will soon be returning to Whitehall – when it does, then so shall I. It is best you go ahead, and prepare for my arrival – for that is how minions should ever serve their lord.'

Milady breathed in deeply. Robert saw her place her hand within her cloak, and he thought of the delicate knife that she always wore there, thought she was preparing to draw it from its sheath. But again she stifled her rage, and slowly turned and crossed to the door. Once there, though, she paused and glanced back. 'You should enjoy your pleasure,' she hissed suddenly, 'while you are still able to, my Lord. It will not long provide you with an excuse for folly and pride. For enjoyment in our breed, if taken too fast, is like the sting of a bee: once lost, it converts its owner to a drone.' She studied him a moment more, then dropped a sudden curtsy. 'In London, then, my Lord. We shall expect you there.'

∽∾∾

'. . . THE MISGUIDED FOLLOWER CLIMBS WITH PAIN
MOUNTAINS OF WHIMSEYS HEAPED IN HIS OWN BRAIN;
TUMBLING FROM THOUGHT TO THOUGHT, FALLS HEADLONG
DOWN
INTO DOUBT'S BOUNDLESS SEA . . .'

The Earl of Rochester, 'A Satyr Against Mankind'

They left that same night. Milady's rage continued icy but seemed tempered as well with a nervous, febrile excitement, so that she was forever leaning out from the window, marking with impatience the passage of the miles. Robert had never seen her so agitated; and he began to wonder what it was she might be hoping for, from a book which she had once desired to see destroyed. Certainly, there seemed no place in her mind for their former minuet of love: she would hold him sometimes, or lay his head upon her lap, stroking his hair; but he could see in her eyes that the game had been suspended, that their dance had broken up. The book, the book; she thought of nothing but the book. And so Robert, absorbing her distraction, found his own mind darkening as well, as though his doubts and fears were a swarm of locusts, stripping him bare once again of all his hope.

Arriving in London, he saw that the marks of the plague did indeed seem less violent; and that life, like the flow of blood through long-cramped limbs, was returning to the streets. The plague's decline puzzled Robert; nor did he contemplate it altogether with relief. For he could not believe that a visitation so deadly in its origin could merely fade away; and he remembered the Marquise's promise of a further terror related to the plague. What that might be, he dreaded to think; but he also knew, approaching Mr Aubrey's address, that he was still unwilling to pay the price she had demanded. For if they did find the book – if Lord Rochester could read its secret script – what need then would they have of the Marquise?

And Robert knew, the moment they had introduced themselves to Mr Aubrey and explained their mission to him, that the book was theirs indeed. For although Mr Aubrey seemed a little flustered, staring at the two of them with evident consternation, he had known at once which book it was that they had meant; and after stammering nervously for a couple of seconds, he had turned and passed into a box-cluttered room. 'I do apologise,' he muttered. 'I have only lately arrived in town. So much still to do – and so little time – for I have never been – alas – the *best ordered* of men.' He began to rummage through the boxes, so that books and papers were soon being scattered round the room, until at last – when it seemed that every scrap had been exhumed – he gave a sudden cry of triumph and rose up from his knees. 'Here!' he exclaimed. He brandished a book above his head. 'Was this the one you meant?'

Milady seized it from him hungrily. 'Yes, yes, this is it.' But as she opened the pages, she shook her head, and disappointment darkened the eagerness in her eyes. She pointed to the script, and glanced round at Robert. He studied it for a moment and then, like her, he shook his head.

'Alas,' said Mr Aubrey, squatting on a box, 'I am afraid it is hopeless. No one even knows what the script itself might be.'

Milady narrowed her eyes. 'In that case,' she murmured, 'you would not object if we were to ... borrow ... it a while?'

'Well,' Mr Aubrey stammered, clearly startled, 'I ... well, that is to say ... goodness me ...'

'We would, of course' – she reached inside her cloak – 'be willing to pay.'

She tossed the purse across and, as Mr Aubrey inspected it, his eyes began to goggle. 'Well ... ha ha ... to borrow it, you say?' He swallowed, then shrugged, then shrugged once again. 'It is not as if – ha ha – I ever read it, I suppose. So yes,' he nodded quietly, '*yes*! – borrow it, please! For of what value has it ever been to me? None. *None*! Although ...' – he frowned, and suddenly paused – 'there was, I suppose, that one occasion once ...'

Robert interrupted him. 'What occasion, sir?'

'Oh, it was nothing, nothing at all ...' Mr Aubrey stammered and laughed. 'But there was once, I remember, a series of crimes ...'

'And these crimes, sir?' Robert interrupted him again,

not bothering now to conceal his excitement. 'Were you asked to help solve them by a militia captain?'

Mr Aubrey gazed at him, startled. 'Why, yes, sir,' he nodded.

'Was his name Captain Foxe?'

'Why, yes, sir,' Mr Aubrey nodded again.

Robert stood frozen for a moment; and suddenly he felt tears prickling his eyes, knowing that his father had not been utterly forgotten, hearing his name be recognised after so long, so long. Robert blinked back his tears. 'Captain Foxe,' he whispered, 'was my father, sir.' He stepped forward and gripped Mr Aubrey's arms. 'Do you not remember me? My name was Robert Foxe. I came once to fish for chub in your stream.'

Mr Aubrey gazed at him in astonishment. 'I . . . you . . . well – I do declare.' He frowned. 'You are very much changed, sir, indeed.'

'Indeed,' Robert smiled. 'Even my name.'

'Yes, yes.' Mr Aubrey nodded. 'For I might then have recognised it, when you left it with my servant. And yet I had thought you were dead – for they told me you were – and that is why . . .' He began to rummage through his pockets and he drew out a key. 'That is why . . .' He hurried out through the door, ran up the stairs; and then Robert heard crashing from the room above, until at length Mr Aubrey came hurrying back down the stairs. 'Here, sir,' he cried waving a thin sheaf of papers. 'If I had known you still lived – I swear it – I would have sought you out long, long before.'

'Why,' Robert asked, as he took the sheaf, 'what is this?'

'A letter from your father.'

Robert stared at it in astonishment. 'When did he write it?'

'On the day that he died.' Mr Aubrey swallowed; then he flushed bright red, and seemed convulsed by his shame. 'If only . . .' he stammered, 'if only I had known . . .' He reached for Milady's purse; thrust it back into her hand. 'Please . . . the book . . . it is the merest compensation, I know . . .'

But Robert took the purse and handed it back; then reached inside his pocket for a purse of his own. As he passed it across, he raised the letter from his father to his lips. He kissed it softly and, as though by transfusion, felt his courage and his sense of resolve redoubled. He thought of his father, of his undaunted will; and he prayed that but a portion of that spirit might be his. Then he offered up a silent vow that, wherever the way ahead might lead, there he would follow it, even to the very bowels of Hell; for he would not, he could not be turned aside now.

It was Robert's determination to keep the book from Lightborn, for he suspected that if he did not, then the precious manuscript would soon afterwards be delivered into the hands of the Marquise. Milady agreed; and it was therefore resolved that, rather than linger in London, they would rent from Mr Aubrey his abandoned Broadchalke home. Pausing only to leave a message for Lord Rochester in Whitehall, they embarked straight away upon the Western road. As their carriage lumbered past Mortlake, Robert saw how Milady gripped the book tightly against her chest, like a tigress guarding her kill; nor would she release her hold until it was clear that no one was pursuing them, and that their discovery was safe.

In the first weeks after their arrival in Broadchalke, however, Robert barely glanced at the precious book; instead he lavished all his care upon the letter, which he imagined, as he read it, he heard spoken by his father. For it had been written, he supposed, to sound from beyond the grave: to plead for his support, to inform him and inspire. Certainly, in almost everything his father had described, there seemed confirmation of the Pasha's tale; confirmation – and hints as well of something more. For Robert could be confident now, as he had suspected earlier, that Stonehenge was indeed the focus of a mighty line of power; and that Tadeus had known this, and had sought to make the power his own. His inspiration, Robert thought, could only have been in Prague; for it was there that Tadeus had practised his arts; and doubtless too had served to rescue his god. Yet the question of how he had done so remained unanswered, along with other mysteries which the letter could not resolve. For the book itself was still unread; and thereby continued the greatest mystery of all.

Then one morning a letter came from Lord Rochester, announcing his intention to arrive the following week. Milady read out the letter with a fierce and naked joy. As she did so, Robert found himself wondering again about the nature of her obsession with the book, for her eagerness – as she stalked the house later, waiting for Lord Rochester to come – seemed as desperate and predatory as the Marquise's had been; and yet when he asked her, she would toss her head, and deny that she wanted anything for herself. 'It is only for you, sweet Lovelace – all for you.' Robert did not choose to press her; for her mood, since their arrival in Broadchalke, had been brittle, and her temper short. Yet despite his fears to the contrary, she seemed not to love him any the less, for she would sometimes hold him in her arms as they worked, or surprise him with a kiss; and Robert, for a moment, would hope their minuet had been resumed. But again he knew better than to press her; for if he did, her eyes would turn to molten ice, and she would shrug him away and glide out from the room. Later he would hear her footsteps, pacing to and fro across the room overhead; and he would wonder all the more what her hopes were from the book, and why she should await them with such impatience and concern.

The week passed, and a second, and then a third; and then at last Lord Rochester arrived. His cheeks seemed flushed and, as he entered the house, Robert felt a tingling in his veins and a stabbing in his stomach. 'I apologise,' said Lord Rochester, glancing at him. 'I had forgotten your guts can sense when I have killed. Yet in truth, I had but little choice in the matter, for I have lately been drunk for several weeks on end. How the devil else was I to cleanse the fumes out from my head?' He glanced across at Milady, who was waiting at the table, the book by her side. 'Let us trust it enables me to read the poxy thing.'

He sat down, and opened the book; but it was clear at once that he could not decipher the script. He stared at the book in silence for a minute; then he closed it again, and leaned back in his seat. 'It may be,' he said at length, 'I shall need another kill.'

'I think not,' said Robert slowly.

Lord Rochester sighed, and rubbed his eyes. 'I have, as I told you, been exceedingly drunk.'

'If you cannot read it now, my Lord, then it will make

no difference how sober you become, for it is clear already that the Pasha did not bequeath you the skill.'

Milady's eyes glittered. 'Disappointing,' she hissed. 'Rather as though the offspring of a stud were not to breed.'

'And yet still,' Robert continued, 'you remain the heir to his powers.'

'Very well,' Lord Rochester glanced at Milady, then narrowed his eyes. 'What would you suggest?'

'We must take the book, and return to Amsterdam.'

Lord Rochester sighed, and shook his head. 'The Pasha left there long ago, for even when we spoke with him he had recovered sufficiently to travel, and had only lingered in the city to meet with me.'

'But are you certain he is indeed gone?'

Lord Rochester nodded. 'I received a letter from him some months ago, telling me of his departure for Constantinople.'

Robert swore under his breath, then reached for the book. 'Well,' he nodded, 'we have no other choice. We must leave for Prague instead.'

Lord Rochester stared at him for a moment; then laughed in derision. 'I shall do no such thing. Damn you, Lovelace, are you not content to have lured me out here, that now you would have me trail all across Europe?'

But Milady reached forward, and took Robert's hand. 'Lovelace, why Prague?'

'Because it is where the Pasha himself was taught to read the book.'

'Yes,' Rochester sneered, 'by a man who has been dead for sixty years.'

'Where else would we find heirs to the Rabbi's

teaching, but amongst his followers in the Ghetto?'

'How can you be certain that he even had any followers?'

'I cannot. But if you have an alternative suggestion, my Lord, then I would be overjoyed to consider it.'

'Are there not Jews or scholars in London, who can read in Hebrew?'

Robert smiled thinly. 'I have some knowledge of the language myself.'

'Then use it, man, use it!'

Robert reached for the book and flicked through the pages; then he shook his head. 'I cannot recognise Hebrew, nor any language, here.'

'Then try harder,' whispered Lord Rochester menacingly. 'For I tell you plainly, Lovelace, I shall not go to Prague. I can think of no purpose that the journey would serve, save to lose us in the bogs and fens of your whimsies.'

'Yet we are already lost, my Lord – and it may be that not even the Pasha could have served us as our guide.'

'Why, sir, what do you mean?'

'Consider, my Lord, this further mystery – that the malevolent spirit who is our deadly foe, who was fought by the Pasha to the very point of death, so that the Pasha himself had believed he was destroyed – was nevertheless somehow saved and restored. How? We know that he was brought here to England by Tadeus; and we may be certain as well that he was brought within a trunk of mortal flesh, the name of which had once been Sir Charles Wolverton – for I saw for myself Sir Charles' face melt, and the creature within him emerge through the bone. Yet by what means, by what magic, was that miracle achieved? We must find out, my Lord, if we are to succeed where even the Pasha could not, and forever destroy our foe.' Robert curled his fingers closely together; then he pursed his lips. 'But we will not discover the answers here. For I say it again – they are awaiting us in Prague.'

Lord Rochester said nothing for some moments, then swore with sudden violence. 'I cannot leave now,' he muttered. 'My affairs are very pressing.'

'Affairs?' inquired Milady silkily.

'I have business at Court.'

Milady stared at him, her eyes glittering with contempt. 'A rare ambition in our breed,' she laughed suddenly, 'to wish to creep and cringe before a mortal king.'

'And yet it is not so rare, after all, Madam, to desire the company and pleasures of mortals.' Lord Rochester glanced across at Robert, then back at Milady. 'What I do not wish, above all, is to be like you, huddled in the shadows, clutching your single mortal toy to your breast. I crave richer and more varied delights – the best women, the best balls, the best visits, the best treats – a wicked town-life.' He stretched and laughed, then rose to his feet. 'Since time henceforth is to serve me as my whore – why then, I shall seek to fuck her all I can.'

'And, like any rake, soon grow impotent.'

Lord Rochester laughed again. 'A pretty moral warning, to come from a blood-drinking bitch.' He waved disdainfully towards Robert. 'I had thought it was he who had been the puritan.'

'So he was,' Milady nodded. 'And it may be, for that reason, he would have served the Pasha better than you.'

'A shame, then, that His Excellency seemed not to agree.'

'Yes,' Milady nodded. 'For his purposes – a great shame indeed.'

There was a silence. Robert stared at Milady in surprise. She met his eye briefly, then looked away, and rose to her feet. 'I am weary of you both,' she whispered suddenly. She turned, and hurried from the room. Her footsteps soon faded away; all grew silent again.

Robert reached slowly for the book, and gazed down at it. 'What is your business at Court?' he asked at length.

'Unfinished,' Lord Rochester answered. 'For I have still to get my wife.'

'Your wife, my Lord? But I thought you had Miss Malet.'

'I seized her, it is true, but I was not allowed to keep her. If I am to make her my own, and still maintain my place at Court, then I must first obtain the blessing of the King.'

Robert nodded slowly. 'And you must indeed have Miss Malet? You cannot let her go?'

'No – for like Milady, I desire mortal company and, unlike Milady, I require my loved one's cash.'

Robert nodded slowly again.

'You need not fear, Lovelace, I shall be as fast about the business as I can. And in the meanwhile, pass your time with studying the book.'

'There would be no value in it.'

'Try,' Lord Rochester whispered, 'only try.'

'And if I do not succeed?'

'Why, when I have bagged Miss Malet, we shall both leave for Prague.'

'You swear it?'

'I swear it – for what that is worth.'

Robert smiled faintly. 'Then let us trust you will soon be a married man.'

'Books are not absolutely dead things . . .'
John Milton, *Areopagitica*

For the next months, Robert followed Lord Rochester's suggestion, and continued with his studies; but as he had feared would be the case, he made no progress with the book. Worse, indeed: for he began to imagine, as he stared at it, that the book was reading him – bleeding his thoughts, feeding on his mind until he wanted to scream, for his brain would seem sucked dry. Milady would sometimes try to comfort him; but if she had recently fed, then her presence would only make the agony worse. For Robert was sensitive now to her every taste of blood, to her every after-glow of pleasure, which he would feel all the more sweetly even as the pain began to stab. Indeed, the ache in his stomach seemed always with him now, and at its very worst as he studied the script, as though the letters were stirring some sharp-toothed parasite awake, to rend and gnaw at the depths of his guts. And so he abandoned his studies, and put aside the book – and waited for Lord Rochester to announce that he had wed.

Yet the months passed; and still the letter did not come. As the agony in Robert's stomach began to grow more searing, so he started to write letters of his own, demanding a reply, even the tiniest scribbled note, until at last his patience dissolved into his pain, and he found himself agreeing with Milady's jibe that it would have been better had the Pasha chosen him. 'Nor is it too late,' he began to think – for if he were indeed to become a blood-drinker, with all the consequent powers,

then what need would there be for Lord Rochester, what
need to wait for him at all? For by now, Robert was
desperate to be on his way to Prague: his pain was
worsening, and summer fading into autumn. Yet still,
both he and Milady were agreed, it would be rashness to
leave without the Pasha's chosen heir; and so it was
decided in the end, at Milady's urgent prompting, that
they would travel first to London and seek Lord
Rochester out, before taking ship and heading onwards
to Prague.

It was a resolution, however, which Robert made
reluctantly; for the danger of discovery, he knew, would
be great. 'It may be,' he whispered, as their carriage
rumbled through Hyde Park and began to shudder to a
halt, 'that they have spies upon every turnpike.' Milady
at once twitched aside the curtain and glanced out; then
she sat back, the book clasped tightly upon her lap.
Robert listened to the cries of the watchmen outside.
Instinctively, he reached for his sword. But then
suddenly, he heard a shaking out of the reins and, with
a violent jolt, the carriage continued on its way. 'And yet
I am certain,' he insisted, 'that they will be hunting
for us elsewhere.' He squeezed Milady's hand. 'Be
careful especially when you approach the wharves, for it
may be they have thought to have the shipping offices
watched.'

Milady nodded faintly, then pulled the curtain back
again. 'We are approaching Whitehall,' she whispered,
squeezing Robert's hand in turn. 'You as well, sweet
Lovelace – be watchful. For I would rather lose even this
book than lose you.' She kissed him softly upon his lips;
then released him again, as the carriage began to slow.
Robert swung open the door, and jumped into the street.

He saw Milady part the curtain briefly, her golden eyes burning from the shadows; and then the carriage rumbled past. Robert did not linger to watch it disappear, but turned and ran towards the Palace gate.

He slipped through unchallenged; then he hurried along the galleries towards that corner of Whitehall where Lord Rochester kept rooms. But as he drew near to the Holbein Gate, he heard his name called out and, turning round, saw Lady Castlemaine. A servant was following her with four yapping dogs; she waved him away, then beckoned Robert near. 'Lovelace.' She surveyed him up and down. 'You are looking very pretty – if not a little pale.'

Robert bowed. 'I have been lately somewhat ill, my Lady.'

'Indeed? I am sorry to hear it. I was thinking I had not seen you abroad for a while.'

'I have been much pressed by urgent business.'

'And was it your business to which you were skulking just now?'

Robert glanced back over his shoulder. 'I was on my way to call upon Lord Rochester.'

Lady Castlemaine arched a thin eyebrow. 'Why, Lovelace, you must have been ill, indeed, to be so ignorant of the news about Court. Did you truly not know that my cousin is gone to sea?'

'To sea?' Robert closed his eyes in disbelief, then struggled to compose himself. 'Why, my Lady? Where is he gone?'

'To be a hero. For it was decided, if he was to be judged a worthy husband for Miss Malet, that he would have to prove himself by whipping the Dutch.'

'When is he expected back?'

'Whenever our fleet is victorious. Judgement Day, perhaps.'

Robert swore violently.

Lady Castlemaine narrowed her eyes. 'Why, Lovelace,' she murmured, 'you sigh as fetchingly as any lady here at Court. Indeed, you are pale as all the rest of us are.'

Robert smiled grimly. 'My Lord Rochester is greatly missed, then, I presume?'

'Oh, exceedingly – it is said that a woman has only to gaze into his eyes, and her reputation is irretrievably doomed. For not only is he the most handsome and witty man at court; he is also the most unprincipled, and dangerous to my sex.' Lady Castlemaine paused; then she breathed a deep sigh. 'I could wish,' she murmured, 'since he is a cousin of mine, that I too had been granted the secret of his appeal.'

Robert bowed. 'Your Ladyship's modesty does you wondrous credit.'

'And yet . . .' Lady Castlemaine smiled faintly. 'It is true what is said – there is a magic to his eye. One might well desire such a charm for oneself.'

Robert did not answer. He thought of Milady: of the feel of her lips upon his own and of how, in Oxford, she had twisted from his grasp. 'One might indeed,' he murmured at last.

He bowed again, and bade Lady Castlemaine farewell; then turned and left through the Holbein Gate. So distracted did he feel that he no longer sought to keep amongst the crowds, but strode along the emptiest, darkest lanes until suddenly, above the muffled clamour of the Strand, he heard the splashing of footsteps hurrying after him. He rounded a corner, and crouched inside a doorway; while still the footsteps came splashing down the lane. As a dark figure rounded the corner, Robert stepped out and tripped it, seizing its arms; then he pointed a knife to its throat.

The figure gave a strangled half-yelp of fear.

Robert frowned, and slowly lowered his knife. 'Mr Aubrey?' he whispered.

The figure nodded desperately. 'Mr Lovelace?' he gasped. 'I saw you . . . as I was leaving my rooms – and I watched – well – it was foolish, sir, of course, to follow anyone down such dangerous streets . . .'

'Foolish, sir? No – the fault was all my own.'

But Mr Aubrey brushed his apologies aside. 'For I was curious, sir – you understand – about Dr Dee's book – and whether you had succeeded in translating the script.'

Robert smiled faintly; then shook his head.

'A challenge, sir,' Mr Aubrey nodded, 'an indisputable challenge – such as would tax the most learned of men. And indeed – it was on that very point . . . when I saw you just now . . . I was struck by the thought – there is indeed a learned man whom you might desire to meet.'

Robert's doubt must have been visible on his face, for Mr Aubrey began to nod ever more violently. 'He is a most remarkably learned and ingenious man,' he insisted. 'And indeed, I am appointed to meet with him tomorrow night.'

Robert shrugged faintly. 'What is his name?'

'Mr John Milton,' Mr Aubrey replied.

Robert nodded slowly. 'Yes,' he whispered. 'Yes, of course. But why the delay, sir?' He paused. 'Why not visit him tonight?'

*

They travelled first to London Bridge, for that was where Robert had arranged to meet with Milady. He saw her standing cloaked in shadow, at the point on the bridge where she had stood many years before, to show him for the first time the vast expanse of London. As he clambered out from the hackney coach, Milady turned round; and lowered the hood which had covered her face. 'Please, sir,' Robert whispered at once to Mr Aubrey, 'stay here, if you will.' Then he slammed the door behind him, and hurried across the street.

'What is it?' he whispered, taking Milady by her hands. He embraced her tightly. 'What has happened?'

'Lightborn.'

'Where?'

'On Pudding Lane.'

'Did he see you?'

'No . . . I . . .' Milady shook her head. 'I do not believe so, no.'

'Then what was his business there?'

'I . . .' She swallowed; then shook her head, and did not reply to the question. 'He was standing at the top of the hill, surveying the street.'

'Was he looking for you?'

Milady shrugged faintly.

'Very well.' Robert frowned, and tried to think. 'The ship, Milady. Is our passage booked?'

She nodded. 'For Lübeck, in three days' time. Our luggage is already being boarded. And in the meanwhile, I have rented us rooms in the Dolphin, by Tower wharf.' She paused again, and arched an eyebrow. 'I am to assume, then, that his Lordship is not yet wed?'

'We must put his Lordship entirely from our minds. And that may mean' – Robert swallowed – 'before we leave, perhaps . . . since there is no other way . . .'

His voice faded, as though his words were morning mist and Milady's stare a burning sun. He looked down, towards the river below; for he could not endure to meet the glitter of her eyes.

'Lovelace,' she whispered. 'No other way but . . . what?'

Still Robert gazed down, at the rapids boiling through the arches of the bridge. 'But it is not yet certain,' he said suddenly. 'There may still be another, a final chance.'

'Lovelace, I do not understand you.'

Robert turned, and met Milady's stare at last. 'The book,' he asked her, 'do you have it with you now?'

Milady frowned faintly. 'Naturally,' she replied.

'Give it to me.'

'Why?'

'Because . . .' Robert took the book from her hands and slipped it beneath his cloak. 'It may be,' he whispered, 'that all will still be well. For if there is anyone who has the learning to read this book – then it is the man I am leaving to visit now.' He kissed Milady. 'Pray for my success.'

'Lovelace, wait!'

But he had already turned, and was crossing to the hackney. Milady cried out after him again; but he paused only to shout back, as he clambered into his seat, that he would see her in their rooms; and then the hackney was rattling up Fish Street Hill, and she was lost to his view. The carriage continued through the City, Mr Aubrey talking at his usual scatter-fast rate, and then out into the open fields past Bishop's Gate. Not far from the road, Robert saw a vast expanse of freshly dug ground, and he recognised it as a pit where he and Lightborn had hunted victims for Milady. Thin patches of grass were already growing across the soil; and Robert wondered how long it would be before the very site of the pit had been forgotten, and all its vast freight with it. And then he thought of Emily; and he wondered where she lay, unmarked as she was, forever lost amidst the myriads of London's dead.

The hackney jolted suddenly to a halt and Robert, woken from his brooding, realised that they must have arrived at their destination. He followed Mr Aubrey out of the carriage, and into a tiny house from which he could hear the sound of an organ being played. They were shown by a maid into a long, low-beamed room. Several guests were already gathered there; and at the far end of the room, his back to them, another man was playing on the organ. At the sound of footsteps, however, he paused, and slowly turned round; and Robert recognised at once his former master and guardian. His steel-grey hair had grown more silver; but otherwise, he seemed utterly unchanged.

Robert remained silent as Mr Aubrey introduced them both. 'Lovelace,' grunted Mr Milton, as he shook Robert's hand. 'Such a name, sir, would seem to suit the Court better than this mean, rude place. I am afraid you will discover no great entertainments here.'

Mr Aubrey interrupted him, to explain the purpose of Robert's visit and describe the mystery of the book. Mr Milton grunted again. 'But I am blind,' he muttered. 'How am I, then, to make out an unknown script?'

'I had thought, sir,' explained Mr Aubrey eagerly, 'that we might copy out a portion of it across an expanse of dirt, which you might then, with your fingers, be able to trace.'

Mr Milton laughed, in the grisly manner Robert remembered so well.

'You find my suggestion' – Mr Aubrey swallowed uncertainly – 'a ridiculous one?'

Mr Milton shook his head. 'No, no,' he grinned mirthlessly. 'But you find us gathered here, Mr Aubrey, to hear a reading from the fruit of many years' labour, in which I have sought to penetrate the mysteries of God, to scale the empyreal air of the very heavens, and now – now you would have me scrabble in the dust. So should all our ambitions be rewarded, lest we forget our humility. I thank you Mr Aubrey. I shall do as you wish.'

He sighed, and stirred, and reached down below his seat, drawing out a thick manuscript. 'But first,' he nodded, 'you shall make your payment, and listen to my poem.' His eyes rolled, as though straining to make out his guests, and he smiled again grimly. 'None of your Court pleasures here, Mr Lovelace. I trust the tedium will not prove too extreme.'

Robert did not answer; for he was remembering those long afternoons when the poet had sat at his desk, measuring on his fingers the rhythms of a secret poem; and of how, on that same evening when they had later been arrested, Mr Milton had left the manuscript unlocked upon his desk. Robert could still recall the lines. *'What though the field be lost?'* He smiled softly to himself. *'All is not lost.'* Perhaps now, he thought, once again, at the great crossroads of his life, Mr Milton's poem would provide him with guidance, and point him a second time towards the way he should take.

He sat down as Mr Milton, fingers brushing across the manuscript as though the pages were a lyre, began to chant from memory the opening to his poem. Robert listened, first in doubt and then in awe, overwhelmed by the scale of the vast design. For it did indeed seem the poet's ambition, as he had claimed it to be, to scale the heights of Heaven; and to plumb, as well, the fiery gulf of Hell. It was into such depths that Satan was described as falling, the infernal serpent with all his rebel host, flung down from heaven with hideous ruin, to gaze for the first time at the dismal penal flames. And yet still, mixed with the rebel angel's affliction and dismay, there seemed pride as well, and steadfast hate; and Robert, listening to the description, felt a sudden stirring of horror as Mr Milton began to read from Satan's opening speech, addressed in defiance to Beelzebub – altered like himself, forever altered and damned. '*If thou beest he; but O how fallen! how changed* . . .' Mr Milton paused; and Robert half-imagined that his sightless eyes were watching him. Then the poet swallowed and began once again, sounding the Evil One's defiance and pain; until at length came the words Robert already knew.

'*What though the field be lost?*'

Robert started, and half-jumped from his chair.

'*All is not lost* . . .'

Robert rose now to his feet.

Mr Milton paused, then suddenly frowned. 'Lovelace?' he whispered, as though in puzzlement.

'You surprised me, sir,' said Robert. 'I had never thought that it was Satan . . . that is . . . that Satan could have spoken with such courage and resolve.'

The frown deepened on the poet's face; and he angled his head, as though to catch a distant sound. 'Evil,' he

answered slowly, 'is never more dangerous, Mr
Lovelace, than when burnished by the embers of a
dying moral sense.' He paused again; and for a
moment, the room seemed frozen by the chill of the
silence. Then slowly, Mr Milton lowered his poem to the
floor. 'Your book, sir,' he whispered. 'Let us make a trial
of its script. For it is good, I think, after a descent into
Hell, to feel the fresh night breezes soft against our
faces.'

He rose to his feet; and Mr Aubrey crossed to him
hurriedly, to lend him an arm. Together they passed out
into the garden – Robert following, and then the rest of
the room. Mr Aubrey was already bending down; he
took the book from Robert's hand and copied a line
across the dirt; and Mr Milton traced it with his
fingertip. He frowned, clearly puzzled; then shook his
head. 'This is no script that I can recognise,' he
muttered. He felt for Mr Aubrey's hands, and took the
manuscript. 'Where, did you say, did you discover this
book?'

Robert glanced at Mr Aubrey. 'It was written,' he
murmured, 'I suspect, by a Jew.' He studied Mr Milton's
face closely, then reached for his hand. 'That was why,
sir,' he whispered, 'I had hoped you might read it.'

Mr Milton stood frozen for a moment; then reached
for Robert's face and began to feel it. 'I, sir?' he asked
slowly.

'Why, yes,' answered Robert. He paused, then
reached in turn to feel Mr Milton's face. 'For it was you,
after all, who taught me to read Hebrew – that . . . and
much else.'

Again, Mr Milton froze; and then suddenly he
laughed, not grimly as before but almost choking, and

Robert saw upon his cheek the silent silver of tears. 'Is it you?' the old man whispered, his voice hoarse. 'Truly you? Master Foxe – who came to me in the bleakest depths of my night . . . and who then seemed lost forever to me.' He laughed again, and gestured with his arms to the circle of his friends. 'For this boy was to me, when all seemed irrevocably dark, without hope of day – he was to me light – and the promise of hope. And yet I never had the chance . . . to inform him so . . .' His voice trailed away; he breathed in deeply and tightened his grip upon the book, so that his fingertips dug inwards and brushed against the pages. At the same moment, he screamed; and the cry was so unexpected, so terrible, that everyone around him seemed paralysed. Slowly, Mr Milton opened the book; he seemed to read it; and then he dropped it suddenly, and slumped to the ground.

At once, the circle of his friends were gathering about him; but Robert brushed them aside and knelt by the blind man, supporting him in his arms as Mr Milton, head rolling wildly from side to side, rubbed at his eyes as though to cleanse them of some horror. 'Oh, beware,' he muttered, 'beware!' He twisted violently, and felt with his fingers for Robert's face again. 'For always ancient darkness waits, hungry to regain her old possession, and extinguish life in nature, and all things.'

'Here, sir,' whispered Mr Aubrey into Robert's ear. 'It may be, this will comfort him.' He handed Robert a glass of wine and Robert, turning back, lowered it to Mr Milton's lips. The old man sipped at it unsteadily; then shuddered; and allowed himself to be helped back into the house. Once seated in his chair, he ordered his other guests away; but Robert waited, then knelt again by the poet's side.

'What did you see, sir?' he whispered. 'For I know what happened – you read the secret script.'

Mr Milton did not bother to deny it, and his expression seemed as chill as marble. 'I saw,' he answered slowly, 'a boy in a small room. The boy was you – the room was my own. You were approaching a desk. On it were gathered the sheets of my poem, my *Paradise Lost*. You lifted the top page, you read from it. You spoke the lines of Satan – the very same lines which startled you tonight.'

'And then, sir? – for there must have been more to have made you cry out.'

'Indeed,' nodded Mr Milton; and his smile now was as mirthless as it had ever been. 'For when you had finished reading, the vision began to change.'

'And what did you see?' Robert hissed urgently. 'What did it show you?'

'Still you. But altered – oh, how altered.'

'How?'

Mr Milton shook his head. 'You were ... still lovely ... for you had been lovely before, like an angel touched with the beauty of God, bright-faced, golden-haired. But your costume now was a Cavalier's, and your looks marred by deadly passions, anger and hatred, envy and despair, so that if you still seemed an angel then it was a fallen one, toppled forever from the joys of paradise – as Satan himself, the Prince of rebels, might have seemed. And even as I thought this, I saw how your lips were bright with blood, and how you licked at them, and I grew certain now that you were a fiend, who had once been so good. And I was overcome with dread – and so I dropped the book, which had shown me such things – for I could not endure to see any more.'

Robert bowed his head; then slowly he rose up to his feet. 'The book,' he whispered, 'try it again.'

Mr Milton shuddered; but Robert gripped his arm tightly and thrust the book into his hands. 'Try it!' he screamed suddenly. 'Try it!' He tightened his grip; then whispered, 'Do it, sir – for there are things I must know.'

Mr Milton bit on his lower lip; but otherwise his expression seemed now perfectly composed once again. With great deliberateness, he smoothed open the book; he brushed his fingers across the page, but still not a flicker of emotion crossed his face. He shut the book again, he closed his eyes. 'I see nothing,' he whispered. 'Nothing but the dark.'

Robert stood in silence for a moment; then prised the book from Mr Milton's fingers. 'So farewell hope,' he nodded to himself.

'Farewell hope?' The blind man frowned uncertainly. 'It is done, then? You are fallen already, and become the thing I saw?'

Robert laughed bitterly. 'What does it matter,' he answered, 'what I am now? For the book does not lie. It represented the past to you faithfully; why should the glimpse of the future not be true?'

Mr Milton did not reply for a long while. 'Virtue may be assailed,' he said at length, 'but never lost. Surprised by unjust force – but never enthralled.'

Robert laughed again, his bitterness now suffused with contempt. 'You fool,' he spat suddenly, 'you old, blind fool! Do you not see, your Satan was right, and wiser than you, though you gave him his speech? All *is* not lost – there *is* still revenge, and courage, and hate. I thank you, sir – for again, in despite of yourself, you have shown me the path of action I must take.' He stood for a moment more, surveying the blind man; then he turned and left, to cross the room. As he reached the doorway, Mr Milton called after him; but Robert was resolved now on what he had to do. Just for a second he paused; and then he continued on his way. He slammed the door behind him, and Mr Milton's cries were blotted out.

∽◦�〇◦∾

'SOME OF OUR MAIDS SITTING UP LATE LAST NIGHT TO GET THINGS READY AGAINST OUR FEAST TODAY, JANE CALLED US UP, ABOUT 3 IN THE MORNING, TO TELL US OF A GREAT FIRE THEY SAW IN THE CITY . . . IT BEGAN THIS MORNING IN THE KING'S BAKERS HOUSE IN PUDDING LANE . . .'

Samuel Pepys, *Diaries*

Robert hurried on foot across London to the Tower. It was dark now; but some mark of deadliness must have gleamed in his eyes, for although he was richly dressed and alone, no one approached him, not even in the meanest, poorest streets; and instead people shrank when they gazed upon his face. He made good time and, once arrived beneath the shadow of the Tower, he was soon able to discover the Dolphin, where he ran up the steps to the room which Milady had rented. He flung the door open and she rose to greet him. Her golden eyes seemed impossibly wide, and there was a strangeness in her expression – a wild, haunted look which might normally have served to freeze him cold. But now he ignored it; and instead he crossed to Milady, and pressed her two cheeks. He kissed her lingeringly, then smoothed back her curls to whisper in her ear. 'There is a matter of great moment we have to discuss.'

'Indeed,' Milady nodded. She reached for the book from his hands, then laid it carefully beneath her mattress. 'A matter of terrible moment.'

Robert gazed at her in sudden puzzlement. 'How could you have been so certain what the fruit of my expedition would be?'

Milady smiled back faintly, then shook her head. 'It is not your expedition which concerns us now, but a far deadlier matter.' She fastened her cloak and, as Robert opened his mouth to demand from her what she meant, she reached up with her finger to still his lips. 'Your business must wait.'

He brushed her finger aside. 'Why,' he whispered, 'what have you discovered?'

'A great horror,' Milady answered. Then without a further word, she picked up a lantern and, with her other hand, led him from the room and out into the street. She summoned a hackney. 'All the speed you have,' she ordered the driver. 'We go to Pudding Lane.'

Something in her voice froze Robert's questionings dead; and he sat in silence as Milady did, staring out ahead, until the carriage arrived outside the house where Emily had died. Robert had not been back there since and, as he stood in the darkness of its shadow, he felt as though his soul were being breathed on by an icy wind. Milady squeezed his hand. 'I have discovered, I think,' she whispered, 'what it was that Lightborn was searching for here.'

Still Robert did not press her, but met her eye fleetingly, and then followed her into the house. The

lock on the door had been smashed; and beyond it, the
darkness seemed moist and unpleasantly sweet. Robert
had not smelt such a darkness, he thought, since
standing in the cellars of Wolverton Hall; and as he
breathed it in deeply, despite himself, so he imagined
that he caught the scent of stale blood. At the same
moment, the stabbing in his stomach confirmed his
impression; and he doubled up, and staggered, and fell
to the floor. Milady reached for him and took him by the
arm; and continued to lead him onwards through the
house.

'We are going,' Robert whispered suddenly, 'to that
room where Emily died.'

Milady glanced round at him, something like pity
glinting in her stare. 'So we are,' she answered, 'poor
Lovelace – so we are.' She paused by the door which led
into the room. It stood ajar, and she pushed it open. At
the same moment, Robert felt his pain redouble, but he
struggled to ignore it. He leant even harder on Milady's
arm, and followed her forward into the room. She raised
the lantern; Robert strained with his eyes.

There came a violent, pain-racked hissing from the
shadows.

Milady drew out her dagger. 'Be careful,' she
murmured. 'For you have seen how they are dangerous –
to my kind as well as yours.'

'What . . .' Robert whispered; but then his question
died, aborted by what he saw in the lantern's flickering
wash. For a creature was hunched in the corner of the
room, cowering before the light, and yet tensed as well
as though ready to leap; and Robert saw how its eyes
were burning with thirst, and how its rotted lips were
moist with a sticky, thick saliva. There were worms still

writhing in its flesh, and mud, intermingled with an oozing, yellowy discharge, smeared all across its body; yet even so, Robert could glimpse on what remained of the creature's skin the unmistakable marks and buboes of the plague. He looked up again into the creature's face; he stared into its eyes. As he did so, he saw the gleam of its hunger start to fade; and he recognised, in the shell of its face, just the meagrest shred still of Emily.

Milady had been studying the creature's reaction intently. 'And so it was in the village,' she murmured. 'For you remember? – you had the power to still the creatures there as well.'

Robert continued to stare into Emily's eyes. By now they seemed utterly frozen and dead. He reached for Milady's hand, squeezed it tightly. 'Where did you discover her?' he whispered at last.

'As I walked from London Bridge,' Milady answered, 'after leaving you. I saw her, a filthy, rotted thing, seeking to break down the door of this house.'

Robert frowned faintly. 'Why should she have wished to return here?'

'It seems in the nature of these dead creatures. For you remember, Lovelace, in the village inn, how the servant girl's father likewise sought her out?'

Robert nodded slowly; then stared back at the thing which had once been Emily. 'You believe, then,' he whispered, 'that all the other victims of the plague will similarly emerge as she has done?'

Milady shook her head. 'Not of their own accord. For it was Emily who brought the plague here – and doubtless, as well, it is she alone who bears the venom which will wake the other corpses from their graves.'

Robert frowned at her suspiciously. 'How can you be so certain?'

'Because I spoke of this matter in the village with the Marquise. I had been interested, since I had never seen such a breed of thing before, to know how the creatures had been roused from the dead. The Marquise answered me that it had needed the first victim to infect the rest; and that then the venom would have infallibly spread.'

Robert stared at her in disbelief. 'And yet the Marquise never thought to tell you – to tell us – that the poison of the undead was the same as that of the plague? That those who bore the one infection bore the other one as well? She must have known – must have done – and so she must have known also what it was that Emily was bound to become.'

'Doubtless,' Milady nodded. 'For you will remember, Lovelace – the last time we visited her – she told us of a secret written in Tadeus' book?' She paused, then gestured to Emily. 'There it is, before us – the Marquise's deadly secret.'

Robert breathed in deeply; brought himself to stare at the creature again. Then, without looking round, he reached for Milady's dagger and took it from her hand. His limbs felt deadened; yet so too, he realised to his surprise, did his grief. It was not Emily, after all, this rotted, dead-eyed thing; Emily was long gone, long sent to her rest.

As he continued to stare at the creature, it began to whimper, as though sensing in him some terrible power. Robert paused fleetingly, to wonder whether she had recognised him; then he stifled all such thoughts to kneel by her side. She was scrabbling fearfully now at the corner's two walls, but still she seemed unable to tear her gaze from Robert's eyes. Suddenly, she froze again. Robert bent down closer. He swallowed his repugnance; he kissed the creature on its oozing gums. At the same moment, he stabbed with his knife.

He felt the blade puncture something soft. He knelt back, and stared down at the creature's chest. A spume of inky blood was bubbling up from the wound. Robert stabbed at it again. The creature was already lying motionless, and seemed nothing more than a shrivelled sack of bones, but still he stabbed up and down, up and down, until at last his arm grew weary, and he slumped forward to rest his head against the dagger's hilt. He closed his eyes. They felt aching and dry. He rubbed them, and blinked; then slowly rose to his feet.

'And so resolution,' he whispered, gazing down at the thing by his feet, 'is fortified by despair.' He turned round slowly. For a long while, he said nothing; then he crossed back to Milady and brushed her hand with his fingertips. 'All is gone now,' he whispered. 'Save only that matter of which I spoke to you before. For that, Milady – that still remains.'

Milady did not answer, but reached for her dagger. She took it, and sheathed it away beneath her cloak.

Robert tightened his grip on her hand. 'You know full well what it is I am talking about.'

She did not answer.

'Very well, then – I must be plain. I would grow, Milady, a being like yourself.'

Milady shook her head. 'This is not the time.'

'When better?'

'When we have read the book.'

'Why not now?'

'Because' – Milady studied him a moment more, then broke away – 'we still have much to do.'

'What?'

She made no reply, but glided from the room and out through the house. Robert followed her, until they were both standing in the street again, perfectly still. Milady closed her eyes, then sniffed the faint breeze. 'Yes,' she nodded. 'It is already spread.'

Robert met her stare for a moment and then, deep in his stomach, felt the sharpening of the agony again. He drew out his sword. Halfway down the narrow street, he could see a baker's shop; the door was hanging half-broken on its hinges. From inside the shop, he heard the sudden clattering of a pan; and at the same moment, the pain in his stomach grew worse. He began to hurry down the lane, but he could only stumble, for it hurt him now to breathe; and it was Milady who passed through the shop door first. Robert followed – and saw ahead of him the corpse of what appeared to be a servant girl. Two creatures, plague-marked and rotten as Emily had been, were bent over her, feeding like dogs. They had hissed as Milady entered; but then, as Robert joined her, the two creatures backed away, and their eyes grew dead.

'Wondrous,' Milady murmured, 'the power which you possess over these things.'

Robert laughed despairingly. 'Yet if the venom spreads to every plague-corpse in London, what value will my power have then?' He stepped forward, and aimed with his sword. 'For I cannot stab a whole teeming city of them – thus.' His aim was a good one; the creature he ran through sighed a soft scream, and collapsed. But its fellow, emboldened by Robert's distraction, leapt suddenly; and he found himself staggering and falling beneath its weight. He twisted desperately to avoid the creature's jaws, and struggled to stab it as he had just stabbed its mate. But the creature was too close, and Robert's sword too long. He felt clammy fingers about his throat, their bones creaking as they flexed – and though he twisted again, this time the creature would not be escaped. Then suddenly, he heard a thud and a smashing of glass; and the creature shrieked and was knocked back across the floor. Robert leapt at once to his feet, and watched as the creature tried to stagger to its own. For a moment it appeared to be succeeding, despite the shards of the lantern in its skull; but the flames were already licking down its body, and the bones in its legs were starting to bubble and collapse. 'Fire,' whispered Milady, stepping back. The heat was increasing, and the flames seemed greasy with melted flesh. She smiled faintly as she backed into the street. 'For what other hope, at this late stage, do we have?'

The flames were already spitting sparks into the night; and as Robert watched, he saw a sudden orange glow from an inn across the street. Its yard had been layered with chippings and hay, and the fire spread across it like the surge of a wave. Soon other buildings too were being licked by the flames; and there came the crashing of timbers, and distant, startled screams.

'The city is so dry,' Robert shouted, 'that if this continues, it will be utterly consumed.'

'Yes!' Milady cried back. Her eyes, like the inn, seemed ablaze with golden fire. 'And if the city is consumed – then so is the danger as well!' She pointed, and Robert could see how the flames were spreading fast down the lane. Then suddenly, stumbling through the sparks, he could make out three, four, five dark figures and, as one of them was caught and enveloped by the fire, Robert glimpsed for a moment its rotted, plague-marked face. Then the flesh began to sizzle; and the creature writhed and stumbled, and was lost upon the smoke. 'So shall they all be served,' Milady cried, 'provided only the fire can spread far enough.'

Robert had no doubt that it would. He stepped back, for the heat of the flames was already intense. He began to walk down Pudding Lane, following the course of the fire, waiting for it to reach the warehouses and sheds along the Thames where oil, and tallow, and spirits were kept. Then Milady squeezed his hand, and raised her cloak to shield her face. At the same moment, there was a deafening explosion; and a sudden ball of fire reached high into the night. The sparks were so bright, and scattered so wide, that Robert too veiled his face behind his cloak; and when he lowered it again, it was to see that London Bridge was ablaze.

Crowds of people were now gathering in the streets. Some were struggling with bags of possessions, pushing barrows piled with crockery and clothes; but already, such was the heat of the flames that buildings were starting to shatter and crack, and suddenly people began to run, leaving their possessions spilled amidst the rubble. Robert seized Milady's arm, and pulled her desperately, for he had seen that they too ran the risk of being trapped by the fire; and even as he did so, there was a crashing from above them, and a wall of burning brick began to break and collapse like a wave. Milady screamed; Robert seized her in his arms; and both of them threw themselves forward into the mud. At the same moment, a heavy beam teetered, and fell; and as it came crashing downwards, Robert heard the hiss of sparks and felt them scorching his cheeks. He staggered to his feet and stumbled forward again, still pulling on Milady; and as he did so, he laughed, for he could see the glint of passion in her golden eyes, as the furnace of London was reflected in her stare. He kissed her, feeling drunk himself with a strange, wild passion; and Milady's lips were hungry and eager in response. She broke away suddenly, for the heat was growing ever more intense; but even as they ran, they clasped each other and continued to laugh. They could see now how the fire was spreading deep into the City; and how the crowds were twisting and widening as though in mimicry of the flames. Robert and Milady were swept along with them; and in the midst of so much terror and despair, still they felt their strange, exultant delirium, so that they would dance, and laugh, and kiss all the more, as the flames rose brighter and brighter into the sky.

By dawn, the fire was still widening in a mighty arc; and not a single rain-cloud marred the blue sky. Robert and Milady began to leave the crowds behind, for although the fire was still a long away from the Tower, Milady had grown suddenly anxious to ensure that the book was secured. Once arrived at the Dolphin, she removed it from the mattress, then continued with Robert on towards Wapping, where their ship was being loaded for the onward voyage. They boarded it and went to their quarters, where the book was carefully concealed once again; then they returned towards the Tower, and their rooms at the inn. There seemed little outward signs of panic in the streets; but from the towers of distant churches, bells were clanging the alarm, and to the west, high above the City, billowing clouds of smoke marked the progress of the fire.

Arrived back at the Dolphin, Robert reached for Milady again. For a moment, the distant blaze was reflected in her stare; and she smiled as she kissed him, and ran her fingers through his hair. He sought to pull her down with him upon his bed; but she broke free, and laid a fingertip on his parted lips. 'A moment,' she whispered; then she smiled again, and left the room. Even as Robert watched her leave, he felt an aching weariness seeping through his limbs, and his eyes begin to close. For a moment he struggled to keep them apart; but he knew that Milady would wake him on her return; and so he surrendered to his tiredness, and at once fell asleep.

When he opened his eyes again, though, it seemed strangely dark. Robert leapt to his feet. He stared about him wildly, but he was alone in the room. Where was Milady? He hurried to his window and, even before he had looked out from it, could hear the crackling of the flames. The fire was still a long way distant; but it had spread violently and, as it burned, its colour seemed like that of blood. Again, Robert stared about him, and wondered with a sudden anger where Milady could have gone. He turned back to the window; stared a second time at the great bow of fire. He swore softly to himself beneath his breath; then dressed quickly and hurried out into the streets.

Dawn was already rising behind him; but the sun's light seemed feeble compared with the furnace ahead. The fire was now so intense that even the pigeons, flapping desperately above their burning roosts, found their feathers singed and fell, tiny balls of flame, into the vaster blaze. Nothing, Robert thought, gazing at the showers of firedrops which marked the inferno's outer edge, would survive such a storm of heat; and he smiled, to think of the horror which had been so utterly consumed. At the same moment, he felt a shiver of that same glee he had shared the night before, when he had danced through the streets with Milady; and he wondered again with sudden desperation where she could have vanished to. He began to hunt her, but he knew – swept as he was on the chaos of the terror-stricken streets – that his search was hopeless; and he abandoned it at last, and returned to the inn. From there he watched the fire, and its continued spread, until at last the sun began to set and the night to return. And still the fire raged; as the stars seemed to melt, and the flames beat high against the purple sky.

Not until next morning did Milady finally return. Robert asked her where she had been, but she did not reply, only took his arm and insisted it was time that they boarded their ship. Robert could read, though, in the flush of her cheeks and the gleam of her skin, what her business had been; and when they arrived in their cabin, she gestured to a trunk. 'There are always easy pickings,' she murmured, 'in times of such chaos.' Robert glanced at her, then opened the lid. There were rows and rows of bottles inside, and he knew at once, from the pain in his guts, what had been mingled with the wine. 'I have always found,' Milady nodded, 'that when embarking on a voyage, it is best to have a cordial ready to hand.'

'And a companion too,' Robert asked, 'to share in such pleasures?'

Milady did not answer straight away. Instead, she closed the lid of the trunk, and then kissed him softly. 'All in good time,' she murmured at last. 'All in good time.'

They left that same night. The ship pulled out from its harbour past tiny, overloaded boats, fleeing down-river towards the darkness ahead. Behind them, though, even the Thames seemed consumed by flames as it boiled with the reflection of the burning city, and sparks like fireflies swarmed above its flow. Only by London Bridge, where the fire had first begun, did the waters seem calm; for there, along the bank on which Pudding Lane had once stood, there was nothing left to be burned, only a heart of blackness abandoned by the flames. Robert stared at it for a long while; then he turned to Milady, and held her tightly in his arms. Over her shoulder, he could see all of London spread out before him: its steeples, and towers, and chimneys, and roofs crumbling, even as he watched them, into the raging arc of the flames, dust to be borne and scattered on the winds. Only St Paul's, the highest and greatest building of all, still seemed to stand unharmed upon its hill, looming dark above the flames; and then suddenly, on its roof, there rose the flickerings of fire. The ship began to swing with the course of the Thames, so that the view of the burning city was lost and nothing could be seen of London, only the hectic bruising of the flames across the sky. But later, the course veered back, and Robert could make out the tower of St Paul's again, now completely enveloped by flames; and suddenly, even as he watched it, he saw a spitting of stones and a portion of the tower began to collapse. Robert turned back to Milady. He kissed her with a sudden, urgent passion; then he broke from her again, and stared ahead into the waiting silence, and the darkness of the night.

IV

VI

'IN HIS LAST SICKNESS HE WAS EXCEEDINGLY PAENITENT AND WROTE A LETTER OF HIS REPENTANCE . . .'

John Aubrey, *Brief Lives*

Dusk was lengthening over Woodstock Park. Faint across the dappled stillness, bells chimed out the summons to evensong; but on the lawns of High Lodge they sounded barely at all, for there was no breeze borne upon the purpling shadows, and the heat of afternoon still lingered in the air. Not even the branches of the oak trees stirred; not even the leaves against the open bedroom windows. Nothing to disturb the calm; nothing to disturb my Lord of Rochester's bad dreams.

And then suddenly, very distant, the sound of a horse's hooves. Lord Rochester stirred. He struggled to raise his head. Then he moaned; the pain from his suppurations was great, his back so sticky that it clung to the sheets. He slumped again on to his pillows. The hoofbeats were drawing nearer now, and there were footsteps too, crunching across the forecourt: servants running out to meet the unexpected guest. Then the hoofbeats came to an abrupt, wheeling halt. Boots could be heard stepping down on to the gravel; the low murmur of conversation; and then the horse being led away to the stables. At the same time – footsteps crossing to the main door.

Lord Rochester was measuring them with each

agonised, racking breath long before he could hear them again, soft across the carpets which led to his room. They paused, just outside the door; and at the same moment he breathed in deeply, to see if he would recognise his visitor's blood. Pray God not his son, he thought, pray God not his son. Yet though he breathed in a second time, there seemed nothing at all, and he frowned. Blood without a scent? He struggled to sit up; and succeeded this time, despite the pain. He cried out to his visitor to show himself.

Slowly, the door swung open. Eyes glittered from the shadows, luminous and cold. A blood-drinker's eyes, Lord Rochester would have said; save that something was lacking; something was strange . . .

He narrowed his eyes, studied the face and then, despite himself, felt a shudder of surprise.

His visitor stepped forward.

Lord Rochester smiled pallidly. 'Lovelace.'

'My Lord.'

'I had been informed you were dead these past fourteen years.'

'And yet here I am.' He drew closer. Hair gold and curling. Skin gleaming with a bright ivory paleness. Lips full; smile amused and cruel. And yet not a blood-drinker . . . so, what, then? *What?*

Lord Rochester could not veil his gaze of astonishment; and then suddenly he felt angry that he was being mocked by the silence of such a mysterious and unforeseen guest. 'Well, sir,' he exclaimed impatiently. 'I assume you have not come here – risen, so it seems, from the very grave – merely to stand and grin at me.'

Lovelace's smile only broadened. 'Indeed not, my Lord.'

'Well, then – what is it? – what is your business? For that you bring the news of some great mystery is evident from your appearance.' Lord Rochester gazed at his visitor again; and again, could not conceal a start of surprise. 'Why, Lovelace,' he muttered, 'how dangerous and cruel you seem now. And yet in all other ways, you appear perfectly unchanged – quite as youthful and full of beauty as ever.'

'While you, my Lord, appear strangely loathsome and lined.' Lovelace laughed, and pulled up a chair, to sit by the bed. He had been carrying a bag slung upon his shoulder; he lowered it now and placed it by his feet, very carefully, as though its contents might be fragile. 'Exceeding ugly,' he continued. 'Yet what can be its cause? You have been cruelly cheated, if you sold your soul, and yet still you grow old.'

'There was a surcharge,' Lord Rochester shrugged, 'which I have found it difficult to pay.'

'What, my Lord, not a spendthrift like you?'

Lord Rochester shrugged again. 'I have recently, to my discomfort, grown infected by squeamishness. I recall, Lovelace, you too once suffered from the complaint.'

'Indeed, my Lord, I was a martyr to it.'

'You will remember, perhaps, a journey we once made together on the Thames, when we discussed the peculiar thirsts of my breed?'

'You know full well, I shall never forget it.' Lovelace paused, then smiled. 'And how is Miss Malet – Lady Rochester, that is? She has performed her function, and bred for you, I trust?'

'I have children, yes.'

Lovelace leaned forward. '*Have* them?', he whispered. 'What, not tasted them yet?'

'You would know, sir, the answer to that question, if you also knew what I have recently found out.'

'Indeed?'

'The cause of my lost looks, sir, my lined and sallow skin, my heavy, dissipated stare is no great puzzle, once you only understand a further secret – that our relatives' blood is prized for much more than its taste. For without it, we grow withered long before our time. But drink it once – only once – and we are ever more preserved by that single precious taste.' Lord Rochester paused; he stretched out the claw-like fingers on his hands. 'In so many ways, then, an indispensable draught.'

Lovelace raised a single mocking eyebrow. 'And yet you have not drunk it.'

Lord Rochester shrugged. 'All men, perhaps, would be cowards if they dared.'

'Where was your cowardice, then, in Amsterdam, when you drained your first victim, and spilled his corpse into the Brouwers Gracht?'

'Submerged beneath the golden floods of my pleasure.'

'And now?'

'The floods are drained away, and there is nothing left to me but a parched dullness, more hatesome than ever for my dread of it is eternal. Within its dust, strange doubts writhe and crawl, like worms of the deep exposed to the light.'

Lovelace smiled faintly. 'Puritan talk, my Lord – most strange and unexpected.' He paused. 'It is true, then, the rumour I heard at Court, that you have lately been closeted with a clergyman?'

Lord Rochester paused. 'I have been speaking with one, yes,' he acknowledged at last.

'And told him . . . what?'

'Everything, Lovelace – everything.'

'Are you not afraid he might betray your confession?'

'You know he would not dare.'

'And what comfort did he offer you, this clergyman, in your damnation?'

'Nothing, of course.'

'Because, as you once proved to your own satisfaction, when we sailed with Wyndham and Montagu, God Himself is a mere silent Nothing.'

'And yet it is Nothing I desire.'

'And the clergyman, you claim, can offer you this?'

Lord Rochester's lips flickered in the faintest of smiles. 'It may be, not even so much. Certainly, it is by his instruction and recommendation that I have forsworn, these past three months, all taste of blood. For he calls me and my kind demons, as contrary to Christian society as wild beasts let loose; and since that much, at least, is irrefutable, his words serve to stiffen my native resolve. And yet . . .' Lord Rochester's voice trailed away as he lifted up his hand once more, its flesh black and dry upon the knobbled bones. 'And yet . . .' he whispered again, 'I do not think my resolve is sufficient. The pain is too great, the goal too uncertain – for I fear my damnation is eternal indeed, and that I shall never find Nothing – that I shall always be myself.'

Lovelace gazed at him in silence for a moment; then he rose, and crossed to the open windows. The night outside was now a deep, silver blue. 'Tell me,' he murmured at last, 'do you pray?'

Lord Rochester frowned in surprise, then nodded faintly.

'And how does God answer your importunities?'

'I remember, one night, when the clergyman was with me and the pain was at its worst – we prayed for resolve.'

'And?'

'Later that night, despite myself, I rose in my dreams. I left my body on the breath of the winds. In the fields beyond the Park, I found a beggar, curled up asleep beneath a hedge. I drank him dry. The next day, when I awoke, my health seemed improved. The clergyman proclaimed the miracle of prayer.'

Lovelace smiled, still gazing out at the night. 'And yet what,' he murmured, 'if your prayers could be answered indeed?'

Lord Rochester narrowed his eyes, and for an interval did not reply. 'I would want to know the means,' he whispered at last, 'by which such a thing might be achieved.'

Lovelace laughed coldly. 'Oh, my Lord,' he answered, 'be under no doubt – you will be told the means, and much, much more. For we have all the night ahead of us yet.'

'And I would want also to know . . .'

'Yes?'

'What the cost might be.'

Lovelace turned from the window. 'Something, my Lord, you might easily afford.'

'Indeed?'

Lovelace smiled, and crossed back from the window. He pulled up the chair again; then leaned forward, and hissed: 'Can you not guess?'

Lord Rochester's face remained perfectly frozen; then he inclined his head, very faintly, just once.

'I am glad, then, that we understand one another.'

Lord Rochester nodded again. 'And yet your folly, sir,' he murmured, 'is wondrous, if you truly wish to grow a thing like me.'

Lovelace smiled contemptuously. 'I thank you, but I have conquered my scruples well enough.'

Lord Rochester shrugged. 'You have had time enough, I suppose.'

'Fourteen years,' Lovelace nodded, 'which I have clearly put to better use, my Lord, than you.'

'How, Lovelace?' Lord Rochester suddenly choked and, racked by his coughs, he struggled to sit up. 'Tell me,' he gasped, 'what has happened to you? Something terrible, I dread, to leave your face so unmarked and yet your soul grown so black.'

Lovelace threw back his head with violent laughter. 'I have said, my Lord – you shall hear it all.' He leaned forward suddenly. 'And then – it is agreed – we shall make our exchange?' He waited a moment; then bent, and picked up the bag from his feet. He laid it by Lord Rochester's side; and his grin grew broader still. '*And then we shall make our exchange.*' He did not inquire now, merely stated a fact. He leaned back in his chair; and as his grin grew more distant and then faded from his lips, so his knuckles whitened; and he began to tell his tale.

◦◦◦

'THE GOD THOU SERV'ST IS THINE OWN APPETITE,
WHEREIN IS FIX'D THE LOVE OF BELZEBUB:
TO HIM I'LL BUILD AN ALTAR AND A CHURCH,
AND OFFER LUKEWARM BLOOD . . .'

Christopher Marlowe, *Doctor Faustus*

'You have said, my Lord, that I seem greatly changed. And yet in truth, I was resolved on my present course even fourteen years ago. It is no surprise,

however, that you have no remembrance of that – for it
was a course thrust upon me by your own negligence and
lassitude, by my gradual understanding that if ever the
Pasha were to have a worthy heir, then it could not be you
but would have to be myself. It was for the same reason
that I had already resolved to leave for Prague without
awaiting your return; and why I asked Milady, even as we
stood on the deck of our ship, watching London burn, to
make me a creature like herself.'

'A request she was clearly unwilling to oblige.'

Lovelace shrugged. 'Her refusal did not surprise me.'

'Indeed?'

Lovelace shrugged again. 'She had already told me,
when I asked her before, that we had first to solve the
riddle of the book. And how, in truth, could I blame her
for her caution? After all, my Lord – she did not want me
to grow like you, distracted from my purpose by a lust for
new-found pleasures. Yet watching London burn, watching so mighty a city's agony, I had felt a keen sense of
what such pleasures might mean – as though my past
were a city, like London, to be destroyed. But as the glow
of the fire faded from our view, as we joined the cold,
black waters of the sea, so I felt my sense of urgency fade
– and I grew content again to wait, as Milady had
advised.'

'Even though you could not be certain what the book
might show you?'

Lovelace smiled strangely. 'Yet for a few brief
moments,' he answered, 'on the night before the fire, I
had already been shown it.'

Lord Rochester stared at him in surprise. 'And what
had it revealed?'

Still Lovelace smiled. 'Sufficient to convince me,' he

answered at last, 'that its magic was real.'

'How?'

The smile slowly faded from Lovelace's lips; he seemed not to have heard the question at all. 'How it tortured me,' he murmured, 'that one fleeting glimpse.' He swallowed; then narrowed his eyes, as though gazing at an object very far away. 'I have said that the sea had cooled my impatience, and yet in truth' – he grimaced – 'it still lingered in my guts. For the pain continued there, like a gnawing, hungry thing, and not even the *mummia* could serve to ease it now. The script, I thought – surely with the magic of the script it might be healed. Not on the ship, though – for the book's presence in our cabin, unfathomable, unread, seemed only to make my agony worse, so that I loathed it and loved it, feared it and desired it, as well one might the cause and cure of one's pain. I am sure, my Lord' – he smiled faintly – 'you will have sympathy yourself for such a condition.'

Lord Rochester did not answer. Lovelace's smile broadened, then he sighed and leaned back. 'Milady, too, infected with her own impatience, had been pacing like a wild thing all the length of our voyage; and our route, it was true, could have been a great deal more direct. Yet it was not only the secret of the text we had to solve; there were other mysteries as well, still dark and unsolved, at the very heart of my longed-for revenge. And so it was that we had taken the ship to Lübeck, across the North Sea and around the tip of Denmark; for it was to Lübeck that my father had dispatched Sir Charles Wolverton.

'But that, of course, had happened more than twenty years before; and our chance of picking up the trail, we knew, would be faint. Yet not hopeless – for we had already, before leaving for London, travelled to

Portsmouth and looked through the records of all the Lübeck-bound ships. There had been, it transpired, only one on which my father could have placed Sir Charles – owned by an Englishman, a merchant in Lübeck – and this merchant, we had been told, though old, was still alive. To whom else would Sir Charles, a penniless arrival in an unknown city, have presented himself, if not such a countryman? And to whom else should we, pursuing Sir Charles, present ourselves, if not the same man?

'He did indeed prove old, but sharp still as well; and I knew at once, as I asked him, that he remembered our man. I recognised the shadow which passed across his face, for my father too had often looked the same, as though reluctant even to hear mention of Sir Charles. We could not, though, now permit the merchant his reticence; and so I left him to Milady, who had soon bled his memories dry. Yes, the merchant admitted, he did remember Sir Charles, who had arrived one morning appealing for help. The merchant, pitying him, had slipped him some gold; Sir Charles, displaying his gratitude, had then robbed the merchant, and fled the city bounds. In the forests beyond Lübeck, there had been many other such fugitives, for it was that time of lawlessness, my Lord, of which the Pasha spoke to us, when Germany was plunged into universal war, and every bond of society had dissolved into blood. In such conditions, naturally enough, Sir Charles had prospered; and had soon become the leader of a notorious robber band. At length, so violent did its depredations grow, so dangerous to the city's trade, that the city fathers had been compelled to raise soldiers to destroy it; and yet in truth, although Sir Charles and his men had soon afterwards left, it appeared they had been bribed, not compelled, to depart. "And where did they go?" Milady pressed. The merchant shrugged. Somewhere towards the south, towards Bohemia, he thought, where the war had been fiercest and the anarchy worst; but beyond that, he could not be sure. Then he paused. "Ask along the docks," he advised, "along the Untertrave. If any of Sir Charles' band returned here to Lübeck, then that is where you will find them – for, like a midden, the Untertrave drains all the city's filth."

'Milady went there that same night. I did not accompany her. Weeks had passed since she had tasted fresh blood; and I had seen in her eyes the familiar glint of thirst. Returning to me the next morning, she seemed flushed and content; but not merely with her pleasures, for she brought news with her as well. In the very darkest and most desperate tavern, she reported, she had tracked down a veteran of Sir Charles' band, maimed and ancient, sitting alone. She had drawn him even deeper into the shadows and then, as with the merchant, had sucked his memories dry. There had been little of direct relevance he had been able to reveal; for he had been wounded before the band had even entered Bohemia, plundering a castle on the Saxon border; and had been left to guard it while his fellows had moved on. For months, though, none of them had returned; and the injured robber had begun to think the castle was his own. Then one night, galloping hard down the road from Prague, a single survivor of the band returned: one Konrad Haszler, Sir Charles' second-in-command. He had at once begun to raise guards, and order the castle refortified, as though in daily expectation of the coming of some foe. Yet for all the evident nature of his dread, he had never chosen to speak of it; and indeed, whenever his injured fellow sought to press him on the matter, Haszler had always been provoked into a violent fury. It had been at the height of one of these rages that he had ordered his comrade slung out into the road; and left him, crippled as he was, to crawl his way back home. Reduced to beggary, the injured man had struggled back to Lübeck at last; but with no fond memories, you may be sure, of his former comrade-in-arms. Certainly, it had required little effort on Milady's part to persuade him to reveal the castle's name; for he had glimpsed, perhaps, in Milady's eyes, a hint of that danger which had reduced Konrad Haszler to such fear.

'We set off from Lübeck that same morning. Although I was still much inconvenienced by the pain in my stomach, I had agreed that we should ride, for Milady was quite as good a horseman as myself and we were eager to make all the speed that we could. Once Lübeck had been left behind, though, the roads soon grew very poor; and the further south we travelled, so the worse they became. The countryside too seemed blasted and despoiled; and as we passed into Saxony, we began to see the shells of villages left utterly abandoned, the towers of churches toppled into rubble, the fragments of houses submerged beneath weeds. Yet the war had ended more than twenty years previously; and I wondered at its nature, and the scale of its horrors, which could have left such visible and enduring scars behind. And I wondered also, my Lord, at what the Pasha had told us – that such devastation would surely be witnessed again, and in England too, if the Angel of Death were not soon to be destroyed . . .' Lovelace paused briefly; his smile was very cold. 'I understand, of course, that such considerations have never weighed with your lordship; but with me, in my weakness, they weighed heavily indeed – for I was reminded, when I glimpsed the ruins where villages had once stood, of the horrors I had seen when I last went to Woodton . . .'

He paused again, and seemed to shudder. 'Beyond Pirna,' he continued at length, 'the landscape grew ever more mountainous. We were drawing near now to Bohemia; and as we wound upwards, I imagined we were travelling through a frozen hell of rock, where all traces of humanity had been transmuted into stone, for the crags which overshadowed us wore fantastical shapes, as though they had been twisted and racked by a terrible pain. And indeed, all that day we saw not a single living soul; for evidently, so total had been the devastation along the road we were now passing that nothing had survived the sweep of ruin, save only the wolves. We would hear them sometimes, their howls sounding from the black depths of forests, howls answering howls, until all the mountains and ravines would seem to echo to their noise. We would then spur our horses faster; for I would wonder, against such implacable foes, what even Milady herself could achieve.

'Yet perhaps I should not have been concerned; for I was soon to have evidence enough of her powers. It was nearing sunset when at last we saw our destination ahead of us – the broken battlements of the castle rearing up jagged against the sky, so that they seemed as bleak and inhospitable as the mountain crags themselves. I found myself wondering again what it was that Konrad Haszler could have seen or done, which had led him to flee to such a godforsaken spot: something terrible, certainly, for as we drew nearer to the castle, we could see that the gateway had been freshly repaired and the gates firmly locked. Milady paused a moment. The faintest smile of amusement played across her lips. "Such precautions," she murmured. "And yet the worst of it must be for him, that he is likely to know how feeble they will prove."

'Then she spurred her horse forward, and together we cantered along to the gateway. Challenges greeted us from the watch-towers above; yet even as Milady glanced up, they were frozen mid-sentence, and without her having to utter a word, I heard the clattering of footsteps, and then the slithering back of bolts. Slowly, one of the gates was swung ajar; and at once Milady was passing through the gap. I followed her. She glanced round at me, then pointed to a tower rising up from the keep. A light was flickering at its very top. "There," she whispered; her delicate nostrils flared. "Even from this distance, I can smell his fear."

'And her senses, of course, were far too sharp to be in error. We found Haszler where Milady had said that we would, at the summit of a winding coil of stairs – his back pressed hard against the furthermost wall, a sword drawn and shaking in his hands. He seemed a brutal, grizzled, battle-scarred man; yet as he met Milady's eyes, he whimpered softly, and the sword fell with a clang upon the floor. He staggered sideways; and I saw how there was a large wooden cross upon a table, which he reached for and hugged very tightly to his chest. "He . . ." The man swallowed. "He has sent you, then?" he asked.

' "He?" Milady arched an eyebrow; then crossed with a measured pace towards a chair, the only one in the room. She sat down in it, and slowly removed her gloves; then fixed her gaze again upon the shuddering Haszler. "He?" she repeated lightly. "Tell me, sir, please, whom you mean by this 'he'?"

' "Ta .. Ta .." the man stammered. "Tadeus, Father Tadeus, I mean."

'Milady arched her eyebrow a second time. "Tadeus," she murmured. Then she shook her head. "No. Tadeus has been dead these several years."

' "Dead?" Haszler stared at her in disbelief. "But he . . ."

' "Was an immortal? Yes." Milady smiled. "So he had thought, at least. But he was dabbling, it seems, in things greater than he knew. And so that is why" – she leaned forward – "we have come to talk with you."

' "But I never . . . it was never me who knew . . . it was . . ." Haszler licked his lips. "You don't want me," he shouted suddenly, "you want Wolverton, and that bloody Jew!"

'Milady glanced round at me, and arched her eyebrow yet again; then she turned back to Haszler, and raised up a hand. "No, no, no," she purred. "Tell me from the start." Then I saw her golden eyes spark, and Haszler screamed despairingly. He dropped the cross as he fell to the ground, clutching at his head, as though Milady's stare were a venomous snake, darting through his sockets and spitting deep inside his skull. Then Milady smiled, and leaned back; and the gleam in her eyes was hooded once again. "Everything," she whispered. "We need to know it all."

'Haszler moaned. He reached for the crucifix, and hugged it again. "It was Wolverton," he muttered, "Wolverton met him first."

' "Met Tadeus, you mean?"

'Haszler nodded.

' "How?"

' "We had gone . . . it was after we had pillaged all the

passes round here – we had gone into Bohemia, and met there with an army of mercenaries and Swedes as they were marching on Prague. So we joined with the Swedes, because we'd already seen how little was left in the countryside to plunder, and we thought we'd do better if the city could be stormed. But the siege was a hard one, and most of our band was killed, and then peace was signed and the invading army left. Those of us still alive, we wanted to go – but Wolverton refused. He had always talked of visiting Prague, for it had a dark reputation for sorcery such as was bound to have attracted him." Haszler swallowed; then lifted the crucifix, and pressed it hard to his lips. "For you must understand," he muttered, "that Wolverton had always been dreaded by the rest of us, as being a master of the secret arts – and indeed, he would not permit anyone to join with us, not until the new recruit had tortured a priest to death and been baptised with the blood into the faith of the Evil One. And to be sure, in return for such devotions, he seemed rewarded with success; for we had all grown rich by following him – and when he stayed in Prague, I was reluctant to abandon him, I and a few others – because we could sense, I think, that he was involved in some great project.

' "What it was, though, he refused to say – not for several months, anyway, during which we barely saw him at all, and the loot we had plundered began to run out. I was thinking we would have to leave, go back to the road; and then one night, as though Wolverton had been reading my thoughts, he came to me and tossed me a small bag of gold. I asked him where it had come from. Wolverton smiled; then he took me by the arm and led me downstairs. Waiting for us in the street outside I saw Kröger, the first person to have joined with me and

Wolverton; and next to him, in the shadows, what appeared to be a priest. I was surprised; for Wolverton, as I have mentioned, was no friend to the Church. But then the priest turned, and I met his stare; and my blood seemed at once transformed into ice. For his stare, Madame . . ." Haszler swallowed, then paused. "His stare, Madame – it was exceedingly like yours."

'Milady nodded faintly. "And the priest?" she murmured. "It was Tadeus, of course?"

'Haszler nodded dumbly.

' "And what did he want from you?"

' "A job."

' "What job?"

'Haszler breathed in deeply, then swallowed again. "He wanted a Jew."

' "Why?"

' "He didn't tell us, just gave us the name. A Rabbi – Rabbi Samuel ben Jehuda Loew."

'As he said this last name, of course, I glanced at Milady, my eyes very wide – just as yours are now, my Lord – for I presumed that this Rabbi was his famous father's son. But Haszler seemed not to have noticed my surprise; and I was careful not to interrupt him in his talk. "Of course," Haszler continued, "we wanted to know, how were we to recognise this Samuel? Father Tadeus answered me by seizing my chin; then by stabbing me, it seemed, very deep, with his stare. And at once I imagined I was standing in the Ghetto, in a narrow alleyway leading from the Synagogue; and I saw, coming towards me, a bowed, white-haired man in a Rabbi's long robes. And then Tadeus released me – and the vision was gone. 'That,' whispered Tadeus, 'was Samuel.'

' "I shrank back from him, then shook my head. "How is it," I dared to ask him, "that you require my help, when you possess such wondrous and unearthly powers?"

' "A shadow seemed to pass across Tadeus' face; and for a moment I was afraid I had angered him. Then he shrugged. 'I am not the only one,' he answered, 'with unearthly powers. That same wisdom I want from Samuel, is also what guards his thoughts from the practice of my own. Yet he is feeble for all that; and in his bodily strength at least' – he smiled – 'no match at all for you.' "

'Haszler nodded grimly. "And that was true enough." He paused, then grinned. "Samuel was just an old man, after all; and for Kröger and me, it was a favourite game, taking people where they didn't want to go. We'd met him by the Synagogue, in the very place where I'd seen him in the vision; and then we brought him, slung like a carpet over Kröger's shoulder, to the ruins of an abbey some distance out of Prague. It was a warm summer evening; but the moment I stepped inside that abbey, I felt frozen, as though the walls had been chiselled out of ice. They were all streaked and daubed with blood; and I recognised some of the symbols, for Wolverton, when he used to desecrate churches, had often painted the walls the same way. He was waiting for us now; and as we joined him, he led us up the nave towards the altar. Father Tadeus was waiting for us there, standing in the shadow of a giant crucifix, which had been painted like the walls with strange symbols in blood. He ordered Samuel bound to this cross; then reached to the altar for a hammer and nails. He smiled very coldly, and lifted a nail before the Rabbi's eyes. 'I want to know,' he whispered, 'where the *golem* was made.' Then he aimed the nail above Samuel's palm, and hammered it in fast, as Samuel screamed. 'The *golem*,' Tadeus whispered again; but Samuel only moaned and shook his head. Tadeus shrugged; then he nailed Samuel's other hand, and both his feet. 'Haszler, Kröger,' he shouted out suddenly. We hurried to join him. Tadeus gestured to the Jew. 'I have been told,' he murmured, 'that you possess certain skills. I would be very grateful, if you would display to me what they can achieve.' "

'Haszler's voice trailed away at this point. He was clutching and pawing at his crucifix again. But I knew he was feeling, not remorse, only fear. I stepped forward. "Well?" I pressed him. "Did your reputations prove to be deserved?"

'Haszler swallowed. "We were very . . . practised," he answered at length. "Samuel lasted better than most, but . . ." – he shrugged – "he was old."

' "And then?"

'Haszler swallowed again. "Samuel was removed from the cross. He was given brandy. And then – he was ordered to take us to the spot."

' "Which he did?"

'Haszler nodded. "That very night." '

Lovelace paused in his narrative. He had been staring for a long while into the darkness; but he turned now, and glanced down at Lord Rochester. 'Samuel led them to a quarry on the banks of the Vltava.' He nodded. 'Yes, my Lord – that same quarry which the Pasha described to us before.'

Lord Rochester met his companion's eye; but then he frowned, and slowly shook his head. 'No,' he murmured. 'This was – what? – more than sixty years after Rabbi Loew's death.'

'As I told you, my Lord – Samuel was his son.'

'Yes, but even so,' Lord Rochester protested, 'how could he have known? Not without the book.'

'There is a great tradition amongst the Jews of knowledge being passed down through the generations.' Lovelace turned, and gazed into the darkness again. 'It struck me, even as I listened to Haszler's account, that Rabbi Loew might easily have shown Samuel the book, and taught him how to read it, for he could not have been certain that the Pasha would appear. Tadeus, I supposed, must have thought the same way – for why else would he have bothered to torture Samuel, if he had not suspected that the Jew might know what he needed to find out?'

'Needed, Lovelace?'

'Yes, my Lord. He *needed* that spot where the *golem* had been made – where the line of power possessed its greatest strength.'

Lord Rochester's frown began to deepen with the silence. 'Yet if Tadeus already knew so much,' he said at last, 'then why had he waited to interrogate Samuel?'

'Indeed,' Lovelace shrugged, 'that had briefly puzzled me. But then Haszler continued with his narrative. Wolverton, it seemed, had been in a febrile and wild-talking mood as they had journeyed to the quarry. He had told Haszler many strange things, which Haszler himself had barely comprehended. But when they were repeated to me . . . well – then I understood.'

'Indeed?'

'Oh yes, my Lord. For Wolverton had apparently boasted that his flesh was to veil the Lord of all the World.'

'By which he meant—'

'Azrael – the Angel of Death . . .' Lovelace paused;

then, slowly, whispered the title once again. 'Who at that very moment,' he continued, 'lay as scattered dust. For remember, my Lord – the war in Germany had just been brought to an end; the times had started, however feebly, to be healed. The Pasha's struggle had been fought; and in the end, it had been won. But not utterly . . .' He paused. 'As Tadeus was to prove . . .'

There was silence. The shadows seemed suddenly to quiver and darken. Lord Rochester shifted uneasily. 'How, then?' he whispered. 'How did he achieve it?'

Lovelace shrugged and half-smiled. 'There is a myth amongst the Jews that a soul can be passed from body to body, becoming a wraith to which they give the name of *gilgul*. It is a vulgar legend, of course; and yet it conceals, it seems, in Prague, the hints of a higher and more terrible truth. For what was the *golem* in the end, my Lord, but a breed of *gilgul*, in which a compound of dust contained a transmigrated spirit? Tadeus too, apparently, had mastered such a wisdom – although darker, in his case, and sodden with blood.'

'That is what he did, then?' Lord Rochester whispered. 'He made a *golem* of Sir Charles' flesh?'

'The Spirit was redeemed from the dust by Kröger's blood. Tadeus had seized him in his gaze; then slashed with a knife across the naked throat. Doubtless it had been his intention to kill Samuel and Haszler as well; yet the merest touch of Kröger's blood had proved sufficient, for immediately the dust had started to stir. Seeing this, Sir Charles had knelt down; then he had cried out exultantly and prostrated himself. At once, the dust had begun to crawl like a plague of hungry fleas across him, until Sir Charles had seemed submerged beneath a seething cloud of darkness. Samuel had already turned;

and Haszler, seeing him flee, had started to slip and
slither desperately after him. He glanced back only once.
The whole quarry seemed enveloped by a storm. Dimly,
Haszler could make out Tadeus, his arms outstretched,
speaking strange words to a figure of clay lying where Sir
Charles had formerly been. Then Haszler turned; and he
did not look round again.'

'So he did not see what occurred next?'

Lovelace shrugged. 'It needs little wit to imagine it,
though. Tadeus would have had Sir Charles' body packed;
and doubtless the dust from the river bank as well – for
you will remember perhaps, my Lord, the mud which my
father discovered in the cellars, and which he wrote had
seemed to suck upon his boots?'

'You think some residue of the Spirit might have
lingered in it still?'

'Why else would Tadeus have transported so much
dirt?'

'But to Woodton, Lovelace? Why so far?'

'Because Woodton is the nearest place to Stonehenge;
that much Tadeus would have learned from Sir Charles.
For do not forget, my Lord: Tadeus was a correspondent
of Madame la Marquise; and the Marquise had been an
associate of Dr Dee. When Sir Charles described to him
the wonders of his home, Tadeus would have recognised
them, doubtless, as the ancient marks of a mighty line of
power. It would have needed no book to discover such a
line; nor, indeed, the torturing of a Jew.'

Lord Rochester pursed his lips. 'And when Haszler
fled the quarry,' he asked, 'did he meet with Samuel
again?'

Lovelace smiled, and shook his head. 'His terror had
been far too great. He had been capable of nothing but a

desperate flight.'

'To his mountain haunt?'

'Where he then sat and mouldered for many years, thinking of the damnable horrors he had seen – and dreading the arrival of a creature such as Tadeus.'

'It would have been a mercy indeed, to put an end to such an existence.'

'Indeed.'

There was a silence. 'You rode, then, I assume,' asked Lord Rochester at length, 'onwards to Prague, to discover if Samuel was still alive?'

Lovelace nodded; then he paused, and smiled again. 'Milady, before we left for Germany, had been growing like you, my Lord – positively womanish with redis-covered qualms. Yet as you have just suggested yourself – it is the quality of mercy that it can sometimes satisfy the appetites as well. Such was the mercy' – he bared his teeth – 'which Milady showed to Konrad Haszler.' The smile faded; he inspected his nails. 'And when it was finished – yes, we continued then to Prague.'

'FOR IT WAS AS RABBI LOEW TAUGHT, THAT IN A ROSE ALL THE SECRETS OF THE WORLD MIGHT BE FOUND.'

Traditional Jewish folktale

'We did not approach the city,' Lovelace continued, 'with any great hopes that we would find the Rabbi alive. He had been old already when Haszler met with him, more than twenty years before; and his sufferings on that night had been terrible enough. I was tempted, as we travelled into Prague, to head directly to the Ghetto, to make certain at once of the prospect of our hopes; yet when I suggested this, Milady refused. You will have remembered yourself, my Lord, how desperate she had been to fathom the book; so you will understand my surprise that she was now insisting we should first find rooms. I stared into her face, and thought suddenly how exhausted and nervous she appeared. I knew that she was thirsty; and yet I wondered as well, passing through the city, whether she had not been infected by a spirit in the air, for there seemed something listless and morose about Prague, as though the shadow of some horror still lingered on the streets. The city's beauty appeared pallid, haunted, spent – such as you might recognise yourself, perhaps, my Lord, when you admire the loveliness of a woman's face even as her life is ebbing softly away.

'We found rooms in a palace, in the shadow of the Castle; and then at once Milady slipped back into the streets. I did not go with her – the pain in my stomach had been growing ever worse. Yet even as I lay curled up on my bed, waiting for Milady to return, I could feel my impatience mounting as well; and at length it triumphed, and I could wait for her no more. Swallowing back my pain, I ventured out into the gloomy twilight. I crossed the bridge, and passed into the Ghetto; and then, just as the Pasha had been, found myself swept upon its crooked, stinking streets until I was brought, without intending it, to the Synagogue's door. I could hear the wailing of a voice from within, and then the mumbling of a congregation's answer. I passed inside, and peered through a window at the house of prayer beyond. I recognised it at once, from the image I had glimpsed before in the Pasha's mind. But the air was greasy now with the stench of oil lamps; and the light they cast was so foggy and wan that I could barely make out the forms of those within. I could understand, though, the words they were singing, a lament for the destruction of Jerusalem – that time when the Wanderer had appeared once before. And now I was standing where he had appeared a second time, bearing the gift of a book within his hands; and I shuddered to think of it, and the secrets it might contain.

'I turned. There was a staircase ahead of me, at the sight of which I felt my heart start to shiver. I crossed towards the stairs, and began to climb them. In the darkness ahead, I could make out the shadow of a door. I reached it, and opened it, and passed inside. At once, I felt the pain like a wall of knives; and at the same moment, even worse, a stifling cloud across my thoughts, which it took me a moment to recognise as dread. All I could see around me, though, were trunks and piles of books, their outlines muffled beneath pale shrouds of dust. I bent down, and touched the floor. Immediately, I felt the pain grow worse; and the surge of some shock passing deep into my blood. I staggered, then stumbled back out through the door. As I did so, from below me I could hear the wail of song again; and it seemed suddenly so mournful, so filled with despair, that my terror was transmuted into a sense of the utmost desolation, so that I felt I would choke if I could not escape it. I descended from the attic, and out into the night. I gulped down air and, as I did so, I recognised the sweetness of blood. Again, the shiver of panic. I spun round. Then I saw that there were butchers' shops all along the street; and at the sight of them, I started to laugh. I turned and hurried on, still eager to purge the terror from my lungs, but finding that the air was foul wherever I went, for the alleyways seemed fetid and dense without end. Next to a brothel I passed a soaking pit, and then a huddle of tanners' shops, and then, beyond them, a single narrow gate; and then suddenly, unexpectedly, I was in an open space.

'I stared about me. Dimly, I could make out strange-shaped slabs – protruding, it seemed, from almost every spot of ground. I walked forward; and realised I was passing through a confusion of graves, impossibly clustered, and crooked like the teeth in an old man's jaw. I had no choice but to keep to the winding path, for the earth on either side was bulging and raised; and I was not surprised to see, filming the narrow gaps between the stones, the faint silver gleam of spiderwebs. I breathed in deeply. The air, at last, seemed wonderfully clear. I paused a moment, and breathed it in again; then closed my eyes and leaned against a tomb, struggling to compose my still fast-beating heart.

' "Although this is a place of death, yet it is also called *Beth-Chaim*, the House of Life."

'I opened my eyes, startled. A man was standing before me: I guessed him, from his beard and robes, to be a Rabbi. I wondered for a moment if he was not Samuel ben Loew; but then I knew he could not be, for he was far too young.

' "Certainly," I answered him slowly, "I have found that life and death may be easily confused."

' "Easily?" The Rabbi frowned. "Then I dread to think what you have seen." His frown deepened, and I realised that he was inspecting me with great attention. "Why," he murmured, "just now, did you climb to the attic of the Synagogue?"

' "It is forbidden?"

' "It is impossible. No one, not since the death of a

former Rabbi here, has had the courage to open and pass through that door."

'I licked my lips. "Yes," I whispered at last. "I felt it myself ... how the shadow of the *golem* still lingers there."

' "You know of Rabbi Loew?"

' "Certainly. I have come here to Prague to meet with his son."

'The Rabbi smiled faintly. "Then you are in the right place indeed." He took my arm and led me along the path, then paused by a grave much larger than its neighbours, shaped like an ark, and the length of a man. My companion bowed his head. "This is the tomb of Rabbi Jehuda Loew. And this" – he gestured to a tomb along its side – "is that of his son." He glanced at my face, gauging the scale of my evident despair; then he bowed down, and reached for a handful of stones. He placed a small pile of them on both of the tombs; then rose to his feet, and bowed his head once again.

' "When," I murmured hoarsely, "did Samuel die?"

' "Eleven years ago ..."

' "Only eleven?" I exclaimed. "Then it was not Haszler ..." I stopped myself suddenly.

'The silence deepened like fog. When I glanced at the Rabbi, I saw that he was frowning at me again, suspicion and puzzlement intermingled on his face. He opened his mouth; then paused, and looked away, gesturing instead towards Samuel's tomb. "You see," he asked suddenly, "how narrow it is?"

'I stared at it; then nodded. It seemed narrow indeed: as though it had been wedged very tight between the neighbouring graves.

'The Rabbi swallowed; and when he spoke again, his

voice seemed strangely hesitant. "It was Samuel's dearest wish to be buried at the side of his father's tomb. Yet there was no space; and Samuel was flung into despair, for it seemed to him – such was the state of his conscience – that he was being excluded from his father's company as punishment for an act of betrayal he had made some years before. Yet then he died; and miraculously, the tomb of his father moved, just a fraction, thereby creating the room for Samuel's grave."

' "A pretty story," I nodded. I gazed down at the tomb. "And yet I am glad," I continued, "that the Rabbi was not punished for the wisdom he had betrayed, for it was no sin what he did, not when the torturers were working for a demon such as Tadeus, who had confused indeed what was life and what was death."

'The Rabbi made no answer at first, save to gather his cloak about him, for an icy wind had begun to blow across the graves. "What is your purpose here?" he murmured at last.

' "Buried," I answered him, gesturing towards Samuel's narrow grave.

' "The book," he asked me suddenly. "Where is it?"

'I turned to him in surprise.

' "Come, sir," he whispered. "The book which the Wanderer brought to Rabbi Loew."

' "How can you know I possess it?"

'The Rabbi seized my arm. "Because I am the heir to these two," he whispered, gesturing again towards the tombs. "I am Aaron Simon Spira, Chief Rabbi of Prague; and therefore learned in the writings of Rabbi Loew. Oh yes," he nodded, "there were secret records left – a true account of all that he had done . . . and a guide as well to that which might yet occur."

' "And this guide," I asked him, not bothering to conceal the sudden blaze of my excitement, "what did it say?"

' "That he had seen you." The Rabbi tightened his grip on my arm, and began to lead me back along the cemetery path. "A stranger from a distant land, in peril much greater perhaps than you suspected – and yet bringing with you too the Wanderer's secret book."

' "And you can read it?" I pressed him. "You can understand the script?"

'The Rabbi paused, then shook his head.

' "But there is someone – or some way – it must have been foreseen . . ."

'My voice trailed away. The Rabbi continued to lead me in silence along the path, until we were standing beneath the narrow cemetery gate. Then he turned to me again. "The writings ended," he whispered, "with the single description of a stranger standing in the Cemetery. But then, pressed between two blank pages – something else" – he paused – "a withered, ancient flower."

'I frowned at him. "What did it mean?"

'The Rabbi smiled sadly. "I was hoping, sir, that you might tell me that yourself."

'I breathed in deeply, as I gazed across the stillness and silence of the graves. "Then all is lost."

' "And yet it has been said," the Rabbi answered slowly, "that even in the smallest and meanest flower, great mysteries and secrets may still be found."

' "Why, sir," I asked him, narrowing my eyes, "what can you mean?"

' "Do you have the book?"

' "Not upon me."

' "Then fetch it and come to me in the Synagogue. I shall be waiting for you there."

' "Why," I called after him, "what do you hope for?" But he was already leaving me, his black robes melting into the dark; and though I might easily have stopped him, I let him go. I stood for a few moments more, gazing at the graves; then I too turned about.

'Yet the book, when I returned to my rooms, was no longer in its place. I stared at where it had been and felt disbelief, like hemlock, slowly numbing my limbs. Milady – where was Milady? Still not back. I began to call out her name wildly; then to ransack every corner of our rooms, even though I knew, as I tore the place apart, that I would not find the book there, that Milady – or someone – had taken it away. At last, I returned to the streets, and sought out all the darkest corners of Prague, all those places where Milady might possibly have gone; yet still I did not discover her. Once, as I called out her name, two figures ahead of me paused, then turned; and their eyes seemed to gleam as blood-drinkers' do. Yet then they turned again, and slipped away; and though I pursued them fast, I could not track them down. I soon grew lost amidst the palaces of Malá Strana, until at length I found myself by the river bank, and saw that dawn was lightening the eastern sky. I had been hunting Milady all night. Suddenly, my limbs felt heavy again; and the pain in my stomach was throbbing hard. I turned, and went back to my empty rooms . . .

'Save that they were no longer empty. Milady was sitting on the side of her bed – the book in her hands.

'I crossed to her, my fury intermingled with disbelief. "Where have you been?" I asked her, my voice very calm.

' "I had business," she answered, not looking up.

' "Business?" I echoed mistrustfully.

' "I have been debating," she murmured, still staring at

the book, "all the length of this night, whether or not I should destroy this thing – destroy it utterly, Lovelace, so that nothing remains. For as much as I have hopes of it – so also I have fears." She turned, at last, to look up at me; and my anger was melted at once by her look. For her face seemed unaccountably delicate and frail; her eyes dulled; her nervousness more evident even than before. I reached for her hands, and kissed her very softly; then leaned across her to whisper in her ear. "We must rise now and go to the Synagogue."

'I felt her start; and as I stepped back to look at her again, I saw how the gleam was returning to her eyes. "You have found something?" she asked.

' "It may be."

' "What?"

'I shrugged.

' "Tell me!" she screamed suddenly, her eyes ablaze now and her pale face mobile with a strange and hungry passion. "What have you found?"

' "Nothing we will know," I answered coldly, "until, as I have said, we go to the Synagogue."

'Milady met my eye; and for a long while, neither of us spoke. Then she gave a faint shrug, and her face seemed suddenly wan with exhaustion. "Very well, then," she nodded. She clasped the book tightly to her breast. "Let us go." '

Lovelace paused; and his lips curled into a self-mocking smile. 'I do not know what we had been expecting. Once we had joined him in the Synagogue, the Rabbi led us not to a storehouse of ancient papers, not to some dangerous, power-haunted spot, but to an old woman lying crippled in her bed. Her face still preserved, in however ravaged a state, traces of an ancient loveliness;

but her mind seemed half-gone, and her hearing with it. The Rabbi must have seen and understood the expression on my face; for he smiled as he crossed to the old woman's side. "This is Jemima," he said, as he pulled up a chair. "Rabbi Loew's grand-daughter – Rabbi Samuel's niece."

'I saw the quickening of my own interest mirrored in Milady's face. "You think, then," she asked, drawing close to the bed, "that they may have taught her how to read the secret script?"

' "In truth," the Rabbi answered, "I cannot believe so. And yet of all those who knew Rabbi Loew, there is only Jemima left alive." He bowed his head in silent prayer; then he reached for the book. Milady, though, would not let it out of her hands, but still kept hold of it jealously, even as she opened its pages and laid it down upon the bed. Jemima continued to stare ahead of her, as though utterly unaware of the book; then she laid a shaking hand upon its edge. She gazed down at it; and her lips began to move. For a brief moment, I felt a surge of hope; but then she blinked and shook her head, still muttering unintelligible words to herself; and Milady snapped the book shut and I saw, stamped upon her beautiful face, a vicious fury and a bitter despair.

'And then, at the same moment, I remembered how Rabbi Loew had once also known despair, when he too had believed that the book would never be read; and how the mystery, one hot afternoon – perhaps in the very room we were all gathered in now – had been suddenly dissolved by the intrusion of a child. I turned to the Rabbi. "You told me of a book, a book in which Rabbi Loew had foreseen my appearance . . ."

' "Yes . . ."

' "Can you fetch it?"

'He gazed at me in puzzlement, then smiled faintly. "There is no need." He reached within his robes, and drew out a tiny, leather-bound volume. He handed it across, and I snatched at it greedily, thumbing through the pages until I came to it – the flower, still there. For a moment I sat frozen, gazing at it; then gently I handed the volume to Jemima. She took it, frowning; then she too looked down and gazed at the flower.

' "I remember . . ." she said suddenly, blinking back her tears. "I remember – the very day when I picked this same flower." She raised it to her nostrils. "The scent is long gone." Her tears were flowing uncontrollably now; she wiped at her cheeks, but at the same moment she suddenly laughed. "I remember," she nodded, "I gave it to my grandfather. Yes. My grandfather . . ." She choked, then laughed again.

'I stared across at Milady. She nodded slowly, as though with dawning comprehension; then smoothed out the pages of the book in her hand, and gave it to Jemima. The old woman dropped the volume she already held; and as she did so, the flower crumbled into tiny fragments, and was scattered as purple dust upon the air. But Jemima seemed barely to notice; for all her attention now was placed upon the script, the secret, mysterious, unreadable script. I saw her eyes widen with astonishment; then her face seemed suddenly to gleam a pale silver, as though lit from deep within. At the same moment I heard a gasp from Milady, a sibilant, triumphant intake of breath. I watched her as her eyes sparked, and I knew she was seizing upon Jemima's thoughts. Suddenly, she moaned softly and closed her eyes; then she opened them again, and their gold seemed now to blaze with fire. She reached hungrily for the book. "Yes," she gasped, as she stared down at the script, "Lovelace, Lovelace, yes, I can read it!"

'I smiled at her weakly. "I am glad," I replied. Then I felt the pain in my stomach pass over me in a tidal wave of red. The room began to swim . . . I felt myself crashing to the floor.

'Dimly, through the crimson banks of pain, I remained conscious of myself; though for how long, how many hours, it was impossible to know, for all sense of time, all sense of place, seemed dissolved. Sometimes, like phantoms glimpsed through a mist, dreams would brush past me. I would see Milady, her face twisted by horror, pressing her hands into the stomach of a corpse, so that the flesh was parted and the coils of gut exposed; and then I would see that the corpse was myself. At other times, I would hear the wailing of a new-born child, and glimpse it dimly, curled, still bloody, like that tiny thing which had been ripped from Hannah's womb, to be found by my father and enfolded in his cloak; save that though I looked, I could never see its face, for as I drew near it, so the dream would start to fade, and I would imagine instead that I was lost on Salisbury Plain. Thick gusts of snow would be burning my face, and I would search for Stonehenge, so that I might find my way home – and then I would understand that I had been mistaken, that I was not by Stonehenge at all but on a remote and barren mountainside, and I would see ahead of me a mighty wall of rock shaped in the profile of an old man's head. How I longed to reach it!' – Lovelace paused and faintly smiled – 'for as I stared at it, somehow the pain would start to melt; but though I staggered forward, I would soon grow blind with the snow, for the flakes would seem sticky and crimson with blood, and my pain would return. Always my pain, flowing deep from my stomach, deep, very deep – until no more dreams came, and I woke up at last.

'Milady was sitting by my side. The book, I saw, lay closed upon her lap. She reached to touch my brow. "You have been sick." Her smile seemed distant, very sad.

' "Have you read the book?"

'She nodded faintly.

' "What did you see there?"

'A strange look, in which pity and disgust seemed equally mixed, passed like a shadow across her face. "I saw," she whispered, "many strange things . . ." Her voice trailed away and she laid the book down on the floor. "I am afraid," she whispered. "Afraid of its power. Afraid I will not know how to control such a power. And yet, dearest Lovelace . . ." She kissed me suddenly. "And yet . . ." She looked away.

' "And yet what, Milady?"

'Shaking her head, she rose to her feet. She had ordered food to be prepared for me. I ate it. We did not talk. Always, though, we both knew, the book was waiting where Milady had placed it, waiting on the floor. "*I am afraid.*" Her voice still seemed to ripple through my thoughts. What had she seen? What did she fear?

' "You should sleep," she said at last. "You have been in fever a long while." She left me alone; I lay down, and closed my eyes. An hour passed. Then I heard her glide up to me; heard the rustling of her dress as she bent down close beside my face. After a minute's silence, she rose back to her feet; and I heard her retire. A door, very softly, was opened, then closed. All was quiet again. I leapt from my bed. The book, I saw at once, had been taken from the floor. I gazed around me. It was nowhere to be seen. This did not surprise me, for I knew where it had gone. I reached hurriedly for my boots and cloak; I slipped them on. Then, as Milady had done, I passed out on to the stairway and down into the night.'

∽∾

'. . . FAIN WOULD I HAVE A BOOK WHEREIN I MIGHT BEHOLD
ALL SPELLS AND INCANTATIONS, THAT I MIGHT RAISE UP SPIRITS
WHEN I PLEASE.'

Christopher Marlowe, *Doctor Faustus*

'I could make out Milady ahead of me, but only just; and it was all I could do to keep pace with her. She continued down the hill towards the river; and then, as she drew near to the bridge, she paused by its gateway and whispered to the shadows. Two figures emerged in answer from their depths. They were cloaked as Milady was, but still, as they crossed to her, I could see the glint of their eyes; and I remembered the figures I had seen the night before. One of them took Milady in his arms; and I was able to glimpse, just for a second as he pushed back his hood to kiss her, Lightborn's face. Then I saw him reach inside her cloak, and pull something out; and though the shadows were very deep, I knew it was the book. Milady seized it back at once; but not before Lightborn had raised it to his lips and kissed it with a laugh of joyous triumph. His companion whispered something; and I thought, as I crept towards them through the shadows, that I recognised the voice of the Marquise. She turned, and led the way on to the bridge. Lightborn and Milady followed, arm-in-arm.

'I could only pursue them as far as the gateway, for on the Charles Bridge itself there was no shelter at all; yet this also ensured that my view was unobscured. Milady halted in the centre of the bridge. She drew out the book, and opened it up; and then I knew that she was starting to read it, for I could suddenly feel the pain in my guts, rising in a wave as it had done before and breaking across my thoughts. But I knew I could not afford to be swept away upon it, for I could see how Lightborn and the Marquise had both closed their eyes, and had a look upon their faces of distant rapture, such as Milady too had worn when she had gorged herself upon Jemima's thoughts; and I knew that it was her own thoughts which were being fed upon now. Then both Lightborn and the Marquise seemed to gasp, and shudder; and the Marquise suddenly snatched away the book. She stared at the open pages; and I imagined I could see – though how, I cannot say – eddies of a pure and invisible light, flowing in a line along the length of the bridge. They seemed to touch and melt with the pain in my guts; and I felt my thoughts melting, as they were lost upon the swirl. But then, as suddenly as it had risen, the pain began to ebb; and the mighty flow of light seemed to fade into the stars.

'I staggered forward, gasping for air. Milady was shouting something at the Marquise; I strained to hear what. She was pointing towards the distance; and then suddenly, she seized the book and began to hurry across the bridge, towards the opposite bank. Lightborn followed her, and then the Marquise too; and I could see now, as she walked, that her back was still stooped and her gait an ugly hobble. It took her several minutes to reach the far bank; and when she had done so, I crossed the bridge myself, then continued to follow her on through the streets.

'Her slowness ensured that I never lost her until, just beyond the outskirts of Prague, I saw Milady and Lightborn each waiting on horses, and the Marquise struggling into the saddle of a third. I watched as she shook out her reins, and then the three of them wheeled and galloped away. I ran forward. The track they had taken was bogged with mud, and the trail of their hoof-prints obvious enough; yet even as I began to follow them, I felt a sense of numbing hopelessness, for I dreaded to think how far the hoofprints might lead. I tried to run; but I was still very weak, and I shuffled and slithered my way through the mud. It seemed to be growing thicker; and soon it was sucking and pulling on my feet. Rounding a corner, I could see the Vltava flowing sluggish ahead. The path wound along its side, rising up towards a straggle of barren trees, and then down a hillside pockmarked with quarries. No longer running, I crept stealthily on. The pain was worsening again. I was not surprised – for I had realised now what it was that lay ahead. And yet I knew as well, for the same reason, that there could be no turning back; and so I continued through the pain, up the path, towards the trees. Three horses had been tethered there; and ahead of me I could see their riders gathered by the river. They were talking violently – arguing, it seemed. All about them stretched a bleak expanse of muddy silt and clay.

'I braced myself: for I knew I was approaching where the *golem* had been formed, and where the Spirit of Evil had been scattered by the Pasha into dust. But I was hungry to understand why Milady had betrayed me; and so I gritted my teeth, and began to descend. Ever more cruel, the pain was gnawing at me now; but still I fought to ignore it, as I reached the tree which stood nearest to the river, and then sank down in agony amidst the tangle of its roots. Sheltered where I was, I could hear the argument clearly now. Milady, it seemed, was reluctant to surrender the book. "You promise," she was hissing, "you promise then, Madame, that you will solemnly keep to the agreement that we made?"

'The Marquise laughed contemptuously. "I have told you, Milady, you shall have all your grovelling wishes made true." Her voice sounded hoarse and cracked. I stole a glance around the side of the tree. The Marquise's hood had fallen back from her face, and I could see that she was quite as ugly as before – all the more so, indeed, for her expression seemed twisted by a desperate greed and her eyes were burning like hungry coals. "Come, Milady." She leered horribly. "Give it to me."

' "How can I trust you?" Milady whispered. "How can I know that you will truly keep your word?"

' "You cannot," the Marquise answered, "and yet what choice do you have? For you remember, Milady, what happened before – when you sought to rule the book, and found that you could not."

'These words startled me, and I wondered what they meant. Certainly, Milady did not contradict them; but gazed down at the book, as though in despair. "Yet I am afraid," she said at last, "that you as well, Madame, will find yourself too feeble for its power."

' "My knowledge and strength are much greater than your own."

' "Yes – but so also is your greed."

'The Marquise shrugged wearily, and sighed. "I have promised you, Milady, that before I pursue my own

ambitions in the book, I shall first achieve your own, as
we agreed in London. So come." She stepped forward.
"Give the book to me."

'Milady breathed in deeply. I thought, gazing at her
then, that she had rarely seemed more lovely – though
why I should have felt that with such sudden force, when
I could see the evidence of her treachery there before me
in her hands, I was unable to explain. I watched as she
passed the book across. The Marquise seized it; she
opened the pages, and at once began to read. And then,
as before, my existence seemed to melt.'

Lovelace paused. 'How to describe it?' He shook his
head. 'There was the great line of power swirling around
us, yet even purer, even more invisible than it had
seemed on the bridge, so that it was the visible world
which grew intangible and unreal, and I could feel myself
fading from it as my pain began to bleed and melt into
the power. I realise, my Lord, I am not making sense; yet
what I felt and saw cannot be framed by mortal words. All
of time, all of experience at that moment seemed dissolved, so that I could comprehend in a single second a
myriad different things – and yet now, in my descrip-
tions, I must anatomise and divide into portions what
was formerly a whole.' He narrowed his eyes. 'There was
my pain . . .' he whispered. 'God's wounds, there was my
pain – and as I felt it rend me, so also I saw images I had
glimpsed before in the nightmares of my sickness: myself
a corpse, my guts exposed; a tiny child, beslobbered with
blood. Now, though, my Lord, I could see the baby's face:
dead-eyed, maggot-faced, with ravening jaws, and as I
stared at these jaws so I doubled up again with pain, for I
imagined they were gnawing at my stomach's flesh. I
imagined blood flowing from my every orifice; imagined

it flooding that mighty swirl of light, so that what had formerly seemed pure now seemed blackened and thick, swirling like a whirlpool towards a single point of darkness, and I knew that point was where the *golem* had been made, where the Pasha had dissolved his foe into dust, the very heart of the great line of power, where blackness seemed bright and fire icy-cold. The Marquise was standing in it, her arms upraised, and she was laughing. "See," she cried, "see!" She brushed back her cloak, and I saw that her face appeared luminous, her former loveliness restored to her, restored to her and more, for her beauty now was terrible to behold.

' "Your promise!" I heard Milady scream.

'The Marquise shuddered, and seemed to flicker upon the ravening darkness.

' "Your promise!"

' "No!" The Marquise flickered again, as though now a part of the fire. "For what can you possibly understand? You cannot see it, not feel it, what I might do, might become!" Still she flickered, fading fast now. "I glimpse Eternity before me." She screamed. "I have it – here – it is my own – in my hands!"

'She was holding the book; and then it was gone, and the Marquise was gone too: fires snuffed out in the onslaught of a gale. Where she had been standing there was a rent of darkness; and I felt my pain, and myself, and all the world passing through it. I saw, beyond the rent, the profile of a face; and I knew it was the rock-wall I had seen before in my dreams. Now, though, it turned to stare at me; and I saw that the face was not made of rock at all. It frowned as it met my eye; and the darkness was suddenly lit by blinding light. Then there was darkness again, and I found myself lost upon a firestorm of pain; and there seemed nothing else, nothing at all.

'As before, I had no sense of the passage of time. Only when a bottle was forced between my teeth, and I felt the taste of *mummia* burning my throat, did I imagine I was waking and escaping the pain; but the relief was momentary, and my senses still obscured. I would be aware vaguely of the rumbling of a carriage; and I would remember the rumbling of a carriage long before, when I had likewise lain upon a silk-sheathed lap and felt a lady's fingers stroke through my hair. Lulled by their ministrations now, I would slip into a merciful oblivion; before the pain, very soon, would flicker back through my sleep, as flames will spread across a lake of oil. I continued insensible to almost all else; save that as time passed, I would sometimes imagine that I glimpsed Milady's face and, opposite me, Lightborn's cold, mocking stare. Then dimly, I remember, I felt a wind against my cheek; and then a rolling and a pitching, like that of a boat. Yet such things still occurred beyond the threshold of my senses; for it seemed too great a challenge to my will, to my powers of resolution, to be anything other than what I already was – the prey and abject slave of my pain.

'And then I felt *mummia* again in my throat. As I swallowed it, I thought how I had not tasted it for what seemed a long, long while. There was the sound of gulls screaming overhead, I realised; and from below me a faint, gentle rocking to and fro. I stirred. I seemed to be lying on bare wooden boards. When I opened my eyes, I was in virtual darkness; but by my side, his pale skin gleaming cold, I could just make out Lightborn. I stared at him. He smiled back at me, but his look was not friendly. "Awake, then, at last?"

' "Where are we?" I murmured.

' "Aboard the good ship *Faithful Pilgrim*."

' "Where are we moored?"

' "By Deptford."

'I gazed at him, so astonished that I could barely speak. "We are in London?" I whispered. "We have travelled so far?"

' "So far, and so long. It has been a ride of many days since we left Prague behind."

' "I remember . . ."

'Lightborn raised his eyebrow inquiringly.

' "I remember – a gash of darkness . . ."

'Lightborn nodded distantly. "As well you might."

' "Indeed?"

' "It consumed the Marquise."

' "She is dead?"

' "Dead and gone – as the book is gone too."

'I stared at him; and felt my pain return. "Then all is lost."

' "It is indeed." Lightborn paused. His smile still flickered very faintly on his lips. "And more so, perhaps, than you have yet understood."

'I frowned. "What do you mean?"

'Lightborn reached for the bottle of *mummia*. He handed it to me. "Drink it again."

' "Answer me first."

' "Drink it."

'I lay frozen for a moment; then took the bottle and raised it to my lips. Lightborn watched me. "Doubtless," he murmured, "you were somewhat surprised to discover that myself and the Marquise were both in Prague."

'I laid down the bottle. "Somewhat," I agreed.

' "You should not blame Milady, for – alas! – all the calumnies are true – it is ever the nature of woman to be treacherous. Be grateful, then, Lovelace, that Milady's deceit was the bastard of her great love for you."

' "Her bastard? Indeed? Bred upon what?"

' "Why, the teeming womb of her fear."

'I gazed at him disbelievingly. "Fear, Lightborn?"

' "That she might lose you."

'I laughed bitterly. "Unnatural indeed, then, for her deceit to have been the offspring of such a dread."

' "And yet there was more at stake – yes – more even than you."

'I frowned. "I do not understand."

'Lightborn's smile broadened. "The Marquise had warned Milady, many months before, that she should return to London at that time you both duly did. A reason had not been given to her; and so when Milady glimpsed me upon Pudding Lane, she was prepared, in your absence, to agree to a meeting, for she was naturally eager to know more. The terms were soon agreed. Milady – that when she had learned to read the script, she would deliver us the book. The Marquise – that she would reveal to Milady where Emily might be found, and the means by which the plague-dead might then be destroyed. A worthy bargain, sir, would you not say?"

'I gazed at him in silence, then shook my head. "Why did Milady not tell me all this?"

'Lightborn shrugged. "Only she can answer that. However" – he paused – "I can hazard a guess."

' "Why?"

' "Because doubtless she wished not to cripple you with horror." He glanced at the *mummia* glass. "For the Marquise, in Pudding Lane, had revealed something more."

' "About me?"

' "Oh yes." Lightborn paused, toying with my dread. "About the cause . . ." he murmured; "the cause of your pain."

'I clasped my stomach; I struggled to sit up. "Tell me," I said.

' "It was something, perhaps, which the book alone could have cured. And so it had been agreed, between Milady and the Marquise, that when the book's power was opened and its secrets read, then the Marquise's first deed would be to heal you of your peril. Alas, though" – Lightborn shrugged – "she failed to keep her word . . ."

'His voice drawled away. I knew that he was watching me very closely, and I turned my head. I could not grovel to him; could not afford him the pleasure of seeing me beg. "Tell me," I asked suddenly, "why Milady could not have employed the book herself."

'I could sense Lightborn stiffening. "She did not have the strength," he murmured at last.

' "Yes," I nodded. "For I remember now, how the Marquise taunted her with the memory of something which had happened before, when she had sought to read the book and thereby brought you back to life." I stared back at him. "What, do you think, could the Marquise have meant?"

'Lightborn smiled coldly. "I would not grow too concerned about Milady now. You have quite sufficient problems of your own."

' "Indeed?" I arched an eyebrow. Still I would not beg.

'Lightborn laughed suddenly. "Shall I tell you, then?" he asked.

' "I wish, sir, that you would."

'He leaned forward, and whispered in my ear. "The

seed of that . . . thing . . . you met with at Stonehenge – it lies buried deep within you."

'I stared at him in mute astonishment; and yet I knew, even as I shook my head, that he had been telling me the truth.

' "You are pregnant," he continued, "with a great load of evil. For the seed – it is growing, and must soon be delivered."

'Again I shook my head. "Delivered?"

'Lightborn laughed with a sudden, naked delight. "Yes, sir – and by its own agency. For the time will come when your baby, Lovelace – your sweet, sweet child – will tear its way out through the mess of your guts, where it has been sheltering and growing all these many years. What else do you think your agonies have been, but a portent of the birth-pangs you must shortly feel?"

'I closed my eyes. I laid my hands upon my stomach. "Dear God," I whispered. "What, then, is to be done?"

' "You must be sent away."

' "There is no hope?"

' "None. For before the book was destroyed, while you tossed in your nightmares in your room in Prague, Milady read the script and employed its power. She gazed at the foetus where it lay within your guts. She saw that the Marquise had been telling the truth – and that she recognised the creature, still unformed as it was." Lightborn paused, and leaned forward close to me again. "Did you not, sir, when you travelled to Wolverton Hall, glimpse dead things crawling in the darkness there, which smiled at you cunningly as they gazed upon your face?"

' "I did," I whispered.

' "Smiles, no doubt, of recognition."

' "You truly believe I can be bearing such a thing?"

' "It is not I who believes it, but Milady."

' "Then I . . ." I swallowed; I closed my eyes. "I must . . . kill . . ." I clasped my stomach. "I must . . . stab this thing, this creature, where it lies."

' "I doubt, sir," Lightborn answered, "that you could murder it now. For think: all your powers, all the marks which have served to set you so apart – what has been their purpose, but to keep your child alive?"

' "Yet we cannot be certain. It is surely worth the attempt?"

' "Yes, sir, but not here."

' "Why not?"

' "Because that thing which you bear . . . it is imbued with the lethal nature of its parent. It is lethal, for instance, even to myself – even to Milady. Suppose, then, that your death does not serve to kill it? No, sir, no . . ." – Lightborn shook his head – "I cannot permit you to continue near us."

'I did not answer him.

'Lightborn suddenly smiled, and reached up to pat a beam overhead. "This ship is due to sail in the next half-hour for America. There is sufficient wilderness there, I would have hoped, for you to lose yourself and your bastard in. And if that should not prove possible – well – the Americans are all devout and Christian men. Who better to have confronting the Devil's spawn than God's own Elect?"

' "No," I said suddenly, "I will not go there. I will not go to America."

'Lightborn tutted. "You have no choice."

' "Milady . . ."

' "Milady?" Lightborn laughed. "But she agrees with

me, Lovelace, that it is the best policy by far."

' "She is not here now?"

' "You know her love for you. She would not have endured to see your departure."

' "I want to see her first."

' "You cannot." As he said this, Lightborn drew a knife; I struggled to evade him, but I was too weak to move and he aimed the point of the blade at my throat. "You will, sir, go to America," he hissed. At the same moment, there came a sudden shouting from the dock, and Lightborn angled his head, then slipped his knife back in his belt. "It is later than I had thought," he said jauntily. "Your ship is due to depart." He rose to his feet; then paused suddenly, and reached within his cloak. "Here," he murmured, as he drew out a further flask of *mummia*. "This is all that is left." He laid the bottle by my feet.

'More cries came from the deck overhead; and I felt the ship starting to rock and move. I gazed up at Lightborn. "You will tell her . . ."

'He nodded, even as he turned and left me. I watched him depart. "You will tell her?" I shouted after him again; but he was gone by now and, if he heard, he did not turn round. I gripped the bottle tightly as I lay doubled up, alone.'

∾◌∾

'. . . MARBLEHEAD, A PLACE OF GREAT WICKEDNESS AND LECHERY.'

17th century New England pamphlet

'The effects of the *mummia* lingered for the next few days, so that I was able to rise at least, and have some consciousness of things other than my gnawing – my ever-gnawing – pain. *The Faithful Pilgrim* was not a large ship, and yet there were upwards of a hundred souls aboard her, Puritans all, bound for a New World. Their leader was a bony, black-clad man, much given to comparing his people to the Israelites, and London to an Egypt damned by plague and fire. The name of this self-anointed Moses was Mr Fortitude Sheldon; and he reminded me somewhat of a Wiltshire man I had known – an old friend of my father, Mr Webbe. Yet Mr Sheldon had taken for himself the best cabin in the ship – something which my father's friend would never have done – and in the violence of his hatreds, the severity of his judgements, there seemed little of that compassion which I recalled in Mr Webbe.

'Nor, as my pain began to worsen again, did Mr Sheldon's compassion grow any more evident. The very opposite, indeed – for seeing my weakness, his manner grew increasingly peremptory, until at length he gave me an order as though I were his servant, or a child. Outraged by his impudence, I struck him. The blow was feeble, and yet he staggered; and his thin face grew very pale. Then he cried damnation upon me, and shouted out to the Brethren that I should be seized, and bound upon the deck. My clothes were stripped from me, and flung into the waves – "For they are the silks of Babylon," Mr Sheldon cried, "fit only for a brothel, not this vessel blessed of God." Then he saw my naked chest; he sobbed a cry of prayer and all the gathered Brethren at once began to moan. I gazed down; and saw for the first time that my nipples were oozing a watery blood. "Oh, be warned!" Mr Sheldon cried. "Be warned! For what are such marks, if not those of the Beast? Let the lash be applied to his back, and richly, that his stripes may bear witness to our most loving zeal!"

'It was done straight away as Mr Sheldon had commanded. Later, now dressed in the black homespun which all the Brethren wore, I was dragged to his cabin and flung down at his feet. Mr Shelden gazed at me with a look of holy approval. "So must you expect to be served," he nodded, "until all the stains of your former life are washed away, and you are rendered as clean as was Naaman by the waters of Jordan."

'I clutched at my belly and, despite my agony, I laughed. "You cannot know what you say."

'He frowned at me. "Are you spotted so foully, then, that you may truly not be cleansed?"

' "I know, sir," I answered him, "that I cannot be redeemed by your god, nor by anyone's, perhaps."

'As before, when I had struck him, his face grew very pale. "I see, sir," he hissed, "that as a serpent you have been smuggled here, into the very bosom of our godly fellowship. Well" – he leaned down close beside me – "your purposes must be scotched. Let us see what toil may not achieve with you, blessed toil, and the guidance of prayer. And if still you should prove to be inveterate chaff – well then, sir – you must be swept into the fire!" '

Lovelace paused, and half-smiled. 'Of course,' he continued, with the faintest of shrugs, 'I might easily have struck him again. But I chose not to – and indeed, in the weeks to come, I was to accept the yoke of his pious tyranny, to toil and pray as he commanded me to do, until he came almost to believe I might indeed be spared the final sweeping. It may be that, even in the depths of my agony, I found the strength to smile at Lightborn's jest, so wittily, so cruelly made, which had seen me restored to my former homespun, praying to my former God down upon my knees – even as I bore within my guts my hellish load. And it may be also, as the weeks began to pass, that I grew to welcome speaking the familiar scriptures, the words which I had learned in my parents' home and had once – as they had done – truly believed. Yet neither of these reasons would have served to stay my hand, had there not been a greater, more certain one as well: that I did not wish to tempt Mr Sheldon's threats – that I did not wish to die.'

Lord Rochester laughed. 'It is as I have said, then. We would all of us be cowards, if only we had the courage.'

Lovelace shrugged. 'Maybe. And yet it was not cowardice alone which made me cling to my life.'

'How do you mean?'

Lovelace narrowed his eyes. 'I cannot be certain,' he murmured at length. 'And yet I can recall, at that very moment when my own whipping began, how I gazed out at the waves being lashed by the storm, and thought how lost, if I plunged beneath them, I might be ... Why search for a wilderness of mountains and trees, I thought, when there was a wilderness before me more terrible by far? And yet then, even as I resolved that I would leap into the sea, I was struck by an unbidden memory of the face I had seen in my nightmares in Prague, which had seemed formed of mountain rock, and yet had turned to stare at me and meet my own eye. And now I imagined it was doing so again; and I knew, at that same moment, as I saw it through the gale, that I would not seek to join with the ocean after all.'

'Why?' frowned Lord Rochester. 'I do not understand.'

'I felt ...' Lovelace paused; his stare grew distant and strange. 'A sense of ... Providence, it may be – of an order of things – spun very fine with invisible threads . . . so that I longed suddenly to see where such threads might not lead.'

'Yet how could you know it was not Providence's wish, that you follow them into the ocean depths?'

'I could not, my Lord; and indeed, I came to fear that such a fate might still be mine. For as the weeks passed, so Mr Sheldon's humours began to worsen, growing violent and icy like the winter storms, and almost, it appeared, as perilous as well. For the lashings, which it had been my pleasure to sample first, were now becoming ever more frequent and severe; and it was Mr Sheldon who would often choose to wield the whip himself. It became his especial determination to root out all adulterous thoughts; and it needed only a sinful glance to have been observed, or a flush of colour brought to the cheeks, for the sentence of guilt to be duly pronounced. And then one day, when we had been at sea for more than nine weeks, and the coast of New England was daily expected, a man and a woman were discovered in the act of adultery; and Mr Sheldon's wrath was a terror to behold. He seemed possessed by some fever; for his eyes were glittering, and his whole body began to shake. In the frenzy of his outrage, he ordered even the adulteress to be publicly lashed, and he applied the whip himself with a strong and godly arm. He dealt with the adulterer in the same manner; then ordered him bound, and lowered into the waves. "Let us see," Mr Sheldon cried, "if such a baptism will not cool the lechery which burns within his loins!" And indeed, it would surely have served to freeze the very fiercest of heats; for it was now the depths of winter and, even as we stood upon the deck, snow and hail were blinding our eyes. We heard the guilty man scream as he was plunged into the waves; and then, it appeared, he began to thrash; and those who were holding him slipped and suddenly fell. They were swept away, and plunged into the waves; and they and the adulterer, although we searched for them, were lost.

'There was no one else taken in adultery after that; and it was fortunate for me that the women were all so plain. And yet it seemed, despite my sobriety, that I might still be drowned, I and the ship with me, for in the following days the storms grew worse, and yet worse, and it began to seem beyond hope that we would ever make the shore. But then one day, the winds began to fall; and almost at once the cries went up that we were come to Massachusetts Bay. I staggered to the deck and saw that it was true, we were drawing near to land. Yet I also saw, coming from the north, clouds blacker than any I had ever seen before; and I knew it would be a race against time, if we were to make port safely. It had been the hope of the Brethren to land at Salem – where, it was said, the Elect of God were thriving; but even as we glimpsed the first faint lights of the town, we were swept off course, back into the bay and then round, as the winds began to veer towards glistening rocks, so that our doom now seemed certain. And then suddenly we saw lights again, and houses upon the shore; and then the outlines of a harbour – and I knew that we were safe after all.

'We had come, so we learned, to a fishing town named Marblehead. It was clear, however, almost as soon as we had docked, that the Brethren would not be staying very long. For there was no hint of sanctity in the place: only a rugged, backward savagery, as harsh as the rocks on which the tiny houses perched, or the gales which lashed spray from the towering waves. One night in Marblehead the Brethren passed, shuddering upon their ship with the cold, and with pious horror as well, for there were taverns upon the shore and drunks upon the streets. The next day, the storm abated, and the Brethren continued on their way. I did not sail with them, however; for at the sight of the drunks, I had at once slipped ashore.

'I passed several days at Marblehead, in a room above a murky, foul-smelling tavern. I struggled as best I could to gather provisions together; yet I had no real plans for where to go, nor when to leave. I had half-hoped to wait until the spring, for the storms were growing ever worse and the snowdrifts piling deeper; and I doubted I would journey very far in such conditions. Yet my pain had been worsening again: the blood was thicker now as it oozed out from my nipples, and across my stomach itself there was a purple discolouring, as though the flesh were growing bruised from within. It was all I could do not to drink from the *mummia*; and yet the final bottle was already almost empty, and I knew I could not finish it – not if I were to have any chance at all of reaching deep into the wilderness. And so I remained where I was, curled upon my bed; and I started to wish I had been shipwrecked after all.

'And then one night, as I drifted asleep, I imagined that I saw the mountain face again. As they had done before, its eyes slowly opened; and at the very same moment, I heard a piercing scream. I awoke with a start. I could hear the muggy hum of the tavern from below me; and then, as I listened, I heard the scream again. I closed my eyes. The vision was gone; the screams too appeared to have been silenced. I rose from my bed and staggered downstairs. The mood in the tavern seemed violent and cruel, the men talking and laughing wildly amongst themselves, and gazing at an open door as it swung in the wind. There was a tall, thin man standing next to it, heavily cloaked, and with a hat pulled down so low that I could not make out his face. As he caught sight of me, he appeared to start; then he turned and slipped at once into the night. I pushed my way across the tavern floor, and followed him outside. The snow was gusting exceedingly thick, but I could just glimpse him weaving through the blizzard towards a hill beyond the village. I frowned; for there was nothing on that hill, I knew, save only graves. And then all of a sudden, from nowhere, I felt a . . . tugging – as though something were – pulling, yes – upon invisible threads . . .' Lovelace paused; then he frowned, and shook his head. 'It is hard to describe,' he murmured. 'Yet whatever it might have been, it seemed real, my Lord, very real, and strange . . . and I found myself turning, without truly knowing why, and running to my room. I gathered together my provisions, then reached for my *mummia*; I paused a moment; I drained it to the dregs. Then I dropped the bottle and returned outside.

'The snow was still falling thickly; but I could see now – though very faint – that there were several tracks of footsteps to follow, all of them leading to the graveyard on the hill. I approached it, and started to clamber up its side; and then suddenly I paused, for I imagined I had heard the sound of cheers and laughter from ahead. I began to creep forward again, grateful that the snow which had muffled the crooked gravestones would serve also to muffle the noise of my approach. I could see figures ahead of me now, gathered in a ring beneath a tree; and in front of them, on a grave, a girl was being forced. It was the girl, I supposed, whose screams I had heard before; but she was silent now, her teeth clenched, her eyes closed, as she reached back with her hands to grip the sides of the headstone. I crept still nearer and realised, from the style of the girl's dress and the darkness of her hair, that she was surely one of the native Indians. She was very lovely and, for all the savage nature of her costume and her looks, there seemed something about her which recalled to me Milady. I watched as her assailant finished with her; and another man stepped forward. At the same moment, I thought again of Milady: of the countless leagues of ocean between us; and then of how she too had once been used, night after night, as these men were now using the Indian girl.

'Almost without thinking, I reached inside my bag. I had a duelling pistol there, preserved amidst my luggage from the voyage. I had been careful to prime it; and now I drew it out and, at the same moment, stepped forward. No one heard me or glanced round. They were all jeering the man in the centre of the ring, who still stood above the girl, shuddering violently, his fists tightly clenched. Now I recognised him as the same man I had seen before by the tavern; and suddenly, as I watched him, I knew who he was. With a strangled moan of prayer, he tossed his hat aside; then he fell upon the girl, his buttocks pumping up and down hard beneath his cloak. At the same moment, I aimed my pistol at his head; then stepped forward. "Let her go!"

'The man froze upon the girl, and did not look round. The other men, though, all turned to face me. "There is no harm," said one of them quickly. "You do not understand."

' "Indeed?" I laughed coldly. "What is there here not to understand?"

' "There are demons abroad."

'Again I laughed. "Are there not ever?"

' "No, sir, for as I said – you do not understand. There have been bodies found about here, emptied of their blood, with wounds upon them such as only the Indians will inflict."

'I started at this, and gazed at the girl with sudden interest. It struck me for a moment that she might be a blood-drinker herself; but then I frowned, and shook my head. "She is no demon."

' "She is a heathen, though, who worships demons and feeds their evil."

' "While you, I see, are good Christians all." I shook my head again, and cocked my pistol. *"You will let her go."*

'Mr Fortitude Sheldon rose slowly to his feet and turned to face me. He met my eyes; then he bowed his head, as though in prayer. At the same moment, the girl too rose up to her feet and, with such speed that no one seemed even to glimpse what she was doing, she pulled out a knife and stabbed the preacher in the back. He met my eyes again, his own staring wide; then stumbled forward, and collapsed into the snow. I watched him as he fell; and then the girl brushed past me and I began to follow her, running down the hill. I could hear cries of violent rage from behind me, and the soft thud of foot-steps following through the snow; and I knew that, even armed as I was, I would surely be caught. I could still feel the glow of *mummia* inside me, it was true; but I wondered where, and for how much longer, I could run. And then suddenly, looming from the darkness ahead, I saw the silhouettes of horses tethered to a tree at the foot of the hill. The girl was already leaping into the saddle of one; she cut the reins with her knife, and then a second pair of reins. As I ran up, she gave me her hand; I climbed into the saddle of the second horse, and then we were both galloping hard along the road, away from Marblehead and into the dark.'

∽०ᘐ∼

'. . . THE GOD OF THE INDIANS, THE SPIRIT NAMED KETAN . . .'
History of Marblehead

'We did not ease our pace, for we were able to see, by the lights of a village we had to skirt, that there were distant pursuers still on our trail. But we passed no further villages, nor even cultivated fields; and soon the road itself was straggling away, hemmed in on either side by a deep wooded blackness. I knew now that we were safe, from our pursuers at least; for we had left the bounds of civilisation behind and, ahead of us, for an eternity of miles, dark and primeval, stretched the mighty wilderness. And still we galloped on; and the forest grew ever thicker, and the undergrowth more wild; and I began to think, so feverish were my fancies, that the realm of Death itself could not seem more sombre nor more chill . . .

'Dawn, as thin and watery as the meagrest gruel, broke at last through the branches of the snow-weighted trees. The effect of the *mummia* was fading from me now; and as I gazed at the infinite shadows of the forest, I shuddered as I suddenly remembered my pain. The Indian girl reined in her horse; she frowned at me, then unfastened her cloak. She offered it to me, but I shook my head and gestured to my stomach; the girl nodded at once, and slipped down from her horse. She passed into the shadows; then she returned, minutes later, with a handful of roots, which she made me eat. For a while my pain was indeed mildly dulled, but it soon returned, more cruelly than before; and the forest, as I rode, began to swim before my gaze. I must have slumped from my saddle, for I woke again to find myself upon the Indian girl's horse, nestled in her arms, while my own horse followed with my bag upon its back. It seemed already to be growing dark again. I remember vaguely, after that, being given more roots; and then the sound of hooves as they splashed through water. But how long we rode, or how far, I could not say; for as in Prague, so now, there was only the pain.

'It never left me; and so I never truly slept. Yet I awoke again to the consciousness of something more, only with a sudden flood of gold within my guts. The agony was very searing, but so also was the pleasure; and I knew at once there was a blood-drinker near.

'I opened my eyes . . .

'He was watching me. We seemed alone together in a fur-draped tent. He wore the skin of a wolf across his shoulders and his hair; his face was painted with swirls of bright scarlet. There could be no doubting he was a Redskin; and yet his face, beneath the paint, was very pale. His eyes, my Lord, burned as brightly as yours.

' "I see," he nodded, "you know what I am." His English was soft and very musically accented. "Yet what you are" – he frowned – "I cannot say."

'He turned and reached down for something, and as he did so I shrieked, for I felt redoubled in my stomach both the pleasure and the pain. The Redskin lifted a cup to my lips. I knew it held blood and I shook my head. "You must," he murmured. "For there is something within you. It is screaming out for this." He tipped the cup and forced me to drink. The blood was cold and very thick. The saltiness made me long to gag. But I brought myself to swallow it; and at once – very faintly, it was true – the agony seemed to dim.

'The Redskin gazed at me impassively. "There are tales," he said slowly, "of a breed of man like you. According to such tales, you bring ruin in your wake."

' "Then kill me," I whispered, "kill me. I could welcome death."

'But the Redskin shook his head. "You must seek out Ketan."

' "Ketan?"

' "You are in great danger from the vengeful spirits of Darkness and of Death. Only Ketan can guide you. Only Ketan can offer you aid."

' "And where do I find – Ketan?"

' "He dwells apart in the Spirit World."

'I laughed hopelessly. "Then you must tell me where that can be found."

'The Redskin too laughed, but very softly. "I cannot." He leaned forward, his face suddenly as impassive as before. "For although it is true that I am older than the oldest tree in all this forest, that I am deadlier and more swift than the firecest of wolves, and that I seem to my people a god, not a man – yet I am not a god. Indeed, I am lower even than certain wise men of my tribe – for I have never been able to meet with Ketan."

' "Then let me talk with these wise men."

' "They are dead – long dead."

'I gazed at him in despair. "What then should I do?"

'The Redskin's eyes glittered; and then he rose, and crossed to the curtain which veiled the entrance to the tent. He pulled it aside and glanced up at the sky. "It is now," he murmured, "the moon of strong cold. It was in such a season, I recall, that the wise men would claim to have met with Ketan. They would walk a great distance, until they came to the hills; and then they would wait alone, amidst the snow. If the Spirit was with them, they would not feel the cold. And then, perhaps, after many days, many weeks . . ."

' "Ketan would come?"

'The Redskin shrugged. "Sometimes. As they said."

' "And then? What did he perform?"

'Again, the Redskin shrugged. He stared at me a moment more, then turned and looked back through the tent-flap at the night. I could feel myself growing delirious again. I reached for the cup of blood and licked it dry; then I staggered to my feet and crossed to the Redskin. I too stared outside. The moon, indeed, did seem strongly cold. It cast silver the ripples of a wide-flowing river. There were other tents, I could see, dotted about the bank – no more, perhaps, than twenty; and a few open spaces cleared from the trees. "The girl," I asked suddenly, "is she safely here?"

'My companion nodded, and gestured to a tent.

' "What was she doing, so far from her home?"

' "Home?" The Redskin laughed with sudden bitterness. "But this is not her home. Her home was Massebequash – which the white men have now named Marblehead, and taken as their own. I prey on them sometimes; for like a wolf which will haunt a vanished wilderness, I do not lightly surrender my ancient dominion. The girl must have followed me – for she too has something of the spirit of the wolf."

' "It is hard," I nodded slowly, "to lose the home of one's youth."

'The Redskin glanced at me, and narrowed his eyes. I knew he could not read my thoughts; yet I felt, for a moment, that he had understood them all the same. "It was lucky," he murmured, "that she met with you."

' "Lucky?" I shrugged faintly. And then I remembered my vision: the vision from which the Indian girl's screams had awoken me, and led me to the forest, where I was standing even then. Turning to my companion, I described the vision to him: the mountain with the face. And as I described it, so I saw his expression alter, so that terror seemed strangely intermingled with awe, and he glanced wildly about him at the tents upon the bank. And then he turned and slipped away, and left me alone; and I wondered all that night what it was that he could know.

'The following morning, very early, the Redskin led me from the camp. Before we left, he had brought me a cup of freshly slain deer's blood, and ordered me to drink it; for, as he had told me, we had a long way to go. He would say nothing more; but I was certain now that he knew where the mountain could be found, for we were following the river upstream and one day, through the trees, I caught the gleam of snowy peaks. I hoped I would not grow too faint to reach them: for although my companion would hunt each night, and bring me fresh blood, the relief it could offer from my pain was growing fainter. "Man's blood," he would nod, touching my belly. "It is thirsty for man's blood." But there were no men to be seen, no settlements at all: only the beasts and the birds of the wilderness. And then one morning we left the river, now just a stream, and began to climb vast boulders up a mountain side; and soon even the beasts and the birds seemed left behind.

'Amidst the bleak expanses of naked snow, my

delirium returned and my legs began to melt beneath me. How or where I continued through the mountains, I do not know; my guide must have borne me many miles, for I remember only waking in his arms and finding the taste of his blood upon my tongue. He had cut his wrist and pressed it to my lips, and although again, as I tasted it, I thought that I would gag, I forced myself to swallow it and keep my pain at bay. But it would not fade; and when I reached beneath my furs, I found that my shirt was sticky with blood – not only from my chest, but from my stomach now as well. I gazed at my damp fingertips, then wildly about me. "How far," I cried, "how far now to go?"

' "Not far," the Redskin answered me. He helped me to my feet; then led me from where we had been sheltering, back into the snows. I could hear a roaring now, like that of ceaseless thunder; and then, rounding a wall of rock, saw a waterfall before me – wild and blinding white, like the streaming tail of the pale horse of Death. My companion paused, and pointed towards the darkness which lay beyond it. "There," he told me. "There you will find the mountain face which you saw."

'I walked forward, then glanced round in surprise. The Indian had not moved. "Will you not come with me?" I asked.

'The Redskin shook his head. "No further," he said. His face, as before in the camp, seemed haunted by a shadow of mingled wonder and fear. "I do not wish to meet with Ketan."

' "Why," I asked him, "what is there to fear?"

' "I remember," he answered, "the wise men of my tribe – they would seek out Ketan, for they knew he could reveal to them the true nature of things."

'I frowned. "And is it evil to know the truth?"

'The shadow seemed to deepen over the Redskin's face. "If I met with Ketan," he murmured at last, "I would ask him a question. I would ask him, is it true, as I fear, that my people must all die, that the Naumkeag must melt into the darkness of things, that they must lie as scattered bones beneath the white man's streets. All this I would ask him; and Ketan would answer me." The Indian paused; and then suddenly he shuddered and cried out to the skies. "But I do not want to hear him! I do not want to know!" The echoes sounded across the barren snows; and then he shouted something else – in his own language, I supposed, for I did not understand the words, and they too sounded across the snows and ravines, before they faded into the cold; and all was silence. "May you at least," he nodded, "find what you seek." Then he turned and left me; and was soon just a distant speck amidst the snows.'

∽◦∾

'O, THAT I COULD BY ANY CHEMIC ART
TO SPERM CONVERT MY SPIRIT AND MY HEART,
THAT AT ONE THRUST I MIGHT MY SOUL TRANSLATE
AND IN THE WOMB MYSELF REGENERATE!
THERE STEEPED IN LUST NINE MONTHS I WOULD REMAIN,
THEN BOLDLY FUCK MY PASSAGE BACK AGAIN.'

The Earl of Rochester, 'The Wish'

'I stood motionless for a long, long while. The Redskin's cry still seemed to echo through my thoughts. Suddenly, I felt a hand upon my shoulder. I turned; I imagined I saw my parents before me: my mother, smiling, and reaching out her hand; my father, very fine, as he had always been. Then snow began to fall; and as the first gust was blown into my face, so my parents seemed to vanish. I walked forward; where they had been standing, there was nothing at all. I continued to walk towards the crashing of the waterfall; and then beyond it – towards a series of crags I could make out dimly through the storm.

'The effect of the Redskin's blood soon began to fade; and delirium returned upon the screaming of the gale. I imagined I could hear a fluttering in my ears, very faint at first, then starting to pound like a tiny heart. Louder and louder it grew, until I could hear nothing of the storm, and blocked my ears, and sank into the snow. I screamed; at once, the pounding stopped. I gazed about me. It was dark. I knew now I would die: for the Redskin had taken our coverings with him, and I had only a gourd of liquor and two bags of food. What hope, then, did I have in such a place, in such a cold? But I staggered on, and waited for the pounding in my stomach to return.

'I walked all night, and heard nothing save the storm. Nor did I drop; but continued on my way as though blown upon the winds, for my being seemed melted into spirit, and my limbs composed of swift-gusting air. Dawn rose. Shadows melted from the snows, and all seemed cast an icy, golden blue. I turned to the east, to gaze at the sun – for I had never thought to see it rise again. And then suddenly I frowned, and turned my head further, for my eye had been caught by a moving dot. It was coming from behind me and, as I stared hard, I could see that it was following my tracks across the snow. My first thought was that it had to be the Redskin, that he must have changed his mind; for I could see how the figure

wore a savage's furs, with feathers in his hair and bright
paint upon his face. But then he drew closer, and I saw
into his eyes. They were brighter than any I had ever
seen, burning like diamonds; and his face, though
unlined, seemed immeasurably old. A shudder of
pleasure flickered through me; and I remembered, my
Lord, as perhaps you may as well, the Pasha's vision of
the Wandering Jew. I knew it was the same man – the
same thing – before me now. As he passed me, he stared
at me; and my pain, I realised, was fading, and then gone.
I longed to cross to him, even to cry out; but I seemed
utterly frozen, and the Wanderer did not pause in his
walk. I watched him as he continued on his way; and
then suddenly, he was gone and I could move once again.
I ran through the snows. There were not even footsteps to
mark where he had been. I gazed about me. A lake
stretched on one side, cliffs on the other; but nothing
stirred upon either water or rock. I stumbled on, my cries
mocked by their own plaintive echoes; and then all at
once – I saw it – the face of the old man.

'As in my dreams, it was a profile of rock emerging
from the mountainside. I walked forward: it seemed to
vanish. I returned to where I had been standing before:
there it was again. I clasped my stomach, raised my
hands. The blood was gleaming sticky and bright. "And
now?" I cried. "Now? Where are you?" Nothing answered
me. And then, very faint, I heard the pattering of a heart
– tiny, remorseless, from deep within my guts.

'I sank into the snow, unable to move. How long I
stayed there, I cannot say; for all sense of myself seemed
utterly lost. There was only the cold, and the pounding of
the heart, and the face on the mountainside, the profile
made of rock. It may be that, like the wise men of the

Indian's tribe, I stared at that face for many days, or even weeks; for that time was passing, I could tell from the heart, which was sounding ever louder and louder in my ears, like that of an infant awakening to life. Yet in a way I cannot explain, such a passage of time seemed frozen and stillborn; for I imagined it shrunk into a single second: measurable not by an endless but by a single beating of the heart. It rose, it pulsed, and then it passed away; and my pain, upon that silence, grew infinite. But I did not faint from it, as I had been doing since Prague; rather it was the agony – and the world – which seemed to faint from me instead. Only the face still remained in the end. Only the face.

'Slowly it turned, as I had seen in my dreams. It was living now, no longer made of rock. I met the Wanderer's stare. His Redskin's paint had gone; so too the furs, and the feathers in his hair. Rather, he seemed dressed like a beggarman, of the type you may see upon any English road. His black cloak was greasy; his clothes old and patched. He clenched between his teeth a thin, curling pipe.

'He gazed at me a long while, his stare unblinking, while tendrils of purple smoke rose from his lips. At last he lowered his pipe. Still the expression on his face did not alter, but seemed as frozen and eternal as the rock itself had been. "Why," he asked me slowly, "should I give you what you want?"

'His accent was one of wondrous melody; more wondrous even, my Lord, than yours. It froze on my tongue all the words I had rehearsed. I swallowed. "For the same reason," I whispered, "that you came to Rabbi Loew."

'The Wanderer raised an eyebrow, and pulled deep on

his pipe. "Indeed?" he answered, as he blew out the smoke.

'I clasped my stomach. It was still oozing blood, yet the touch of it somehow seemed to give me back my will. "You know what is here," I said, "the seed of whose evil. Did you not appear before to the Jew, to save him and the world from the sickness of such a thing?"

'The Wanderer shrugged amusedly. "There is sickness enough in the world as it is." He gestured with his arm; and where before there had seemed to be nothing at all, I could now see the mountain and the lake once again, and a great expanse of forests. "How long," he asked me, "will the Redskins still come here, to seek me out as you have done? Not for long. Like a mist before the morning sun they must retreat, and then fade. It is the order of things – the sickness of the world."

'I shook my head, and hugged my stomach more tightly than before. "Yet you came to the Jew."

'The Wanderer leaned back. He shrugged again. "What of it?"

' "You gave him a book."

' "Well, sir – your point?"

' "It offered the path to a hidden world – for, as I have learned, the world men live in is but a shadow of the truth. In the hidden world – your world – there are creatures of dream. I do not know what you are, sir – whether an angel, or a god, or a demon yourself – but that some of you are demons, I have seen all too well."

'The Wanderer smiled mockingly. "Demons? Why, sir, who can you mean?"

' "You know."

'His smile lingered; and he shook his head. He rose and drew close to me, then took my hands. "It is true," he whispered very softly in my ear, "that there are forces in this world full of power and great strangeness – stranger, certainly, than you will ever know. For we are not to be comprehended by mortals – no, nor by blood-drinkers either, who were once mortals themselves. The creature you talk of – he is very great, but he is not so great as me. He is not, as you put it, a creature of dream. And yet – he sought to be. He sought to be . . ."

'I felt a great horror creeping through my blood; yet at the same moment, an exultation as well. "And this desire," I whispered, "this ambition of his – is it that which has served to make him what he is?"

' "As moths are shrivelled by a candle flame, so souls are blackened which draw near to our world."

' "He was a mortal once?"

' "A mortal who grew a blood-drinker – and now – a nameless thing."

' "Yet even blood-drinkers – I have seen it – may be destroyed."

' "Be warned, then – for you are not even one of them. Do not draw too near."

' "I must die anyway, if you do not give me the powers which you gave to Rabbi Loew."

'The Wanderer gazed at me; then he laughed.

' "Give me the powers," I hissed, "and I will slay him, as he slew my parents and destroyed my world."

'He laughed again. "Why should I care what you would do?"

' "I cannot say," I answered. Then I frowned. "And yet you do."

'The smile faded from the Wanderer's lips and he leaned close to me again, his cheek against my own.

' "Why would you have come to the Jew," I asked him

slowly, "when there is so much else in this world, as you have said, which is sick? Why would you have given him the book? Why would you have given him the power?"

'I turned to face him.

'He did not reply.

' "To destroy the demon," I continued, answering my-self. "So much is clear. Yet why? Why should you have cared? Is it possible, perhaps . . ." – I turned to face him again – "that the responsibility for his fall was somehow your own?"

'The Wanderer's stare seemed immeasurably deep.

' "Who was he?" I whispered. "How did he fall?"

' "That," the Wanderer murmured, "is another tale."

' "And yet it is not altogether," I replied. "For if you did cause his fall – then you caused my own fall as well."

'The Wanderer gazed at me a moment more; then rose suddenly to his feet. "You cannot understand what it is that you request."

'I breathed in deeply. "Yet I ask for it all the same."

' "Be warned, then," he nodded, "lest you become like the thing you are seeking to destroy."

' "I will brave that risk."

'The Wanderer smiled very faintly. "And so it ever is," he whispered. "Forbidden fruit will always be plucked." He leaned over me; he pressed his hands upon my stomach, then raised them before my face.

'I gazed at the gore, my own, upon his fingers. "What," I whispered, "would you have me do?"

'His smile broadened. "Why," he laughed, "have not your own scriptures taught you, that the Blood is the Life?"

'Then he turned, and began to walk away from me. I watched him go; even as I stared, he seemed to be fading.

"What should I do?" I screamed. Still he did not pause. He was melting now into a shadow of cloud. "What should I do?" I screamed a second time. He continued to dissolve; he did not look round. He seemed nothing now but a haze of mountain mist. And then very faint, like an echo, came his voice: "*The Blood is the Life.*" And then he was gone.

'At the same moment, I heard the beating of the heart rising from deep inside me once again; and an icy dampness seeping from my skin. I touched it. My blood was thickening; it seemed almost black. I parted my lips, I extended my tongue. Then I brought up my finger; I licked the very tip.

'At once, the mountains seemed to shudder. The dampness was growing all over me now; the heartbeats sounding with a deafening pitch. When I struggled to sit up, I seemed to be sitting in a spreading pool of gore. I reached behind me. Blood was flooding out as though from an open wound. "No," I screamed, "no!" I bent back my head, as my muscles seemed to tear. Faster and faster the heartbeats were pulsing, louder and louder, as they slipped out on the pain. I clasped my stomach. It was pulsing up and down now, soggy with blood; and I began to lick my hands desperately, to suck upon the gore. As I did so, the mountains shuddered again; they writhed, and melted, and disappeared. I gazed about me. Briefly, I saw the forms of giant standing stones; and then they too were gone; and there seemed nothing but light, in straight burning beams, washing my thoughts where I lay within their heart. The light was mine, I realised; I could control it as I wished. "Ease the pain," and the pain at once was eased. "Purge me – purge me clean!"; and I seemed to shimmer and leave my own flesh. I could see my body laid out before me, and I resolved to play my own anatomist. Yet I needed no knife; I willed it, and it happened – my stomach was sliced apart. There, deep within the guts, the gnawing foetus lay. It twisted its corpse-white, thick-veined head; and then it hissed and spat, as though appalled by my gaze. And well it might have been; for I had never seen a thing I hated so. I ripped it out, bloody and unformed; and as I did so, I heard a violent screaming which was not my own, and I found myself restored to the veil of my own flesh. Again, though, I heard the scream, and again it was not my own.

'And then it faded, and there was only silence; and then, very soon, there was not even that.'

⌒⌒

'AS EVER YOU DO HOPE TO BE BY ME
PROTECTED IN YOUR BOUNDLESS INFAMY,
FOR DISSOLUTENESS CHERISHED, LOVED, AND PRAISED
ON PYRAMIDS OF YOUR OWN VICES RAISED
ABOVE THE REACHE OF LAW, REPROOF, OR SHAME,
ASSIST ME NOW TO QUENCH MY RAGING FLAME.'

The Earl of Rochester, Valentinian

'I woke again at last to feel the sun against my face. I blinked painfully. The sky was a burning blue; the trees which spread below me vivid shades of green. Of snow there was not a trace. I blinked again, in disbelief. How many days, how many months, could have passed?

'I rose to my feet; and as I did so, I felt how my clothes seemed sodden. I shrugged off my thick cloaks, then ran my fingers between my thighs, which were damp and sticky with blood. I frowned. How was it possible, if it was indeed summer, that the gore should still be fresh? I looked around me. There was more blood lying in pools amidst the rocks, and I could see that it was streaked with gobbets of jelly; and then, behind me, I found a thick trail of the stuff. It led towards a mound of something – as though a creature, veiled beneath the slime, had sought in vain to escape it by crawling away. I crossed to the mound . . . I prodded it with my toe. And then I thought that I would vomit with disgust – for the mound, I could see now, had been a little child.

'I breathed in deeply, then turned the corpse over. Again, as I looked down, I thought that I would retch. For the thing appeared less a child than a homunculus, a tiny monster fully formed, with razor teeth in a bared grimace, and a face which seemed, even frozen in death, expressive of the most loathsome cruelty and thirst. I knew at once where I had seen such faces before – in the darkness of the cellars at Wolverton Hall – and I offered up a prayer of thanks that the thing by my feet would never join their ranks now.

'I knelt down beside it; then reached out with my finger. The gore which veiled the creature oozed at my touch; and at the same moment, the air seemed to lighten and the mountains to pulse. *"The Blood is the Life."* I touched my finger with the tip of my tongue. At once the brightness grew more burning, and I felt it ripple and caress through my thoughts; and I knew, if I desired it, that I might make its power my own. But I remembered the Wanderers' admonition, not to employ his gift with too much prodigality; and so I rose to my feet, and felt the brightness start to fade. I crossed back to my furs, and brought out from beneath them the gourd and the sacks of food. I transferred what I could into one of the two sacks; then I filled up the gourd from the pools of blood, and scooped the foetus into the empty sack. That done, I turned and began to climb down the mountainside, towards the wondrous green trees and a distant silver stream. I felt a strange and joyous strength within me; and I imagined, as I walked, that my veins were filled with light.

'I soon found the stream, and began to follow it through ravines and over giant rocks. I remembered, from my journey upriver, that there had been an Indian settlement at the foot of the hills; and when I arrived there, I was able to steal more food and a boat. After that, I made rapid progress – very fortunately, as it proved, for there were no more settlements, nor Indians at all. There were clearings, it was true, but they were all overgrown, and the soil often charred; and I began to wonder again how much time could have passed. One evening, to my astonishment, I saw a stockade ahead of me upon the bank, and inside it the gutted ruins of log buildings. I landed, and walked through the abandoned streets. Just as the clearings had been, they were charred and over-grown; and yet I was certain, on our journey upriver, that we had never passed such a fort; for there had been no one but Indians living in the woods.

'I was not many miles distant now from where the blood-drinker and I had first set off for the hills. It did not surprise me, when I arrived at the site, to find it as abandoned as all the other settlements had been. It was late now; and so I moored my canoe, and prepared for the night. But before I lay down, I unfastened the sack and laid it, still open, upon the edge of the bank. There was a light breeze ruffling the grasses. I hoped it would also serve to carry any scent.

'The Redskin came to me in the dead of the night. I woke suddenly to find him as I had done before, seated by my side, staring down at me. "So you met with him," he murmured. "You met with Ketan?"

'I half-rose, then gestured to the bag.

' "It has been a long time since I left you in the snows."

' "How long?" I whispered.

'He gazed about him. "Since then," he murmured, "twelve winters have passed. And upon those winters – so have other things passed too." He picked up a handful of dust, then scattered it upon the breeze. He watched as the river was pockmarked by the dirt, and muttered strange words I did not recognise. Then he glanced up at me again. "For ever more," he whispered, "if I am to be understood in my own tongue, I must speak it to myself." He paused. "I wish now I had come with you to meet with Ketan."

'I told him nothing of what the Wanderer had said to me about the future of his race; but reached for the sack and handed it to him. "Taste it," I ordered.

'He frowned at me. "Why?"

'I explained the secret nature of its power.

' "The scent is rotten," he muttered. But he dipped his finger into the blood all the same . . .'

Lovelace's voice seemed suddenly to fade into a smile. He reached for the bag he had laid upon the bed, and settled it instead upon his lap; then he leaned forward and narrowed his eyes. 'The taste of it, my Lord – it made him start to choke. He grinned at me in sudden pain and disbelief; then he moaned, and staggered, and fell at my feet, scratching at his throat all the time, as though to tear it apart and cool it with the breeze.'

'Indeed?' Lord Rochester glanced at the bag. 'Might not blood have proved an easier cure?'

'Naturally,' Lovelace shrugged, 'I tried that more — sanguinary — alternative. As the Redskin had done for me, so now I did for him, nicking my wrist and pressing it to his lips. Yet he needed more. He was able to gasp in my ear, while his senses were still his own, that there was a fort a few miles further downriver. Then, at once, his convulsions returned.'

'You were successful in discovering the medicine?'

'I located a supply. Yet it took me time; and when I returned to the Redskin, where I had left him in the boat, his fever seemed so violent I was certain he would . . . die.'

The final word seemed to linger in the air; and Lord Rochester glanced again at the bag. Then suddenly he shook his head and sneered. 'Yet he did not die, did he, Lovelace, not in the end? For he was immortal — a blood-drinker — he could never have died.'

'You cannot know that, my Lord. I saw his convulsions and his sickness for myself. If I had not brought fresh blood to him in time, then, yes, he would have died.'

Lord Rochester laughed contemptuously. 'And that claim, Lovelace, is the basis for your boasts?'

'That claim, my Lord — and what I hold here in this bag.' He raised it aloft, kissed it very softly; then laid it again by the side of his feet. 'For I need not tell you the mystery it contains.'

'On one point, certainly, your savage was right — it stinks of rottenness.'

Lovelace smiled mockingly. 'Are you not tempted, then, to test its other effects?'

'Why, Lovelace, most certainly, if you will only vouch

for me that you have seen any of my breed be slain by its taste.'

'I have told you, my Lord, that the Redskin survived; and yet, for all that, I can swear that its taste will destroy you.'

'How can you know?'

'Even should the venom on its own not prove fatal . . . well' – Lovelace shrugged – 'there are other ways as well.'

'And for those ways at least you are able to vouch?'

'Indeed, my Lord. But patience.' Lovelace held up a hand. 'For I am not yet finished with my history.'

'Well, then.' Lord Rochester sank back upon his cushions. 'We have world enough, and time. Continue. You were saying, I believe, that the Redskin did not die?'

'No, he did not.' A smile shimmered faintly over Lovelace's lips. 'For do not forget, my Lord, that he had been poisoned by only the barest of tastes – and with a settler fresh from the fort on which to succour himself, his recovery soon proved certain enough. He rose at length, and tracked fresh blood; and I told him, as he fed, that I would leave the next day, for I was eager to return at once to England, and Milady. The Redskin nodded; then he warned me to be careful, that there were men abroad still hunting for me. When I asked him what he meant, he answered that a New York man had lately journeyed to the fort, asking if anyone had seen me or knew of my fate. I was puzzled by this news; for I could not see what interest it could have been to such a man, that a murder had been committed in Marblehead more than ten years before. I asked the Redskin where the New York man had gone. The Redskin smiled. He rose from his meal, then led me a short distance from the river towards a road. On the other side of it, in the shelter of a

cave, he pointed to a corpse. "There," the Redskin smiled.
"He will never find you now."

'I bent down by the corpse's side. Around its neck
there was a leather bag, very thick with mildew but still
preserved. I unslung it. Inside I found a sheet of paper,
folded and stamped with a seal; yet when I broke the
letter open, it was to find that the ink had run and faded
with the damp. I dropped the letter; then felt again inside
the bag. There was nothing else there, save only a ring. I
drew it out, and held it to the light; then felt a hollowing
wrench of astonishment. My first thought was that I had
surely been mistaken – yet even as I held it to the light
again, I knew that I had not been, for the meaning of a
ring does not fade as easily as that of ink will do. It still
gleamed as brightly as when I had seen it before, seen it
and kissed it on Milady's finger.'

Lord Rochester started at the sudden mention of the
name. 'And there was no other clue upon the corpse,' he
frowned, 'as to what the fellow's business might have
been?'

'Nothing save the ring, and the seal upon the letter.'

'What then did you do?'

'Why, my Lord, what do you think? I journeyed at once
to New York.'

'And what did you discover there?'

'That it was, to my relief, a flea-bite of a town. I had
heard mighty boasts of it, and been afraid that it would
prove a great metropolis; yet there were only a few streets
of handsome houses, very like those of Amsterdam,
huddled on the tip of an island of rock. It was therefore
no great task, in such a place, to have the seal identified;
and within an hour of my arrival in New York, I had
discovered the identity of the corpse who had borne it –

and more, had gained entry into his house. He had been a Dutchman, I found, only twenty years old, the son of rich parents who seemed untroubled by his fate. He had fled them, they told me, to live with his whore; and they had resolved never to see nor to hear from him again. They did not know what he might have been doing in the distant northern woods; nor what his interest in myself might have been. When I asked them where his mistress might be found, they shuddered and grew indignant at the very question. As I left their house, though, a pretty young servant girl ran after me. She was in tears. "On Long Island," she whispered, "beyond the village of Breuckelen. A farm with peach-trees. His mistress lives there."

'I left on the ferry for Long Island that same night. The heat of day still lingered in the air, and the stars were prickling like silver drops of sweat. They cast a ghostly light as I passed through Breuckelen, and then, beyond a small and ugly church, came to a field full of heavily laden peach trees. I began to hurry through their shadows. Suddenly, I could see the outline of a building ahead of me, and in front of it what seemed to be a long expanse of lawn. I began to walk more slowly; I could hear the murmuring of voices now. I paused. Just then, I heard a low, soft laugh, and I knew it was Milady. I crept forward again, and gazed out at the lawn.

'She was standing pressing the hands of a young man. She kissed him lingeringly; then stepped back and unfastened the clasp of her necklace. I recognised it at once: we had bought it together at a fair once in London. "And when you meet with him," she instructed the young man, "do not forget – you must give this to him." She handed it across. "For only then will he know that you have truly come from me." She kissed him again; then stepped away. As she did so, the young man stumbled after her; and I saw for the first time how haggard he seemed, how pale and wild-eyed. "Please!" he beseeched her. "One more – one final – kiss!" But Milady shook her head, and brushed him lightly away with her fan. "Only when you bring me Lovelace," she whispered. She smiled. "Now go." The young man choked something; then suddenly he bowed, and turned, and fled. Milady watched him run. Then she walked softly forward to gaze out at the night: at the distant glimmering of the lights of New York, and at the vast and empty darkness beyond.

'I smiled to myself and, drawing out her ring, I stepped from the trees and threw it so that it arced above her head, arced and fell upon the grass just before her. She froze; then stepped forward, and picked up the ring. She gazed at it a moment; then turned round, her eyes very wide. She stood frozen again; then laughed chokingly. "Lovelace!" I stepped forward. "Lovelace." I reached for her, her lips met my own; I held her, felt her, her body's soft lines. She was still laughing, even through our kisses, and sobbing as well, and I broke away at last to brush the tears from her cheeks. She blinked up at me. I could see the patterns of a myriad different emotions crossing her face. "How unchanged you seem," she said at last. She laughed again; then frowned and shook her head. "How is it possible, Lovelace," she whispered, reaching up to stroke my hair, "that you are still as youthful and beauteous as when I saw you last?"

'I gazed at her. Hair rich and black; lips very soft; eyes more lovely than the brightest gold. "You too, Milady," I whispered in her ear. "You too are unchanged."

' "Yes, Lovelace," she answered – "but you know what I am."

'I gazed into her eyes; then looked over her shoulder at the darkness beyond. "I have seen many wonders," I murmured at last. "Gained many strange powers."

'She nodded faintly. "So much, at least, would seem evident."

'I smiled. "They are yours, Milady, now." Then I tried to lead her from the lawn towards the doorway of the house; but she would not come, and instead she took me in her arms again. Her eyes were gleaming as she studied my face, but her lips seemed parted in puzzlement.

' "What is troubling you?" I asked.

' "I need to know what happened. I need to be certain it is you."

' "Why," I shrugged, "who else might I be?"

' "I cannot say." She smiled crookedly. "And yet I was certain, sweet Lovelace, certain you had died."

'I glanced at the ring she had placed back upon her finger. "Did you share that certainty with those you sent to find me?"

'Milady tossed back her hair, as though indignant at the question. "Of course not. For I have ever, as you know, been a loving mistress. Indeed, Lovelace, just consider – it would have been a greater cruelty to have kept them by my side. For they would then have sunk to utter lunacy – while as it was, their love had begun merely to fester."

'I smiled; then took her arm again, and this time began to lead her to the house. "Yet still, you might have spared yourself much heartache, and your lovers much wandering, if you had come with me at first upon *The Faithful Pilgrim*."

'I felt Milady start. "You cannot believe," she whispered, "that I knew where you had gone."

'I frowned. "So Lightborn told me."

' "Then Lightborn lied. As he also lied to me."

'I halted, and turned to face her. "Why," I asked slowly, "what had he said?"

' "That you would die unless we found fresh *mummia*. We had both agreed, we would only find the stuff in the Marquise's house. That was why I left for Mortlake the moment we had docked."

' "You would have done better, I think, to have looked in Lightborn's own trunk." I laughed. "Yet at least he was not such a villain as to deny the bottle to me. And he must have told you as well, upon your return, where it was that I had gone?"

' "He did not want me to find you. He would say only that you had left for a New World."

' "Indeed?" I murmured softly. I felt my belly; then reached up, without thinking, to touch the bag across my shoulder. "Then so far, at least," I said, "he told you the truth."

'Milady's gaze had been following the movement of my hand. She glanced back at my stomach; then brushed it, very gently, with her fingertip. "How?" she whispered. She reached up suddenly for the bag; but I jerked it away from her, and took a step back. "How?" she said again. Her face seemed suddenly predatory and eager; and her stare as desperate as before in Prague, when she had first watched the secret book be read. I seized her wrists. "There will be time enough," I whispered, "for all this business – for whatever it is you still seem to desire. But first, Milady" – I brushed her hand against my cheek – "we have other business to finish as well."

'She seemed almost to flinch, and I felt her stiffen. Then I kissed her brutally, crushing her lips, and seized her in my arms, hoping to squeeze the strange resistance from her. The tension in her body began to soften, and her kisses suddenly to grow as thirsty as before. I felt her teeth bite my lip; she licked at the blood and moaned, head tossed back, her burning eyes half-closed. She pressed harder against me, so that I staggered, and fell. I laughed, and seized her wrists again; then took her in my arms. I climbed the stairs and, on the passageway at their summit, found an open door which I passed through. There was no bed, but there were cushions spread across the floor, as Milady had always loved to have them, and a balcony open to the summer night. I laid Milady on the cushions by its edge. "No," I heard her moan softly; then she kissed me again. I began to kiss her throat; then down, towards the perfect rounding of her breasts. I ripped her bodice open. Milady shuddered, as I pulled the dress down and eased it off her arms. Then I reached with my hand up her petticoats. At once, the muscles in her thighs seemed to stiffen again. "No," she said suddenly, "Lovelace, no, not yet." She sat up hurriedly; then pulled back her dress to conceal her naked breasts.

'Well, my Lord . . .' Lovelace snorted, then shrugged. 'What was I to think? I gazed at her, of course, in utter disbelief; and left my hands where they were upon the curve of her thighs. Then I asked her, very icily, what virtue she could possibly believe she still possessed. She made no answer, but laughed despairingly and shrugged her dainty shoulders. So I felt with my hands across her thighs some more; and then put it to her that it ill became a creature such as her, so ripened on blood and mortal sin, to be playing the prickteaser.'

'And what was her reply to such an eloquent appeal?'

'An insistence that I remove my hands at once from her thighs.'

'Did you obey her command?'

'I am always a gentleman, my Lord. But I did it with reluctance.'

'And then?'

'She reminded me of my promise, that all my new-found powers might be hers. I stared at her with even more bafflement than before. "As you wish it," I nodded coldly. "For I, Milady, choose to keep my vows." I seized her by the hair, and reached for my sack. I unfastened it; then held Milady's head close above it, that she might better see its contents. She breathed in deeply, then closed her eyes. "I have never smelt such a poisonous stench," she said at last. "What must I do? Suck upon its wounds?"

' "You can do nothing," I answered her. "Its taste would be your death."

'She frowned. "I do not understand."

' "Tell me what you wish. I will then achieve it for you."

' "No." She smiled in a suddenly soft, despairing way. "No, that is not possible."

' "I assure you that if you want its power, it is not only possible but your only choice. Smell it again." I thrust the bag close against Milady's face, then described how the Redskin had almost died from its taste.

'Milady turned away, her face a blank wash of misery. For a long while she gazed out at the night; and I thought, watching the frozen profile of her face – and for all the frustration and the anger that I felt – how lovely she seemed, even in her wretchedness. Softly now, I reached out to touch her arm. "What is it?" I whispered. "What is it that you need?"

'Still she did not meet my eye. "I had hoped," she murmured, "that with the employment of the book, there might never have been the need for you to know."

' "The book is destroyed."

'She laughed with bitter irony. "Indeed?" She turned to face me at last. "Do you know why I betrayed you over it?" she asked suddenly. "Why I never revealed my pact with the Marquise?"

' "Yes," I nodded, "Lightborn told me."

' "But not all of it, I swear."

'I felt a touch like a frozen finger down my spine. "What do you mean?"

'She smiled again, her twisted smile of before. "I had believed the Marquise's proud boasts, you see, believed and trusted in them, when she had claimed to have the mastery of the book's secret powers. For I had already discovered, Lovelace, that I did not possess such a mastery myself."

'I gazed at her in puzzlement. "You had *already* found out?"

'She nodded faintly. "Many years before. On the occasion in Mortlake, when I saved Lightborn's life." She paused a moment. Absently, she began to trace the curve of her breasts. "For I have already told you of how Lightborn took me from the brothel, to have me perform as an actress in his masques. So much was the truth. And yet, sweet Lovelace – I did not tell it all." '

Lovelace paused. His own smile too seemed suddenly crooked and strange. 'Naturally,' he continued at length, 'I asked her to reveal what this hidden truth had been. She answered me that she had also been an actress on a stage – that Lightborn had written not only masques, but also plays.' Lovelace paused again; he studied Lord Rochester from the corners of his eyes. 'It was to join the actors he had chosen her – the *actors*, my Lord – not the actresses at all.'

Like a serpent waking from a hot day's slumber, Lord Rochester's lips stirred and twitched very faintly. 'I am sorry?' he inquired with a display of great politeness.

'You heard, my Lord, exactly what I said.'

Suddenly, Lord Rochester began to laugh. 'Of course,' he whispered in a long, mocking hiss. 'There were no actresses – no girls upon the stage – not before the reign of our own much-fucking monarch. Of course. *Of course!*' He began to laugh again; and as he glanced at Lovelace, so he laughed all the more, until the tears were coursing down his lined and withered cheeks. Lovelace himself leaned back in his chair and made a great show of inspecting his nails. 'I am glad, my Lord,' he murmured at length, 'that your decline has not affected the pleasant nature of your wit.'

Lord Rochester grinned. 'You would surely not deny me the simple pleasure of laughing at you, Lovelace, and jeering you roundly? And yet in truth, the jest could have been more amusing still. Certainly, speaking for myself, I would rather have a mistress who proved to be a boy than do as some fools will, and permit a mistress to become a wife. Your error, at least, was less egregious than that.'

'You are ever a profound and learned moralist, my Lord, and in your judgement, of course, you are perfectly correct. I had no regrets.' Lovelace shrugged. 'For even as a boy, Milady was still the prettiest woman I have ever known.'

'Her breasts, sir.' Rochester leaned forward. 'Dammit, sir, her breasts. How the Devil did she come by those?'

'Since, as I think I mentioned, she had been stroking them at the moment when she made her revelation, I was not disinterested in resolving that question for myself. And yet, of course, she had already given me the answer.'

'The book?'

'Exactly so.'

'Yet how had it occurred – the transformation?'

'You will remember, perhaps, how Father Tadeus, when he came to Wolverton Hall, had given himself the false name of Faustus?'

'Yes.' Lord Rochester frowned. 'But I fail to see . . .'

'There is a play of the same name. It may be, my Lord, that you have seen it for yourself? You will recall, then, how Faustus is a learned man who sells his soul to the Devil in return for great powers. A suggestive conceit, I am sure you will agree – especially in view of how it came to be written . . .'

'Indeed?'

'The author, my Lord, was none other than Lightborn – at a time when he went by the name of Marlowe. Whether it was the obsession he had inspired in Milady, or whether that their minds had somehow grown intermingled, I cannot say; but Milady, when she read the book – Lightborn dying on the floor beside her – found the world she had opened to be slipping her control. She could see its patterns of pure light, not as strong and mighty as those we found in Prague, but present all the same; and Lightborn – Marlowe – still lying huddled on the floor, washed by the flow of one of the lines. Milady crossed to him; except of course that she was not yet Milady, for all her gown and curling locks, but still a boy. She – he – knelt by Marlowe's side. Marlowe turned, and grinned at him horribly. Even as he did so, the flesh appeared to be shrivelling from his face. "Sweet Helen," he whispered. At the same moment, the boy imagined he was kneeling on a stage; and the very act of thinking so made it seem he was. He imagined he was garbed as he had often been, when he had performed the part of Helen of Troy, summoned from the underworld by the lust-stricken Faustus, to syrup with pleasure the dread of damnation. "Sweet Helen," Marlowe whispered again. His grin now seemed more than ever like a skull's, for the gums had rotted utterly away and the few shreds of flesh wept and stank upon the bone. "Sweet Helen . . ." he rattled a third time. He paused, his eyes rolling blindly in their naked sockets. Then he whispered as though with his last gasp of breath, "Make me immortal . . . immortal with a kiss . . ."

'The boy bent forward. As his lips brushed the teeth of Marlowe's skull, so the flow of light began to shiver and refract, and its purity to dissolve into a myriad of colours, shifting and mutating before the boy's astonished gaze; and he found that they altered with the patterns of his thoughts. He sought to caress Marlowe with them, to bring him back to life. At once, the lights began to spiral away in infinite double coils. The boy sensed, somehow, that he should bend them to his will. "*Sweet Helen, make me immortal with a kiss.*" He did so. As he saw it in his mind, so it happened before his stare. The flesh was restored to Marlowe's lifeless skull, the gaping wound above his eye socket healed. And then the light began to fade, as though ebbing away upon the return of Marlowe's breath; and the boy blinked, and saw the room again, and Dr Dee's face, and how the Doctor seemed filled with mingled horror and awe. There was a mirror upon the table. The Doctor reached for it and, without a word, held it up. The boy stared into the glass; he shook his head – and then he screamed . . .'

'He?'

Lovelace grinned. '*He* no more. And yet neither, not wholly – forgive the pun – a *she*.'

'And it was that, then – her prick – which she wanted you to cure?'

'Who better to fulfil such a wish for her than me?'

Lord Rochester frowned. 'But she did not wish to be . . .?'

'A boy again? No' – Lovelace shook his head – 'for she had been an almost-woman far too long to wish that. After all' – he shrugged – 'why waste the practice of a century in skirts?'

'She had no regrets at all, then, for her former life?'

'In one sense only.'

Lord Rochester arched an eyebrow. 'Indeed?'

'Yes.' The grin still lingered on Lovelace's lips, but with all the amusement suddenly bled from it. 'She wished' – he paused – 'to be a mortal again.'

Lord Rochester arched his eyebrow a second time. 'Indeed?' He drawled the word with prodigious slowness, then he nodded to himself. 'And your success, sir? Tell me. Tell me your success.'

Lovelace stretched, then rose slowly to his feet. He crossed to the window; and for upwards of a minute stood in perfect silence, gazing out at the night.

'Prodigious,' he whispered at last, not looking round. 'I swallowed no more than a mouthful of the foetus's blood; and yet at once, I saw the hidden lines of power revealed and, in the night outside, visions of strange and magnificent substance. What before had seemed dark now appeared dotted with lights; and upon the island of Manhattan, for as far as I could see, were towers of impossible beauty and height, which seemed to brush the very heavens and filled me with delight, for I could feel, as I beheld them, strange powers flood my soul. I turned away from the rapture of such visions, back to Milady; and I saw how her golden eyes seemed luminous, as though with anticipation of pleasures to come. As she had done to Lightborn, so now I did to her: I brushed her lips with a magic-honeyed kiss. Then I reached with my hand up her thighs; and beyond . . . and this time – this time – she did not cry "Stop!" '

Lovelace turned round at last. 'So, my Lord – all things, you see, are possible.'

'Milady, then . . .'

'Is pregnant even now.' He laughed with sudden delight. 'Yes, my Lord, yes – she carries my child.'

Lord Rochester nodded with wonder and dread in his eyes; then he half-rose from his bed, and swallowed very hard. 'And her other desire?' he whispered. 'To grow a mortal? Was that fulfilled as well?'

Lovelace snorted with contempt. 'Naturally,' he shrugged, 'I might have performed it for her with consummate ease – so please, have no fears on that count. Yet it was unworthy of her, as it is unworthy now of you – and so I pretended, to Milady at least, that it could not be achieved . . .' He grinned; then he crossed the room suddenly with rapid, weightless steps, and returned to his chair, pulling it up close so that he could whisper softly in Lord Rochester's ear. 'For I will need, through the passage of eternity, a companion. I would not have Milady grow withered and ugly, sir, like you.'

Lord Rochester smiled coldly. 'You are resolved, then?'

'Absolutely.' Lovelace leaned back in his chair. 'For why else do you think I got Milady with child? The bastard will serve to keep my own youth fresh.'

Lord Rochester's smile faded. 'And Milady?'

'What of her?'

'What does she think?'

Lovelace shrugged. 'She does not wish me to become a blood-drinker, that is true enough.' He shrugged again. 'But why should I care? This recent womanish softness of hers – it is derived, perhaps, from that softness newly gashed between her legs. Whatever the reason, though – in the end, she will accept the nature of my choice. God knows' – he laughed – 'there will be centuries enough, and more.'

'Yet she would not transform you herself?'

'I am certain I could have . . . persuaded . . . her. But no, my Lord . . .' Lovelace picked up the bag; he nursed it in his arms. 'It has to be you.'

'Why?'

'You are the Pasha's heir.'

'You still seek to become that yourself, then, sir?'

'I would be fitter in such a role, my Lord, than you.'

'Then it is still your intention . . .'

'To fight with my great enemy? To destroy him?' Lovelace nodded curtly. He leaned forward, his face suddenly twisted by a fierce and deadly passion. 'Every inch of strength I have,' he hissed, 'every power, every thought, is devoted to that single goal of my revenge. You, my Lord, have failed; allow me, then, to succeed. Give me what I want, and I . . .' – he smiled – 'I will grant you your death.'

Very softly now, he laid the bag upon the bed. He unlaced the fastening to expose what lay within. 'Can you not breathe it?' he whispered. 'The scent of your extinction?' He drew close over Lord Rochester; he lay upon him; he kissed him suddenly, very hard. 'I should have known you like this,' he murmured, 'many years before – when your lips, perhaps, were less withered and dry. And yet still, my Lord, still – your charms are very great.'

'It is fitting you should think so,' Lord Rochester answered, 'since all that I have and all I am will soon be yours.' He reached for Lovelace's cheeks, and pulled him down again. Through their kisses he began to tear at Lovelace's shirt; and then at the golden, naked skin. Lovelace screamed, a cry of mingled ecstasy and pain. He shuddered; his body arched; he moaned very softly at the feel of his own blood.

Lovelace turned, for he could feel the world melting into the flood of his wounds, and he wanted symmetry, his own eternal life to be born from the moment of Lord Rochester's death. He dabbled his fingers in the bag, then sucked upon the gore. He laughed softly, for he could feel it now: knew he would succeed. Upon the thunderous pounding of his own naked heart, he leaned forward again to brush Lord Rochester's lips. For a moment he heard a second heart beating with his own; and then the sound began to fade, to pulse and ebb away, so that in the end there was silence and nothing else – impossibly still, as though the very universe had been dimmed into nothingness, as though all of creation itself upon that silence had grown dead.

And then – at last – from the depths of that silence: a pulse again – the beating of a heart.

But it was single now: single and alone.

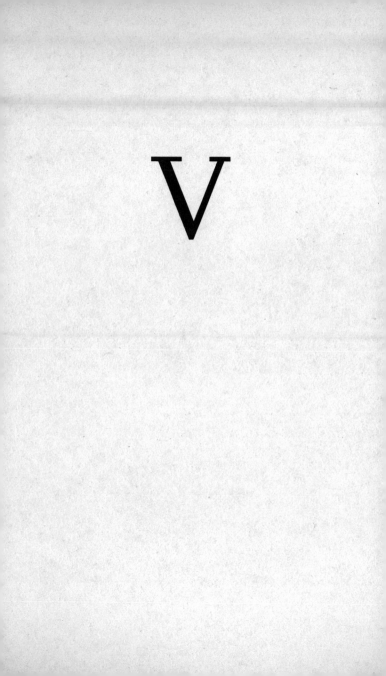

V

'AND SOME ARE FALLEN, TO DISOBEDIENCE FALLEN,
AND SO FROM HEAVEN TO DEEPEST HELL.'

John Milton, *Paradise Lost*

'The afternoon of May Day. I could have wished, Milady, you had come sooner than this.'

Milady smiled with chilly politeness. 'If I had known how desperate you were for the delights of my company, sir, then I would have jumped to your summons even sooner than I did.'

Lovelace grinned. 'You are perfectly aware, Milady, how I have regretted every second of these long months you have not been by my side. And in truth' – he opened the carriage door and clambered in – 'it is good to see you again.' He folded her in his arms and kissed her, just long enough to feel her surrender to his embrace. Then he released her; but as he sat back, he kept hold of her hands and started to kiss each slim finger in turn.

Milady watched him a moment, then pulled her hands away.

Lovelace looked up as though bitterly wounded. 'A woman's love, they say, is ever as fleeting and unreal as a dream.'

'It was not I who betrayed our love.'

'Indeed?' Lovelace's grin broadened and he struck a pose. 'You do not find me improved by my transformation?'

'You seem as deadly and cruel a thing now as myself.'

'Oh, worse, Milady – worse. For I have such a business now in hand, such a matter of revenge, as . . . well – as you shall see very shortly for yourself.' He nodded in emphasis; then leaned out from the carriage window and struck its side with his hand. As the carriage began to rumble through the Salisbury streets, he continued to lean out, craning his neck, to make certain that the wagon following them did not grow lost; and he only resumed his seat when they had left the city gates behind. 'It is loaded, then,' he asked, gesturing back through the window, 'just as I requested it to be?'

'To the very letter.'

'Save for . . .'

Milady angled her head.

'There is one thing I requested which I perceive you have not brought with you.'

Milady did not answer, but looked away.

Lovelace leaned forward, took her by her chin. 'And how is she?' he whispered. 'How does our little child?'

'I have not set eyes on her,' Milady answered distantly. 'Not since she was born. It was temptation enough, scenting her presence in my womb. But you, Lovelace – if you had not been changed – *you* might have tended her.' She widened her gaze. '*You* might have been a parent to our child.'

Lovelace's own gaze widened as well. 'Is the pleasure in her blood,' he murmured, 'truly so dangerous as that?'

'It is not to be endured.'

'And yet you know full well, I have no intention of enduring it. For there is only one certain way to abolish temptation – and that is to surrender to it.'

Milady brushed his hand away, but Lovelace leaned forward closer and seized her chin again. 'Why would you deny her to me?' he asked slowly. 'I have not seen you growing wrinkles, Milady.'

'No!' Again, Milady struggled to free herself, but Lovelace would not release his grip.

'I want to be as you are, eternally young.'

'But with the blood of *our* child, Lovelace – the offspring of *our* union? Can you not do as I did, and get a child upon some flinty-hearted whore, who will not care what you do to her bastard?'

'Your sensibilities, Milady, are worthy of a nun.' Lovelace leaned forward even closer, tightening his grip. 'Where is she now?' he whispered.

'With Lightborn.'

Lovelace smiled unpleasantly. 'It is a pity, then, for his purposes, the bastard was not a boy.'

'Yet he will cherish her all the same – the child being what she is, my daughter. For still, sir, he loves me – as you no longer seem to do.' She pushed his hand away, and this time Lovelace did not seek to hold her again. She leaned her head against the carriage window, and for a long while she said nothing more. 'I could wish,' she murmured at last, 'wish it with all my heart, that you had not paid your visit to Lord Rochester.'

'You know I had no choice.'

She turned to stare at him again, narrowing her eyes. 'I wonder.'

'No, Milady. Be honest with yourself. For you must understand, in the depths of your soul, that if I am to succeed in my revenge, then I require all the powers and the strength that I can seize.'

'And yet . . .'

Lovelace silenced her by taking her hands. As he had done before, he began to kiss each finger. Then he entwined them with his own. 'Wait until you have arrived at Woodton,' he whispered. 'Then you will see the fruits of all my preparations. Then you will see how my transformation has not been in vain.'

Milady parted her lips again, but Lovelace silenced them with a kiss. He crossed to sit beside her and, kissing her a second time, began to stroke with practised hands. 'Let us discover,' he murmured, 'how my gift to you fares.'

Milady gasped. Lovelace grinned. So easy, he thought, as he pulled back her petticoats and felt Milady shudder, and cleave to him tightly, parting with her own hand the skirts of his coat. So easy – as everything had seemed easy since the change. He glanced out through the window. They were still a distance yet from Stonehenge. More than time enough. He did not need to wait for Woodton to demonstrate the scope of his new powers. Let Milady feel them now. And when he had finished with her . . . well . . . then let her complain!

'There,' he asked afterwards, as she lay upon his lap, 'was that not better than a mortal's fuck?'

She smiled up at him faintly. 'I felt no difference.'

He laughed, and looked away, knowing that she was lying. As he stared out through the window, he saw that they had passed Stonehenge and were drawing near to the trees which served to veil Woodton. 'We are almost home.'

Milady stirred, and sat up as the carriage jolted to a halt. 'Where are we now?'

'By the gates. They have to be opened.'   •

'They are still guarded?'

'Yes – but by my own soldiers now.'

'Your own?'

'I could not permit the villagers to escape.'

'Why? You have need of them?'

Lovelace nodded and grinned. 'As you shall witness this evening.'

Milady did not answer Lovelace's smile. The carriage was now rumbling forward through the gates, and then out of the trees into open land; and she saw, as she looked, how there seemed no change at all. Rubble was still scattered everywhere, and fields and village alike appeared a wilderness of weeds. She turned to Lovelace in puzzlement. 'Where are the marks of the great transformation?'

He pointed towards a manor house silhouetted beyond the village. 'There is the house where Emily grew up. Where Sir Henry Vaughan was quartered with his guards.'

Milady stared at it. 'But that was standing here before.'

'True,' Lovelace grinned. 'So that is one change at least.'

Milady narrowed her eyes; and realised that the building was indeed abandoned, its beams charred by fire, its windows dark and empty. She turned again to Lovelace, to ask him what had happened; but he was leaning from the window, shouting at the coachman to come to a halt. As the carriage began to slow, Lovelace pointed at a second house. It stood on the edge of the village green, on the very spot where before three gallows had been placed. The carriage halted beside it. Lovelace climbed out. He waited to take Milady by the hand; then led her past two guards and into the house.

Gazing about her, she could see a few of Lovelace's

familiar things decorating the room. 'What is this place?' she whispered.

'My parents' house, where I was a boy.'

'But, Lovelace ...' She turned to him. 'That was destroyed.'

'As you can see' – he gestured with his arms – 'I have had it rebuilt.'

'How?'

'It was a condition I made.'

'Condition?'

'I have grown a great benefactor to this village. Come.' He took her by the arm; led her across to the doorway again, and pointed. Men were unloading crates from the wagon, piling them in a line along the edge of the green, while guards in tattered uniforms and rusty breastplates stood beside them on watch. 'And if you have indeed done as I requested you to do, and brought the finest delicacies that London can afford, then I shall soon be able to demand even more. For you will see' – he pointed to the labourers – 'how although they are fuller than they were, there is still very little flesh upon their bones.'

'They are the wretches I saw before in the fields?'

'And from the pens by Wolverton Hall.'

'You freed them?'

Lovelace grinned crookedly. 'In a manner of speaking.'

'How do you mean?'

'Say rather – I bought them. For I understood, when I first came here following my night with Lord Rochester, that the villagers might easily be seduced – not by wealth, as Faustus had seduced them, but more simply, by food. They could not leave the village; no one else could enter it; only I had the power to pass to and fro. It was therefore a simple matter to control the entry and supply of bread.

'And yet you said, you *bought* the villagers?'

'Naturally – for as they themselves had shown me long before, everyone has his price.'

'What did you demand?'

Lovelace narrowed his eyes. A shadow of hatred passed across his face. 'Sir Henry Vaughan.'

'He was still alive?'

'Oh yes. He and his men.'

'Yet they were armed.'

'True.' Lovelace grinned. 'And so, of course, it was a difficult struggle for the slaves: between their natural terror, and their ravening greed. Yet in the end, some grew brave enough. They came to me, I supplied them with arms, and they stormed Sir Henry's house. They captured him, and all his men. I gave my own men the abandoned uniforms.' He gestured through the window at the soldiers outside. 'As you can see for yourself.'

'And the other slaves?'

'They were freed as well. For I supposed, from all that I had learned, that the Dark Spirit, my enemy, fed on mortal suffering; and that if I could only ease that, then I might also serve to weaken his power.'

'And that was your only motive?'

'Reason enough, would you not say?'

Milady did not answer for a moment, but stared out through the window at the bone-thin labourers straining with the boxes. 'And your supposition,' she murmured at length, 'do you know if it has proved justified?'

'I am certain it has done.'

The note of triumph in his voice made her turn, surprised. 'Why,' she asked him, 'you have evidence?'

Lovelace nodded. His smile seemed very thin. 'I have

mentioned, I believe, how Sir Henry and his men are my prisoners?'

'They are still alive, then?'

Lovelace's smile broadened. 'Not so many of them as there were. Three only now.'

Milady frowned. 'You have been feeding on the others?'

'Upon the lucky ones, yes. But there were some whom I remembered had been seduced very early by Faustus' gold, and must therefore have been the leaders in the plots against my father – and for those I found a crueller, far more fitting fate. The first of them I killed upon Yuletide, in the heart of an ancient site named Clearbury Ring.'

Milady gazed at him, appalled. Lovelace caught her expression; and he snarled with sudden fury and contempt. 'Do not, please, Milady, goggle as though it is somehow a crime to spill blood.'

Milady answered him distantly. 'But to spill it, sir, as your great enemy did?'

'And yet that was how, Milady, he recovered his greatness – and I too, by its consequence, have increased my own strength.'

'How can you know?'

'Because after I had left the body dumped on Clearbury Ring, I drank the abortion's blood, and at once felt a surge of power such as I had never previously known. I rode directly to Wolverton Hall. I entered it for the first time since I had been there with you; I found the library filled as it had been before. The creatures I slew – I slew them, Milady – which was more than you or the Marquise had been able to achieve. Their victims I freed; and then, not wishing to exhaust my strength, I left the

Hall and burnt it to the ground. The cellars, though, I knew, would still remain; and so on Childermas, I slew a second man, and left his body in the Lady Chapel. I returned to the cellars. Again, I slaughtered as many of the creatures as I had the strength and power to kill. A further visit, though, I knew would still be required. Candlemas came. I left the body this time beneath Old Sarum. And upon my return to the cellars, I completed the slaughter – I destroyed utterly the creatures which the darkness had been nurturing, so that none of them – none of them at all – still remained.'

'And . . . the Dark Spirit?'

Lovelace shrugged. 'What were those creatures I slew, save the emanations of his evil and of his very self? I know that to be the case – for after all, I bore one of them once within the depths of my own belly. And now they are gone. How much feebler, then, do you think, their author must be now?'

'And yet still he remains.'

'True.' Lovelace paused. 'But do not forget – May Day has come.'

He met Milady's stare a moment more; then turned abruptly and left the room.

'What will you do?' she cried after him.

'Come and see,' he answered. 'For it is almost sunset – and everything now is done.'

She followed him outside. Lovelace was walking towards a guard. He had words with him, the guard bowed his head and turned at once; and then, sounding across the green, there rose the remorseless, steady pounding of a drum. Straggles of villagers began to gather on the green – forming, as if by instinct, in a circle round its edge. Their haggard faces seemed twisted by greed, their nostrils twitching as they sniffed at the breeze. Milady walked to join Lovelace. She could see that the boxes from the wagon had been opened, and the meats, and wines, and delicacies laid out. Lovelace smiled at her; then snapped his fingers. Two horses were at once brought forward. 'Please – Milady.' Lovelace gestured with his hand. He watched as she climbed into her saddle; then climbed into his own. Side by side, the two of them rode forward.

As they did so, the drum was silenced, and the villagers sank at once to their knees.

'Have no fear.' Lovelace raised up his hand. 'For you have seen what I have brought you.' He gestured with his arms towards the food and, as he did so, the villagers began to mutter amongst themselves. 'Please!' cried out a thin and desperate voice suddenly. 'What would you have us do?' A chorus of other voices echoed the cry. Lovelace smiled, and again he raised his hand.

'You know full well,' he answered. 'I would see the marks, the certain proofs of your regret, for the crime which you or your parents committed, when my mother was burned here more than twenty years before. Well?' He suddenly raised his voice. 'Show them to me! Show me the proofs!'

He was greeted for a moment by a deathly silence. The ring of faces, so desperate, so worn, seemed utterly frozen. Then an old woman stepped forward, pulling at something round her neck. There was a glint of gold; and then she tossed the necklace away, so that it was flung into the centre of the green. Lovelace spurred his horse forward; he bent down from his saddle and plucked the necklace up. He was laughing wildly as he wheeled and trotted back to Milady. As he did so, there was a glitter of jewellery and coins from all around him – arcing, then falling in a shower of gold upon the grass. Lovelace halted again by Milady's side; he raised the necklace, and placed it against her naked throat. 'I would give you this,' he said, 'as I would give you all the world, my dearest love, but . . .' He raised the necklace again, and held it to the sun. It was caught by the dying rays to become a deep red. 'And so it was caught before,' Lovelace whispered. 'Stained by blood, as though in mourning for the innocent.'

There was another deathly silence; and then Lovelace nodded, and the drum began to sound. It rolled slower now and the crowd, as though sensing what it foretold, half-fell to their knees as they had done before. Several on the edge of the green began to back away; and through the gap they created, a column of guards emerged. Milady pricked her horse gently forward. She could see now that the guards were leading two men weighted with chains. They staggered forward into the centre of the green. Behind them, through the gap which had been made in the crowd, she could glimpse a great pile of wood, and on its summit two stakes.

The guards pushed the prisoners forward, so that they fell by the foremost hooves of Lovelace's horse. They blinked and gazed about them, as though too enfeebled by hunger to know where they were. Lovelace prodded the nearest with the tip of his boot.

'Is it true,' he asked in a ringing voice, 'what these others here have told me, that you were the first in all this village to accept Faustus' gold?'

The two men blinked up, as bewildered as before; while from the crowd there rose murmured jeers of condemnation. Lovelace sat motionless all the while in his saddle. Then suddenly he leaned forward, and struck the man nearest him about the face with the necklace. 'Answer me,' he hissed. 'I want to hear the admission of guilt from your own lips. Were you the first to accept Faustus' gold?'

The man nodded hurriedly, and muttered something.

Lovelace struck him again across the cheek. 'Louder!'

'Yes,' he stammered, 'yes, it is true, we were the first.'

His companion writhed and sobbed. 'Yes,' he echoed. 'We both took the gold.'

Lovelace nodded to himself; then sat back in his saddle and gazed round at the crowd. 'Well?' he demanded. 'What punishment, then? What punishment? *Decide!*'

There was silence again; then three or four voices, at the same moment, gave the answer: 'Burn them! Burn them!' Lovelace smiled; he gestured at once with his hand. Two of the guards stepped forward; they tugged on the chains. The condemned men fell, then staggered to their feet. They were dragged across the green to where the two stakes were waiting. The crowd began to break and re-form around the pyre. Lovelace's grin broadened. 'And in this manner,' he cried suddenly, addressing the villagers again, 'it may be that you will serve to burn your own guilt away. Whoever lights the fire – let him or her have first portions from the feast!' He sat frozen a moment more, watching the sudden surge of excited villagers all clambering forward to snatch the tinder-box; and then he wheeled his horse round again. He glanced at Milady. 'A pretty sight,' he laughed, 'fit subject for the moralising you seem now to enjoy.'

She gazed at him bleakly, then shook her head. 'This is not the way.'

'The way?' Lovelace answered. 'No – for this was the

merest excursion. The way, Milady? The way lies ahead!'
He laughed again; then spurred his horse forward and
began to gallop down the road which led from the village.
Milady glanced behind her. She could barely hear the
screams of the dying men above the villagers' cheers, but
beyond the crowd a pall of black smoke was now starting
to blot out the sun. Milady smiled very thinly; then
wheeled her own horse round, and followed Lovelace
down the road. She watched him ahead of her, dis-
appearing into the wood, and knew, riding side-saddle as
she was, that she could not hope to rival such a pace. Nor
did she try; for she was certain already of their destination, and of what would be waiting on the far side of
the trees.

She cantered briskly through the wood, and past the
now abandoned gates; and then, emerging into open land
again, saw the silhouette of Stonehenge ahead of her,
black against the deepening purple of the sky. It seemed
circled by fire and, nearing it, Milady saw a ring of
guards, all holding torches, and Lovelace, lit by the glare,
dismounting from his horse. He passed between the
guards into the ring of stones itself, and was lost amidst
the shadows. Milady shook out her horse's reins and rode
towards the torches, until she too was lit by their glare.
The guards seemed to shrink at the sight of her; but one
stepped forward to hold her horse. She slipped down
from the saddle; then followed Lovelace into the shadow
of the stones.

There was a naked man by his feet, face down upon
the grass. The wretch was shrieking uncontrollably; but
for all his writhings, he could not escape, for a gleaming
metal hook had been driven through his ankles. The hook
was attached in turn to a rope; and Milady saw how it

passed across a lintel of the stones, and descended again into the hands of a guard. Lovelace made a sign, and the guard began to tug. As the rope tautened, the man was dragged across the grass and then pulled into the air, until he was twisting and bucking like a fish upon a line. Lovelace approached him; seized him by his hair. It was long and matted, and exceedingly white; and as Lovelace jerked the head round, Milady was not surprised to recognise Sir Henry Vaughan. 'He has grown damnably ancient,' said Lovelace, releasing his hold. 'See, Milady, the leathery skin. Any blood he has will be sluggish and cold. Yet still' – he shrugged – 'I am certain it will serve.'

'Lovelace.' Milady approached, and took him by the arm. 'Do not do this.'

'Why not?' The gleam in his eyes was perfectly dry; yet his voice, as he spoke, seemed almost to catch. He met Milady's stare a moment more, then turned to gaze at Sir Henry again. 'You know what he did.'

'What did he do?'

Lovelace breathed in hard; he shuddered violently, then started to laugh.

'What did he do?' As Milady echoed her question, she reached to seize Lovelace by his other arm. He continued to laugh, and she shook him. 'Do you not see,' she cried with mounting fury, 'what is happening to you?'

'I know it full well.'

'You are content, then, to become a second Tadeus?'

'No. For I am wiser, stronger, greater than he.'

'Yet Lovelace, listen, for I have been considering this matter greatly. The power of the book . . .'

'The power?'

'Yes, which you have since found in the blood of that creature which you bore . . .'

She paused suddenly; for Lovelace had raised his hand to quiet her, and his face seemed twisted with scorn and contempt. 'You presume,' he hissed softly, 'to instruct me on such a thing? You, Milady? You, who could not even approach the secret power without transforming yourself into the image of a whore?' He laughed bitterly; and as she sought to keep hold of his arms, he brushed her away, then raised his hand and struck her across the face. She was knocked to the ground and lay a moment where she had fallen; then reached with her finger to the side of her mouth. She felt blood. She licked it away; and gazed up at Lovelace. He was standing perfectly still, his face as frozen as one of the stones. She narrowed her eyes. 'You are damned indeed,' she whispered. 'Damned as surely as Tadeus was.'

Lovelace tensed, as though uncertain which way he should move; then he shook his head faintly and took a step back. 'No,' he whispered. 'I shall not be damned. For I do not come as Tadeus did, a feeble suppliant, but to invoke the powers of this place for my revenge. The spirit which destroyed him – I shall destroy it now in turn.'

He tensed again; glanced round at Sir Henry, who was twisting no more, but hanging limply like a butcher's carcass.

'Please,' Milady whispered.

She saw a tremor of something, a shadow, cross his face. But he shook his head. 'No,' he answered. His voice seemed suddenly, strangely tender. 'Leave me, Milady. Where I am going – you cannot come. Please go – go far from here – for you are all I have left to me still of life.' He reached beneath his cloak, and drew out a flask. He unstoppered it; and at once Milady felt its stench burn her throat. Through the stinging of her eyes, she saw how

Lovelace was smiling at her very sadly now; then he raised the bottle, as though in a toast. He brought it to his lips; he began to drain it; and when he was finished, dropped it on the grass. At the same moment, he raised his hands to the sides of his head; and, closing his eyes, he began to gasp.

⟡

'WHICH WAY I FLY IS HELL; MY SELF AM HELL;
AND IN THE LOWEST DEEP A LOWER DEEP
STILL THREATENING TO DEVOUR ME OPENS WIDE,
TO WHICH THE HELL I SUFFER SEEMS A HEAVEN.
O THEN AT LAST RELENT: IS THERE NO PLACE
LEFT FOR REPENTANCE, NONE FOR PARDON LEFT?'

John Milton, *Paradise Lost*

He had known, even as he started to drink the liquid, that the vision of power it was opening to him, a blazing wall of infinite light, would be greater than any he had made his own before, greater even than the very first, the Wanderer's, which had served to melt the abortion from his flesh – that same thing which, crushed, he was gulping down now. He swallowed more of it; and saw the light shimmer into a thousand colours, flickering and changing into a line of dark fire, still bright about the edges and with amber at its heart. The standing stones, just a shadowy façade, spanned the line from side to side; and then Lovelace blinked, and they faded and were gone. He finished the liquid; and knew that the line, its power, its space, were his. He gasped, for he had felt the line pass through him, and seem almost to become a part of himself. He clasped the sides of his head; he closed his eyes; and felt the world ripple in obeisance to his thoughts.

Yet not utterly. For even as he seemed to behold, within the depths of his own mind, the burning light of the universe of things, so also he felt a blackness polluting its gleam, a spillage of terror staining the flames. He knew from where the blackness was coming – from a creature which was feeding, like himself, upon the line, seeking to bend to its own will the blaze of power. Lovelace sensed the creature's mind for a moment blankly; then dared to meet, to engage with its spread. At once the blackness was spilling across his thoughts, heavy like a fog, so that only pinpricks of silver were left of the former blaze, casting weak and ghostly shadows; and Lovelace dreaded that even those might soon be lost. He sought to protect them; and at once the blackness seemed to weaken and turn. Encouraged, he strained harder. The contours of the line began to glimmer again and, as they strengthened, so the blackness grew thinner, and retreated all the more. Lovelace did not pursue it utterly – the time for that would come – but it had soon faded all the same to the margins of his mind. Lovelace smiled to himself. He could be certain now, certain. He was ready. The line was all his own.

He opened his eyes again, willing the world of the everyday to return. It appeared before him, indistinct but unchanged. He turned at once. Sir Henry was still hanging from the meat-hook. Lovelace raised his hand, gave the signal to a guard. A knife was drawn and Sir Henry's throat severed; blood, in a thick shower, fell upon the grass. As it did so, Lovelace sensed a thickening of the blackness again, billowing inwards towards the stain upon the grass, a mist of predatory and fell intent.

Now, he knew, was the great moment of truth: for the Dark Spirit was coming, drawn again – as Faustus had once drawn it – by the scent of blood within that ancient place of power. Lovelace could see the figure before him, still shadowy but visible now; and he braced himself for the moment of attack. The line, he reminded himself – the line was all his own. He summoned all his strength, all his reserves of will and hate; then sought to make himself one with the light.

Suddenly, he could feel the attack. The creature's presence was all about him, and then he saw it: the figure from the coldest depths of his memories, its face deformed and gleamingly pale, its jaws gaping wide, its eyes as before an unpitying index of measureless power. It screamed as it felt itself washed by the light; and Lovelace felt the grip of its hands around his throat. But the grip was not tightening; and the light grew ever brighter, and the grip began to fail. The figure staggered back, a silhouette again; and then Lovelace saw, across its body, the glistening of blood; and its shriek was terrible to hear, as its limbs began to dry and crumble into dust. The blood lay upon the great line of light, a dancing cloud of crimson motes; and Lovelace smiled, for he could be confident now that the light was still his own. He raised his eyes to the corpse of Sir Henry Vaughan. Its flesh was drinking up the cloud of blood. The creature shrieked again, then Lovelace cried out too. The light was starting to burn his mind, for its brightness was too great and the flood of its power was scorching his thoughts. Yet he could not relax now, not ease his efforts; for the creature had virtually crumbled away; and his blood been drained almost wholly from the light. Lovelace gazed at the *golem* of Sir Henry's corpse: it was twitching uncontrollably.

Very close, Lovelace thought; very close to success. Yet the agony in his skull was unbearable now; his hold upon the light was fading; and then he felt a terrible explosion of pain, and he screamed again, for he knew his hold was gone. At the same moment, the limbs of the corpse were rent from inside; blood, in a black rain, blotted out the light; and Lovelace saw before him the creature's face once more.

It lingered for a moment, a pale imprint upon an impossible darkness; and then it too faded, and all was utter black. Lovelace closed his eyes. He sought to recapture the flood of the light. The darkness pressed undimmed, and the light did not return.

He imagined he heard sudden laughter.

He started.

He had imagined it was his own.

'Did you not understand, sir, that all your designs of revenge will serve only to succour me, and make me more whole?'

Lovelace opened his eyes. The darkness was still as total as before; yet there seemed to be, before him, a shadow of even greater darkness, wearing the form of a human figure; and then it turned, and Lovelace saw its face. It appeared, like the laughter and the voice, to be his own.

The face mocked him with a smile. 'Had you truly not comprehended that malice and hatred are what I feed upon? And what a dish, a rich dish, you have brought to me of both.'

Lovelace closed his eyes again. Still the darkness; still no light.

He felt the touch of something cold running sharp against his throat; and then a thin cravat of dampness, and the softness of a tongue. He sought to shrink away, but found it impossible to move. Only his eyelids could be stirred. He flickered them apart. There was a figure before him, the very image of himself, down upon its knees, lapping at the wound; then leaning back, lips damp, its smile very cold.

'A pretty dish indeed.'

Lovelace gazed at the picture of his own face with revulsion and disgust; and as he did so, saw how the strength of its evil seemed to grow. He could not even close his eyes now; had no choice but to stare at the grinning mask. He struggled not to hate it, struggled to purge his mind of every thought. But he knew it was too late now; and the smile before him grew steadily more cruel.

Still Lovelace sought to annihilate his hatred.

'Too late,' the smile whispered. 'Too late, too late.'

Lovelace knew that it was true.

He struggled to put such a thought from his mind.

The smile grew broader still.

And then suddenly, from distant depths: the sound of footsteps.

The smile did not waver. 'Everything,' it whispered, 'must redound upon itself.'

The footsteps again; drawing nearer.

The smile parted, curling back from the teeth.

The footsteps echoing on flagstones now outside.

Suddenly, Lovelace stirred, and found that his paralysis seemed gone. At once he shrank back from the face. He felt soil underfoot, very powdery; and then behind him, rough brickwork; and looking around, he knew where he was. Above him were the ruins of Wolverton Hall; behind him the cellars where the dead things still stank, slaughtered weeks before by his own avenging hand; and ahead of him and all around, the lair and refuge of his enemy – that final cellar he had never dared to enter. And the enemy was with him there now; and Lovelace knew that in that reservoir of evil and power his own powers would be as nothing, that a fly might as soon seek to destroy a spider in its web. And so he tensed himself for the end that he knew was surely coming; for the end – or for a beginning more terrible yet.

And then suddenly he heard the footsteps again. He looked round as he heard them stop; and he saw, standing in the doorway, a figure – shadowy and indistinct, as figures had always seemed indistinct before, when he had sought to glimpse them through the veil of power. Yet the power now appeared to be ebbing; for even as Lovelace watched, he saw how it was eddying and swirling away, so that the figure was growing ever less indistinct; he imagined that he recognised Milady. Yet he could not be certain; for he found it impossible to imagine what strength she might have, which could serve to dim the power of his adversary. And indeed, no sooner had he glanced at the figure than he heard in his ear a hissing, hell-like moan, and he saw, as he turned back again, his own face, its smile now vanished utterly and its jaws opened wide. Desperately, Lovelace twisted away, and fell into the dirt as the jaws bit air; then twisted once more, and leapt back to his feet. To his astonishment, the creature appeared suddenly frozen. Lovelace watched as his own looks faded from its face. He could see now how its skin was ashy white, and its eyes no longer blank but shaded by deep pain. It appeared even more hollowed and deformed than before; so that he wondered suddenly what wounds he had inflicted; how near to success he might have been after all.

Just as suddenly, he realised that he could hear the distant drip of water, the sound of a world beyond the cellar walls; and then, from behind him, footsteps again. He turned, despite himself. *Milady. It was her.* He stood frozen in astonishment. At the same moment, she screamed at him; and then he felt a pain slash across his back and a weight, icy cold, send him crashing to the floor. At the same moment, he heard a piercing shriek; and he felt the weight tense, and release him from its grip. As he had done before, he twisted free, and then round. He saw Milady with her dagger. It was dripping blood. She raised it again, and then stabbed it down; and again the creature tensed, as the blade was driven in hard. It staggered backwards as she pulled the dagger free; and then staggered again as she slashed across its throat. A spurt of blood hit her in the face; she screamed, and raised her hands to cover her eyes. The dagger clattered upon the stones of the floor. The creature seized her by the hair; it bent back her head, then bit into the naked curve of her slim throat. Deep it drank; deep and very hard; and then staggered back as Milady collapsed into the dirt.

'No!' Lovelace screamed. 'No!' He ran to her. She was curled up in a tiny, motionless ball; but he could see that her blood was seeping out across the floor. She was moaning softly, hands still raised to her face; Lovelace knelt beside her and gently brushed her hands away, then bent down closer to inspect her face. It was hideously pitted: wherever, it seemed, the creature's blood had splashed, there the flesh had been corroded even to the bone. Milady stirred at last, and struggled to smile through her shrivelled lips.

'Lovelace.'

He glanced up at the darkness; then laid a finger softly upon her lips.

'Lovelace . . .'

'Do not try to speak.'

But she shook her head. 'The power . . .' She started to choke and he tried to quiet her, but there seemed something urgent and desperate in her eyes. She swallowed frothily. 'The power,' she whispered a second time. 'It is born, Lovelace . . . do you not see? . . . the power is born from love.'

'From love?' He stared at her in confusion. She had closed her eyes. 'Please,' he begged her. 'I do not understand.'

Milady opened her eyes dreamily. 'Love,' she murmured again. 'The surprise of it – the shock . . . the truest way to power . . .'

She began to choke again, more violently now, then suddenly started to vomit up blood. Lovelace gazed at her helplessly, clutching her in his arms, as she shuddered and seemed to grow more frail beneath his touch. 'The surprise of it?' he whispered. 'Of love?' He frowned, and shook his head. And then all at once he thought of the Pasha's account of Rabbi Loew, brought a flower by his tiny daughter; and of Mr Milton, recognising the long-lost companion of his dangers; and of how both had suddenly made sense of the script, and found in its mysteries the hidden power. And then he thought of Milady; how as she had approached it, the blackness had started to fade from the cellar; and he knew that she too had come armed, not with hatred but with love.

She retched again.

'No,' Lovelace whispered. He rocked her in his arms.

'Milady – no – what must I do?'

She smiled at him very faintly, even through her spasms. 'Our child . . .' she whispered. 'Lovelace, please . . . our child . . . no.'

'Never,' Lovelace vowed at once. 'Never, I swear it!'

She smiled again, and reached up for his hand.

'But you will live,' he whispered.

'No,' she answered. 'I . . .' She sought to entwine her fingers with his own. 'Peace, Lovelace. Peace . . .'

He gazed at her in disbelief. 'But you are immortal, Milady. You will never die.'

She was still smiling; but even as he stared at her, he felt the grip of her fingers start to fade.

'You will never die,' whispered Lovelace again. He kissed her. Her shrivelled lips were parted, but he could feel no breath. He kissed her again; then leaned back upon his heels. 'You will never die!' he screamed suddenly. 'You *can* never die!'

Nothing answered him.

He gazed into the black silence of the cellar's depths, then eased Milady's head very gently from his lap. He reached for her dagger; and as he did so, saw how her blood was still slipping across the floor, slipping until it met with another pool of blood, flowing from the shadows, wide and very black. Lovelace gazed into the darkness again, but there was still no sound; and so he placed the dagger beneath his coat, and turned, and hurried at once from the cellar. He picked his way over the corpses littering the passageway, climbed the stairs, emerged into the night, and the charred remains of the Hall. He ran fleet-footed to Woodton. The smell of ashes still lingered above the green, but Lovelace barely paused to glance across it, and at the bodies of drunken villagers slumbering in piles. Instead, he passed into his house, opened his trunk, and drew out a slim – the final – flask of blood. He gazed at it a moment, holding it to the moonlight; then turned and retraced his steps back to the Hall.

By the entrance to the steps, he paused and drew out the knife. Even with his blood-drinker's sight, the darkness seemed thicker than it had been before; but he saw nothing as he descended the stairs, and began to make his way through the corpse-strewn cellars. By the entrance to the final cellar, he paused again. There was nothing ahead of him that he could see, save only darkness and the pale, cold gleam of Milady's naked skin. He glanced down at the blade of her dagger: so slim, so elegant, so lovely. He kissed it very softly; then he drew out the flask and drained its contents in a single gulp.

At once, the darkness seemed to eddy and thicken. Lovelace passed into the cellar. He glanced down at Milady, and felt a sudden lightness burning through his veins. He looked up again, and gazed ahead. The darkness waited, as thick as before. He tensed himself, then walked towards it.

He realised he was treading through the pool of black blood. At once, he froze; for he remembered how its touch had been fatal to Milady – had the power to incinerate even a blood-drinker's immortality. At the same moment, he heard a hissing moan; and then the darkness flickered as it had done before; and he saw the shadow of his enemy, its hands clasped to its wounds. They glistened very brightly; and Lovelace knew for certain that they were cruel and very deep, and that Milady's death had not, perhaps, been wholly in vain. He felt a thrill of pleasure and desperate hope; and, stepping forward, he aimed his dagger at the creature's heart.

At the same moment, with a sudden rush, the creature flickered and grew, as though formed of black flames. Lovelace staggered back, for he could feel himself washed by its touch, so that his blood seemed turned to ice and his limbs to iron. He staggered again, then felt himself stumble. Glancing down, he saw that he had tripped over Milady's corpse. Milady! He sought to empty his mind of all other thoughts. As he did so, he felt the lightness start to grow once more; to ripple and then flood in a blinding stream. At the same moment, he heard the creature shriek and saw, as he had done before within the stones, a sudden glistening across the blackness of its form, and then, in the air, a faint mist of blood. Lovelace felt a second surge of pleasure and hope; and then again, immediately, the creature's touch, as chill as before, and the pressure of something like jaws against his throat.

He screamed, and tried to bend his neck away, but the creature clung like an icy sweat, and even as Lovelace twisted and writhed with all his fading strength, he felt the teeth again – and this time they drew blood. Again Lovelace stumbled back, out through the cellar doorway, so that he fell amongst the corpses of the slaughtered dead; but the creature was still upon him, pressing down and then tearing at his neck, lapping at his wound. Everything was starting to seem distant and faint; and even as Lovelace sought to break free from the weight upon him, so his own limbs too were growing steadily duller, so that at last he could not move them, could only lie still as the weight grew heavier, and the darkness more chill.

From where he lay he could see the cellar walls ... they were starting to fade. He traced the patterns of the mould upon the brickwork with a strange, distracted concentration, knowing they would doubtless be the last things he would see. He followed with his eyes a long and glistening stain, from the edge of the floor to the side of the doorway; and then suddenly, by the arch, he saw a cross drawn in chalk.

He gazed at it with a rapt and astonished awe.

He could move again now, despite the weight; and he saw as he did so, upon the archway's other side, scrawled likewise in chalk, a second cross.

Where could they have come from, he wondered, such marks? What were they doing in such a hellish place?

The weight was fading on his chest; the light was returning.

Lovelace still gazed in wonder at the two chalk crosses; and then, as he stared at them – suddenly, he knew. There was someone before him: the figure of a man in a militia uniform, the sash of a captain tied about his waist. The figure was bent by the archway, drawing with a piece of chalk the outline of a cross.

'Father,' Lovelace whispered. 'Father.'

The image of Captain Foxe rose, and slowly turned round. He was smiling, even as he began to melt away. Lovelace closed his eyes. The flood of light was blinding him. He could only feel, not see, how he drove the dagger home. But then he opened his eyes again; and as his sight adjusted, so he could make out the cloud of blood in the air. He watched as it fell in a mist-thin rain; fell, and settled, and was swallowed by the soil.

Two days later, upon the Channel, dawn had almost broken. Robert Lovelace gazed across the waters towards the eastern sky. He waited, his hand at the ready. Then it rose, a ray of sunlight; and Lovelace brought his hand down. Two sailors cut the ropes, the coffin fell into the sea; it splashed, and sank, and was lost beneath the waves. Lovelace turned to the captain, and gave the order. Back to Portsmouth. Back at once to land.

As the ship began to veer towards the distant coastline, Lovelace brought out from his coat a tiny casket. He opened the lid and gazed at the soil inside; then touched it very lightly with his fingertip. As he did so, he imagined that he felt it sucking upon him; and instinctively he held it away from himself, as though he were gripping the head of a snake, its fangs damp with poison. And yet in truth, Lovelace thought, no serpent's venom could rival what he held; for it possessed the power, perhaps, to kill even blood-drinkers. All that night, he had been disposing of the soil from the cellars: the soil, and the deathly freight which it bore. Each hour, he had given the order; and a fresh coffin-load had plunged beneath the waves. And now all that was left, he was holding in his hand. All that was left of the blood which might yet kill him.

For it was still within his power, he thought, to be at one with Milady – with Emily – with his parents – in the calm and rest of death. He gazed at the casket a moment more. 'Peace, Lovelace, peace.' He imagined for a second he heard Milady's dying words.

He shook his head. He knew that in truth he had heard nothing but the shrieking of the gulls; and as he gazed at the birds wheeling above the sea, the freshness and joy of things seemed borne upon the winds. Lovelace tightened his grip as he closed his eyes; and then he opened them again and flung back his arm. Forward he hurled the casket; forward and upwards, so that soil was scattered in an arc across the waves, before the casket itself hit the water and was lost. He watched the spot where it had fallen, as the ship was blown onwards, and then began to veer. The place was lost. He breathed in deeply. He began to laugh.

He turned and walked along the ship to the prow. Portsmouth ahead; and the road to London.

And in London – his daughter.

Lovelace smiled; then he laughed once again.

I first conceived the idea of writing *Deliver Us From Evil* at a party held in John Aubrey's Broadchalke home; and his twin obsessions with the biographical and the bizarre have been a constant inspiration during the writing of this novel. Numerous people have helped me in my own attempt to fuse the two, above all my brother, Jamie, whose knowledge of the life and works of Lord Rochester has proved invaluable. It was he who pointed me towards some of the more suggestive features of Rochester's career – the abduction of Elizabeth Malet, the bargain with Wyndham before the Battle of Bergen – and I would like to apologise to him for having turned his hero into a vampire. To try and make up, I have dedicated this book to him.

Keeping things in the family, I would also like to thank Sadie, my wife, not only for being wonderful – that goes without saying – but also for the added bonus of her in-depth knowledge of the Voynich Manuscript, which has proved an excellent plus. The Voynich Manuscript, part of which has been reproduced on the inside covers of this book, is one of the most extraordinary and baffling documents in existence. It first appeared in Prague in the reign of Rudolf II; and its mysterious script has never been cracked. It was Sadie who first pointed out to me its supposed connection with John Dee; and thus, however tenuously, with John Aubrey, whose grandfather had indeed been a close associate of Dee's. Such links are always a pleasure to make: they allow one to feel that one is on the right track. Of course, since Sadie does not believe in magic, it goes without saying that the interpretation I have put upon the Voynich Manuscript is entirely my own.

For advice with regard to Prague itself, I am indebted to Harriet Castor, whose knowledge and love of the city is unfailing. It was she who helped set me up on my first journey there, so that I could see for myself Rabbi Loew's seat in the Old-New Synagogue, and stand by his grave, and that of his son. She also introduced me to Angelo Maria Ripellino's wonderful book, *Magic Prague*. For anyone interested in the legends of Rabbi Loew and the Golem, I cannot recommend it highly enough. I would also like to thank Mr Meyer Sheinfield, for helping me with details of Jewish history and folklore.

Finally, a big thank you to three American friends. First, Amy Conklin and Mark Dolny, who drove me to Marblehead, and then supplied me with endless details on its grim condition in the 17th century, and on the Native Americans who had formerly occupied the site. Also to Jim Schnabel, who has a knowledge of the weird sites of Wiltshire which comes from several summers' on-the-spot field-work. For anyone wondering whether there is indeed a ley-line running from Clearbury Ring to Stonehenge, I would advise the following: buy a good map of the Salisbury area, a ruler, and find out for yourself.